THE
WINDS
AND THE
WAVES

THE
WINDS
AND THE
WAVES

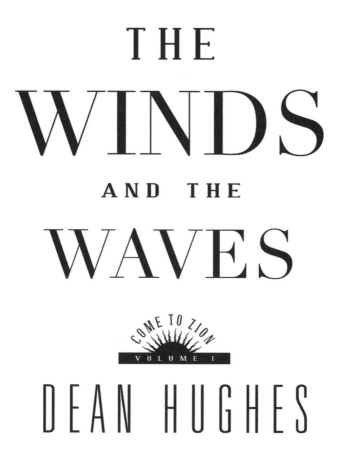

COME TO ZION
VOLUME 1

DEAN HUGHES

DESERET
BOOK

SALT LAKE CITY, UTAH

For my grandson,

William "Billy" Hurst Hughes

© 2012 Dean T. Hughes

This is a work of fiction. Characters and events in this book are products of the author's imagination or are represented fictitiously.

Visit us at DeseretBook.com

Library of Congress Cataloging-in-Publication Data

(CIP on file)

ISBN 978-1-60907-058-8

Printed in the United States of America
Malloy Lithographing Incorporated, Ann Arbor, MI

10   9   8   7   6   5   4   3   2   1

CHAPTER 1

Will Lewis heard a wailing sound, faint and distant. When it came again—sharper this time—above the noisy scrape of his plow blade, he shouted, "Whoa!" He reached with his stick and tapped the rumps of his oxen. "That's it, Nick. There's a good lad, Nimble. Take a rest now." The oxen settled to the ground, still yoked.

Will looked down the hill to the south end of the field, where he thought the cry had sounded, but he saw nothing. Then he heard it again, and he saw movement close to the south hedge. By the time he recognized that an arm was waving, he was already running. There was a pinched insistence in the voice; something was wrong.

Will stumbled and wobbled as he ran over the heavy clods in the plowed soil. "Help," someone was yelling. "Here. Here, Will. By the stile."

By then he could see that it was his father, Morgan, dressed in his farmer's long smock frock. He was rolled up on his side, looking like a pile of white linen. "Dad, what is it? What's happened?" His father was gripping his right leg, which was bent toward his chest. Will dropped down next to him.

"I can na' get up," Morgan said, but he no longer sounded quite so desperate. "I was crossin' the hedge an' jumped down from the stile. But me knee give way. I've torn somethin' inside, Will. It burns like a fire." He tried to straighten his leg, but he grimaced and then grasped it tight again.

"What were you meanin', jumpin' off a stile?"

"I can still climb a stile, can na' I? An' jump down too. I come down wrong, that's all."

"You're near fifty, Dad. It's time to think on that."

But Morgan was looking away from Will, toward the sky. "I prayed, son. I called out, but you could na' hear. That's when I lifted up me voice to God an' called again—and the Spirit carried the sound to your ears. It's what I've said so many a time. God does—"

"Pray next time that you'll know better'n to make such a jump. That's the prayer you should be sayin'."

"What I pray—more'n anythin'—is that you'll soften your heart and not talk so."

Will didn't want to hear another of his father's sermons. "Let's get you to the house," he said. He got his hands under Morgan's arms and hoisted him upright, and then he slipped his shoulder under his right arm. "Can ye place a little weight on that leg, or do I need to pack ye on me back?"

"I can manage a little, I think, if I . . ." But when Morgan tried to straighten the leg again, he gasped and tightened his grip around Will's neck. Will knew the damage must be serious, and his mind was already running to all the troubles that lay ahead. For now, though, he needed to get his father to their cottage, on the other side of the hedge. He moved in front with his back to his father and got the man's arms over his shoulders. Then he bent forward. "Hang on to me," he said, and he grabbed Morgan's left leg and pulled him up. He heard another gasp. "Is that hurting ye too much?" he asked.

"I'll last it out," Morgan gasped.

"Say another prayer," Will said, and he wasn't mocking. He trudged forward along the hedgerow, his boots sinking into the damp soil. "I'm heading to the gate. It's a long way about, but there's no other way I can go."

"I know. Keep on agoin'."

And that Will could do. He was twenty-two, the oldest of the seven Lewis children, and he had been carrying the heaviest load for the family for the last four years. He was a powerful man, built like those oxen—thick and hard in the shoulders and limbs—but there was none of their bovine indifference in him. He looked forceful when he walked, and whenever he strode into Ledbury for church meetings, or even just strolled past booths on market day, he turned the heads of the young women in town. His hair was almost black, his skin tanned from the sun, but his eyes were bright and intensely blue—always a surprise when someone first looked at him.

Will made it to the gate, used his free hand to unlatch it, and then headed past the old brick barn and the hayricks. He was already thinking ahead. He needed to take care of his dad, but he also needed to get a lot more work done before the rains started again. Clouds had been gathering all day, and by tomorrow he might not be able to get back into his fields. It had gone that way so far this spring, with rain falling more days than not and the soil never quite drying out. Spring was often like that in this part of England, but it was April, and most years Will had planted his barley by now.

"How bad is the pain?" Will asked.

"God's helping me." But Morgan was breathing hard, moaning a little with each step Will took.

"There's Daniel," Morgan said. "He can help."

Will was already heading around the cottage, so he didn't need Daniel now. But before he reached the front gate, Daniel hurried past and opened it. "What's gone amuck?" he asked, sounding curious more than concerned.

"Give Will a hand. I've hurten me knee."

"Do na' bother," Will grunted. "Open the door. And tell Mum we're acomin' in."

Daniel was already at the door, but the old latch caught; he had to shake it before it let go. He stepped in and called, "Mum, it's Dad. He's hurt his leg. Where do you want us to lay him out?"

Will bent low so that his father's head wouldn't hit the doorjamb, and then he stepped into the dim light of the cottage. His mother had just stood up from a chair by the front window. "Oh, Morgan," she said, "whatever have you—"

"Never mind all that, Nettie. I'll be right as rain. Send Josiah ta town, fast as he can run, and bring back Brother Watkins."

"Do you want him in the back or out here?" Will asked. The cottage had only two rooms—a bedroom in back and beds in the main room too, along with the fireplace where all the cooking was done.

"In the back room." She touched Morgan's shoulder. "Is it your ankle, or—"

"Nay. Me knee," Morgan said. "It's somethin' inside what's pulled apart. I felt it give way. But God'll heal it."

Will didn't say what he thought about that. He merely bent to get through another door and then stepped to the bed. He crouched and at the same time let his father's good leg slide from his hand down to the floor. He balanced him, turned him on one foot, then slipped around him so they were face-to-face. "I'm going to take your weight now and let you sit down on the bed."

But his dad did most of the work, all but hefting his right leg onto the bed. When Will did that, a muffled little cry emitted from his father's throat, but nothing more.

"Oh, Morgan, you're badly hurt," Nettie was saying. "I'll call Josiah, but we better send for Doctor Eldredge. You might have broken a bone."

"No. I do na' need him. Brother Watkins will rebuke the pain and I'll be walkin' again in that very moment."

Brother Arthur Watkins was a lay preacher for the United Brethren. Morgan had been raised as a dissenter from the Anglican Church—a Wesleyan Methodist—but he had joined an offshoot group called "Primitive Methodists," and then he had discovered the United Brethren. A lay preacher named Thomas Kington, a Primitive Methodist himself, had formed an organization—a group of believers—who sought "light and truth," as they liked to say. By now, in 1839, many branches of the organization, with several hundred members, had spread across Herefordshire, Gloucestershire, and Worcestershire, mostly in the Malvern Hills.

Will, with the rest of the family, had begun attending services in the Ledbury, Herefordshire, branch of the United Brethren, which met in the home of Brother Watkins. Nettie and the younger children seemed happy enough with the choice, but Will was skeptical and Daniel was mostly uninterested. Morgan had become far more resolute in his faith in recent years, and to Will he seemed fanatical, as did many of the other United Brethren. At every service and prayer meeting people reported their dreams and visions, spoke in tongues, or testified of faith healings. But Will doubted that God fussed with day-to-day aches and pains. His parents—and everyone at church—had been asking God for weeks to hold back the rains so that spring planting could commence, and what had come? More rain. So Will had started plowing before the ground was really dry. He wasn't about to wait for all those prayers to slip through the dark clouds and penetrate heaven.

"Bring Brother Watkins," his dad was mumbling again. "That's all I ask of ye." But his eyes were closed and his jaw clenched. "It's like a knife stickin' in me."

Will was suddenly sorry for his impatience with his father. The man did work hard. And he accomplished a great deal for someone his age.

Nettie seemed to be thinking much the same. "Oh, Morgan, I'm sorry this has happened," she said. "I'll send Josiah, and I'll make a brown-paper poultice. That might cool the pain a little, for now." She turned to Daniel. "Find Josiah, quickly as you can."

Daniel nodded, but he was smiling as though he saw something comic in the scene. He left the room without showing any sign that he was in a hurry.

Will wanted to get back to the field. The house seemed to be getting darker, those clouds surely continuing to build, but it didn't feel quite right to leave so soon. "Dad, is there anything I can do for you? Can I hold your leg or—"

"No. Do na' touch it." Morgan took a long breath, then added, "Go on with your business. You can na' do a thing for me here, and when the preacher come, you will na' add nor a penny's worth of faith to his blessin'."

"I guess there's enough truth in that," Will said. He stepped from the bedroom and found his mother down on her knees, searching in a cupboard by the fireplace. Will had seen her put together poultices before—wheat bran and vinegar, more often than not. She had plastered Will with her concoctions all his life. He had never been certain that they helped him any.

Will watched, still wondering whether he ought to stay and help. But it was the longer view that was setting in as a reality now. "This is a bad time for this to happen," he told his mother.

"When's a good time?"

"Never, I guess. But right during the planting season, that's about the worst."

"You always do the plowing. He hasn't done any of that for two years." She had found the tin container she had apparently been looking for. She started to use a hand to get up. Will reached and took hold of her elbow, but she got up under her own strength. She was a little younger than Morgan, but she had always been more delicate. Nettie's father had been a merchant in Ledbury. He had operated a chair-making business and had sold his furniture in a little store at the front of the family house on Homend Street, the main street of town. He was considered above the "working class," a craftsman, and Nettie—Neath was her actual name—had received several years of education. At twenty-three she had found no husband, and she had met Morgan. He was the son of a tenant farmer from Wellington Heath, a lovely green valley just north of town. Morgan was socially beneath her, but he was handsome and strong, and he had humbly professed his love. She had convinced her father that she shouldn't miss her chance to marry and have a family.

Nettie had told all this to Will—told him probably because she could talk to Will better than she ever could to Morgan. And what she had also told him was that she had felt for many years that her husband was disappointed in her. She hadn't come to the marriage with many household skills, having had "help" in her house, so she had learned everything as a wife. She had worked hard, learned from other women, and devoted herself to her children, but she had not really understood what it would mean to live as a tenant farmer's wife. She had also not realized that Morgan would be so hard to know. She had settled into a quiet life, often alone with her thoughts, even though she was busy with her duties. She had done her best to cook and sew—even taking in sewing to add a few shillings a week to their income—and she had worked in the fields during harvest. But she wasn't the woman Morgan's mother had been, and, in little ways, he had made that known to her.

Will could see that Nettie was aging. She was forty-six now and much too thin. She lived with more pain all the time—rarely admitting to it, but showing it in the way she moved about the house. She would stitch for a time, stop to rub her fingers, and then go right back to her work. Since the day she had married Morgan, she had been working from sunup until long after sundown. Father was adamant about not doing farm work on Sunday, but he never noticed when Nettie cooked and even churned butter or salted meat on the Sabbath. Will doubted that since her wedding day she had ever spent two daytime hours in one stretch just resting—not even when she got sick.

"Dad's the one who keeps things agoin' around here," Will said. "I can do the plowing, but with Dad staying in bed, Dan will sleep under the old sycamore out back. They all will—'cept the girls."

"Will, don't start all that again. Daniel does his share. He starts slowly, but he always gets to his work, in time."

"That's fine. I will na' say another word. But when he finally comes 'round to his work, it's Dad who, more'n not, gets him to it."

"Don't speak like a farm boy, Will. You have been taught better than that."

Will couldn't help smiling, but he didn't reply. He *was* a farm boy; he could speak the Herefordshire dialect as well as anyone. It was when he had tried to speak his mother's way that the lads at school had teased him. Still, Nettie had corrected him all his life. She believed that Will would better himself someday, and for that, he needed to speak correctly.

The door opened, and Sarah and Esther stepped in, the gray light from the open door making silhouettes of them. They were wearing white aprons and caps, both having spent their day in the little dairy that was attached to the back of the house. "What's happened to Dad?" Sarah asked. "Daniel said he's hurt himself."

"He's sprung his knee," Nettie said. "Badly, I fear."

"He'll be laid up for quite some time," Will said. He took a hard look at the girls, hoping they would understand that more would now be asked of everyone. Sarah was sixteen and Esther only eleven, but they were used to working hard. They milked two cows every morning, and that meant separating milk, churning butter, molding cheese. They fed animals, too, and they weeded in the garden and topped turnips. Josiah, who was fourteen, did some of those things as well, but he had plenty of work just cleaning out the barn, keeping the yard tidy, and doing all the other chores Morgan gave him.

"We'll hope for the best," Nettie said. She had assembled her ingredients on the dinner table in the center of the room and had spread out a scrap of brown paper.

"I'll tell you this much," Will told the lasses. "He couldn't get up, couldn't even make his leg go straight. I'll wager he won't walk for a fortnight and won't work for a month. When a man his age makes a muck and muddle of his knee, there's not much anyone can do to make it right again."

"He thinks God'll heal him," Sarah said. "That's what Daniel said."

Will looked down at the floor—the smooth-worn paving stones. "Well, I hope he's right."

"But you don't believe it, do you?"

"I don't have his faith. Father just told me that himself." Will meant to say no more, but he couldn't help adding, "Still, I'm thinking we're all going to have to work harder around here."

"Dan can fill in for Dad," Esther said, and she laughed. Sarah laughed too, and Will finally smiled. He knew the girls loved

Daniel—probably more than they loved him—but everyone knew how Dan liked to dawdle.

"That's enough of that," Nettie said. "All three of you. Someone go see how your father is doing."

So the girls walked to the back bedroom, and Will said, "I better see about the oxen. I left them in the field. Do you need water from the well, or—"

"Not right now. Go back to your work before the rain starts. I can see it coming." As Will turned to go, she said, "I know what you're thinking."

Will looked back at her.

Nettie looked up from the concoction she was mixing. She brushed some loose gray hairs out of her eyes with the back of her hand. Will had heard from others how pretty his mum had once been, with flaxen hair and bright blue eyes like his own. He could still see some of that beauty, but she was tired, and her eyes had lost much of their brightness. Her skin had turned leathery, especially along her throat and around her eyes. The last few years had been difficult. Tenant farmers with small parcels of land—like the Lewises, with only twenty acres—had struggled to feed their families. It was not just the work, but the worry, Will thought, that had taken a toll on her.

"What am I thinking?" Will asked.

"That you'll never get away from us now."

Will didn't answer.

For a long time Will and his mother had talked about his hope to find another way to make a living. As the oldest son, he was the one who would normally take over the tenancy and continue to farm the land. Squire Riddle, the young man who had inherited twelve hundred acres that he rented out to tenants, was not obliged to pass the tenancy to Will, but Will stood in line to be the fourth generation to farm the parcel the Lewises lived on. More than that, he was more skilled and knowledgeable about farming than any young man in the valley.

The problem was, Will wanted more. He had watched his family struggle to get by all his life. The enclosure laws that Parliament had passed had taken away the chance for tenants to graze cattle, to hunt, or to gather firewood from the lands that bordered their farms. Time was, a tenant could run his small farm, share his income with the landlord, but also help provide for his family by using adjacent lands. Now, the gentry had been allowed to make those lands part of their own property. This meant better efficiency and more production, which was seen as a positive by Parliament, but it also meant that tenant farmers were forced into deeper poverty. They could sometimes manage to keep a pig and some fowl, and they could raise a small garden, but all this took away from the land they could cultivate— and landlords pressed them to plant every inch of their rented land. The Lewises kept two cows and sold some of the butter and cheese. Squire Riddle didn't like that, but Morgan persisted. The tiny dairy didn't offer much profit, especially since the cows were aging, but he wanted to keep his daughters close—not off working in some mansion, servants to the gentry.

The elder Squire Riddle had been a fair-minded man, but he had died rather young, and his oldest son had taken over the estate—the expansive manor house, gardens, barns, and coach house on a prominence overlooking the valley. The young squire liked to live well, and rumors were that he spent more than he took in. He was trying to bleed every farthing he could from his tenants. He had raised his rents twice since taking over, and he was strict about any use of common lands. He had hired a gamekeeper, whose job it was to stop poaching but also to watch for anyone hauling off wood— even just dead limbs.

For years Will and his mother had discussed Will's leaving to learn a trade, but Morgan had not been willing to hear of that. In his mind, the tenancy was a family legacy not to be lost. He always believed that better days were ahead and that the new squire would soften with time.

Will had actually learned one non-farm skill from his father. Morgan had taught him to lay brick and stone, enough to build an outbuilding or to repair a wall. Morgan and Will sometimes took on small jobs and added to their income. What Will had been mulling over for years was the idea of pursuing this masonry trade. He had talked to the stonemasons in Ledbury about working with one of them, but he was too old to be an apprentice now, and masons were not interested in training someone who might soon compete with them—not in such hard times.

"There's something I've been thinking about," Will said. He waited for his mother to look up at him. This was probably the wrong time to introduce his idea to her, but she had raised the question. "I'm thinking of heading off to Birmingham or Manchester to work in the factories. It's not good work, I know, but I might, in time, become a manager. The bosses earn a pretty penny, from what I hear."

"What are you saying? When would you go?"

"Not now. That's certain. I can't even think of leaving until after this year's harvest."

"But aren't factories closing up?"

"I hear those things, but I can't say for sure. If a man is young and strong and willing, maybe there's hope for him. If I stay here, my hope is dead already."

"But Will, I doubt you would be happy in a factory, far away in a big city."

"Maybe not, at first. But I have more education than most of the workers in those places. I talked to a man in Ledbury who said I might have a chance to make something of myself."

It was true that when Will was younger he had attended school in Ledbury each winter after harvest, and he had gone to a Methodist Sunday School where children were taught to read the Bible. More important, Nettie had always taught him at home. He was a good reader and had a natural knack with arithmetic. Still, it was only a little more education than most farm boys had; it probably wasn't enough to get him work as a clerk or a bookkeeper.

"Is it the farm you hate so much, or is it Liz Duncan you love so much? Which is it that makes you want to leave us?"

"Mum, you've always told me it's what I ought to do—rise a little in the world."

"I know. But not in a factory. And I don't want you to go so far away from us."

Will let his breath blow out. He didn't know what he could say to his mother. She had no idea how unhappy he had been lately.

"Do you think you can win Liz over if you hold a position in a factory?"

"No. Nothing will win her over. I'm not thinking about that."

"Will, I watch you at church meetings. You light up if she so much as speaks to you. I know she's pretty, but is she worth all the pain you put yourself through?"

"Who said anything about pain?" Will didn't want this.

The poultice was ready now, and Will had thought his mother would hurry off to her husband, but instead she was still watching Will. "I think you're taking me wrong," she said. "In my mind, you deserve her. I just don't want to see your heart broken. Her father wouldn't hear of his precious daughter marrying a tenant farmer's son. And Sister Duncan thinks that being a solicitor's wife makes her better than anyone else in our church."

She picked up the poultice, ready to take it to Morgan, but she kept watching Will. He felt her pity, and he appreciated it and hated it at the same time. "That's how it is with religion," Will said, with more bitterness in his voice than he usually let his mother hear. "We all go to meetings together and hear sermons about loving our neighbors, but the 'better classes' *will na' mix wiff us what's beneath 'em.* God blesses them all the same. And things only get worse for us."

"Oh, Will, I fear you take some of your attitudes from me. We really are God's children, and that is what matters." It was all the same old talk. Will didn't want to hear any more of it. He walked to the door before his mother said, "I pray every day that something will change—that somehow you will be able to have what you want."

"Mum, it's better not to talk that way. You should tell me plain to give up on things I cannot have. It's what I tell myself, and it's what I need to believe."

"I still pray." She hesitated, as though she wanted to find the right words to encourage him, but then she said, "I must go to your father."

"Aye. Do that."

As Will stepped through the door, he heard his mother say, "Morgan, has the pain calmed a little by now?"

Will didn't hear the answer. He headed back to the field. He could see the oxen where he had left them, still bedded down. He wondered whether he could get them going again now. He wasn't sure he could get himself going, but he could still feel the rain in the air, and he needed to try.

As Will passed the barn, he heard Daniel laugh. He stopped and looked through the door. Daniel was wrestling with Edgar, who was seven, and little four-year-old Solomon. They were trying to grab

Daniel and pull him down, but he was holding them off and laughing at their inability to move him.

"Dan, I suppose it would na' help matters if I told ye we have more work than ever now."

"It would na' help at all," Daniel said. He pushed Edgar away and then turned around, smiling. "I know that as good as you. I was workin' when you was whilin' away your time in the house with Mum. These little badgers took me on, though. I plan to make short work of 'em." He poked Solomon, who laughed and then jumped at him. Daniel caught him and pushed him back. "And do na' forget, we have no worries. Brother Watkins will fly in soon, like a angel. One touch with his magic hands and Dad will rise up and do the plowin' himself—no oxen needed—an' then do me chores."

"And is that what you hope for, Dan? Someone to do your work for you?"

"Do na' start with me, Will," Daniel said. His smile was gone. "Just get back to your oxen. You're the chosen one. You get to plow; I get to dig ditches and muck out chicken coops."

"If I can ever leave this place, you can have the farm—if you think there's such a bright future in it."

"More future than laborin' for some other man."

Will knew that might be true, and at times he did pity Daniel, who had little to look forward to but farm labor, the lowest-paying work of all. But Daniel might have tried something by now, not having been required on the farm as Will always had been. Will was sick of his whining. "I work hard, Dan. Every day. And you play with the lads in the barn."

"I've heard that story afore. Dad tells it to me all the time. But I say this. You do me chores and I'll be happy to plow those fields—any time you want to trade."

Will felt rage fire inside him. "Tell the truth, Dan. You can na' hold a plow straight, can na' cut two furrows without runnin' one o'er the top of t'other. An' you walk away five minutes after you make a start."

"That's a lie, Will. It's what you allus say 'bout me, and it's na' any of it true. If you think you're so good with a plow, tell me how good ye be with two fists." Daniel stepped up face-to-face with Will.

"Do na' tempt me, Dan. I could end all this talk with one blow."

"Let's see it, then. But make it good, or six more will be flyin' back at ye."

But Will couldn't hit his brother. He didn't look away, but he knew that the little lads were standing near, probably frightened. This had to stop. "I can na' waste me time with this," he said. "I'm goin' to plow a li'l more afore the day is gone." He turned and strode away.

As he reached the door, Will heard Daniel laugh and say, "Take heart, big brother. You can allus marry Liz Duncan. Maybe her dear ol' father will take you into the solicitor's trade."

Will spun around. "You know as well as I do, Liz Duncan would never stoop to *touch* someone as lowly as me."

"Or if she did, her father would slap her hand." Daniel's voice had changed, as though he understood how raw Will's pain was.

Will stood for a long time, looking into Dan's eyes, and then he looked at his little brothers, who looked concerned. "We do na' have a future, do we?" he finally said, softly. "Not one of us."

For once, Dan didn't smile. "Nay. An' that's the truth on it," he said, barely loud enough to hear.

Will worried what the boys would think of such an assessment. Edgar was a frail little fellow who liked to joke with Daniel, but he took life far too seriously. He had the same dark hair as Will and Morgan, and brooding eyes. Will could see that he was worried. "We still have to do our best," Will said. "Right now, we have to keep things movin' fo'ward 'til Dad is up and agoin.' And who knows, maybe things'll get better one of these days."

He didn't believe his own words, and surely his brothers must have known that. Still, there was nothing else to say, so Will walked around the shed, used the stile to cross through the hedgerow, and then hiked up the hill to the oxen. He talked to them, told them they needed to plow a few more furrows before dark. The oxen got up as though they understood, and the three of them trudged back across the field, Will fighting the plow in the damp soil and feeling so tired he could hardly keep up the struggle.

Half an hour later, Will felt the oxen losing strength. He pushed on a little longer, but finally a light rain began to fall. He unyoked Nick and Nimble and led them down the hill to their corral. On his way to the house, he saw Esther coming for him. "Brother Watkins is here," she said. "Dad says for all to come in."

"He do na' want me," Will said. "He tol' me so. Tell 'im I'm still aplowin'."

"In the rain?" Esther was always much too quick to believe Will, even when she should have known he wasn't serious. She was a pretty girl, with her mother's eyes and wispy hair that shaded toward yellow, like an early cowslip bloom.

"It's not rainin' now," Will said. It was true that the shower had passed over quickly, but darker clouds lay along the west hills of the valley. Still, Will had no intention of going back to work. He walked all the way to the top of the hillside field and then sat down under the great sessile oak near the upper hedgerow. The sun was not far from setting now, and the clouds over the hills were orange and pale yellow, with streaks of misty light shining through, reaching across the valley, turning everything golden. South, toward Ledbury, he could see the fields in varied shades, and white hawthorn blossoms in the hedgerows, shading yellow in the angled light. Mixed among the shades of green were cottages in little groups, red-tiled or thatched. All of it was like pictures rich people liked to hang on their walls. Mother said that the valley, Wellington Heath, was as beautiful as anything she had ever seen. Will thought she might be right. But he had never seen anything else, and the truth was, Mum hadn't seen much either. He had no idea what the rest of the world looked like. He only knew he would like to find out.

For Will, this valley was a snare. He was caught like a hare, one leg in a trap, with no way to break loose. Across the valley he could see Squire Riddle's manor house with its many windows and chimneys, and all the red brick buildings: a coach house, stables and half a dozen outbuildings, plus living quarters for the coachmen, who dressed in livery and drove the squire around as though he were the new young Queen Victoria herself. The squire had servants to cook for him, to tend his fires, to wash his bedding, probably to scratch his back. The man had done not one thing to earn anything he had. He had only been born to it, and Will had been born to the plow that was still sticking up in the ground where he had left it. He could find a wife someday, bring her here, and work her hard until she grew old—all too fast—and he could raise up a family and make all the children work as hard as he always had. And when life was over, what would he have, and what would his children have? He still wouldn't own the land he worked, and his income would be as meager as ever—hardly enough to keep clothes on his children and bread on his table.

His mum said she was praying that things would change, but Will had tried praying too, and he had never seen any results. Maybe hares prayed when they were caught in a snare, but he had never known one to escape.

CHAPTER 2

Jeff Lewis got home to the apartment before his wife, Abby, did.
Now, for half an hour he had been waiting, nervous, rehearsing different ways he could break the news. He was sitting on the couch in their little living room when she opened the door. He felt self-conscious, not reading, just sitting there, so he stood up. She looked pale to him, and tired, but she was smiling. "You won't believe what happened today," she said.

He didn't say anything. He tried to smile.

"You know that yellow swatch that I said was too bright? The one for the Boltons' kitchen?"

Jeff didn't remember, but he said, "Yeah."

"Well, Mrs. Bolton didn't like it. Mary was all, 'Oh, I wondered. It is a little bright. But you like the concept, don't you?' So Mrs. Bolton—she's like super quiet, and won't give her opinion most of the time—she just kind of shrugs, like she isn't really sure. I was standing behind Mary trying not to laugh." But Abby's smile was fading. "What's wrong?"

Jeff decided he might as well just say it. "Well . . . Mr. Hart called me in this afternoon. I didn't think much about it at first, but then he started talking about the bad economy and how the company was going to have to cut back on their computer people—you know, let some people go." He lifted his hands, palms up. "He said I'd done a good job for them, but since I've been there less than a year—and I was the last guy hired—I'm the one he felt he had to cut. I'll finish out the month, but that's all."

"Is it just a layoff, or . . . what?"

"He said that in case they get busier again, or if anyone should leave, I should keep in touch—but I don't see that happening for a long time."

"What are we going to do?"

One reason Jeff had been dreading this moment was that Abby always worried so much. Her pretty, dark eyes were brimming with tears already, and that crushed him. He walked to her and took her in his arms. Abby's head fit under his chin. She pressed her face against his chest. "I wouldn't worry too much, Ab. I did all that contract work when I was still in school. I'll start calling those people in the morning. I'm pretty sure I can get enough work to keep us going for a while."

"What about insurance?" She stepped back from him. It was like her to think of the practical things. In some ways, she was more the grownup than he was.

"I wondered about that," Jeff said. "But it shouldn't be a big problem. I don't think I'll be out of work very long. We're both healthy, and—"

"I don't dare do that, Jeff. Something could happen."

"Well, okay. I talked to Personnel. The woman said I could get some COBRA thing through the government—it's the same insurance we've had, but we have to pay for it ourselves. It lasts eighteen months if we need it that long."

"Did you say you would take it?"

"I told her I'd think about it. I was just hoping that maybe we could . . . but that's okay. I'll get back to her in the morning and tell her we want it. Don't worry, though, Abby. We're going to be fine. A Stanford degree means a lot. I'll find another job."

"You don't know that, Jeff. My Stanford degree got me a part-time job at Saunders' Carpet and Floor Coverings."

"But honey, think about it. You knew when you went into art history that you'd have to get more than an undergraduate degree."

"Still . . . I thought I could get a job in a museum or something like that."

Jeff didn't want to argue with her. The only museums that might have been interested were in San Francisco, and he and Abby had chosen to live close to his work on the peninsula, near Stanford, in Sunnyvale. They had agreed not to have her look for jobs that would mean a commute all the way into the city.

Anyway, that was not really the point. Abby was scared. If there was one thing Jeff had learned about her in the last year, it was that she needed the security she had grown up with. She'd been raised in Teaneck, New Jersey, and her father had ridden the same commuter train into New York City—and had worked at the same advertising firm—for almost thirty years. Security to Abby was like the water that flowed from the faucets in the beautiful home she had grown up in. Jeff had watched her, after they had married, seem to realize—as though it were a whole new concept—that not everything was certain all the time.

It wasn't that she was spoiled. She had worked hard in high school and college, and she'd worked summer jobs all those years. She liked making her own money and not relying entirely on her parents. She thought for herself, too, sometimes almost more than

Jeff had been ready for. But she simply had never experienced anything but security.

Abby had come to Stanford as a churchgoing Methodist, but she had had a best friend in high school who was LDS—a girl who had impressed her—and then she had become acquainted with a Mormon in her dorm. A long talk about religion had led to her taking missionary lessons. Jeff had spotted her at church and decided immediately that he'd like to do a little "fellowshipping." She was quite skinny, and she was cute more than beautiful, with dark brown hair and a dimply smile. Jeff had liked her immediately. She was smart and she liked to talk about ideas. The two of them could talk about anything and everything. They hadn't been dating a month before Jeff knew he wanted to marry her.

Abby had been a little less certain about him. For one thing, she didn't want to join the LDS church just because she was attracted to a good-looking guy. She attended church for the better part of a year before she was finally baptized. But maybe half that year was spent getting her parents to accept the idea. They kept finding anti-Mormon information on the Internet and e-mailing it to her. That did raise a lot of questions for Abby, but she took the questions to Jeff and he kept providing perspective, if not always easy answers—as did a lot of other really bright students in the Stanford singles ward.

On Valentine's Day of their senior year Jeff had finally asked her to marry him and Abby had accepted, but she asked that the wedding be held in New Jersey, since they couldn't get married in the temple for a year anyway, and neither of them wanted to wait that long. Jeff had met her parents a couple of times and had spent a little more time with them when they came to California for graduation, but it was during the days in Teaneck that he seemed to experience a breakthrough with them. John Ramsey enjoyed talking to Jeff, and he told Abby he was amazed at how many things Jeff, young as he was, could talk about intelligently. Even more, he liked that Jeff had helped his father build the Lewises' house in Las Vegas. He said that Jeff was a "solid guy," and *that,* according to Abby, was Dad's highest compliment.

Mrs. Ramsey—Olivia—had warmed to him too, if not quite so enthusiastically. She was Italian and had been raised in a Catholic family, but her parents had divorced, and she remained skeptical of men's promises. "I love the way he treats you," she had told Abby, but she had added, "Just make sure it doesn't change."

Jeff had thought a lot about that. His own father was certainly a solid guy and a good husband, but he wasn't one to show a lot of affection. His mom sometimes teased him: "Come on, Alan, kiss me in front of the kids. They need to know you actually love me." Jeff and his three younger sisters would all say, "Oh, yuck," but Jeff knew now that it was a good thing to tell Abby he loved her, and it was important to remember days that were special to her. Abby kept track of the months they'd been married, and Jeff tried to preempt her at mentioning that it was their "monthaversary." What he sensed already, though, was that he was more like his father than he had realized, and he could easily slip into complacency about such things if he didn't work at it.

Jeff had grown up an active Latter-day Saint, involved in Scouting and all the Young Men activities. He had served a mission in British Columbia and been an assistant to the president. He was every Mormon's wish for a son in most ways, and yet, he sometimes felt uncomfortable in Church discussions. He was a little too much like his mother—who never stopped raising questions. She could drive a Sunday School teacher crazy with her little queries that would start with something like, "I'm sure that's true, Brother Jones, but on the other hand . . ." She couldn't help inserting reality into a conversation that the teacher would have rather concluded with, "Well, I guess you just have to follow the Spirit."

Jeff had thrived in his college ward, where questions had been valued at least as much as answers. But that wasn't always easy for Abby. She was still trying to get lots of things straight in her head, and Jeff tended to make things complicated for her. He had majored in computer engineering, but he had taken every class in history and literature that he could work into his schedule.

"Do you want to go get a sandwich or something—and talk through this whole situation?" Jeff asked. "I've been thinking a lot about it. I really feel like it might be the best thing for us."

"What do you mean? How could that be?"

"Well, that's what I want to explain. Why don't we just run down to—"

"I'm not hungry, Jeff. And we can't spend the money. I'll make you a sandwich, if that's all you want, but I don't want anything right now."

"It's not that. I'm not that hungry either. But I have some things I want to tell you—or, you know, talk over with you." He took her hand and led her to the little couch they had bought at a secondhand shop in Palo Alto. Abby had a knack for finding old things and making them fit her decorating scheme, but she didn't always look carefully at the structure of the furniture she chose. Jeff had warned her about the couch, but she had liked the pattern of the beige and red fabric. The thing was breaking down now, and there was a depression in the springs where Jeff usually sat and read under the light of the fancy Victorian floor lamp Abby had also chosen. He sat down in that gully now, still holding Abby's hand, and he pulled her next to him.

"I know you're upset," he said.

"It's okay. It wasn't your fault. Mr. Hart said that, didn't he?"

"Well, yeah. He said he'd write me a good letter of recommendation and everything. But that's not what I mean. I'm just saying, I know it's kind of scary. When he first told me, I was blown away. I'd known it could happen, but—"

"You didn't tell me that." Abby's voice was soft, but the glance she had thrown his way seemed a little too accusing. He knew she was calculating her small income, setting it off against their bills. He had to be careful not to sound naïve. But she didn't have to assume the sky was falling, either. He found it a little hard to be patient when she got that way.

"Okay, here's the thing. I'm sure I can get contract work. The companies I did work for always threw more work at me than I could handle. And that wasn't very long ago. I've got all the phone numbers. I'll start working through them in the morning."

She nodded.

"Sometimes, though, something like this is just what a person needs in order to move ahead in life. The thing is, I've never said too much about it, but I didn't like my job that much. You know how I've been in the mornings. You keep asking me what's wrong, but I just hated doing grunt work. I was trained to do creative stuff—real programming—and I don't get a chance to do that."

"You always said that was okay—since it was just a first job and everything."

"Hey, I was relieved to find a job as soon as I graduated. It gave us a start. But I always felt like a fish out of water. Most of the guys I worked with were the real geeks they're supposed to be. If I said something at lunch about—you know, almost anything—they'd start in on me about being the 'Stanford boy.'"

"You told me that didn't bother you."

Jeff sat back, let go of Abby's hand. He knew already that he couldn't tell her everything he'd been thinking all afternoon.

"Well—you know—it didn't *seriously* bother me, but I didn't feel like I fit in, either. The main thing, though, was that the job was just not challenging. And it had no future. It was always just a stepping-stone. To get anywhere, I always knew I'd have to look for another job."

"But this isn't a good time to be looking, with the economy the way it is."

"I know. I wouldn't have quit. That's the thing—now I'm forced to look for something better, and that might be my chance to move in the right direction."

She looked at him again, and he could see resolution in those brown eyes. She had made up her mind about something. "Let's have a prayer, okay? I think things will work out if we have enough faith."

"Of course. I do too." He pulled her to him and kissed her on the side of her head, his bottom lip catching the top of her ear. "In fact, that's one of the reasons I thought we ought to eat something. Maybe we could start a fast before I make those calls in the morning."

"Okay." But she sounded hesitant.

"Or maybe that wouldn't work, with you having to work tomorrow."

"No, no. I want to do it. I think I can." Fasting had been a new thing for Abby when she joined the Church. Actually, she never ate very much, but she would become weak and even dizzy when she tried to miss two meals.

"No, honey, you don't have to. We'll be okay. I'm so sorry this happened." He knelt down in front of her and looked up into her eyes. "I'll make everything all right. Trust me, okay?"

"I do. Don't think I don't." Tears spilled onto her cheeks. She bent forward and kissed him.

He held both her hands in his and said, "There's something I want you to think about."

"Okay."

"I've been wondering this afternoon whether this might be the right time for me to go back to school. We've always said that we both need to do that at some point. But maybe it's easiest to go now, when we're young and don't have kids."

She sat up straight. He knew he had scared her again, but he hadn't expected her to be quite so surprised by the idea. Still, he decided he might as well say it—get it out on the table—and then let the idea sink in for a while. "I'm thinking, if I go to grad school, I might not want to stay in computers. What I'd love to do is to go on for a PhD in history. I've always thought I'd like being a professor. The whole computer thing was just a way of playing it safe. Everyone said there were plenty of jobs in the field." He hesitated, unsure what she was thinking; she was avoiding eye contact now. "But here's the thing. Maybe we'd both be happier if I was doing something I really loved."

"Jeff, we didn't do that last year because we couldn't afford it. How can we afford it now?"

"Lots of people keep going to school after they get married. I might be able to get a fellowship of some kind, and I could still do contract work part-time. We could take out student loans if we had to."

"We looked into that. People are spending their whole lives trying to pay back their loans. When you found a good job, we decided that was the answer." She looked frustrated. "Remember everything we talked about? And how we prayed about it?"

"Sure I do. And I am going to start looking for another job. But maybe it's a better time to move ahead with my education. Everyone says that you never lose when you invest in education."

"Jeff, I want to start a family. That's what matters most to me. You know that."

"That's what I want too. It's the most important thing there is in life."

"But the doctor said I had to control stress—get more rest and everything. She said that might be the reason I haven't gotten pregnant." The first several months Abby and Jeff had been married, they had held off on Abby getting pregnant, and then they had decided together that they wanted to get their family started. But nothing had happened. Abby had finally seen a gynecologist, who had said there was no reason to assume infertility problems yet. Abby had always been rather irregular with her periods, and that was probably the problem. The worst thing Abby could do was worry too much about it.

"Do you think it would be stressful for you if I went back to school?"

"If we had some savings, or if you knew you had enough work—or maybe a fellowship or something—maybe it wouldn't. But it scares me to think of jumping off into something without more of a plan."

"Hey, I agree. We'd have to figure a lot of things out. I'm just saying, maybe we should start thinking in that direction. But I'm with you. I want kids. I'll never put my own priorities ahead of that. It's just that I'd like to enjoy my work, too. Is that wrong?"

"No." She looked past him.

"Tell me what you're thinking."

"I *want* you to be happy. And I've noticed it a lot lately. You just haven't been."

"It hasn't been *that* bad, honey. If it's what I need to do, I'll just take whatever job I can get. But let's not decide anything yet. I'll fast, and we'll pray, and we'll try to get some answers about what we ought to do. I'll get all the contract work I can, for now, so we won't have to worry about having enough to get by."

"I want to fast too."

"Only if you're sure you can." He watched her face for a time. She was clearly preoccupied, and he wondered whether she wasn't wondering about him, doubting that he would ever give her the life she wanted. "Are you upset with me?" he asked.

"No, Jeff." But she still wouldn't look into his eyes. "We'll do what we have to do."

"The Lord will help us, honey."

"I know."

Jeff decided he'd said enough. He was actually more worried than he was letting on, but it was hard to understand why Abby couldn't empathize a little more and imagine what it was like for him to do a job he didn't like—to go there day after day, counting hours all day, never feeling challenged. He had always thought he could do something big, or at least creative, but he wasn't developing software programs the way he had expected. He had ended up in a sort of glorified IT job, supporting the accounting department and helping the office staff when they couldn't get programs to run correctly.

"Let's pray," Abby said. She slipped off the couch next to him, knelt, and took hold of his hand. He said the prayer and asked for help and guidance. Then he held Abby again and reassured her as best he could. She said the right things too, with more life in her voice, and she kissed him again. "I'll fix us something to eat, okay? But if you don't mind, I'll wait just a little while. I'd kind of like to lie down for a few minutes."

"Sure. In fact, you do that and I'll fix dinner."

She smiled. "I was hoping you'd say that."

• • •

Abby did rest a little while, but she kept asking herself what lay ahead for them, and she couldn't sleep. She could smell bacon frying and knew Jeff was making up one of his pancake breakfasts as a dinner. There was something really sweet about that—but not all that appetizing.

Abby knew better than to call her mother, but she found herself digging in her purse for her phone. She decided she might as well give her mom the bad news and get it over with. So she called, talked about other things for a time, and then, as casually as she could, said that Jeff had lost his job but that it wasn't a big problem; they were both sure he could find something else.

Mrs. Ramsey didn't take the news in stride. She asked lots of questions, and by the time she was finished had Abby more nervous than ever. "I've heard about a lot of computer people out of work lately," she told Abby. "The way the economy has shut down, from what I'm hearing, people could be out of work a long time."

"Well . . . thanks for those encouraging words."

"It's just reality, Abby—something young people don't like to recognize. I hope you have some savings."

How were they supposed to build up savings this first year of marriage, with so many things they had had to buy to get their apartment set up? Abby only said, "We'll be fine, Mom. I wanted to let you know, but I'm not worried at all."

"You sound worried."

Abby took a breath. "Well, you know . . . it's not what we'd like right now. But we're handling it all right."

"Don't go without food out there, okay? We can help. In fact, I'll—"

"No. Don't send money. We're okay for now. You helped me get through college, and that cost way too much. I've got my degree now and I'll be fine."

"At the carpet store?"

Abby wasn't going to answer that one. It was a stab, and they both knew it. Mrs. Ramsey had wanted Abby to wait to get married and go on for an advanced degree immediately. Of course, she had also hoped that Abby would end up back on the East Coast, not all the way across the country. It really seemed that every choice Abby made bothered her mother in some way.

"Look, I'm sorry," Mrs. Ramsey finally said. "It's just hard for me not to worry about you."

"That's okay. I understand."

"I love you, sweetheart. I really do."

"I know." Abby waited. She knew better than to end the call too quickly and make it seem she had only called about the layoff. She asked a few questions, tried to seem chatty.

Her mom talked about this and that—Abby's sister, Maria, and her husband, and some friends of the family. "Hey," she said, "did you hear that Tracy Mower is pregnant?" The Mowers were family friends from their neighborhood in Teaneck, and Tracy was their oldest daughter. She was five or six years older than Abby.

"Actually, I did. She posted it on her Facebook wall."

"You've got to be kidding. This world is getting away from me, I swear. Why would she put it on the Internet?"

"She's happy about it."

"I don't know why. They want to buy a house and I don't see how they'll do it. I'm just glad you're not pregnant. That's the worst thing that could happen right now."

"Mom, what a terrible thing to say. There have to be worse things than having a child."

"Children are wonderful, Abby—when the time is right. But don't let this Mormon thing get you thinking you have to start early and pop out a dozen kids before you're finished."

"Mom, we *don't* want to wait too long." Abby had never had the courage to tell her mother that they had been trying. She knew what kind of reaction she would get if she said anything.

"Abby, I don't like the sound of that. Even if Jeff finds another job, he'll have to start all over again with a new company. I'd be very sure he's in a stable situation before you start thinking about a baby."

"Mom, I'm a grownup now. Don't talk to me like I'm a teenager."

"Well, maybe I know a few things you don't—even if you are clear up in your *twenties*."

Abby decided it was time to get off the phone. She was only getting angry.

"Do use your heads, the two of you," her mom continued. "That's all I'm saying."

"Okay. We will. Well, look, Jeff cooked tonight. I've got to go see how much damage he's done to the kitchen. Don't worry about us, and please don't send money. I'll let you know how things are going."

"Honey, I'm sorry. I know I've upset you. But I do love you."

"I know. Thanks, Mom."

Abby had lost control of her voice a little, and her mom must have heard her shakiness. She really was scared, but there was no one she could say that to. She needed to go out to the kitchen and convince Jeff that she wasn't a frightened little girl. She would stand beside him, and the two of them would figure things out. But she was crying again, and she didn't want Jeff to see that.

CHAPTER 3

It was May 1, 1839—Fair Day in Ledbury—and the weather was perfect. Good weather meant that Will could get a hard day of work in. The night before, however, Nettie had asked him to drive Sarah and Esther and their wagonload of cheese into town early in the morning so they could set up their booth at the fair.

"And why not have Daniel take them?" Will had asked.

"They want to leave at four-thirty, and you know what a fight I have to get Daniel up at such an hour."

Will thought she was entirely too easy on Daniel, but he didn't say so. The truth was, he actually wanted to go and had worked hard all week to make the time. He longed for a day away from the farm, and he had allowed himself to think a little about who might be there and what might come of that.

So he slept in the barn loft, got up in the dark and yoked ol' Nick and Nimble, and then chained them up to the wagon, which the girls had already loaded the night before. When he opened the cottage door, he saw that his mother was up too. She had cooked barley porridge, and now she was standing behind Sarah, who was sitting at the dinner table. Mum was braiding her hair so she could wear it up under her cap. The girls had taken a bath the night before and washed their hair—as though it were already Sunday.

Esther was brushing her long hair, looking at herself in the little mirror on the wall by the bedroom door. She was going to be prettier than Sarah, and she seemed to know it already. She had learned from her big sister to talk about the lads in town, and clearly hoped they would notice her.

"Have you two eaten anything?" Will asked the girls. "You won't be having dinner for a long time."

Nettie pointed to the hanging blanket that divided the room at night. Daniel and Josiah slept in the bed behind the blanket and Sarah and Esther on the side where the fire was. Will had slept with Daniel and Josiah for many years, but it was all that crowding that motivated him, in warmer weather, to sleep on a straw tick in the barn. Dad said it was a waste of tallow candles, his sleeping out there, but now that the days were getting longer, that didn't matter so much. "Don't wake the boys," Mum whispered.

"Them two can . . ." Will saw his mother's reaction and corrected himself. "Those two can sleep through anything. They won't hear me." It was little Solomon who woke up more easily, but he slept along with Edgar on a straw mat in the bedroom where Mum and Dad slept.

It took some doing, but Will got the lasses to move along and eat their breakfasts. He gulped down his own porridge with a pint of buttermilk, along with a thick slice of buttered bread, and then he walked out ahead of the girls and drove the wagon up to the cottage. He waited a minute or so and then jumped down and walked back to the door. "It's the two of you who said four-thirty, and it's past that now," he said.

"We're comin'," Sarah said. "Is there a fire some'eres I don't know nothin' about?" But she was happy; Will could hear it in her voice. She and Esther sounded like peeping little birds as he drove the oxen down the Ledbury road. The rutted road made the wagon bounce and sway, but that didn't slow the chatter.

The lasses would be busy all morning selling their cheeses, but he knew how they would spend the afternoon—strolling along High Street where all the booths would be set up. They would watch whatever performers might be in town and, more than anything, gossip with their friends. Sarah's friends—girls she knew from church, or ones she had gone to the town school with years ago—would want to talk about the farm lads in town or, even more, the young men from Ledbury, apprentices and sons of merchants.

Nettie had said that she would probably walk into town a little later with Edgar and Solomon. Josiah could walk in with Daniel. Morgan would surely be staying home. It had been over a week since he had injured his knee, and he was not much improved. Brother Watkins, according to Daniel's account, had placed his hands on Dad's knee and commanded, "Morgan Lewis, arise and walk." Dan had imitated Watkins, roaring like a wild man, his chest puffed out like a crowing rooster. And according to his account, Dad had jumped up instantly, his face all alight, and almost as quickly had crumpled to the ground, crying out with pain. Nettie had stopped Daniel at that point and had denied that Morgan had made any sound at all as he had fallen, but she couldn't help smiling a little at Daniel's reenactment. Will assumed that, for the most part, it was true.

Dad was hobbling about these days, putting little weight on his right leg, and he was saying nothing about faith healing. Will knew what he would claim—that in time they would all understand why the Lord had not healed him as quickly as he had hoped. But Will's skepticism had proven more accurate than his father's faith, and he took some satisfaction in that. The trouble was, all the problems he had foreseen had also come true. Daniel wasn't helping any more than he ever had. In the coming weeks, maybe months, there would be no change to that, Will was sure.

But he wasn't thinking about that today. He was wondering whether he could create an opportunity to talk with Liz Duncan. He often tried to do that at church, but Brother Duncan watched him like a guard dog. Now and then Will had chatted with her all the same, and those were times that he savored, rehearsing them over and over in his mind as he plowed or harrowed. She actually seemed to flirt with him at times—teasing him, smiling slyly as she talked. Will always tried to say something clever—even practiced ahead of time so he would have something to say—but he doubted himself afterwards, wondered why he hadn't come back with a better response, why he hadn't said the things he had thought up.

The Ledbury road turned into Homend Street at the edge of town, and Homend turned into High Street. The long, wide lane was lined with homes and shops. In the dark, Will could barely make out the timbered, two-storied buildings and pubs—The Swan and The Little Crown and several more—or the bay windows on the storefronts. He had been walking or riding down this street all his life, and still, it represented excitement to him. Liz lived on Southend Street, a further extension of High Street, but it was not far from where the road widened into a triangular marketplace—the site for the fair. Her father's office was on the first level of their home. Will had never been inside her home, but he had looked at the solicitor's office through the window, and the furniture was finer than anything he would ever own in his life.

At the marketplace, Will helped the girls set up their booth and lay out their cheeses. Once everything was ready, Will watched a line of horses trudging down Homend Street, tethered head and tail, led by a trader. Horses would be auctioned or bargained in front of The Feathers, a pub in Union Lane. Cattle and hogs would be sold at the Horse Shoe Inn, not far from the fair, and sheep even closer, near St. Katherine's hospital. Will could remember days when Butcher's Row stood in the middle of High Street and animals were butchered in the street, the blood running over the cobblestones.

The market area was coming alive with people setting up wooden poles, covering them over with canvas to make booths. The spring fair was never as big as the one in October, but still, all kinds of items would be for sale: baked goods, sweets and nuts, toys, glassware, pottery, jewelry, purses, trinkets of all sorts. Hucksters would offer watch chains and knives. Costermongers would shout out their wares: fish or fruit or early vegetables.

When Will had been a boy he had seen magic shows at the fair, juggling acts, animal menageries, bull baiting, cock fighting, wrestling and boxing matches, gypsy musicians. But hard times had changed everything. No doubt, there would be a puppet show and some other entertainments, but nothing these days was ever as grand as he remembered.

"I'm agoin' to find a bit of grass for Nick and Nimble to graze," Will told his sisters. "I'll stop back now and again, to be sure you're doin' all right."

So Will took care of the oxen, and then he walked about to see who was there today. He had no interest in the wares he saw, and no money to buy anything, but he saw plenty of people he knew, and he talked with some of them. He stopped back a few times to make sure the lasses were all right. They were pleased that their cheeses were selling fast. They wanted to take money home to please Dad. Even more, Will knew, they wanted to be free of the cheese and able to roam about.

It was late in the morning, after the church bell had rung eleven, when Will finally spotted Liz. She was in the middle of a gaggle of young women, one of them Liz's sister, Mary Ann. They were laughing and talking, and all were dressed in Sunday clothes. Will felt self-conscious about his own clothes. He refused to wear the knee-length smock frocks old-fashioned farmers like his father still wore, or a felt "wide-awake" hat with its wide brim. On working days he wore a moleskin jacket and corduroy trousers, along with a cap, but today he was wearing his Sunday best. But his waistcoat was pulling apart at the seams, and his frock coat, made of a heavy fustian fabric—the only kind of suit he could afford—was fraying at both cuffs. What embarrassed him most, however, was his heavy boots, the same ones he wore in the fields. He had blackened them and tried to put a shine on them, but they were worn and cracking, too old to look decent.

Liz, on the other hand, looked beautiful. She wasn't wearing the blue merino she had worn to church all winter. She had on a rose-colored dress, mostly covered with a dark cape, but he could see her face, framed by a bonnet the same color as her dress, and he could see how brightly she was smiling as she talked with the other lasses. As he worked his way through the crowd, drawing nearer, he could feel the thump of his heart. He wanted to appear as though he had come across the girls by chance. He told himself he would doff his cap and say something offhand—and not seem overly pleased.

He worked himself into a good position without being seen, and then he stepped out of the crowd and strolled past a line of booths, all the while taking in the items for sale and never glancing in the direction of Liz and her friends. What he hadn't expected, however, was that they had started walking his direction, coming upon him sooner than he had expected. He didn't have to pretend surprise when he looked up, and he forgot to doff his cap, forgot what he had planned to say. He ended up nodding, nothing more, and Liz gave him only a quick glance.

She had almost passed before Will tried to salvage what he could of the situation. "Hello, Miss Duncan," he said. "It's a nice day, isn't it?"

Liz's friends all burst into laughter, and Will knew why. He had sounded hopelessly formal—and anything but himself. Some of these girls attended his church, and all of them knew him. He was a tenant farmer's son, not a gentleman, and he couldn't pretend otherwise.

"Ah, Mr. Lewis, it *is* lovely," Liz said, just as formally. "A day to inspire poetry!"

Will was lost. Not a word came to his mind, and certainly not to his mouth. The girls—six of them, counting Liz—were greatly entertained.

"I hope you are not following me, Mr. Lewis," Liz said. "That would be unseemly."

"I do believe he was trailing after us," Mary Ann said, but she couldn't keep a serious face the way Liz had done.

Will was standing straight, his arms hanging at his sides. He felt like a scarecrow. He wanted a rejoinder—just anything—but it wasn't there, and the lasses were still giggling.

Liz took a couple of steps to walk on by, but then she stopped and looked back, as though she hoped Will would come up with something.

"Actually," he said, and he tried to smile, "you're all very charming, but I don't allow young ladies to address me unless we have been properly introduced."

Will's face was burning, but he was rather pleased with himself. The girls were laughing *with* him, and they seemed impressed with his little pretense. He certainly was a farmer's son, but he had read the books his mother had brought to her marriage—novels about the gentry and their social manners. He could sound educated when he chose to.

There was something else Will knew. He *was* handsome. He had been told that all his life, but even more, he could see it in the girls' faces, their bonnets all turned toward him, their eyes lively under the brims. Liz may have thought of him as being beneath her, and maybe the other town girls thought so too, but he suspected that they wished he weren't.

"What are you saying?" Liz asked. "That you are not coming to tea?"

"I'm afraid not. It's the opera for me. I must be off to London on the next coach."

"Then you must be a coachman."

The girls liked that one, but Will was feeling more confident now. "No, ma'am. I'm a baron. And a duke. And an earl besides. I have so many titles, I could never list them all for you."

"What about 'blaggard'? And 'ne'er-do-well'? Does that remind you of some of your titles?"

He could see the girls waiting, all thrilled with Liz's challenge. He finally doffed his cap and smiled. "None of those, ma'am. But I have been called a ladies' man. You must take care that I not try to steal a kiss."

This caused a squeal among the girls, but Liz smiled confidently. "A kiss takes two," she said. "There's no stealing without complicity." She smiled and waited, then added, "But who knows? I just might comply."

"Liz!" Mary Ann said in a gasp.

Will was startled. Was Liz actually suggesting the idea—or only toying with him? He wasn't going to walk away from the door she had opened. "Would you like to walk out with me, young lady, and test whether such complicity couldn't be attained?"

"Oh, no. There'll be no talk of that—and no taking arms. But I don't mind walking out with you."

This was more than Will could have hoped for. She seemed to mean it. All the girls were looking at her now, obviously convinced that she really was serious, and all shocked by the possibility.

"Liz, you shouldn't," Mary Ann said, but she was giggling.

"Let us walk," Will said, and he motioned for her to join him, not offering his arm even though he wanted to.

Liz looked from one girl to the next, clearly enjoying the sensation she had caused, and then she turned back to Will. He was sure that the show was over now, but she said, "Then, sir, let us walk. As you mentioned, it *is* a fine day."

"You need to take one of us with you," Mary Ann said, now sounding serious.

"Oh, it's nothing," Liz said. "I don't need a gooseberry watching after me. Will and I are old friends."

Will understood that for her to call him "Will" was to put him back in his place. In polite society a suitor was always called "Mister" until betrothal, but Will and Liz had known one another since they had been children, and referring to him by his Christian name confirmed that she only thought of him that way—merely as her friend. But why would she walk with him? He knew there was more to it than she wanted to admit. He had seen it in her eyes more than once; she did take an interest in him.

Liz stepped up next to Will, and the two walked away, not touching, but close enough that they might easily brush one another's arms. And Will hoped at least that much would happen. But he said nothing for now. He headed away from the market square past the black-and-white timbered market house that had stood in

Ledbury since medieval days. He decided to walk up Church Lane toward the parish church, St. Michael and All Angels. He knew a path beyond that, in Dog Woods.

"I didn't think you would walk with me," Will finally said, all the laughter gone from his voice.

Liz held on to her facetious formality. "Why wouldn't I walk with an earl?" She fluttered her lashes and smiled. Will loved her pale green eyes.

"I've wanted to walk out with you for as long as I can remember," Will said.

She touched his arm, and he looked to see that her face was serious now. "Don't talk that way, Will. You're my friend from church. That's all there is to it. Be an earl, if you like, or tease me about coming to tea—but don't say anything serious."

Will walked. He told himself to abide by her rules. At least he was with her. He walked up Back Lane from Church Lane, and on to Dog Hill. The path took them to an overlook, and Liz stopped to gaze down on the town and the fair, and then, as though she assumed herself in control, she moved on into Dog Woods, where the path narrowed. Will clasped his hands behind his back, but she bumped against his arm at times. It was more than enough.

"And speaking of church, oh Earl of Lewis, I've noticed you nodding off in meetings a good deal lately. I don't think our traveling preachers like that. You miss all their admonitions and warnings. That's the road to hell, you know."

"Oh, yes." Will deepened his voice to imitate the style of the preachers. "Repent, sinners. The day will come when you shall answer for your sins. You shall burn in hell, and the fire never will go out."

"Will! You shouldn't make fun of them. You're lighting the fire that will burn you."

"Is that what you believe?"

She laughed, but then she looked his way and said more seriously, "Not exactly. I believe in God, and I believe in being kind to others. I just can't imagine that God would burn us forever, especially for the little sins the preachers seem to worry so much about."

"You mean, for instance, if we stopped and you *complied?*"

"Oh, no, sir. A kiss would be a great sin—and we very well *might* burn for it."

But she sounded playful again, almost as though she wished that he would try it. Still, he had no idea how he could approach something of that sort.

They kept walking. The woods were cool and dark, and the growth under the trees alongside the path was thick. There were massive oaks and elms and chestnuts. Birches and flowering buckthorns grew beneath the higher trees. Ferns reached into the path. Will felt alone with Liz in a way he never could have imagined. He wondered what she intended, what she was thinking, but he dared not ask.

"Are you really such a doubter, Will?" Liz asked. "Your father testifies almost every week, and you never do."

Will hardly knew what she had asked. She had taken off her bonnet, and he could see her pretty dark hair. He wondered why she had done that. It would certainly make a kiss more reachable.

When he didn't answer, she said, "Tell the truth. What do you believe?"

"I don't know. It's actually my father, and all his ranting, that makes me doubt."

"There are a good many ranters in our little group," Liz said. "Some of my friends are Anglicans, and they tell me no one acts like that in their church. Sometimes I think I'd rather stay at home and pray. That's when I feel best about God—when I can just talk to him. I don't like the God Brother Kington and Brother Watkins tell us about."

"I wish I could talk to God and believe He was actually listening. He doesn't seem to hear my prayers."

"What do you ask for?"

"Do you really want to know?"

"Yes."

"Not much, really. I only want him to help me put my foot on the first rung of the ladder. After that, I can do my own climbing. I'm trapped at my farm for now, and there's no getting out."

"Our preachers say there's more to life than riches."

"But I notice that they bow deep when they meet up with Squire Riddle. And God seems to answer all the squire's prayers."

"Will! Such bitter words. We must love our betters, not be jealous of their worldly possessions."

He glanced to see how serious she might be, but she let her eyes drift to one side and she smiled. He took all of it in: the crisp curve of her cheekbone, her soft skin, her dark brown hair, and the rich hue of her green eyes behind such long lashes. But he looked away and said, "That's what religion is all about. It's to teach poor people to stay poor, and to teach aristocrats that they deserve what they possess."

The words had come out with more intensity than Will had meant to express. He wondered whether he might have offended her. But Liz said, "And what does it teach someone like me? I'm not poor, but I'm also not a lady. No duke will ever pursue me, and a poor man can't give me the life I want. I've not been taught to churn butter or bake ash bread in a fireplace. Maybe it would be good for me to do humble work. Maybe it would bring me closer to God. But if a duchess doesn't have to do it, why do I?"

She had put him back in his place again with those few words, but he gave her the answer he wanted to believe. "Maybe a man can change the way things are—at least for himself. And he can give a woman the life she wants—whether he was born to it or not."

"It's nice to think so, Will. But it doesn't happen. Not really. Footmen don't become squires. The rules are set for us and we can't change them."

"I don't accept that, Liz. Sometimes the rules don't hold."

"Yes. And love conquers all. Do you believe that, too?"

"Maybe I do."

Liz stopped. The path was full of last year's leaves, and they were damp. "We should go back," she said. "I'll ruin my boots in here."

"And someone might notice that you've been gone with me too long."

"Yes. That, too." But she didn't turn back. She looked at Will, her eyes seeming sad, but soft. "Do you love me, Will?" she asked.

"You know I do. I don't have to tell you."

"Tell me anyway."

"I love you, Liz." He was embarrassed that his voice had become so shaky.

"But it's not to be, is it, friend? So tell me what a nice day it is."

"It's been nice for me," he said, hearing only sadness in his own voice.

"Oh, Will, I don't want to break your heart. You're so wonderful to look at—so I haven't been able to resist looking—but you know how things are. You know what my father tells me every time he catches us talking."

"I do mean what I say, Liz. I want to make something of myself. I've been thinking about it for a long time. I could rise in some kind of work once I make a break of it with my father."

"What work, Will?"

"I could start out in the factories, in Manchester or somewhere like that. I could make good, maybe become a foreman, and then a manager."

"Even an earl."

"No, not an earl. But if a man is worth his pay, if he works hard, he can rise above—"

"He can become a lead horse, but he's still harnessed to a rich man's coach. You'll work hard all your life, Will, and I know you'll be a good husband to some woman, but she will have to work just as hard. And I want more than that. I'm sorry to say it, but it's true."

"Just give me some time. See what I can do."

Liz began to walk, and this time she stayed a little ahead of him on the path. "You'll have time," she said, without looking back. "No one's knocking at my door. No one is making proposals to my father."

"But you're so beautiful."

"Well, yes. I do turn a few heads. But in the end, it's money—and station—that decides such things. I have too much money for you and not nearly enough for those who seek a fortune to match with their titles."

"My father hurt his knee last week. I can't leave him right now, but before long I will, and I'll see what I can do."

Liz stopped and turned around. "Will, I wish it could happen. I've wished it for a long time. But let's not pretend. We can't walk out again, and we can't ever talk this way again. I wanted to have this one chance, but that's all." For a long moment she hesitated, looked closely at him, and even leaned a little toward him, as though she wanted to "comply," but Will didn't dare, and she turned and walked away.

The two said nothing as they returned to town. When they reached the marketplace, Liz saw Mary Ann and her friends. She waved to them. She laughed and walked away, only saying, "Good-bye, Will," in a whisper.

So Will walked about, could hardly see, couldn't think. When he found his sisters, he told them he would take apart their booth and carry it back. They could stay in town and then walk home with Daniel or with Mum. He needed to get back to the farm.

When he came up to the booth, Sarah seemed to sense that something was wrong. "We saw Sally Morehead, from church. She said she saw you walking with Liz."

Will didn't say anything. He only shrugged.

"Did something go wrong?"

He made the same little gesture, then said, "Don't walk back alone. Mum would be unhappy about that."

"I'm sorry, Will. But she isn't right for you. She thinks she's better than us."

Will had no idea how to respond to that. "I'll be agoin' now," was all he said. He turned away and walked back to his wagon and his oxen. He drove the animals back to the marketplace and then on to Wellington Heath. Along the way he tried to tell himself the truth. Liz was right about everything she had said. He was "working class," so he might as well get back to work. He had some hours of sun left and plenty to do. He would rise with the sun—tomorrow and every day—and work until the light was gone. It was what he was born to do. Why pretend there was anything more to hope for?

CHAPTER 4

When Liz returned to her friends, they wanted to know what had happened. "I've broken the poor lad's heart," she told them, "but what can I do? He thinks I'm beautiful, and who knows? He could be right." She laughed a little too hard, not wanting them to think she cared about him.

"You *are* beautiful," her friend Molly Drake told her. "But did he dare to say so?"

"Oh, yes. He said that—and much more. But I had to tell him that I'm simply out of his reach." She laughed again, and so did all the others, but she was ashamed of herself. She knew how badly she had hurt poor Will. She spent another hour with her friends, saying little, and then she made an excuse and left Mary Ann and the other young women. She walked home.

She found her mother in the parlor, sitting by the fireplace, doing needlework. The woman spent her life making doilies and embroidering pillowcases. Little was required of her in her home, thanks to her domestic help, so the handwork was something to keep her busy. Liz had no desire to while away her life the same way.

Sometimes she looked at her mother and saw her own face—with most of the beauty gone—and she dreaded what passing years with so little purpose would do to her.

"Where's Mary Ann?" Mrs. Duncan—Jane—asked.

"She's still walking about with Molly and the other girls."

"How was the fair?"

"It was . . . fine—about the same as every fair, every year."

"I thought you enjoyed the fairs." Jane finally looked up, seeming curious about Liz's tone of voice.

"It's like everything else, Mother. It comes around year after year, always the same. Nothing in this town ever changes." Liz sat down on a velvet high-backed chair not far from her mother's rocker.

"One thing was different this year," Jane said, and she looked back to her stitching.

"What was that?"

"I'm told you walked out with Will Lewis—left the marketplace entirely and walked up to Dog Woods."

"How could you know that?"

"People see things, Liz. And people talk. In this case, I'm glad someone stopped by and talked to me. Let's hope she won't talk to others."

"And what if I did walk with him?" Liz asked with defiance in her voice. "So what if I wanted to do something just a little different for once?"

"Do I have to answer that question? You know what people will be saying."

"What? That I'm a loose woman? Well, I'm not. We walked a little. We're old friends. There was nothing more to it. I didn't even take his arm. Now I wish I had."

"People will think that you two are courting. They'll say you're promised to a tenant farmer's son, and then who will come calling on you?"

"No one comes calling, Mother. That's just the problem. At least Will Lewis loves me. Maybe I like to see it in his eyes, how much he cares for me. It's better than nothing at all."

"You only gave him hope. It was a *terrible* choice. I can't think what your father will say when he finds out."

"I don't care what he says. I'll do as I like."

"And ruin your life."

A long silence followed. Liz heard the ticking of the old cherry-wood clock, like the pounding of a hammer, knocking down hours and days and years. But there was carpet on the floor, and she liked carpet. Will Lewis would never be able to carpet his floors, buy fine-crafted furniture, hire help for the kitchen, or light his rooms with oil lamps. Every time she thought of a life with him, she saw clearly that she would *not* be happy, but when she thought of life without him, she wondered whether she would end up embroidering in this parlor all her life, sitting in this room next to her mother.

Finally Liz said, "Mother, I gave him no hope. I told him he shouldn't think of me that way. But you must know. He has aspirations. He's gone to school more than most tenant farmers. He thinks he can leave the farm and do something more with his life."

"Liz, his father farms only a few acres. They live in a broken-down cottage. I've seen it. The thatch on the roof is falling in, and the path to the door is nothing but mud. The Lewises are good people, but they have nothing. What can he aspire to?"

"He has plans. Hopes."

"And did you encourage him in those hopes—so he might win you someday?"

"No. I stabbed him in the heart. I told him it wasn't possible to change his station in life. And I told him we could never go walking again."

"But don't you see, by talking to him this way, you're making him hold out hope whether you tell him to or not. He'll be off seeking his fortune, thinking that you're waiting for his return."

"No. He knows better. I set him straight on all that." Liz's voice broke, and suddenly tears were on her cheeks. She thought of the broken look she had seen in Will's eyes.

Now Jane was looking up again, watching Liz, seeming to assess what she had just heard. "He's a lovely young man, Liz. He's good-looking, strong and manly, and he loves you with all his heart. Anyone can see that. And all that is very appealing. But you've been accustomed to a certain way of living, and—"

"I know all that, Mother. I told him so. I was cruel to him, if you want to know. But I had to say something to him. I didn't want him to think of me that way—with that look I see in his eyes every Sunday."

"Well . . ." Jane leaned back in her rocking chair. "It was not wise to walk with him, Liz, but since you did, it's good that you made yourself clear. Some things simply aren't meant to be."

"Why, Mother? At church we say that we're all brothers and sisters—all God's children. Then we come home and say, 'That's all well and good, but some of us are better than the rest.'"

"It's not that. We're not better. But God, in his wisdom, offers different roles to different actors. We must serve as best we can, and love our neighbors—but accept the station in life God has granted us."

Liz stood up. "I don't believe that," she said. "Grandfather was a clerk, and he saw to it that Father read for the law. That moved him up a little in the world. It's snobbishness that rules our lives—not God."

"Liz! Don't let me ever hear you say such a thing again—and certainly never speak that way to your father."

Liz was crying now. She didn't want to show such weakness, but everything was so very frustrating, and nothing was ever going to change.

Jane stood up and tried to take Liz in her arms, but Liz held stiff, wouldn't put her own arms around her mother. "I'm sorry, Elizabeth. I really am. Any girl could have her head turned by such a young man as Will Lewis. But please don't encourage him ever again. Will you promise me that?"

But Liz wouldn't promise. She pulled away.

"I'm going to have to tell your father about this," Jane warned.

"Tell him what you want," Liz said, and she headed for her bedroom.

• • •

Will worked hard the next few days. He had to take advantage of the good weather. He felt little joy as he worked, and yet, when the barley and wheat and turnips were finally all planted, he did feel a sense that he had done his duty for his family. He was proud that he rotated crops and used chalk and crushed bone to build up the soil he left fallow. His father didn't care about science, didn't bother to learn about new methods. The man prayed for good weather and said that was all that was necessary. But Will had seen better production since he had taken over the plowing and planting, and he wished his dad would acknowledge that. All the same, he found more satisfaction in a good crop than he liked to admit.

Will attended church every Sunday all summer—primarily because it was too hard to live with his father if he didn't. He noticed that Liz responded to church services much as he did. The Watkins family had a parlor big enough to allow the twenty or more

Ledbury members to gather there, but it was not like sitting in pews in an Anglican chapel. It was easy to look about and see the faces of everyone there. If Will attended all the meetings, it meant three a week—two on Sunday and a prayer meeting on Tuesday evening. But prayer meetings were too much for Will. About forty preachers, both men and women, rotated through the circuit, and even though they each had a little different manner, they followed a similar approach. They would interrupt their sermons to call on people to pray, sometimes more than one at a time, and the excitement in the group would become almost frightening. The preacher would call out, "Have you repented, really repented?" and those who felt their sins too strongly would sometimes collapse on the floor, wave their limbs and roll about, all the while raving about their sins. Finally, the preacher would shout, "Believe! Believe, and you shall yet be saved." And those on the floor, more often than not, would leap to their feet and shout words of praise to God, having felt the saving power.

"Glory!" the preacher would shout, and the repentant person would spin and dance and praise God.

Will was not about to go to those extremes. He never had. Members of the little group knew it, too, and sometimes hinted to him that it was time for him to accept salvation. Will responded by avoiding Tuesday meetings. He always told his father there was too much work, and Morgan knew enough not to push Will too far. So Will usually attended the 2:00 P.M. service on Sunday but rarely returned for the Sunday evening meeting. What Will had noticed was that Liz usually kept more or less to the same schedule. Once, when she had been younger, she had dropped to the floor and admitted her sins. But Will had watched her change since then. Sometimes, when he looked at her across Brother Watkins's parlor, he could see her eyes expressing her impatience with the sermons. But she avoided him now after the meetings, and he rarely had a chance to do more than wish her a good day.

One Saturday evening in early August Nettie heated water and had the boys carry it from the fireplace to the bedroom, where they poured it into a tin tub. Will had to help Morgan in and out of the tub, but he was getting about fairly well now, though he walked with a serious limp. Nettie and the two girls took turns bathing after that while all the others waited in the main room. Then Will demanded that the brothers help him empty the tub outside and refill it with fresh water. Will took his privilege, bathing first in the hot water. Each boy ended up with dirtier, colder water, even though a freshly heated dose was added from time to time, but Will always told his brothers that they would have their turn at clean water whenever they grew to be older than he was. The little boys didn't really understand the joke and always argued that they never would. It was Daniel who saw no humor in Will's claim to preeminence.

After Will bathed and dried himself that evening, he dressed in some old clothes he kept in the house for nights when his work clothes were wet and muddy. He then walked out to the other room where the only mirror in the house hung on the wall next to the bedroom door. The family was all there, the girls looking shiny, and the dusty boys waiting their turns. Will had washed his hair and dried it roughly, but as he tried to comb it, he found that it was all in knots. He pulled the old wooden comb—the same one all the boys used—through his hair until it was finally slicked back, and then he turned to his mother, who was sitting by the window where she always tried to catch a little evening air and the remainder of the day's light. She was mending stockings. "Mum," Will said, "could you bring your scissors and cut my hair?"

"I certainly can," Nettie said. "I've told you for two weeks that it needed cutting."

Will knew he had thick hair. He had even heard one of the lasses at church say something about that. He liked to let it grow a little long, down over his Sunday collar. But he worried now that it was getting wild.

Nettie got up from her rocker and set her mending aside. But when Will turned to wait for her, Sarah said, "Esther, do na' look at Will. It's like looking at the sun. His beauty will hurt your eyes."

"He must be pretty for church—so Liz Duncan will notice."

"Do na' start that once again," Will said.

Sarah and Esther were sitting by the west window on a little bench near Nettie's rocker. They had taken turns brushing one another's hair, and now they both had books in their laps—ones they had borrowed from the squire's wife, who fancied herself a kindly woman, willing to assist the poor. The Lewises didn't like her attitude, but Nettie told the children to take advantage of her willingness to let them borrow books, and both girls did love to read. But light for reading was almost gone now, and Morgan didn't like to use up their candles any faster than necessary. Rush lights could bring a glow to the house, but the spots of light they threw off didn't help much with reading.

"Do na' get your hopes up, Will," Sarah said. "I hearn Henry Parker is after Liz. His father's a rich horse trader. Girls are sayin' she's sure to be promised ere long now."

"Sarah, please," Nettie said, "I've taught you better than that. Speak properly. And that's also enough on that subject."

But Will was already asking, "What girl says so?"

"All her friends say it. Me an' Esther—" Sarah looked at her mother. "Esther and I were in town on market day, and one of the girls from church—Molly Drake—told us. She said, 'I hate to say it, but Liz Duncan is going to break your brother's heart. Before long, she'll be marrying Henry Parker.'"

Will turned his back. He let his mother cut his hair. He didn't want the girls, or his mother either, to see him show emotion. But he wondered whether Molly knew what she was talking about. Did Liz like Henry Parker, stout as he was, and so stuck on himself? But Will also wondered, did everyone in town talk about him this way—the sad young man, lovesick and spurned by Liz Duncan?

"Henry Parker's not pretty," Esther said, and she giggled. "All he has is a purse full of sovereigns."

"For someone like Liz," Sarah said, "a pocket bulging with money makes a man prettier than even Will."

"You don't know that about Liz Duncan," Will said. He was trying to breathe evenly and not show how annoyed he was. "So don't talk about her."

"Oh, my," Esther said. "We must take care. We must not speak ill of his true love."

"Esther!" Nettie said. "Stop. You too, Sarah. It's time to finish up your chores. You haven't washed the dishes."

"Mum, no," Esther said. "Not yet. You said we could read while the light lasts."

"The light is almost gone. And there's no need to burn up rushes just to clean the dishes."

The girls didn't stop reading immediately. They took a few minutes before Morgan said, "You lasses do what your mother tol' ye. Get up now and wash them dishes."

They didn't argue with their father. They got up immediately. But when they were finally across the room, talking to one another, Nettie whispered to Will, "I can't picture Elizabeth Duncan marrying Henry Parker. I just can't. Molly talks too much. And she doesn't always know what she's speaking of."

"Liz will marry someone one of these days," Will said, trying to sound stoic. "What does it matter to me?"

"It matters a great deal to you. And it matters to her too. I know it does."

"It only makes things worse if I think so."

"But some things are meant to be. Some things are the will of God. You need to pray about this and ask the Lord if it can't happen."

"I've tried enough prayer, Mum. I've learned my lesson on that one."

"Oh, Will, don't say that. Keep asking—not just for Liz, but for guidance, so you'll know what's best."

The truth was, Will did pray. No matter how skeptical he was about religion, he did ask God over and over that he might find a way to marry Liz. But he didn't tell his mother that, and he strongly suspected that God didn't bother with such matters.

• • •

Thomas Kington, superintendent of the United Brethren, was the visiting minister at church services the next day. He lived in Dymock, just a few miles south of Ledbury, and he was someone Will had heard preach many times. Will liked the man, too. He was kindly and humble. He wore the same sort of worn-out farmer's suit of clothes that Will and Morgan wore, and boots as heavy as Will's. He was not a young man, probably about the age of Will's father, and that year he had finally married a woman not all that much younger than himself. She didn't travel with him when he walked about the preaching circuit, but Will had met her at the annual United Brethren gathering called the "love feast." It was meant to unify the members in Christian love. The woman—Hannah Pitt had been her name before she married—was as unassuming as her husband.

But Thomas Kington was a different man when he stood up to

preach. He wore a flaring beard, streaked black and white, and when he admonished his people, his teeth would flash through that beard, and his little eyes would glare. He had a thin voice that became high and strident when he preached repentance.

As usual, he repeated his story of how the United Brethren had come to be and how the movement continued to grow. He was entertaining, in his way, if only because he started quietly and then raised his voice in passion as he built upon his thesis for the day—which was always about the same. The United Brethren were committed to study and pray and wait for truth to be revealed, but they could only receive that truth if they repented, and they were wicked people living in a wicked world. He would list the failings of the people, their tendencies to profane, to desecrate the Sabbath day, to imbibe too much alcohol, to commit whoredoms, and to make light of the things of God.

There was also nothing he loved more than to describe the folly and wrongheadedness of the Church of England. "What is Christianity in our country today?" he was shouting now, as Will folded his arms and leaned against the wall. He had been forced to stand because the parlor was packed with people. "The church has been made *convenient* for those who would rather not exert an effort. Where are the disciples of yesteryear—healing the sick, casting out devils, blessing those who need comfort? They've been replaced with *comfortable* rectors and vicars, who receive a *living*. They hobnob with the wealthy, play at whist and drink port, and tell their parishioners on a Sunday morning that all is well. Why would they upset those who pay them to preach?"

Will certainly agreed with this assessment of the Anglican clergy. Kington and the other ministers of the United Brethren were not paid, and they didn't oblige their members in quite the same way;

on the other hand, Will sometimes wondered whether some of them weren't just a little mad.

"When Jesus Christ walked this earth, he called apostles," Brother Kington said, his voice becoming a shriek, much too loud for the little room. "And they went forth among the people, led by the Holy Spirit. Jesus Christ commanded the winds to cease, he changed water into wine, and he raised up the dead. And what miracles do our modern priests perform? They turn indolence into money.

"But last week I was in Frome's Hill, meeting with Brother Benbow, and he told me that he had met a man who was sick unto death, about to depart this life and leave a family destitute. He commanded this man to arise and . . ."

Will didn't want to hear it. It was always the same. He wished that he could see Liz's eyes from where he was. He wanted to know whether she was as doubtful as he was about some of these stories. Of course, another question was bigger in his mind at the moment: Was she actually entertaining the thought of marrying Henry Parker? Could she give herself away to such a dolt?

When the meeting ended, Brother Kington made his rounds among the members, shaking hands, wishing everyone well. Will shook hands with him, managed to say as little as possible, and then slipped through the crowd and on outside.

Liz soon came out, ahead of her parents. She nodded, politely, greeted some of the other members who were leaving, and then turned as though merely waiting for her family, staying a few feet away from Will. He was about to speak to her when she whispered, "Happy birthday, Will. I heard you turned twenty-three last week."

"Who told you that?"

"Your sisters. They were in town on market day." She was wearing the rose-colored dress and bonnet she had worn at the fair.

Her face was blossoming with the same color, as though she were happy for this chance to speak for a moment—after avoiding him all summer.

Will nodded. He knew his sisters had talked to Liz's friends, but he didn't know they had actually talked to Liz. He wondered what else the three had talked about.

"I'll be nineteen next month," Liz said.

"I know."

"How do you know?"

"I just know."

Liz glanced at the door. No one was coming out at the moment. "I don't know what to do, Will. Henry Parker has been calling on me, and my father wants me to accept his hand in marriage."

"Are you going to do it?"

"I don't know. My father doesn't want to give me a choice."

"Can't you stand up to him?"

"For what? You tell me that you want to make something of yourself. Are you doing anything about it?"

"I . . . I have to run the farm right now. I can't leave yet."

"Fine, then. At least Henry has some money. He's a pompous prig, but I could have my own home, and I could raise a family."

"With *him?*"

That stopped her for the moment. She turned toward him, and he saw the pain in her eyes. "Will, if you can do anything, you have to do it now. I have to have some reason to believe you could make a life for us."

And then she stepped away. Her parents were shaking hands with Thomas Kington, near the door, and she obviously didn't want them to look out and see her with Will. So Will turned and walked up Homend Street and on up the Ledbury road. His feelings were so jumbled he couldn't think. Hadn't she professed her love for him more openly than ever before? Hadn't she said, in effect, that she wanted to wait for him? And yet, what was he supposed to do about it? He couldn't leave the farm now—and even if he did, what was it he could do? Was there really any opportunity for him in the factories?

But he did pray again, and he did ask for a miracle. The problem was, he said the words sarcastically, as though to challenge God—to say to him, "Fine, then, you claim you can bring about miracles? Let's see one."

When the harvest began, late in August, the weather was nearly perfect. All the family worked hard every waking hour; even Dad was able to help a little. The older boys cut the grain with scythes, and Mum and the girls bundled the sheaves. Then everyone worked together to haul the sheaves to the ricks by the barn, where they could dry. The work took more than three weeks, and everyone was exhausted before it ended. But the crop was good. The problem was, grain prices had dropped a little, so the winter would be just as lean as it had been the last few years.

Threshing would soon begin, and another cutting of hay was coming up, so the work wasn't finished, but Will was glad to have a few days for everyone to rest—including Nick and Nimble. He also had time to think, but that was not what he needed. He had finally told his father that he wanted to set out for one of the factory towns as soon as the heavy work was over. Morgan had been furious. "I will na' permit such a thing," he had shouted, and then he had talked of the evil in such places.

But he had also asked, "Would ye go off an' leave your family, just when times is so hard?" Those were the words that had stayed in Will's head. He knew he would have to defy his father to leave, but, more than that, he would have to leave his mother, his family, with only Daniel to lead out. He couldn't do that. He had no real choice.

Dad thought things would get better in time, but Will didn't believe that—and he also knew he had no time. What he wanted would soon be gone.

So Will stayed to himself for a few days—stayed at the barn after evening tea and slept in the loft even though September nights were getting cooler. Late one afternoon he found he was losing his light in the barn as the sun went down. He walked to the door, leaned against the doorjamb, and looked out to the west. Pink was showing in some bumpy little clouds on the horizon, and a layer of mist in the bottom of the valley was beginning to glow. It was all very beautiful, but his old thoughts came back to him: It was the same sky, same valley he looked at every day. He would never know anything else. Suddenly he felt a need to break out, to defy someone, to do as he chose. The only thing that came to mind was his animal traps. He knew his father would be outraged if he ever found out Will had set them, but he didn't care. He wanted to enter the woods, feel the old excitement he remembered from when he was a boy. The squire would claim that such trapping was poaching, but Will didn't believe it. The small game in the woods mattered nothing to the man. Why couldn't tenants have a bit of meat to eat?

Will found his traps, quickly greased two of them with bacon fat, then grabbed a spade and dug in the garden until he found a couple of old turnips that had been missed in the early harvest. They had a strong smell. Will thought they might attract a hare from some distance. He cleaned the dirt off them at the well and then grabbed the traps and used the stile to cross the hedge into the field beyond. He took a look, saw no one, and trudged up along the west hedge to the top of the hill. He didn't think anyone could see him, but he watched the road for a time and listened for the sound of anyone moving about in the woods. He knew that the gamekeeper watched mostly at night. He would never expect a poacher to walk into the woods before the twilight was gone.

It was all too easy. Will worked his way through a narrow opening in the hedge, walked a little way into the woods, baited the traps, and staked them to the ground. He had heard no one, felt none of the excitement he had longed for. Still, he liked the feeling that he was saying no to the squire even if he could never do it to the man's face.

CHAPTER 5

Jeff and Abby had been living with Jeff's parents in Las Vegas for a couple of weeks. It was May, only about six weeks since Jeff had learned that he had lost his job in California. But other bad news had forced them into occupying the "grandma's apartment" in the basement of his family's home. When Jeff had started looking for contract work with some of the companies he had worked for before, he had found little available. He had picked up a couple of small programming assignments, but it was hardly enough to pay for health insurance, let alone for rent. Since the lease on their Sunnyvale apartment was running out before long, it had seemed a bad time to renew. On the last day of April they had loaded everything they owned in a rental truck and headed for Las Vegas.

The advantage in living with Jeff's parents was in having no rent or utilities to pay, along with getting some big help on groceries. The disadvantage, of course, was that Jeff and Abby had lost a good deal of independence. Abby really liked Alan and Alicia—whom she usually called Dad and Mom—but they were strong people with strong opinions, and she sometimes felt as though she were in over her head with their intense discussions and their tendency to offer advice, even though most of it was directed at Jeff. Jeff's three sisters were also forceful, each in her own way, and they usually stayed up very late. Much of their noise—their music, their movies, their laughter, their piano and violin practice, and even some angry arguments—had a way of reaching the bedroom downstairs, and Abby had been tired lately, not ready to try to wait them out.

Rachel, the Lewises' oldest daughter, was home from BYU for the summer, and Julie and Cassi were both in high school. Abby had fun with them sometimes, but they also made her feel old. She was already feeling out of touch with what was happening with electronic gadgets, music, styles—but then, she had always separated herself to some degree from what was "going on." She had grown up with just one sister—Maria, three years older than Abby—and the two of them had been in choirs and orchestras, both of them much more in tune with classical music than they were with the latest trends in rock music.

Jeff and Abby were trying to stay to themselves as much as possible, but Abby longed already for the day when they could move into their own apartment again and life could get back to what had become normal for her. She had been looking for work since they had arrived in Las Vegas, but lots of people were out of work, and her degree in art history didn't really open any doors. The truth was, Abby was even more worried than she admitted to Jeff.

"Jeff! Abby!" Alicia was yelling from the top of the stairs, "Dinner's ready. Come on up."

It was Sunday, and Alicia had invited Jeff and Abby to eat with the family, which Abby appreciated but also sort of dreaded. She had always been confident in social situations, and she certainly wasn't uncomfortable with the Lewises, but she felt engulfed when the whole family was together, as though everyone had more than enough to say, and Abby was the quiet kid in the corner. She did have things she wanted to say at times, but she just wasn't good at forcing her way into the conversation.

She and Jeff walked upstairs and sat down at the big dining-room table. The Lewises had a beautiful home in the northeast hills, far from the Las Vegas strip and fairly close to the temple. Alan had taken a job as a civil engineer with the city long before the enormous building boom. When things had taken off, he had risen to a position of prominence and had watched his salary climb. Still, he had built this house, doing much of the work himself, and he had taught Jeff a lot about house construction in the process. Alan was very handy with tools, and Jeff had the same aptitudes even though he hadn't had as much practice. It was one of the things that Abby loved about Jeff, that he thought about everything, loved art and good music, but he could also fix a dripping faucet or replace the bathroom tile in their apartment. If he didn't know how to solve a problem, he would go online and look for answers, and he had the confidence to attack the job.

Abby could see that Jeff had learned confidence from his mother as much as from his dad. Alicia had a flair for decorating, never worrying much about what others might think of her choices. She liked bold colors and eclectic mixes of patterns. The dining room was painted a dark red and the chandelier over the table was massive, brass and glass and, to Abby, too overpowering. But then, Alicia's personality was pretty much the same way.

"Jeff, would you say the blessing on the food?" Alan asked.

"He always asks you on Sundays," Cassi, the youngest sister, said. "He thinks our prayers are insincere."

"Maybe that's because you say the same thing every single time you pray," Alicia said. "And you rattle it off like you're afraid the food won't be there when you open your eyes."

"Who says I shut my eyes? I keep at least one eye on the food—before Julie starts grabbing everything." Cassi was like her mom, both of them probably a little heavier than they would have liked, but both quick to laugh, and both seemingly in love with rings and bracelets and bright fingernails.

"Oh, right. You're the one who—"

"Girls," Alan said. "Never mind. Jeff?"

So Jeff said a nice blessing, probably taking a little more time to give thanks than he usually did, and then the family passed the food around. Alicia had cooked stuffed lamb chops with her own little concoction of stuffing, plus a salad laced with artichoke hearts and perfectly prepared asparagus. Alan was actually a meat-and-potatoes kind of guy—born and raised in southern Idaho—but he rarely got the roast he would have preferred for Sunday dinner.

The talk was vigorous, with more than one conversation going on at all times. Rachel, who seemed to have reacted against her mother's style by choosing to wear shades of beige and almost no makeup, was the only one who tried to include Abby, but Abby was in no mood to assert herself today.

Alicia was asking Alan and Jeff about the discussion in Gospel Doctrine class that day. "Don't you think Brother Handley got too political? Why is it a guy like that can get way off on the far right and no one says a word about it, but if I say one thing that someone thinks is a little too 'liberal,' I get chastised for it?"

"Maybe that's because you say things that are *very* liberal," Alan said, laughing.

"Oh, yes. Feed the hungry, clothe the naked. That's really liberal, all right. I think I got that admonition from the *scriptures.* I seem to recall the Sermon on the Mount says something about it."

Jeff was smiling. "Don't trust those hungry people, Mom. They're all faking just to get a handout."

"That *is* what Brother Handley thinks. I've told him before, he bought the edition of the Book of Mormon that cut out King Benjamin's sermon. It must have been the abridged version."

And she launched in again, questioning how the Church had become so Republican in recent years. Then, as though the transition were completely natural, she raised her voice and said, "Jeff, there's something I need to talk to you and Abby about. Could everyone be quiet for just a minute?"

Julie, as the middle daughter, always worked hardest to be noticed. She kept right on talking, telling Cassi about her Laurel teacher, who was "about the coolest woman I've ever met, but like, really, really spiritual too."

Alicia waited for a time and then said, "Please, girls, this is important."

"Okay, okay," Julie said. She rolled her eyes, as though she resented the interruption.

"Today I was talking to Harv Robertson," Alicia said. "He just got called to be a mission president."

"Is that your big announcement, Mom?" Julie asked. "Because the bishop announced it in sacrament meeting. You ought to pay more attention." She was a freckle-faced sixteen-year-old with a smile that was full of good will, no matter how sarcastic her comment.

"No. That's not my big announcement." Alicia pretended to glare at Julie for a few seconds before she looked at Jeff, then Abby. "Harv was telling me that he and Susan bought a house in Nauvoo, Illinois. They plan, sooner or later, to live there part of each year. But now they're going to be gone three years, and they would like to rent it out—except that the place needs a lot of remodeling."

"Wow. This *is* really interesting, Mom," Cassi said. She widened her eyes and opened her mouth, but after a second or two, she couldn't help breaking into a smile.

"Shush." When Rachel and Cassi laughed, Alicia said, "All of you, shush." But she was smiling too. "Here's the thing. Harv had heard about you losing your job, Jeff, and he asked whether you had found anything yet. When I told him you were doing what contract work you could find, he said, 'If he's interested, he and his wife could go out and live in my place in Nauvoo—no rent—and I'd pay him to do some of the remodeling I want to do.'"

"Was he serious?" Jeff asked.

"Sure he was. He knows that you helped build this house. He said the work he needs is stuff you could handle."

"Is the house a decent place to live—you know, before I could get started fixing it up?"

"I guess so. I didn't really ask him about that. You'd have to talk to him. Why don't you give him a call and see what he has to say?"

"But Jeff," Abby said, "what if you found a job and we had to leave right away?"

"That's exactly what I asked Harv," Alicia said. "He said it wouldn't matter. Anything you took care of would be to his advantage. I think really, though, he's mostly just looking for a way to help you out. My guess is, he'd pay you more than you're worth."

The girls made some sarcastic remarks about Jeff being worth an awful lot as a *Stanford* grad, but Alicia didn't let that bother her.

"Actually, that might not be a bad idea," Jeff said. "We could certainly use the income, and you know me: I'd love to live in Nauvoo for a while."

Abby was thinking that it would be a way to get out of her in-laws' basement—but she hated the idea of making the move and then being there only a short time. More than anything, she wanted Jeff to find a job, and this might be a distraction from his search.

"I'll tell you what worries me about it," Alan said.

"Uh-oh, here it comes," Rachel said. "In case you don't know yet, Abby, Dad's our official worrier. He can find something wrong with any idea."

"Yeah, like you coming home for the summer," Alan said without cracking a smile. "But what I was going to say was, I can picture Jeff getting out there and just spending all his time studying Church history." He actually said this to Abby, but then he looked at Jeff. "You would have to be very disciplined to get your contract work done—especially if you start finding more of it—and work on Bishop Robertson's house at the same time."

"You know me, Dad. I'm a workaholic."

"Yes—when you're doing what you want to do. But sometimes you 'put off' what you *don't* like to do. And the other thing is, you've never lived in that kind of humid heat. I'm not sure you'd like it out there."

"A Las Vegas boy afraid of heat?"

Abby laughed. "You do know heat," she said. "You don't know misery. The humidity out there might do you in."

But Jeff let that one go. Abby could see already that Jeff liked this idea, and she wasn't really that opposed to it. She wondered how soon they would be leaving.

"I'll tell you honestly what worries me most, Jeff," Alan was now saying.

"Here it comes, Jeff," Julie said. "I heard him clear his throat. One of his long speeches is on the way."

Actually, that was true. Abby had heard him clear his throat too, and she had the same impression, even though Alan was shaking his head as if to deny the whole thing. "No long speech," he said, "but I do have a little advice." He set his fork down and wiped his mouth with his cloth napkin.

Jeff nodded, and the girls seemed to sense that it was time to back off.

"You really do have a way of letting things distract you. You're way too interested in every book you come across, every lecture, every museum—and every other thing in this world. That's great. I admire that quality in you. But right now, you need to concentrate more than anything on finding a job. I keep hearing you talk about going back for a PhD, and I understand why you would want to do that. But it's a long row to hoe, and when you finish, you can assume right from the beginning that you'll never make a great salary. I can see you going on for grad work in computers—or even an MBA to go with your computer background—but I'd be awfully careful about going after a doctorate in history."

Abby wasn't at all surprised by Alan's opinion. In fact, she had probably had some influence on his coming to those conclusions. She and he had talked one day that week, and she had told him that she worried about all the years of study if Jeff went after a PhD.

"I'm not sure I agree with you, Alan," Alicia said. She had been chewing, so she held up a hand, chewed some more, then swallowed.

That gave Cassi a chance to say, "Oh, good. Now we're going to have a fight."

Alicia gave Cassi an incredulous glance before going on. "Jeff's only twenty-four. I'm not sure he'll ever really be happy until he's a professor—theorizing about all those interests he has. If he's going to go back to school, now might be the right time to do it."

"I'm too late for this year, Mom. I'd have to start applying this winter for next year."

"Same thing. I still say it's better to go on soon than to get ten years into your career and then try, with a young family, to go back."

"I'm not saying I disagree," Alan said. "But if that's what he's going to do . . ." He looked at Jeff instead of Alicia. "If that's what you're going to do, get after it hard. Get accepted to a grad school, then get in and knock yourself out to finish as fast as you can. Every year of student loans now will hold you back for years to come."

"Why don't you just pay for it, Dad?" Rachel said. "That's my goal, I know—to stay in school as long as possible and have you foot the bill."

"Actually, I do want to address myself to that issue," he said, and he clearly was serious this time. "When Jeff got accepted to Stanford, I told him that it was going to cost us dearly. I would support him in going, but he would have to figure out his own way to pay for grad school. Rachel, I could support you at BYU for ten years for what I paid Stanford for four."

"Okay, so that's the deal? I get to stay for ten years?"

"Hey, remember, you've got two sisters coming up who have an *outside* chance of getting into BYU—or at least *some* school."

"And I want to see the world," Alicia said, laughing. "Dad says we can't afford to travel until he gets you all through college. Of course, he just says that because he'd rather stay home anyway."

Alan paid no attention to all of this. He was looking at Jeff, who said, "I know, Dad. I have no intention of coming to you for more money. If I went back, I'd have to get a fellowship or a teaching assistantship—or maybe some kind of grant money. I agree that I'd rather not build up a big student-loan bill."

"Jeff," Alicia said, "it's not like me to be the voice of reason in this house, but remember, you don't have an undergraduate degree in history. You'd probably have to go back and get more credits before you could even get in. Why would they give you a fellowship?"

"Yeah, I know all of that. I just . . . wish . . . in some ways that I had stayed in history and never moved into computers. That had a lot to do with the 'voice of reason' I heard around here, too."

That brought on some silence. Everyone knew about Dad's long talks with Jeff when he was younger, always with Alan preaching that computers were the future and academic degrees were a dead end.

Jeff held both hands up. "Look, I'm sorry. You did put me through Stanford, and I'll find another job in computers. I'm sure I'll thank you someday." But it didn't sound very convincing, not to Abby, and surely not to anyone else. All the girls were eating now, looking at their plates. It was Jeff, again, who broke the silence. "It's just that . . . life is long, and I'd like to do something I enjoy. Dad, don't you ever wonder whether you shouldn't have found a way to make a living with your music?"

"I play in the community orchestra, and I get my satisfaction that way. And I make a good living as an engineer. It's the best of both worlds for me, and not some sort of compromise. You can read history all your life—for your own interest—but you can make a better living with your computer skills."

Abby had heard Jeff say that his dad's happiest hours were spent in playing his viola. He went to work each day and did his job, but he never said anything about it at home. He was already starting to talk about the day when he could retire. Jeff didn't want to do life that way. He didn't say that, though, and Abby knew that was because of Alan but also because of her. She was too practical herself. She really was worried that she was robbing Jeff of who he wanted to be.

"Honey," Alicia said, "don't listen to us *too much,* okay? I think you've tried too hard sometimes to prove yourself a good son. If you feel like you have to do something that seems impractical to your dad and me, then do it. It's your life and your heart. The saddest thing I know is watching people who work out their mortality with no joy."

Abby watched Jeff. This last little plea hadn't changed his mind.

He had given up. What was worse, she had something to tell him that would be the last straw.

· · ·

Jeff wanted to get away from the table, but he stayed for the dessert, and he tried to enter the conversation just enough to let everyone know that he wasn't pouting. He thought he would talk to good old Bishop Robertson—*his* bishop when he was growing up—and at least arrange to get out of his parents' basement. Maybe he was already getting too much help right now; his father probably thought it wasn't part of the deal for him to come home after getting that Stanford degree. He didn't want to be mad, but he was a little tired of hearing, for the millionth time in his life, that he was too impractical, too full of ideas, and not focused enough on one thing. He was going to buck up, do his duty, and look for a *solid* job. It was not just Dad—and even Mom, to some degree. It was also Abby. Maybe mostly Abby. She was just too scared, and he couldn't add to that. He had to find a job, with insurance, and then hope that it was a job with some room to rise.

When he and Abby got back downstairs to their apartment, Abby came and sat by him on their couch—the beige and red one they had brought from California. "Jeff, I'm sorry," she said. "Everyone's ganging up on you right now. I think we have to do what we feel right about. Why don't you sign up at UNLV and get some more credits in history, and then start sending out applications?"

"What about all the student loans we'd have to take?"

"I don't care. You can't do something you hate all your life. After you go back to school, I will, and we'll both work. We'll get the loans paid."

Jeff knew what Abby was doing. But he also knew that she wanted to have a family, and she didn't want to work when the kids were young. What would happen to all that? "No, honey. That's not the answer. I think we should go out to Nauvoo, just for the experience—and for the extra income Bishop Robertson would give me. I'll start working every connection I have to find a job. Let's just hope and pray I can find something that will be a little more interesting than what I was doing in California."

"Jeff, I know what you're doing. Inside right now, you're saying, 'I'm sacrificing the life I want, but I'll do it for my wife.' I don't want that."

"No, that's not true. We'll make it work. Let's find out what it's going to take for you to have a baby. Maybe that's what I need more than anything—to stop thinking so much about myself and worry more about raising some kids. That's what happens in life. We think too much about ourselves when we're young. The real job in life is to raise good kids and to bring them up in the gospel—create a righteous posterity."

Now he could see something happening to Abby. She was trying not to cry, but tears were filling her eyes.

"What is it?" he asked.

"Jeff, there's something I haven't told you. I thought for a while that it was a false alarm, but I'm sure now it isn't."

"What?"

"I'm pregnant, Jeff. I'm almost sure I am."

"Have you taken one of those tests?"

"No. Not yet. When I missed my period, I thought it was just the same old thing I've gone through before, but I'm feeling different this time. I can actually feel that something's going on in my body." She waited a moment, and Jeff could feel her watching him. He didn't know what to say. The timing was not that great. "I'm sorry," she said, and tears filled her eyes.

"What do you mean?" But he wasn't looking into her eyes. They both knew what she meant.

"You just said that we needed to find a job first, and then start thinking about a family."

"I know. But it didn't happen that way. We don't have a lot of choice in the matter. Still, it's what we wanted. It's great." He knew he hadn't managed to pull it off, though. His voice had been entirely unconvincing.

Now Abby was crying hard. She pulled away from him a little and pushed her face into her hands.

"Oh, honey, I mean it. Really. We're having a baby. That's great. Honest. It's exciting."

He still sounded phony and he knew it. He tried to let the joy come, so his feelings wouldn't contradict his words, but the baby was a worry. He really did have to find a job now. Life was going to be very different.

"Hey, I'm going to be a dad. Can you picture that? I think I want either a girl or a boy. What about you?"

"Jeff, I'm sorry it worked out this way."

"Hey, you didn't do this by yourself. I was actually there at the time."

"I don't mean that. I just know what you're thinking—that you can't go back to school now. But this doesn't change things as much as you think. We can still figure out a way. Lots of couples do it. You told me that yourself."

Jeff wondered. But he knew, more than anything right now, he had to stop thinking so blasted much about himself. "Abby, thank you," he said.

She looked up, her face wet, her cheeks and eyes red.

"Thank you for making me a dad."

"You're not one yet."

"Almost." Suddenly he realized something. "Have you been scared to tell me?"

"A little. I've only waited a few days, though. I wanted to go buy one of those tests, but I couldn't do that without telling you. We need to get one tomorrow—so we'll know for sure—but there's not much doubt in my mind about it."

"Ab, I am so sorry you didn't feel you could tell me. It's a good thing. It really is. I want to be this really great dad."

"Just don't decide right now that you won't ever go back to school. Let's keep thinking about it—and praying. We'll know what to do."

"That's right. Let's pray now, okay? Let's thank the Lord."

Before they prayed, Jeff pulled Abby into his arms, and the two clung to one another for a long time. Jeff really was excited when he thought about having a child to love, but he was frightened, too. It was just very important that he didn't say that.

CHAPTER 6

Liz Duncan was sitting in the upstairs parlor with her mother and Mary Ann. It was September now, and mornings had been cool. Mrs. Duncan had instructed Sally, her maid-of-all-work, to lay a fire each morning. By afternoon the room was always overheated, as it was again today, but there was no convincing Mrs. Duncan to change her habits. Liz had always loved warm days, when the sour smell and smoky haze of coal fires didn't hang over Ledbury. But her mother wasn't the only one building fires now, and Liz noticed when she and Mary Ann took strolls along High Street that she was starting to come home with a fine black dust on her bonnet. And sitting here in the parlor with all the windows shut tight, she could smell the fire more noticeably than she could the sweets sitting on the table or the steaming tea in the pot.

Mrs. Duncan was embroidering . . . something. Liz had no idea what. The woman did so much needlework, it was a wonder she could still see to stitch. Liz and Mary Ann were both reading, except that Liz was mostly just staring at the pages and thinking about the awkward situation she was about to face. Henry Parker was going

78

to call on Liz—again—and she knew she had to let him know that she did not welcome his courtship. Mrs. Duncan had invited him to come by for tea that afternoon, and for some reason she had chosen market day, when Liz and Mary Ann liked to walk to the market and greet friends. Neither was eager to spend her precious time with Mr. Parker.

"Mary Ann," Mrs. Duncan said, "could you serve the tea? I have some things I need to do. I'd rather not sit here the whole time Mr. Parker is here."

"Then let me take care of whatever it is you have to do," Mary Ann said. "I don't want to be here either."

"Better yet, let me do it," Liz said. "I *especially* don't want to be here."

Mary Ann laughed, but Mrs. Duncan said, "Liz, please don't judge Mr. Parker too harshly. He may not be a handsome man—"

"But he has money." Liz waited until her mother looked up at her, and then she said, "Isn't that what you had in mind, Mum?"

"That *is* part of it, Elizabeth. He has the means to care for you—to provide you with a nice home. And he attends our United Brethren group, so you know that your children would be taught as they ought to be."

Mary Ann was still giggling. "It's *creating* those children with Henry Parker—that's what Liz doesn't like to think about."

"Mary Ann! What a dreadful, improper thing to say. I've raised you better than that."

Now it was Liz who was laughing. "Well, really, Mother, let the idea run through *your* mind."

"I won't have this conversation," Mrs. Duncan said. She stood up. "There are things more important than physical *appearance*. I've tried to teach you that all your life."

"But Daddy was a handsome young man. I've heard you say that many times."

"And you were a beauty," Mary Ann said. "That's how you managed to marry a solicitor—and improve your station."

Mrs. Duncan stood straight, her chest high as she drew in plenty of breath. Liz knew that she was hearing the argument, feeling the truth of it. But Liz was taken aback when her mother suddenly broke into a smile and then couldn't stop herself from laughing. "Oh, Liz," she finally said, "I know Mr. Parker isn't much to look at, and I know how I felt at your age. But looks really do turn out to be less important than they seem. We all lose our looks in time, you know."

"You never have." Liz knew she had said the right thing. The fact was, Mrs. Duncan had always been vain about her pretty figure and her lovely dark hair and eyes. She liked to wear nice frocks; she even added a little color to her cheeks and lips, even though preachers in the United Brethren always spoke against such brazen behavior. She didn't seem to mind when men paid her special attention, either, even though she never flirted with them, as some married women did. Today she was wearing her turquoise dress with fancy beadwork around the neck and across the tight-fitting bodice. She looked pretty.

"I was fortunate," Mrs. Duncan said. "I found a man I could love as well as honor." She glanced at each of the girls and then took a long look at Liz. "You're beautiful, Liz. Any man would find you attractive. But it's very important that you find someone who can give you the right kind of life. Men with means are not abundant— and they aren't always handsome. Try to judge Mr. Parker by his heart. I know he loves you."

"He thinks I'm pretty. That doesn't mean he loves me. He hardly knows me. Once he learns that I have a sharp tongue and that I'm arrogant—as Father has so often described me—he'll run for cover."

"Oh, Liz, can you not hold back just a little?"

"Not to win over Henry Parker. The prize is not great enough."

"But who else is there? The young men in our church are nice enough, but they're laborers and mechanics. I was able to come up a little in the world. Do you really want to lose what I gained—just because certain young men are nice looking?"

Mary Ann, who was looking down at her book by now, said, "I think she means Will Lewis, Liz. That's my guess. I told you to stop encouraging that brute. He's *so far* beneath us. And by the way, please stop being so arrogant."

Mrs. Duncan shook her head. "I don't know how to talk to you two," she finally said.

"Mary Ann has a point," Liz said.

"I know she does. But I was a tradesman's daughter. My father was a good man who worked hard and died young. My mother was left with little to live on. Even so, she lived better than tenant farmers do. You may think I'm putting on airs, but the thought of seeing one of you manage a farm with a brood of children under your feet and a broken-down cottage for a home—it makes my heart hurt to imagine it."

That stopped Mary Ann, and Liz too. "I understand, Mum."

"Just be nice to Mr. Parker. See if there's not a little more to him than you suppose right now."

Liz didn't accede to that, but she also didn't say she wouldn't. So Mrs. Duncan left. Mary Ann tried to tease Liz about encouraging Mr. Parker, but Liz was feeling serious by then. She thought of her mother growing up in the home of a hardworking tanner who cured skins and turned the leather into shoe tops and soles and even sewed gloves himself. The chemicals had hurt his lungs—or something had—and he had become consumptive by the time he was in his late thirties. He had lived long enough for Liz to know him, but she only remembered him being deathly pale and always coughing. Her mother might well have ended up a housemaid in some landowner's mansion if she had not been able to employ her good looks to win a man of law. Liz had always imagined herself going one better—finding some squire's son to marry, or even the son of an aristocrat—and yet she was having daydreams about a man who didn't own so much as a decent suit of clothes. No wonder her mother was alarmed.

"Mary Ann, maybe I do need to think about this from Mother's point of view," she said. "Henry Parker will have his father's business. He's going to be rich. I know no one else I can say that about—at least no one who comes calling on me."

"You don't have to choose someone from the United Brethren. Mum makes too much of that."

"All the same, how many suitors do I have—of any kind?"

"I'll admit, Mum's right about one thing. I don't think you should judge Henry Parker by his looks alone. You should also consider his stupidity."

Liz couldn't help laughing. She did appreciate Mary Ann's directness. She sometimes suspected that Mary Ann would find a man more easily than she would. People said that Mary Ann's appearance was "pleasant," or that she was "quite attractive." But some man was likely to be charmed by her humor and honesty and notice how perfect her skin was, how enticing her smile. Liz would watch her talk sometimes and think, "She's the prettiest little thing I've ever seen. I wish I looked more like her." Mary Ann *was* small, but maybe it was her coloring that made her less noticeable than Liz. Liz's dark hair and smoky green eyes, she knew, had an effect on people. Mary Ann was lighter, her hair brownish, her eyes a pale sort of gray. It was the animation in those eyes, and in her smile, that Liz envied.

Liz also wondered, if she rejected Henry Parker, would another suitor come calling? The years for finding a husband passed very quickly. Mother was probably right; she probably should grant Mr. Parker the benefit of the doubt. But then he pulled the bell rope, and Sally opened the front door for him and led him upstairs to the parlor. The sight of Henry changed Liz's thinking instantly. He was certainly well over thirty and soft as a feather pillow, with rounded cheeks and puffy hands, and under his waistcoat were curves like a woman's. He had on a fine suit of clothes, of good fabric—dark, with a gray waistcoat and white shirtfront, collar, and cravat. He held gray gloves in one hand and a tall black silk hat under the other arm. That was all very well, except that the tailor hadn't allowed for his ample limbs and waist—either that, or Mr. Parker had added some padding after the suit had been cut. Liz thought of Will, with his threadbare suit and his hard muscles beneath the rough fabric.

Mr. Parker was straining to stretch his face into something that could be called a smile. He had little eyes that peered out from under bushy black eyebrows. He bowed slowly toward Liz and said, "Miss Duncan." Then he turned and bowed to Mary Ann. "Miss Mary Ann Duncan. I'm so happy to make your—or . . . I mean to say . . . to see you again. It certainly is a fine day, if you don't mind my saying so."

"Why should we mind?" Mary Ann said, laughing a little. "Say it if you wish."

It was the worst thing she could have done to poor Mr. Parker. Clearly, he didn't know why they should mind. It had only been a little rivulet of words that had spilled from his mouth. "That is to say," he muttered, "certainly you wouldn't mind. I only meant to comment that it's a lovely day. A few clouds have gathered, and rain may not be terribly far off, but it's . . . aside from being a little cooler than one might prefer . . . perfectly . . . or at least passably pleasant."

"Yes, it is, Mr. Parker," Liz said. But she glanced at Mary Ann, and both of them had to look away from one another to keep from laughing.

Sally took Mr. Parker's hat and gloves then, and Liz said, "Mr. Parker, would you like to sit down for a few minutes? No doubt your day is busy, but perhaps you can spend five or ten minutes with us."

"Oh, much more. Much, much more." He sat down in one of the velvet parlor chairs. He tried to sit up straight, but his softness spread to both arm rests. Liz saw panic in his eyes, as though he realized that he had said the wrong thing. "I don't mean to say that I'll become tiresome. I certainly won't linger any longer than you young ladies . . . would enjoy. Or would seem to enjoy. Not that you are ones who would be so impolite as to say that I was growing tiresome. It would be I, of course, who would perceive that I had overstayed . . . and take my leave, according to your wishes. Or that is to say, the wishes that I would, by then, have perceived."

Liz had no idea what to say to that, and a painfully awkward ten or twelve seconds passed. Liz heard the ticks, suddenly seeming very loud. Mr. Parker's eyes looked confused, as though he were searching his head for something else to say. Finally, what came out was: "I buy and sell cattle, you know, Miss Duncan." He nodded to Mary Ann. "*Both* Miss Duncans."

"Yes. I believe you mentioned that," Liz said.

But Mary Ann, with an innocent face, said, "Oh, really? How interesting. Could you tell us all about that?"

Henry seemed to notice no irony in the request. He nodded to Mary Ann again, and then to Liz, and he cleared his throat. "Well, I must say, there is a great deal to it, you know. You may think it's only buying an animal and then selling it to someone else. But there's really much more that goes into it."

For the first time he sounded almost confident. But Mary Ann stopped him short. "I thought you said it was buying and selling. So what else can there be? Buy a cow as cheap as you can, and sell it as dear as you can. Isn't that the idea?"

"Well, now . . . it's not all cows, you know."

"What else is it? Pigs?"

"Yes. Mostly cattle and hogs. We've handled horses at times, too."

"No sheep?"

"Uh, no. Mostly cattle."

"And so you buy them for a low price and sell them for a higher one. Is that how it goes?"

Liz was ducking her head, trying not to watch any of this, but when she finally did glance up, she saw that Mr. Parker's big cheeks had reddened and his mouth was moving—popping open and shut like a fish's mouth.

"Yes, yes, of course. But what do you town ladies know about feeding animals, fattening them, and understanding just how much a man can invest in an animal before he loses everything in the exchange?"

"I don't know a single thing, Mr. Parker. Do you, Liz?"

"No, Mary Ann. I cannot say that I do. Maybe Mr. Parker will tell us. How much can a man invest in an animal before he loses in the exchange?"

Liz watched Mr. Parker raise himself up a little, seem to draw in all the self-importance he could project. "It's all a matter of . . . calculations," he said. "A man must look at an animal and recognize immediately just what it will cost to have it ready for the market— and calculate the price he can get at the same time. And it all must happen in a few seconds. That sort of capacity comes only with years of experience. I'm happy to say, I've acquired that experience. My father puts a great deal of trust in me."

"Let me see if I understand," Mary Ann said. "If you pay more for feed than you can gain back in the price you get for the cow, that's bad business."

"That's exactly right, young lady."

"Well, then, I suppose I do understand a good deal about buying and selling cattle. I might take up the trade."

"Oh, well. . . ." He laughed. "A young lady is not likely to recognize the qualities that make an animal salable. You have to grow up with cattle, know their—"

"I think I know a pretty cow when I see one."

"Oh, Miss Duncan, you would have much to learn. I don't think you would like getting manure on your . . . or, that is to say . . . excuse me. I should not have used that word. I should never use such words in the company of ladies. I only meant to say that—"

"That we wouldn't like stepping in cow dung?"

"Well, yes. Of course. But *dung* isn't a word to be spoken here. I wouldn't—"

"You didn't say it. I did. It's all part of nature. Liz might be embarrassed to speak of it, but I'm certainly not. Are you embarrassed, Liz?"

"No. Not at all. Go ahead, Mr. Parker. Tell us all about stepping in manure and feeding cows, and selling dear—and all those things."

"Oh, well . . . now . . . I'm certain we can find something more fitting to discuss in your lovely parlor." But he was edging toward the front of his chair, rolling his softness forward. "Ladies like to hear a man tell them . . . other things . . . I'm sure."

Mary Ann grabbed at that one immediately. "What things, Mr. Parker? Whatever they are, tell us some of them."

Mr. Parker clearly wanted out now. Liz could see him look about, as though to make his plan. But he still had to face Mary

Ann's question. "I'm not a flatterer, you know. I'm not one to say a lot of pretty things."

"Is that what comes from working with cattle and hogs? Does it make a man more down to earth, so to speak?"

"Perhaps so. It's not that I am incapable of extending a compliment."

"Such as, 'What a fine sow that is, sir!' That sort of thing?"

"No, no. I meant . . ." But suddenly he thrust himself forward. "Well, now, I should not take up your entire day. I do need to meet with my father . . . and . . . confer about matters of business."

"But you haven't said one pretty thing to us," Mary Ann said. "Please now, Mr. Parker, you can surely do better than that."

His mouth was going again, as though it might emit bubbles at any moment. "Well, now . . . what should I say? You are both very charming, you know. It's been more than pleasant to spend this hour . . . this few minutes . . . with you."

"Now, tell the truth, Mr. Parker. It *is* Miss Elizabeth you admire. Tell her how beautiful she is. Tell her that her eyes are the color of the sea, and her lips as red as—"

"Mary Ann!" Liz said. "Don't tease Mr. Parker. He thinks no such thing."

"Well, now . . . I would not say that. I am not likely to use such terminology, but you are quite . . . impressive, Miss Duncan. You are very . . . attractive."

"Oh, please, Mr. Parker," Mary Ann said. "You could say that about a nicely formed milk cow. It's time to speak out and say what you feel deep inside yourself."

"Mary Ann, that's enough." But it wasn't Liz who spoke the words, although she was about to. It was Mrs. Duncan who had stepped to the open door of the parlor. And then she tried, without making things worse, to apologize for Mary Ann. But Mr. Parker took the chance to retreat. He had almost made his way out the door before Mrs. Duncan reminded him of his gloves and hat, which he did stop long enough to receive, but then he headed down the stairs without an escort.

When he was gone, Mrs. Duncan turned around quickly. "I ask you to be fair to this man," she said, "and what do you do?"

"Liz was congenial," Mary Ann said. "Mostly. I was the one who ran him off. I couldn't help it. Someone had to do it."

"I don't understand why you—"

"You're right, Mum," Mary Ann said. "He does have money. And with such a fine brain for business, he'll go far. If Liz doesn't fancy him, I'll take him. What I know now is, Mr. Parker and I have *so much* to talk about."

Liz could see her mother fight the impulse for a few seconds, but then she started to laugh. "Oh, Mary Ann, you are so terrible," she said. "You had the man so flummoxed he couldn't speak." And then she put her hands over her cheeks and eyes, and she laughed hard.

But it was Liz who said, quite seriously, "He might *provide* for me very nicely, but at the end of the day I would have to *talk* to him. How would I do that?"

"I understand what you're saying, Liz. Just don't tell your father. I'll tell him Mr. Parker didn't show much interest. He only stayed a few minutes."

"Thanks, Mum," Liz said, and the two smiled at one another.

"But, girls, you *were* terrible. You needn't have been so cruel to the man."

"He's too thick to notice, Mother," Mary Ann said. "I hope he knows enough not to call again." She turned to Liz. "Let's walk to the market now. It's a lovely day . . . except for the gray skies . . . and the cold . . . and the imminent rain."

So Liz and Mary Ann walked to the marketplace. They usually

shopped for nice produce, or whatever Margaret, their cook, asked for—or ribbons and bows and the like—but mostly they used market day as an excuse to see friends. Liz always watched for Will, who sometimes drove his sisters into town with their cheeses. But Sarah and Esther weren't there this afternoon, nor was Will. Liz was a bit disappointed by that, but she was also feeling some disappointment in herself. She kept thinking that her mother was right. They had been cruel to Henry Parker. She wondered how humiliated he must have been.

The weather really was threatening, so the girls didn't stay long. They were about to start home when they met their friend Molly Drake. "What are you two doing here?" Molly asked. "I thought your gentleman caller was stopping by today."

"He did stop by," Mary Ann said, "but I scared him half to death. I ran him off in about ten minutes."

"What did you do to frighten him so?" Molly was a sturdy young woman of seventeen—the same as age as Mary Ann—with a good, broad smile. Her father was a wainwright, not a business owner. As a skilled laborer, he fared reasonably well, but Liz was aware that Molly looked up to the Duncans. A solicitor didn't hold the prestige that a barrister would, but in a country village, only a wealthy landowner ranked higher. Still, Molly had attended school every year and was now a teacher herself, teaching her first year in the town school. She was a clever girl, and lively, and a favorite of Liz's and Mary Ann's.

"I asked him to profess his love," Mary Ann said. "As rightly he should, I think. But he played Falstaff and chose the 'better part of valor.'"

"He's fit to play Falstaff," Molly said. She laughed. "All the same, you can send him to call on me. I would enjoy his money ever so much. I'd marry him, send him off to buy cows, and then hire a staff of servants to do all my work."

"But what about when he came home at night?" Mary Ann asked.

"Well . . . that wouldn't be the best time of the day. Maybe it wouldn't be worth the money."

Liz was feeling that this had gone far enough. "He's not such a bad man," she said. "He means well. We made him so nervous, he didn't know what to say to us."

"I think you're right," Mary Ann said. "He's better at talking to cows and hogs."

"Mary Ann, he *is* our brother in the gospel," Molly said. "Brother Kington wouldn't be happy at all to hear us speak ill of him."

That stopped Mary Ann for a moment, but then she said, "It's his pompous manners I don't like. And his pride. He could do well to lower his own opinion of himself."

"But it's also prideful of us to look down on him," Liz said.

"That's true," Molly said. "I know I don't like people to look down on our family just because my father works for a living."

"There's nothing wrong with working," Liz said.

"I wish that were true. But it marks a man as being lower than the privileged classes."

This was awkward. No one spoke for a time. A solicitor "worked," in a certain sense, but that was not the same as plying a trade.

"It doesn't matter," Molly finally added. "We didn't make the world the way it is. And we can all love one another. It's what our preachers always tell us."

Mary Ann said that was true, but Liz hardly knew what to say. She didn't feel superior to Molly, but she also knew that her mother would never invite Mrs. Drake into her home. They could sit in the same chapel and worship, but afterwards they returned to their own social circles.

Molly laughed, clearly hoping to lighten the mood. "I'll tell you this much. If Will Lewis ever called on me, I wouldn't turn *him* away—whether he works hard or not. I think I could be a very happy farmer's wife if I could look at his blue eyes every morning and have those big strong arms around me at night."

Liz felt a pang of jealousy. She didn't like to imagine Molly having Will. "Good looks aren't everything," she said, actually only to say *something*.

"Maybe not. But money isn't everything either. I may joke about that, but I want to marry a man I love. I may be a working-class girl, but that's all right. I can work hard all my life if I have a good man who'll work beside me—and one who loves me more than anything in the world."

"I want that, too," Mary Ann said. "But I still hope the fellow has a little gold in his purse."

They all laughed, but Liz was feeling the first little drops of rain, soft as mist. "I think we'd better hurry home," she said. "The rain's finally coming."

They said good-bye and Liz and Mary Ann walked on up High Street. But Molly's image was still in Liz's head: A man who loved her more than anything in the world. A man she loved. And one so wonderful to look at.

"It isn't fair, is it?" Mary Ann asked.

"What isn't fair?"

"That some people look down on Molly and her family."

"You mean, the way we do?"

"I love Molly," Mary Ann said. "I don't think of her as—"

"Would we consider her brothers as possible suitors—if they were old enough for us?"

Mary Ann didn't give the answer they both knew was correct.

"Mary Ann, what makes me better than Will Lewis? Mother and Father believe in Jesus Christ—but not in mingling with God's *lesser* children."

"But Molly's right," Mary Ann said. "We didn't make the world the way it is."

"And isn't it lovely that God made us better than the Lewises or the Drakes?"

"Liz! Now you're the one saying things you shouldn't say. I'm the one who's supposed to do that."

But neither was laughing.

CHAPTER 7

It was nearing October now. The last hay cutting had begun, and Will was starting to worry about his traps. At first he had checked them each night; he had found no game so far. Now, putting in such long days in the fields, he had let a few days go by, and that was dangerous. If John Carpenter, the squire's gamekeeper, happened to spot one of the snares, he would surely know who had set it. John had stopped Will one day that summer and had asked him whether he had ever seen anyone moving about in the woods above his field. Will had told him that he hadn't, but John had nodded knowingly and asked, "And if'n ye ever zeed such a thing, ye'd tell me sure, wouldn't ye now?"

John was a big man, nearly six feet tall, and square as a woodshed. He was not forty yet, but his hair was gray, his eyebrows black, and there was a coarseness in his face, like a rocky cliff.

"I'd tell ye, sure," Will had said. "You know me, John. Allus willin' to do what's right—an' ta show love ta the squire." He had smiled just a little, daring John to accuse him.

John had only said, "Mark that ye do. I'd not like ta see ye get run off this land after your people has lived here s'long."

There had been no doubt in Will's mind that the man suspected him, but Will had only said, "An' why would I take such a chance, with you watchin' out all the time? You're like the squire's hound, runnin' about sniffin' and barkin' an' lickin' his hand."

That had brought color to John's craggy face. "Ye best be careful, Will Lewis. I do watch. An' one night when a fox comes out from its hole, this hound'll be waitin'. An' that fox'll have its tail hangin' in me barn that night."

Will had only nodded and continued to smile. At that time, he hadn't been setting any traps; he only liked John to think that he might. His attitude was different now, and danger wasn't quite the deterrent it had been before. Still, there was no use pushing his luck too far. He decided he had better pull up his traps.

After an hour or two of cutting one morning, rain had set in rather hard. That was the last thing Will wanted, but it did allow for catching up a little in the barn. Will sharpened scythes and let the lads rest for a time before he got them back to their threshing. As soon as they were doing that, and the lasses were busy in the dairy, he hurried up the hill toward the east hedgerow.

Will didn't like what he found at his first trap. A little fawn, only a few months old and still in its spots, had caught its foot, obviously thrashed about a great deal, broken its leg, and finally died. But it hadn't been dead long.

It was one thing to take a hare or a grouse—quite another to kill a deer. Will's first thought was to dig a hole and bury it, but a disturbance in the bracken would be hard to hide. He would be better off to get the little carcass back to his farm and bury it there. So he found his other trap and pulled it up—empty—and then carried the fawn and the traps back down the hill, this time staying close to the hedge, hidden from the road. He tried to avoid anyone seeing him as he dug a hole behind the barn, but the rain had stopped, and Daniel stepped outside, probably to find out what Will had in mind for the boys to do. "What's that you got there, Will? Are ye lookin' to get yoursel' locked up in jail?"

"What if I do?" Will said. "At the least, I could sit mysel' down for a day or two."

"Aye. An' longer."

Suddenly Will was angry. He decided not to bury the fawn. There was more meat on it than on any hare, and his family might as well enjoy it. He knew what he would face from his father, but he had heard all that before. What difference did it make?

So Will gutted the little animal and skinned it, and then he took the carcass in the house to the dry sink and butchered it as best he knew how. "Please don't do this," Nettie kept saying to him. "Get rid of it. Don't let your father see it."

"Boil it up, and we'll tell 'im it's a four-legged chicken," Will told her, laughing. He almost looked forward to the anger that he would surely inspire.

And the anger soon came. Father walked into the house and then across the room to see what Will was doing. He stared at the meat for a few seconds and then, astonished, asked, "What ha' ye gone and done, Will?"

"Don't worry yoursel', Dad. It's all as it should be. This poor li'l fawn caught its leg in the fence at the hog pen. I found it, dead but still warm. So I brought it in to cook—so as not to waste the meat." But all the while he was smiling, never for a moment thinking that his father would believe him.

"That's a lie," Morgan said. "It's poachin', plain and simple. You can na' bring the squire's meat into this house."

"But no use wastin' the meat now that I've gone an' done it."

"I tol' you not to set them traps, Will. An' you promised you ne'er would."

"Aye, it's true. It's odd how sinners turn back to sin, like hogs ta the wallow. You best preach to me again, and this time with all your heart—an' hope I can yet be saved fro' destruction."

"You blaspheme, Will. An' you're not e'en afeard. But we shall na' eat that meat. We can lose our place—lose everythin' we have."

Will took a long breath. He stood staring at his father for a time, and then he looked over at his mother. He could see the fear in her face. "Fine, then," he said. "I'll get rid of it."

Will took the carcass back to the barn and buried it with the entrails and hide—every trace of the animal—and then he spread dirt and hay and manure over the hole he had dug.

Showers came and went the rest of the morning, and Will worked with the lads in the barn. When the rain finally let up, Will knew the hay would be too wet to cut for another day or two. But then, in the middle of the afternoon, John Carpenter showed up.

Will spotted him from a distance, riding up the road from the valley in his donkey cart, pulled by a thin old gray horse. Will walked out to the front of the cottage and waited, more frightened than he wanted to be. Still, he tried not to show it when John got down from his carriage and walked toward him.

"What's for supper?" John asked.

"Thin gruel, I 'spect," Will said. "Why? Are you stayin' to eat?"

"No venison with that 'ere gruel?"

Will tried not to give anything away with his eyes, his face. "An' how should we come to have venison, John?" But he heard the tightness in his own voice. He wasn't going to win this one.

"Will, I pay a man to stan' in these woods fro' time to time. He told me you marched yoursel' into the trees today an' after'n a while come back with a spotted fawn in your arms. So do na' tell me a lie. This time I have ye."

"I did find a li'l deer, John. It was chewed up, like a dog had gnawed on 'im."

"An' you carried him home for supper? Is that it?"

"No. Me father said you might think the worst. He told me to bury the poor feller and pray over 'im—give 'im a proper sendoff to'ards heaven."

John wasn't buying the story. He might have been smiling; it was hard to tell. But those deep eyes had more life than usual. "Then tell me how it come that you had traps hangin' over both shoulders. Help me ta un'erstan' that."

"Traps?" Will gave up. He smiled. "Who thought it was traps? If'n I remember right, I had a chain slung over my shoulders."

Will heard a voice behind him. "I've heerd enough o' this."

Will looked back and saw that his father was in the front doorway of the cottage. "Me son's lyin', John. I told 'im not to poach the squire's game, and he's done it all the same. But his lies shame me more'n his poachin'. He only told one thing true. He brought a fawn in, an' I said no, that the family would na' eat it."

"So where'd he throw it?"

"He told me he digged a hole and throwed it in."

John walked to Morgan and pointed a finger in his face. "An' why is it he hid that poor li'l deer? Warn't it to bury away the proof agin 'im? An' agin you, too?"

Will saw the chagrin in his father's face. He was about to lose everything he'd built up in his life. But he looked John in the eyes and said, "Aye, it's so, John. I'm afeard I joined in me son's lie. I'm 'shamed of that, too."

"That's all well and good, Morgan," John said. "But start

packing up. A new tenant will have to finish cuttin' your hay. You're done here."

"Wait a minute," Will said. "I set the traps, and I took the fawn. Don't punish my family. Punish me."

"That's not for me to say. You'll be off to jail. That's the law. But your family has to pay, too. Poachers is set off the land. Ye know it's so."

Mother had come to the door, and Will could see that she had been listening. She took her husband's arm, held it tight. Tears were on her face. This struck Will hard. "John, give me a minute with Squire Riddle. He can do as he wants to me, but don't take my father's home away. He's lived here all his life, and so have all my brothers and sisters. There's nothing for them but the poorhouse. Don't send my mother there."

"An' why did na' ye think on that when ye carried traps into them woods?"

"You're right about that, John. But give me two minutes with Squire Riddle. I worked his land hard for all this time. I should have a hearing."

"You'll talk to the squire aw right. He's the magistrate here-abouts, an' you'll stan' afore him in court. Tell 'im that story an' see what it gets ye." He looked past Will to Morgan. "Expec' the squire here in no more'n a hour. It's him who says how soon you clear out." John walked back to his cart and got in. He shook the reins and gently spoke to his horse. He looked back at Will one last time, still seeming pleased with himself.

The squire showed up in less than half an hour, and that was a relief to Will. He had been trying to console his mother but mostly had had to listen to his father's righteous anger. And for Will it did finally have the ring of righteousness, however unyielding. All his family had gathered into the cottage, and everyone was broken down with fear. Morgan kept saying that they had nowhere to go, no way to make a living. Will saw that the color had gone out of his sisters' faces, and the younger boys were crying, clinging to Nettie. Even Daniel seemed more frightened than judgmental.

It was Nettie who took Will in her arms. She didn't tell him how wrong he'd been. She only clung to him and whispered, "Oh, Will, what will they do with you?"

Squire Riddle arrived in a much finer carriage—a black gig pulled by a matched team of black horses. John was driving the horses, and Squire Riddle, in a tall top hat, was sitting next to him, looking stiff and serious. Will stepped outside immediately and approached the gig when it came to a stop. "Sir," he said, taking off his cap, "before you decide what to do, I'd like to say a word to you. I've admitted to John that I trapped the fawn. But you need to know, it was I alone. Hold me for judgment—and punish me as you see fit—but please don't send my family away."

"See what I told ye," John said. "He's humble as a little lad caught with a finger in his mum's pie. But he's been poachin' all along and his family's been eatin' the meat that's rightfully yourn."

"That isn't true," Will said. John stepped down from the carriage, came around it, and stood before Will as though he were about to grab him and carry him away. Will stepped to the side and looked at the squire, who remained in the carriage. "There was a time when most everyone hereabouts took a hare or a grouse from time to time, and your father didn't mind. But when you took over, you laid down the law, and my father told me never to trap game again. He told me the animals were not ours, and wrong to take."

"But Morgan don't mind eatin' what you poach," John said.

"No. That's not true."

"You zed it yourself. You—"

"Be quiet, John," Squire Riddle said. "I'll handle this matter."

The squire was about half the size of John Carpenter, but his metallic voice carried more authority. He was dressed in a full suit of clothes, with a gray cravat tied up around his collar and a gray waistcoat under his dark frock coat. He wasn't carrying his silver-headed walking stick today; his bare hands were gripped across his front, and his skin was pink with emotion even though his voice was under control. "John is right about this," he said. "You've poached my animals and your family has feasted on them. Now you want me to forgive you merely because you plead for mercy."

"That's not it, sir. I went against my father when I set those traps. I didn't expect to take a fawn, but I did. So I plead for no mercy for myself. I only ask that the punishment be rendered where it's deserved."

The squire looked off at the sky for a moment, as though he were considering the justice of the case.

"Ask why they been keepin' them traps about, if'n they warn't goin' to use 'em," John said.

The squire turned and pointed at his gamekeeper. "John, not another word out of you." He looked toward Morgan, who was standing a few paces behind Will, Nettie clinging to his arm again. All the children were standing closer to the house, more or less in a line. "Morgan, did you eat the fawn?"

"I did na', sir. But I told me son to bury the carcass, and I was wrong there. Still, I told 'im, in the strongest words I know, ne'er again to take an animal of any kind."

"And you claim this happened only once?"

"Yes, sir. But I'm afeard I'm the one who taught me son to thieve these animals, years ago. Me heart changed when I turned mysel' to God, an' I ne'er stole since ye come to the manor. I was wrong to tell me son to bury the fawn, but I gave way to fear, sir." Will heard his father's voice break and saw tears fill his eyes. "Me family has farmed this field for gen'rations, sir, an' withou' it, I have no way to feed me children."

"I'm not an unfair man, Morgan, but I have to consider what will happen if my other tenants learn that I allowed you to get away with this crime. Your son told the truth when he said my father wasn't stern enough in these matters. He let his tenants believe that they could do as they pleased, and they almost destroyed our game. I can't—"

"And what makes it *your* game?" Will shouted, surprising even himself. He could see where all this was heading. This self-righteous *gentleman* was about to throw his family off the farm, and his father would probably thank him for his kindness in teaching them all a good lesson. But Will was outraged. "The animals live on common land, and there was a time when all could have them, rich and poor. But that's never good enough for the *better classes.* They have to send men to Parliament to do their bidding—pass laws to enclose the land and give *everything* to those who already have the most."

"Will, don't say such things," Morgan said. "Sir, it's not what I believe."

The squire calmly looked toward Morgan. "So you've raised a socialist, and you can't imagine how?"

"I can na' say who's talked to him so, or who might ha'—"

"No one has *talked* to me," Will said, but not with the same force as before. "I watch what's happening. Tenant farmers barely get by. Gentlemen ride to the hunt and kill off foxes for sport—and they cover their tables with a spread of food that would feed half the poor people in the county."

"It's the talk we hear from labor unions and Chartists," the squire said to Morgan, and then he looked back at Will. "I could hire laborers to farm my land, but I choose to provide a cottage and sheds and a barn for your family, and you begrudge me a chance to serve a nice meal to my friends."

"No. I don't mind that you have more than we do. But there was a time when tenants could get by. Now you've taken more and more to yourself, and taken it out of the mouths of those who make a living for you."

"Sir, sir," Morgan was saying, stepping in front of Will. "None o' this come from me. I ne'er said such things. Me grandfather was a tenant to your grandfather, and me father to your father. I owe all I have to your family. That's my honest feelin'."

"It is, sir," Will said. "He's telling the truth. I'm the bad apple. Get rid of me and you'll never hear talk like that again. Please let my family stay."

The squire finally stepped down from the carriage—slowly and rather ceremoniously. He stepped up close to Will. He looked less imposing now, shorter than Will and slight of build. "You've accused me wrongly, young man."

The words seemed comical to Will. The squire was only thirty or so, and he looked even younger. "I have always sought to be fair with my tenants, and I know nothing but good about your father. My father told me long ago that he was the hardest working man who lived on our estate, and as loyal as any man alive. I have no desire to harm him or his family."

Will nodded. He looked at the ground and said, "What your father said was true, sir."

"But I think your characterization of yourself is quite accurate. You are a bad apple and I want you off this farm."

"Yes, sir."

"You have one hour to gather together whatever is yours and to leave my land. I could hold a court and sentence you to a long term in jail. And perhaps I should. But I see the tears in your mother's eyes, and the worry in your father's, and I'm willing to give you another chance in this world."

Will looked up, unsure what he meant.

"Leave. And never come back. If I ever see you on my estate again, I shall try you as an admitted poacher."

"That's fair, sir."

"But I thought we gentlemen were incapable of fairness."

"I don't think there's much fairness in this world, sir. I don't think the poor have much chance, but in these circumstances, you might have acted much more harshly."

"Thank him," Morgan said.

But Will wasn't going to do that. He gave a little nod, and that was all. What he knew was that he had very hard days ahead. He might never see his family again, and a pain was spreading through him as he realized that, but at the same time, at least his life would not continue on the same. He could leave and try to make something more of it.

The squire was still talking, pompous and satisfied with himself, and Morgan continued to apologize and express his gratefulness. The words would normally have been annoying to Will, but he could hardly hear them now, with his mind on everything else. And yet, Will understood something in a way that he never had before: his father meant every word he was saying. He was grateful, and he really believed that God made some people rich and some poor, and that it was not his place to try to change that.

The next hour was the strangest of Will's life. He would later remember it with pain, and yet, as it was happening, he was almost emotionless. He was going away, and his mother, his sisters, his little brothers, even his father and Daniel, were devastated. Everyone cried, embraced him, but it was his mother who was breaking with pain. "Oh, Will," she told him, "you were my first, and I didn't know anything about caring for a baby. You were so sick that first winter, and I thought I was losing you. I begged the Lord, and he let you stay with us, and now . . . this. How can it happen?"

Will heard the words, but he would only think about them later. He went about his business. His mother gave him an old carpetbag she had brought to her marriage. He stuffed an extra work shirt into it—his only extra shirt—and his father convinced Will to put on his Sunday suit. That made sense to Will only because it was easier to carry that way, and he might need a suit of clothes. But he hardly knew what else to take. He had only one pair of boots, and almost nothing in the house actually belonged to him.

He did have a few coins in a drawer, two sovereigns and a little pile of shillings that he had saved with the hope of setting out this way, if not under these conditions. He stuffed the coins into his coat pocket, and his mother gave him some sheets of paper and a quill so he could let them know where he was as soon as he stopped somewhere. Sarah kept asking him where he would go, but he didn't know, so he didn't answer. He was trying to think about that, but what kept coming to his mind was that he had to let Liz know what had happened. So he finally asked everyone to give him a few minutes alone. They left him in the back bedroom, seeming to understand what he wanted to do. He sat down and wrote out a note to Liz.

When he came out, he still had some time left in his hour, but there was no use staying any longer. "I'll be going," he said. "I'm sorry. If I can earn some money, I'll send you what I can." He looked at Daniel. "You can na' go on as you have," he said. "Look after the hay-making. Work hard, Dan."

He was surprised by the tears in Daniel's eyes. "I'll do it, Will. I promise."

"Stop a li'l yet," his father said. "We need to pray together."

Will didn't want to do that; he knew what was coming. But he knelt with his family. His father's prayer was full of reprimands. "Let Will learn from this," he told the Lord. "Let him repent and find your grace." And later, "When he comes to his senses, and gives up his sinful ways, forgive 'im for all he's gone and done."

Will listened to it all, let it pass through him, and then he embraced everyone one more time. After he took Sarah in his arms, he gave her a sheet of paper, folded, and asked her to take it to Liz on Sunday, or sooner if she found a way.

Nettie brought him a flour sack full of bread and cheese. When he embraced her, she didn't want to let him go. He finally let Daniel take her from him, and then he stepped to the door. He tried to think of something to say, but he had already told them that he loved them and that he was sorry. He couldn't tell them that he would see them again.

But Morgan had his own words ready. "Will," he said, "I love ye with all me heart. You ha' worked like a man sin' you was a lad, and you ha' kept our family agoin' when I could na'. I shall miss you ever' day of me life. What I ask is that ye turn back to God an' take your solace in 'im. Repent, an' ye still might be forgiven."

Will nodded, and finally tears came to his own eyes. He saw his mother clinging to Daniel, and he watched as Daniel lowered her into a chair, and that would be the memory of her that stayed with him as he walked away. He was a few rods up the road before he felt his knees get weak, and he almost dropped to the ground. He was alone, he realized, and he had never, until now, understood the meaning of the word.

●　●　●

When Liz walked with Mary Ann to church services on Sunday, she knew that she would not see Will there. The story of Squire

Riddle sending him away had spread through the town. Liz had heard the story with more shock than she let on, but her reaction was more anger than unhappiness. She had known that nothing would ever work out with Will. At least now the matter was finally put to rest for certain. He was likely to find work as a farm laborer somewhere, and that would be his future—a step down from the status he had known, which was low enough. So that was what she told Mary Ann, and it was what she told herself: that she would think of Will no more.

But her stomach didn't feel right from the moment she heard the story. Even though she had known she would never marry Will, there were the glances at him at church, the occasional meeting on market day, his handsome smile, his unforgettable blue eyes. She couldn't help thinking of that day she had more or less invited him to kiss her and he had not been brave enough to do it. She wished now that she had kissed him once, just to know what a kiss felt like. She had always liked to think of him taking her in his strong arms, and that wouldn't happen now. What she did feel was a sense of emptiness, of longing for a change in her life that may never come. She was not going to marry Henry Parker no matter what her father thought she should do, but she did want to marry someone, and there was no one in her life.

When she approached the Watkins house, she saw Sarah Lewis waiting outside. "Liz," Sarah said, "do you know about my brother?"

"That he's banished? That he can't ever show his face here again? Is that what you want to tell me?"

"Well, then, you do know. But he wanted me to give you this." She handed Liz the folded sheet of paper.

"What's this?"

"It's what he wanted to say to you. I wanted ever so much to read it, but I didn't."

Liz nodded. She saw the tears in Sarah's eyes. "You miss him, don't you?"

"Aye. More than you can ever imagine. He's such a wonderful brother—so good to me, and such a good man. I'll miss him forever."

Liz could only nod. She didn't want to show any reaction.

"He will make someone a wonderful husband," Sarah said. "He's strong, but he's gentle and kind. He'll work hard all his life, and I think he'll make something of himself."

Liz knew what Sarah was saying, but she didn't try to get any words out. She pulled Sarah to her and held her in her arms for a time. Sarah fought back her sobs with little choking sounds, and Liz fought back her own tears by biting down on her lip.

Liz walked inside, and she and Mary Ann joined their parents in the parlor. She didn't look at the letter because she knew her parents would ask her what it was, so she had to sit through a very long, very ordinary sermon from a visiting preacher—a howling man named Jones—before she could make her way outside in the dreary light of an overcast day.

Liz and Mary Ann waited until their parents had gone on ahead of them, and then they walked a little way and stopped. Liz opened the letter. "Let me read it with you," Mary Ann said.

"No. I don't know what he might say."

"He'll promise to come back someday and cover your lips with kisses."

"Hush."

The note was very short. It only said: "My dear Liz, by now you must know what has happened to me. I don't know whether I can ever be worthy of you, but I plan to try. I do not have the right to ask you to wait for me to return. I may not ever do that. But know, as I leave, that I love you and always will, and I shall try to better myself."

"Did he ask you to wait for him forever?" Mary Ann asked.

"No. He didn't have enough courage. He wants to 'better' himself. He wants to be 'worthy' of me."

Mary Ann laughed. "How long is that going to take?"

"I don't want to talk about it."

"Is your heart broken?"

"Not at all. And that's all I'm going to say."

They walked for a couple of minutes, neither speaking. Finally Mary Ann asked, "So here's what I want to know. How is his handwriting?"

Mary Ann seemed to think that was funny, but Liz was weary of Mary Ann making light of everything. "His writing is *girlish*," Liz said, and she tried to sound disdainful. But the tears finally came, and she looked away so that Mary Ann couldn't see under her bonnet.

CHAPTER 8

Will had never traveled far beyond his valley. He only knew that Birmingham and Manchester, the great factory cities, were well north of Worcester, which was across the Malvern Hills northeast from Ledbury. So that was the direction he decided he would go—northeast, over the hills. But that wasn't his first worry. He didn't know how long he would have to make his money last. If he traveled in a coach and paid to stay in taverns along the way, he might have little left to live on while he tried to find work. The truth was, he had no idea how much a passenger paid to ride in a fancy coach or to stay at an inn, and he wasn't sure where to ask. So he hiked the hills to the north, and then east, pretty sure that he could catch the road from Ledbury to Great Malvern. He knew that was the direction he had to travel to reach Worcester.

He followed footpaths until he reached a road wide enough for wagons, all the while climbing higher. When a farmer came along in a wagon, he accepted an offer for a ride. He was pleased at first not to be making his own way up the steep hill, but the old team of horses trudged along too slowly for his liking. Will was actually relieved when, after a mile or so, the farmer said he was turning off the main road.

Will asked the man if he knew how far it was to Worcester, and how far after that to Birmingham or Manchester. Will was fairly sure that Birmingham came first, but he couldn't say for certain. The man raised his head a little and peered out from under a sagging straw hat. Then he took the hat off and ran his fingers through his sparse hair as though he were contemplating a great question. "Can na' say," he finally offered. "I heerd tell Worcester is up this road some'eres, so it can be, Birm'n'ham and Manch'ster is that same way."

Will thanked the man, though he had learned nothing from him, and then he walked hard the rest of the afternoon. He had enough to eat for two or three days, at least, but nothing else was clear to him; his mind refused to concentrate on matters at hand. He had the strange sense that Will Lewis had died that afternoon, and he had no idea who would arise and take his place. He tried not to think about his family, about Liz, about his farm—about anything. He looked at trees and farms, let himself take everything in, told himself how beautiful the valley below him was, even told himself that he had started an adventure. But no matter how hard he looked, the scenery wouldn't sink into him, as though nothing was exactly real. He wished, in a way, that he could cry—out here where no one could see him—but he felt empty, more than anything, and very scared.

The sun was setting quite early these days, and a cool evening was coming on. The weather was dry, which was fortunate, but Will knew the night would be cold. He thought of seeking out a hayrick or a barn where he could lie down, but nothing offered itself. Farms were scattered on this higher land, and, as the dark deepened, he couldn't see much beyond the trees or the hedges along the road. So he kept walking.

It was late when he came upon an inn with candlelight flickering in a window. He peered in and saw that a fire was still burning in the fireplace, so he opened the door and stepped inside. Only one table was occupied. Four men were seated near the fire, all of them laughing about something. They turned from their tankards of ale and looked at him, seeming surprised, their faces orange in the glowing firelight. One of the men stood up. "What can a' do for ye?" he asked.

"I'm cold," Will said.

"Aye. An' will a pint warm ye?"

Father had joined the temperance movement even before he had joined the United Brethren. When Morgan was younger, he had sometimes drunk too much, but he had turned against alcohol entirely and didn't allow it in his home. Will had tried ale and beer a few times but had never learned to like them. He also knew his father wouldn't want him to start drinking now. He shook his head, not sure what to say.

"Are ye wantin' a bed?"

"How much?"

"Sixpence."

Will turned to leave.

"A groat, then. That's as low as a' go."

Again, he shook his head.

"I can na' help ye then, can a'? Ye've warmed yourself a li'l, so move on."

But a little man in a baggy suit of clothes, without so much as looking at Will, said, "I'll stan' the four pence. Give the lad a bed."

Will thought of turning down the offer, but the words didn't come. He only said "Thank you, sir," and the proprietor led him to a tiny room with two beds in it. Will sat on one of the beds. He stared into the dark for a time, and then he stretched out in all his clothes. He thought of eating a little something, but the next thing he knew he was waking up to the sound of a loud grumble. Someone was snoring, someone very close to him—on the same bed. Whoever it was reeked of alcohol, and the odor from his body and clothes was disgusting.

Will lay quiet for a time, still trying to remember exactly where he was, and then everything came back to him: his departure from home, his mother clinging to him. And now it was clear. He would wake up every morning of his life without his family. He might not always be alone, but it seemed so at the moment. He wanted to take everything back, to hurry back to his home and beg the squire to let him stay. But all that was impossible. The tears had started now. They rolled from the corners of his eyes and into his hair. He knew he had to get up and going.

Will found his flour sack and his carpetbag in the blackness, felt his way to the door and opened it, and walked carefully down the dark, squeaking stairs. He found no one downstairs, so he sat at a table and pulled out his loaf of bread and a wedge of cheese. He broke off some of each and actually ate more than he had the whole day before. Then he tucked the food back into his sack, and he set out. He walked all day. He passed through Great Malvern, an old town, much like Ledbury, and he reached Worcester. It was the biggest city he'd ever seen, and he felt strange to be among so many people in one place. He stopped just long enough to ask a constable for directions, and then he trudged on through the city and set out for Birmingham.

Will slept in an old shed that night—one that hadn't been used in years. The sagging roof seemed as though it might fall in, and there was no door on the hinges, but he felt lucky to be out of the wind, anyway, especially since a storm was evidently blowing in. He curled up on the dirt floor and fell instantly asleep, but sometime in the night, water began to drip on him. Only a light rain was falling, but the thatching on the roof was falling apart and it didn't stop much. Will worked his way to a drier spot and tried to go back to sleep, waiting for the dawn, but it was hopeless. The dripping soon reached him again. So he sat up, ate a few bites, and then set out once more.

All morning it rained. The water gradually soaked through his frock coat and shirt, but there was nothing to do but to keep tramping ahead. He spoke to farmers along the way who told him he was heading the right way to get to Birmingham. One of them offered him a place by his fire, inside, to dry out. "You can sleep the night, too, if ye have a mind to," the good fellow said, but Will resisted. He wasn't even sure why. He only knew that he wanted to get to Birmingham, see what his chances were, and maybe find some reason to hope.

Early in the afternoon he thought he had reached the city, but the smokestacks were still in the distance. He walked another hour before he reached the first of the huge factory buildings. By then the rain had let up.

Looking around, Will wondered whether he hadn't walked into some part of hell. He had never seen such a vast place, with houses stacked nearly on top of each other for miles. The first of them had seemed well cared for, but the ones deep in the city looked like pens for hogs. They were built of brick, mostly, but the roofs sagged and the window frames were shedding their paint. Many of the windows had been broken and stuffed with rags or boarded over. Everything was covered with a heavy layer of coal soot, and filth was in the air, too, hanging over the city like a brown fog. The houses were most often built in double rows, slapped together side to side and back to back. Will wondered how any light could get inside. In the streets he saw children, sometimes playing, but with little joy in their faces, and all of them dirty. Few had shoes, and their clothes were as gray and worn as the buildings, the streets, the sky.

What shocked Will most, however, was the stench. He had grown up around manure. He had spread it on his fields and shoveled it from his barn and pens. It was the smell that made him think of his farm, his home. But the odor in Birmingham was human, like the stink of a privy. It permeated the sooty air and filled up his lungs until he wondered whether he could keep breathing. Black water ran down the center of the streets, or along the sides, in rivers that smelled like night slops. More than once he saw a woman or a child carry a chamber pot to the street and dump it out into the running streams of sewage.

Will had made his way toward a tall smokestack he had been using as a guidepost for at least a mile. What he found there was a huge brick building, built like a box, with rows of windows four stories up. He didn't know where he would sleep that night, and he didn't know how to start his search for work, but this was a factory; he was sure of that. It seemed the right place to ask. The problem was, the building was fenced off with a high brick wall, and when he walked around a corner, he found only a closed gate and a man in a little office next to the gate. Will looked in through a window and nodded at the man, who raised the window sash about halfway. "Aye. What is it ye want? If it's work, we ha' nothin'."

Will nodded. "Well, then, could you tell me—"

The man's hands were still on the window sash. He pushed it closed again.

Will was left standing, wondering. He finally turned and looked about himself. He saw a man dressed in a ragged suit of clothes walking toward him. "Sir?" he said.

"Sir, is it?" the man said. "It's not what I be, lad. I'm 'zackly nuffin', if yo want to know the plain troof of it. I'm called Jed, if ye need ta call me sumpin'."

"I'm sorry. I'm looking for work and I—"

"Who ain't?"

"Are there no jobs here?"

"None for a body to lay hold on. Them what's workin' ne'er earn enough to live, and them what's not, want the jobs aw the same."

"So where can a man find work?"

"Not anywheres here. Could be in the potteries. I heerd that, anyways."

"Where is that—the potteries?"

"Stoke and Burslem an' those places—towns norf fro' here. It's them what make dishes and pots and aw."

"And you've heard that there's work there?"

"Aye. I heerd a man say't, but that do na' mean it's so."

Will had no idea what to make of that. "Jed, have you made a long search for work here? Is there really *nothing* to be found?"

"What's long? I go aboot ever'day, ha' done for awmost a year. I'm agoin' out back to ax here now, but I won't find nuffin'. I know that afore I ax."

"I asked the man at this window, but he said—"

"It ain't the right place. It's a door out back where a man knocks. Coom. We can bof ask and be telled the same. But don' ask like a gen'leman, the way yer talkin' now. They ain't lookin' for them what read and write. Don't let on like yo can do it."

"I'm no gentleman."

"Yo do na' dress like one, but yo talk like't. And it's them what read and write what start talkin' of unions and aw. The bosses don't like't."

Will knew that he had spoken rather formally, maybe because he was addressing a stranger, or maybe because he wondered whether people here would understand his Herefordshire speech, but he was glad to learn, from the beginning, that he shouldn't sound too educated.

Will walked down an alley with Jed and they stopped at a door. A sign tacked on the door read: "No work. Do not knock." Will began to read the sign out loud, but Jed said, "I can read that much wiff ou' knowin' a single letter. Them signs is all over Bum'n'am."

"So wha' can be done, if we can na' even knock on the door?" Will asked, trying to sound more down to earth.

"What work ha' ye done afore?"

"Farm work."

"The harvest is mostly done. Yo can maybe cut some hay here an' there—out on the land."

"But nothin' comes from it. I want ta work my way up a li'l. If I can get a place in a factory, it might be I can be a foreman in time. It's what I've heard."

"Go home, lad. Farmers eat aw right. That's more than yo can do here."

Will let the idea sink in. He had told himself for years that something better than his farm was out there somewhere. It had given him something to hope for. But maybe it was all a lie. He couldn't even think which way to walk, what to do. He needed someone to turn to, some friend, some answer. He felt his breath coming faster, and he told himself he couldn't break down, not here before this man. "What do ye say, Jed?" he asked. "What can you tell me? Is it worth lookin' here, or better to keep walkin' to the potteries—or maybe Manchester?"

"I can't say shor, but I know where nuffin' is, and that's here. But if ye have a home, go there. That's the best."

"I can't go home," Will said, but he didn't explain. He merely got directions for the road north to Stoke, and he set out again. At least the weather had cleared, and his clothes gradually dried. He slept in the woods that night and lasted until the cold got into his bones and he had to get up and walk again.

Will hiked a long road, crossed low hills, and splashed through streams where there were no bridges. He learned that Wellington Heath was not the only green valley in England, that there were lots of pretty places and nice villages. But it was hard to take much pleasure in sightseeing, and when he asked himself which place was best, he still thought his valley, and Ledbury, were the best he'd seen.

Will found the potteries—in Stoke-on-Trent, Hanley, Burslem, and other towns in what he learned was Staffordshire—but he found no work. He also heard, from many a man whom he asked, that there was no work in Manchester, either. But he spoke to one fellow who didn't see everything as being quite so dark. Will was out of food, so he stopped at a street stall in Burslem to buy a hot potato and some pickled eel. The vendor was a well-spoken man. He told Will, "I agree, times are hard in Manchester. Demand for cotton cloth is down, and the weaving mills have been letting workers go, but there are still a good many people working. Manchester has all kinds of factories and warehouses and businesses. Jobs open up from time to time, and if a man knocks on the right door at the right time, he might find something. You're young and strong, and that's what I wasn't. I had to move away, but it was lads like you who took my job."

Will didn't like to think of it that way—that he would be taking someone's work—but he did like to think that there were many doors to knock on and that one day, when he arrived on the right day, he would find something. Maybe it was just a matter of trying all day, every day, until something turned up.

So Will walked on to Manchester. He didn't know how far he'd walked from home, but he thought it must have been more than a hundred miles. His boots were showing the wear, too, a hole having opened up in each sole. His feet were already sore, but now, with his stockings soaking up water from the streams he had crossed, they were cold and getting blistered. Worse, however, was the ache and confusion he felt in his head. He hadn't slept well—or long—any night since he'd been traveling, and he had been gone from his farm six days, if he remembered right.

Manchester was like Birmingham, big and sooty and putrid. And people lived the same way—or maybe worse. He found his way to the Ancoats section of town, where smokestacks were thick and people were piled into broken-down housing. He told himself that he had at least made it to his destination, and he had spent little of his money getting there. Now he could make a serious, daily search until he found something. And he *would* find something. But for the moment, he was hungry—and too tired to start knocking on doors. What he didn't know was where he would sleep that night. He wondered about his health in a place like this, with such terrible air and so many diseases that could spread through the people. He stopped on a corner of Great Ancoats Street and looked about himself. He couldn't think what to do next.

Will noticed that a woman and her little daughter—not more than six years old—were walking in the street, bending down and picking something up, putting it in a burlap bag the woman was carrying. He wondered what it could be. The street was paved with cobblestones, but everything was coated with mud and straw. Ash heaps and rubbish piles were scattered here and there. He walked a little closer and watched the woman. He felt a wave of sickness pass over him when he realized she and her daughter were picking up horse manure, most of it still quite fresh. The woman's hands were bare, and filthy, as were her clothes, and the little girl was dressed in rags. But the two were assiduous in their work, filling up the bulging bag.

Will assumed there must be sale for the muck, somewhere, but he couldn't imagine that anyone would pay more than a penny or two. Did the woman do this every day? Did she feed her little girl—and perhaps other children—by gathering dung? Will had watched his sisters pitch manure, and they had worked around cows and hogs, but this seemed lower, more disgusting than anything he had seen before. He wondered how far a person would go, just to find a way to survive. He had wanted to find a better place in the world, to rise to a higher rank. Now he wondered how much further he could fall. What might he have to do the rest of his life, just to keep from starving?

"Needin' a place to stay?"

"What?" Will looked about. A lad of fourteen or so—like Josiah—was standing next to him. He was wearing a tattered frock coat, much too small for him, and no shirt underneath it. His trousers were half a foot too short, not reaching his ankles, and he was wearing wooden clogs on his feet, as most people did in the city. As people walked, the wood hit the paving stones and made a constant clacking sound.

"Needin' a place to stay? We has beds, tuppence a night."

Will had been thinking about this. He needed to clean up as best he could before he looked for work, and he needed a good night's sleep. He had thought of a boardinghouse, but he wondered how much that might cost. What if he couldn't find work for weeks? Two pence a night was surely cheap, and it would get him inside tonight. After a night of sleep—in a bed—he could think better about what he wanted to do.

"Where is this place?"

"Doon the street, na' far."

"Is it a tavern, or . . . what is it?

"It's where I stay."

"What? A room in your house?"

"A bed. Coom and see. Talk to Mum. She makes breakfas' too—an' it won' cost ye much at aw."

Will thought for a moment. He doubted this was a good idea, but he had no others. If he wanted to find a boardinghouse, he needed the strength to look. "Can she make me something to eat now?"

"Aye. Good food, too. Follow me."

The boy strode away, and Will followed. But when they left the main street, they turned into a lane lined with the same decrepit dwellings he had seen everywhere in Manchester. The buildings were "one-up, one-down," with one-story houses alternating between two-story structures. The privies were out front, close to the street, and the smell from them was thick in the air.

When finally the boy stopped and said, "Here w'are," he didn't enter the front door. He ran down a flight of stairs that led to a basement entry. He turned back quickly and said, "It's aw right, sir. An' on'y tuppence. Think on that."

He opened a door that seemed not to fit quite right. It hadn't been entirely shut, and Will wasn't sure that it could be. Will followed the boy into a room without light. He squinted to see but could only make out piles of things he couldn't identify.

"Young man, this will na' do," Will said.

A woman's voice answered, "It'll do when ye coom to it. Yo on'y need to set yor mind right. If ye have a shillin' to stay some'eres better, then go. If not, tuppence is a fine price."

Will's eyes were becoming accustomed to the dark. He could see the woman now, wearing a dark dress, standing in a doorway.

"For a penny, I give ye a candle. An' for a groat, bread and taters and bacon for supper. What say ye?"

"Where's the bed?"

"It's not rightly a bed. It's a mat. But many has slep' good on't. There's no rats, and it's dree for the mos' part, at leas' when the day is fine, like today."

But Will could hear a scratching noise in the dark, and he wondered about the rats. "No. I'm sorry. The lad said it was a bed. An' I haven't slept in a bed for many nights. I need one t'night. An' I need to get a bath. Do you know of a boardinghouse?"

"Not like you want. Not in these places. Not in Ancoats, I wager."

"Where could I look?"

"On the edge of toon, where the rich people live."

"I'm not rich. I—"

"If ye think on such a house, yor rich—at leas' for now. When yor doon to nuffin', that's when ye coom back, shor."

Will could not see the woman's face well, but he heard the despair in her voice. It occurred to him that he *was* rich—that he had never known anything like this. He looked again at the piles in the room. "What is all this?" he asked.

"Rags, mos'ly," the lad said. "I find what I can in rubbish piles and behin' fact'ries, an' we sell it aw to them what cooms in our street buyin' such thin's—rag-and-bone men." The lad sounded rather proud of himself. Will thought of his own pride at that age when his father had told him that he was a hard worker.

"I can na' stay, I fear," Will said. "But I can pay the tuppence as though I did, an' a groat more for the supper."

"Pay for supper," the woman said, "but not fo' not stayin'. That rich yor not."

"But you need the money," Will said. "Does your husband—"

"My husban' is dead. Killt by breathin' in cotton fluff in the mill where he worked 'til consum'tion took 'im. I los' two li'l girls, too, both with whooping cough. But me and the lad keeps on agoin', and not by beggin', neither."

"Do you have work?"

"I had work. An' los' it. My fact'ry shut doon."

"I came to look for work," Will said.

"Yor yoong. Sometimes they want lads yor age."

"But it's not fair. Everyone needs work."

"Fair?" the woman asked. "You think anythin' in this world is fair? Aye, yor young, aw right."

"I'm older than I was a week back," he said without explaining. But he stayed to eat, and while he waited, he talked to the lad, whose name was Nathan. The boy had never been to school, he said—had never been out of Manchester or, for that matter, Ancoats. When Will tried to tell him about Herefordshire and Ledbury, about his farm in a green valley, the lad couldn't seem to grasp what it was like. He had seen trees, in a park, and he had seen oxen and horses, but he had never seen a valley, or a farm, or a barn.

"That I'd like, to see sich a place," he said. "Me and me friend, we talk on sich things. We hope ta be sailors, and go about in the worl', but the sea is far from here an' we do na' know how to go there."

"It's not far," Will told him. "Liverpool is only a few miles that way." He pointed to the west.

"Then we'll go someday. Me and Thomas."

Will thought of himself at the same age, longing to go somewhere, and now he had done it.

When Will left the basement, not happy with the sour potatoes and the tiny bit of bacon, he knew night was coming on and he had to hurry to find a place to stay. He was out of strength; he needed to go to bed. But Nathan and the woman were still on his mind. He wondered how this could happen, that people had to live as they did. And he wondered why she didn't give up.

He walked back to Great Ancoats Street and found a public house, where a room could be had for half a shilling, and a bath would cost fourpence. He paid for both, and for another meal of roast beef and roasted potatoes. He knew he had spent far too much, but he needed to feel ready for the day tomorrow.

When Will finally got to bed—early, but much later than he had intended—he was thankful that it really *was* a bed, and he was glad he had left another tuppence under his plate for Nathan and his mother. But he had to start earning money soon. He was only a couple of sovereigns away from living as they lived.

CHAPTER 9

Will was standing in a queue with other men and women, waiting behind a huge factory building. He was starting the day the way he had each morning since he had been in Manchester. It was November now, and mornings were cold. The sun was not fully up, but several men had arrived in the alley before him, and they were waiting at an unpainted door at the back of the building. The damp air, almost black in the alley—and yellow gray in full light—filled Will's eyes and nose and throat. He had started coughing soon after arriving in the city, and he couldn't stop. All around the weaving mills in the area, the steam engines banged and rattled. Will wondered what the noise must be like inside those places. He had been close enough to hear the roar when the doors came open. He had also seen the cotton fluff floating in the air like a snowstorm, and seen how many small children were working around the weaving machines, crawling under them to splice broken threads.

"You coom off a farm?" a man asked.

Will realized the man behind him had posed the question. He looked back. "Aye," he said.

"From 'roun' here?"

"No. Her'fordshire."

"What brought you oop here?"

"I was ahopin' to find work." He was trying to speak like a working man, not give the impression he was educated.

The man wore a cap with a brim. From what Will could see of his face, and from the sound of his voice, he seemed to be forty, at least, and worn out, his hands as battered as his clothes. "That's a long trip for nuffin'."

Will nodded, but he still didn't want to think there was no hope at all.

"An' did yo spend everythin' just to get yorseln here?"

Will didn't want to admit to having any money. He had learned already that there were thieves about who would knock a man down and clean out his pockets. "I did na' have much," he said. "I walked. An' I took my sleep where I could. I took a room here, but I do na' know how long I can pay for it."

The man might have nodded. He was silent for a time. "Yo ha' some schoolin'?" he finally said.

"Just a town school. A few years."

"But yo can read and write, I wager, and yo talk good."

Will wondered how he could possibly sound less educated.

"If'n yo fin' a job, that ain't so bad to speak good. They might make ye a boss. But do na' show it much at firs'."

"I been telled that afore. But how can I get a start?" Will asked.

"Hard ta say. Too many is stan'in' in these queues. And mos' is just like you an' me. We farmed, went broke, an' then we coom here, thinkin' somethin' might turn oop."

Will waited, hoping maybe there was something else to say. But the man was like all the others he talked to every day. They had no answers. He shrugged his shoulders, and that was the end of the conversation. In another few minutes the door opened, only a crack, and a thin, half-angry voice said, "No hiring. No writin' doon names. Clear away fro' the door."

It was what Will had heard everywhere. All of England was like this, some said. Demand for cloth was down, not just in England but on the continent and in America. That put weavers out of work, and the economic troubles had spread to every industry. At the same time, corn laws kept the price of bread high. That helped the big landowners, but working people lived mostly on bread, and they had to pay dearly for it. On top of that, the potato blight in Ireland had sent thousands of the Irish poor across the Irish Sea into England, adding to the numbers of people willing to work for almost nothing.

Will walked from the alley back to a wide street. The stink was not so noticeable to him as it had been at first, but the dreariness of everything seemed to fill his chest, his head, his every thought. What was becoming clear was that he could stand at back doors every morning until his money was gone, but the hope of being at the right place at the right time was seeming ever less likely.

Will stood by the road, looked both ways, and tried to think where he could go. Off to his right he heard a man talking in a loud voice. He was saying something about God, which didn't interest Will or, seemingly, anyone else. Those who had jobs were already at work, and even those who were only loitering about were paying no attention to the preacher. Will leaned against the wall of a building. He was curious what sort of man would make a fool of himself that way.

"God is not silent," he was saying. "He speaks to man. He has called a prophet, just as he did in olden times. And he has brought back to earth all the true teachings that have been lost from the earth."

The man was dressed in a cheap suit like Will's, although it was cleaner than his, not so worn, and he did sound more educated than most of the poor people in Manchester.

"Apostles and prophets walk the earth again. Come to our meeting this Sabbath day and hear of the miracles that have already occurred." He was holding sheets of paper, waving them, apparently to advertise the sermon he was describing. This idea, that prophets and apostles should return to the earth, was what Will had been taught by the preachers in the United Brethren. He could see what was happening here. Some set of fanatics—or imposters—was going one step further, claiming themselves to be God's chosen. No doubt it was a way to bilk people out of the pennies they needed to feed themselves.

Will looked the opposite way down the street, deciding to head that direction in order to avoid passing by the man. But he hesitated and thought again where he might go. And then he did something he had been doing often these last few days, never really believing that there was any hope in it, but trying anyway. "Lord, help me," he said in his mind. "Show me what to do." Then he waited, hoping he would feel something, that some idea would come into his head, some sense of what to do.

"My friend, I noticed you were listening to what I said."

The preacher had walked over to him.

"No. Not really," Will said. "I have no interest."

"Looking for work?"

"Yes."

"Out of money?"

Will didn't want to fall into a conversation with the man, but he was a little surprised at the look of him. He was actually smiling. Will realized that he hadn't seen anyone do that here in Manchester. People rarely looked into his eyes, but this man was acting like a friend. He was good at what he did, Will supposed. "No," Will said.

"I'm getting by." He doffed his old cap. "Good day," he said, and turned to walk away.

"I heard about some work this morning," the man said.

"What work?"

The man smiled again and held out his hand. "Timothy North," he said. "I'm a missionary from The Church of Jesus Christ of Latter-day Saints."

"I'm not interested in—"

"I understand. I wasn't either—not at first."

"But what's this about work?"

"I heard some men talking about it. Railway tracks are being laid not far from here. It's a new line from Manchester to London. The company laying the tracks is looking for navvies."

Will had heard of navvies, but he wasn't quite sure what they did. "What kind of work is it?" he asked.

"It's hard work, mostly on a shovel or a pick. In this case it's probably grading for the tracks. From what these men had heard, there was a black powder explosion in a tunnel and some men were killed. Now they need new men, and there's many who won't take the chance of getting killed themselves. So it's not good work, but you look strong. Maybe you could keep yourself going for a while that way. Navvies are rough men—hard drinking and profane—but those hiring might like a better class of young man like yourself."

"Where do I go?"

"South of town, past Gatley, toward Wilmslow. That's all I was told. You could ask around once you get down there."

Will nodded. He thought he was probably too late, but it was something to do today, some little wedge of hope. "Thank you," he said.

"I hope you listened to what I was saying. God has spoken to man again. There's a prophet, and what he teaches can bring you more happiness than anything you've ever known."

"I'm really not—"

"I know. But remember, there is a prophet on the earth. His name is Joseph Smith. He lives in America. The ancient church of Jesus Christ has been restored. And remember me—Timothy North—and don't forget that I tried to help you. Sometime, when the opportunity comes along again, listen to what we have to say."

"I think I better get on my way."

"Yes, yes. You get along. But shake my hand first, and look in my eye. I'm telling you the truth, young man. I testify before the God of heaven that the truth has been restored to the earth, and the only road to happiness is through Christ Jesus, the Holy Messiah, and through the door of baptism by one having authority, a priesthood holder in His church."

Will nodded. He was surprised by the man's sincerity, the confident look in his eyes. Will told himself that some madman in America was imagining himself a prophet, and this Englishman had no more sense than to fall for it. Still, he shook North's hand, and as he walked away, he felt himself lifted a little. The man hadn't had to offer him this help. He seemed a good man, and sometimes Will wondered whether there were many of those still about.

Will spotted a carriage and hired a man to take him to Gatley. It would cost him a good share of the money he had left, but he had to get there fast. Although it was a gamble, he had a good feeling about taking the chance.

Two hours later Will had a job. A hulking man with wild, black side whiskers and whiskey on his breath at ten o'clock in the morning looked him over and said, "Yor what I like—not these worn out farmers that coom 'roun'. I need a man what can work twelve hour and shovel rock like it's sand."

"I can work hard. I've done so all my life."

"Yo soun' too much like a gent'men. Watch out our lads do na' knock some of that out of ye—all for sport."

"I can keep up with any man. And if men don't like me, that don't worry me. I'll hold to mysel'."

"Might be better if yo drink with some of 'em a night or two, and show yor a good feller. That's better'n hidin' out."

Will didn't tell him that he wasn't about to drink away the money he earned, but he was relieved when the man said, "Yo will na' las' long, I fear, but I do na' mind givin' ye a try. I'll show ye yor tent an' yo can stow your gear . . . or do ye have anythin'?"

"I heard about the work and came here as fast as I could. I'll have to go back for my things—back in the city."

"That'll do. I'll show ye yor tent, an' yo can go. But coom back fast. Yo can start early in the mornin'. We pay half a crown a day, and we feed ye, too. If'n we work six days in a week, that's fifteen shillin's, an' if'n we work Sunday, e'en more. We charge a penny and a half a night for yor bed, or on'y a penny a week, if you sleep on a mat. But you'll wan' a cot, won't ye?"

"Aye. I will."

"That's smart. Be shor to get some sleep t'night." He grinned as though he expected Will to break down before the next day was over.

"I will, sir."

"Do na' 'sir' me. And do na' let these navvies hear ye talkin' pretty like that. Yo'll pay dear for't."

Will only nodded. And then he walked the six or seven miles back to the city. He had a feeling that he had found an answer to his prayer—but not a very good one. He didn't know whether to thank God or to laugh at His joke.

When Will arrived back at the camp, after the same long walk, the men in his tent were mostly asleep. The odor of their bodies was heavy inside—that and alcohol and tobacco. It was like the smell of a pub. Some of the men had stretched out on the cots in all their clothes, and they seemed to like bright neck scarves and vests, as though they thought of themselves as dandies.

The air in the tent was cold. A candle was burning, probably for a little heat, and maybe to send off a tallow smell to block out some of the stench—but it was accomplishing neither objective. A man sitting on a cot on the opposite side of the tent looked up at Will and said, "Yo the new lad?"

"Aye."

"Yo will na' las' long, I s'pect."

"I can work."

"But yo ain't rough enough for us. Yor pretty as a spring lamb."

Will shrugged. He walked to his cot and set down his carpetbag and his flour sack. Mrs. Michaels, at the boardinghouse, had given him a quartern loaf of bread to carry with him. She had also given him back the balance of the week's rent, even though she wouldn't have had to.

A man was sitting on the cot next to his. He looked a little old for this kind of work, and tired to the bone. He was staring ahead and hardly seemed to notice Will until he said, "George is my name. George Fisher."

"Will Lewis."

"Stay close to me," George said. "They'll test you, right off—don't let them see it if it bothers you. Show 'em you can work. That's the most important thing." He sounded rather educated himself, and certainly not from Lancashire.

"All right, then."

George had already pulled off his boots, but he lay back on his cot without taking off his shirt or his trousers. He pulled a heavy quilt over himself.

Will decided to do the same. It was cold already and surely would get colder in the night. But it wasn't the cold that kept him awake. It was the ferocious snoring, and it was thinking of the morrow and what his life would be like now, and it was wondering about George's words: "They'll test you, right off."

Will also thought of his mother and all his family. He had written once to say that he was in Manchester, but he hadn't told them anything about the trouble he had already experienced. He didn't know what to say to them now. How could he tell them he was a navvy, living in a tent with men who lay on their backs snorting for air, looking like beasts of burden? He hadn't liked his life at home, but he hadn't known how much worse things could be. When he shut his eyes, what came back to him were visions of his valley, of glowing green and gold at sunset, of grain rippling like water in the evening breeze. And he saw his family, his mother, sitting by the fire. It was too much to bear to tell himself he would never see those things again. He opened his eyes and stared at the smoke-stained roof of the canvas tent.

Will didn't sleep for hours, but then he awoke much too soon to the clatter of something like a bell—someone beating on a tin pan, as it turned out. Some of the workers had to be shaken out of their sleep, but they all lumbered out of bed after a minute or two. They rubbed their faces, stared ahead, and then pulled on their boots, seeming only half alive. One big-shouldered man took a glance at Will, hardly seemed to take notice, but then said, "Keep up or I'll bust your legs with a shovel. Yo hear?"

"Do na' worry yorsel' about me," Will said, staring back at him.

Now other men were looking at him. There were two rows of six cots in the big tent, and more than half the men had turned when Will had spoken. "What are ye?" one man asked. He was not tall, but he was massive, with a big, round head. His face seemed rounded off, too, his nose flat and his eyes shallow.

Will looked at him, not knowing how to answer.

"What talk is that?"

Will tried to think what he had said. "I'm from Her'fordshire. Near Ledbury."

The man looked around at the others. "He sounds like a lass— an' looks like'n besides. He knows how to curtsy, I'd wager. He best curtsy for me. An' if'n he don't, I'll knock him on his back—twice a day, just ta keep 'im lively."

The men laughed in something like a grumble. It was too early to be merry.

"I been raised on work," Will said. "I will na'—"

"Straight off the farm, are ye?" another man said. "An' missin' some li'l calf you fell for? Do na' bellow for her, lad. We can show you where to buy plenty a love, once you get paid."

"For a shillin', ol' Max here can give ye a sweet kiss," the big-headed man said.

Max was a little, hard-looking man, with a bandanna around his neck and a scowl on his face. "Shut yor mouf, Arnold, or I'll rip it off'n yor face."

"Try't, Max. Coom here an' try't."

At least the attention was deflected from Will. He pulled on his boots, and when the men started moving outside, he followed George, who got in the queue for oatmeal gruel, served in a tin bowl, with a thick slice of bread. The cup of tea was what Will wanted most, but it tasted like mud.

Will stayed by George, who was saying very little this morning. They sat on a pile of rocks and ate. George finally said, "Get more if you want. The food isn't good, but they'll give you all you want. By dinnertime, you may wish you had eaten more."

Will didn't think so. The gruel had sand in it, or something gritty, and the bread tasted of mold. Still, most of the men went back for more.

It wasn't long before a man in a suit of clothes came along and said, "All right, don't take the whole morning eatin' your breakfast. We have ta put some miles behind us today. We're far back from where we're planned to be."

"It's what he says every day," George said. "There's no such thing as ever backing off a little."

"Who is that?"

"His name is Lake. *Mister* Lake to us. He's the boss. He never works, and he knows nothing about setting grades or blasting rock. All he does is work men to death and then throw them aside."

"Does he—"

"So is the new lad joinin' up with ol' George?" Arnold asked, his voice like the scraping of rock on rock. "Don't take to his ideas, lad. He's a dang'rous man."

George told Will, under his breath, "Don't answer him." But Will had already known that he wouldn't.

The men began to get up from wherever they had found a place to sit among the debris from an earlier excavation. The sun was starting to rise, and Will could now see what looked like a roadbed. Back to the north he could see tracks laid, and ahead to the south, a cut had been made through an outcropping of sandstone. The scattered rock had been partially cleared, but there was more of that to do.

All the excavation seemed a scar in this green valley, where meadowlarks were singing and a little stream was sloshing in the willow trees not far away. Will could see a farmer across the way, pitching hay over a fence, where a couple of jersey milk cows were corralled. It was hard for Will to resist the thought that he would rather trade places with the man.

"We're working in the tunnel," George said. He gestured to the south.

Beyond the outcropping, maybe half a mile to the south, was an opening in a sizable hill. "Who's going to clear this area?" Will asked.

"Another crew. One crew grades, one lays track, but our crew does the heavy work—tunnels and anything that has to be blasted." He glanced at Will and, for the first time this morning, showed a little life. "We have all the luck, don't ye see?"

"I heard that some men were hurt in a blast."

"Two killed and three better off if they had been. Five more on top of that, hurt too bad to work for quite some time."

"How many new men were hired?"

"Seven or eight, so far. Most of them sleep in another tent. We have two dozen, when we fill out the crew."

"How did I end up in the tent with the experienced men?"

"I told ye. You have all the luck." He laughed a little more this time. And then he added, "We had an empty cot. That's all I know."

But it registered with Will—as hard as it was to admit to himself—that maybe his mother's prayers were being answered. It seemed more than luck that he had found George.

The men trudged down the track bed. Some were carrying lamps that smelled of coal oil. For the moment, everyone seemed to have forgotten about Will, and he was glad for that.

Once inside the tunnel, Will felt a discomfort he had never experienced before. He wondered how he could be sure that there was no loose rock above his head. Someone had built a wooden structure, posts and cross beams to hold the rock in place, but the poles looked puny compared to the mass of rock. There was also something about the eerie flickering of the lamps, the yellow light cast into the dark, showing the silhouettes of the navvies and the yellow of their faces when they turned his way.

A man named Jack Kincade was the crew boss, but he only told Will to work hard or he wouldn't last long, and then he walked away. George told Will that Jack worked mainly with the black powder men and didn't say much unless the shovel men failed to keep up. So it was George who demonstrated the work, which was simple at this point. Shovel men simply scraped up the smaller debris and cast it onto a flatbed wagon pulled by a team of oxen, or they hefted larger rocks by hand. "At some point this morning," George said, "we'll all go out and wait while the powder men set off a blast."

"What happened that some of the men were killed before?"

"Black powder. It goes off when it chooses sometimes. Since we shovel the smaller material, we're not as close to the blasting. If it goes off, we might get through, the way I did a few days ago."

"Didn't it hurt you at all?"

"Just my ears. My head is full of ringing. Might be forever, for all I know. But that's enough talk. Don't let the men hear you saying much. Just shovel—and move more rock than anyone today. But stay steady, don't push yourself so hard you can't get up tomorrow morning."

And that was what Will did. He put his back into the work and moved rock, steady and hard. At first he thought it was not very different from the work he had been doing all his life. He tried not to think about the dark, the rock over his head—or the future. He merely set out to prove himself. But it wasn't long until he understood what George had told him. His back ached. When he stopped from time to time to straighten up and stretch his muscles, he realized how much pain he would have to live with if he worked this way from sunup until sundown every day.

What Will had not expected was for Jack to announce mid-morning that the men could take a break. Tea and another slice of bread were carried in by the cooks. Both tasted better than the first time around, but even better was the chance to sit down.

George sat next to him again, but they didn't talk. Every word could be heard now, with all the shoveling and picking stopped. "Arnold," one of the men said, back in the dark, "how did the lad hold up?"

"Any lad can work for a few hours. But he won't stick long. Yo know how many coom an' go 'roun' here."

"Maybe. Maybe not. I wager he's more a man than yo be. Yo scratch in the dirt like yor doon somethin', but that's about aw."

Will recognized that it was Max speaking, the same one Arnold had insulted first thing that morning. Max was deeper in the tunnel, only a dark outline, but Will saw the man's muscles react—a little jerk in his shoulders. "I ain't goin' to hear that from ye, Max. Yo can't say them things to me wiffout I bust yor head open."

"Yo know where I am," Max said, his voice strong. "But if ye coom for me, bring a shovel. Yo ain't man enough to face me with yor fists."

"Come oot in the light. Right now."

Now George said, "Let's not have this. We got enough trouble with black powder and falling rock. We don't have to beat on each other."

But Max was on his way. Will heard his boots scrape in the loose rock, and then he saw his little silhouette. He was half the size of Arnold, and crazy to take him on. "Yo think yo can do as ye please 'roun' here, but some of us is sick of it. Yor big, but yor slow. I'll hit you four times afore yo pull yor arm back."

Arnold stood up. Will could see the rage in his face.

"Let's stop this right now," George said. "Lake likes nothing better than to see us turn on ourselves, so we won't ever organize to work together."

"Ol' George, the Chartist," someone in the dark said. "It's allus the same talk fro' him. Go ahead, Max. Take a swing. I wanna see this."

The two stepped toward one another, and now their faces were not far apart. George stood, but he had stopped talking. Will wondered where Jack was, why he wasn't trying to stop this.

Suddenly little Max did strike first—quick and hard, right on Arnold's nose. Will was close enough to feel a spatter of blood. And Max did hit Arnold twice more before Arnold grabbed him up like a bag of flour. Will heard a great grunt come out of Arnold and a gasp from Max. "Yo like that?" Arnold asked, his voice deep and ugly.

Will realized what he was doing, crushing Max's body, squeezing him, smashing his ribs, maybe breaking his arms. A scared little howl came out of Max.

"Yo won't breathe again in this world, Max. I'm taking yor breath, an' when I drop ye, I'll drop a dead man."

There was a whimper, a seeming acceptance that Arnold could do it.

Suddenly Will knew he couldn't sit by and let this happen. He jumped up and grabbed Arnold by the shoulder. "Don't kill the man," he shouted. "Please. You can't do this." He tried to get hold of Arnold's arm to pull it away.

"Get the lad off me," Arnold said.

But Will had gotten his hands in around the big arm, and he was starting to pry it loose. And then something struck him square in the back and he dropped to the ground. He didn't know what had happened, but he felt a pain in his back as though a horse had kicked him, and his own breath was gone. He gulped for air, trying to stay conscious, but his mind was spinning.

For a time—maybe only a few seconds—Will did slip out of himself, but then he was gasping for air again and coming back to the surface, like a man under water.

"It warn't his fight," someone said. "He should a knowed that."

"You didn't have to hit him with a shovel, Ned." That was George. And Will suddenly understood. It had been the flat side of a scoop shovel. That was why the pain was so broad across his back.

And Arnold was laughing. "I didn't kill 'im, lad. I broke 'im up a li'l, is aw. Yo want to be next, do ye?"

CHAPTER 10

Will suffered all day and all the next week. The bruise on his back was huge—purple and yellow—and it gradually spread down his back and onto his backside. He struggled to get going each morning, his muscles stiff and sore, but he would push on and manage all right during most of the day. By evening he would feel the stiffness return. Still, he didn't say anything about it to anyone, not even George, and he kept up his pace, the same as that first morning. He wasn't going to let Arnold—or Ned—think that they had gotten the better of him.

George had helped Max out of the tunnel after Arnold had crushed him and dropped him. Max had never returned. He surely wouldn't be able to work for a time—maybe never. Will didn't know whether he had family to help him or a place to go and recover. He could see what George had meant about using people up and then casting them aside.

One thing was certain: Arnold had no regrets. As Max had lain on the ground, gasping and moaning, Arnold had offered his only opinion on the subject: "You axt for me, Max. An' you got me. I wouldn't a' squashed a little mouse yor size if yo hadn't axt for it."

But Arnold seemed to know what Will and George thought. He didn't talk about Max after that, but he never stopped harassing Will. "Is that aw the rock yo can move?" he would ask, not having any idea how much work Will had done. "Lad, yo ain't holdin' oop yor end of the job. Yo don't do better, we'll get us some'un who can."

George would say sometimes, "That's enough, Arnold. He's movin' more rock than anyone in this tunnel," but Arnold paid no attention. Will, himself, said nothing. He merely made it through his days and then slept as much as he could. He would lie down at night and think for a few moments about the trap he was in. He was earning a little better money than factory workers did and not spending much of anything. That was good, but it would take for-ever to build up enough savings to mean anything. He was a laborer now, one of the lowest in the social order. George had explained to him that "navigators," as they were first called, had dug the canals of England and had come to be called navvies. The men on navvy crews were usually castaways, immigrants from Ireland in some cases, mostly men without families, and some of the roughest lot in all of England. So Will had left his farm hoping that he might make something of himself, only to slide into a deeper hole.

But Will didn't think very long about any of this. He would slip away into sleep while the other men were wandering off to drink. He heard them at times, drunk and loud, laughing and challenging one another as they returned to the tent. But he had learned to put all that aside and go back to sleep. The smell of the place no lon-ger bothered him. He didn't even notice the odor of his own body, which he washed well only once a week. He awoke earlier than the other men almost every morning, and it was then that the pain in his back, in all his muscles, was worst. It was then that the sound of all the snoring, the disgusting smell of chamber pots, the awareness of another day of drudgery, all combined to break him down. The air was getting colder all the time, and by morning, his quilt couldn't keep the cold away from him. He would lie in the dark for a time and think of Liz and her pretty house, try to imagine her sleeping in a feather bed, her breath gentle as a bird's. He thought of her delicate skin, and he thought of her lips that he hadn't dared to kiss. He didn't tell himself that he had lost all hope of her; he didn't have to put the thought into words. She was simply gone, and he was lost in some other world that she couldn't have imagined.

But Will survived a few weeks, and the pain in his back gradually diminished. When Sundays came, the crews usually didn't work, so he slept in later than usual and spent the day resting. He didn't think of going to church. He sometimes walked a little in the countryside, just to get away from the men and to smell fresh air, but winter seemed colder here than in Wellington Heath, and rain or snow fell often. The lanes in the area were often deep in mud and ruts, so he soon had to leave off walking. A stove had been brought into the tent now, and the men built a fire in it at night, but it didn't vent properly, and it filled the tent with smoke.

When Christmas came, on a Wednesday, it was a day like any other, hardly mentioned by the other men. But Will thought all day about the special meal his mum always served that day. And he even though about the special Christmas church service with the United Brethren.

At least Sunday was a day when most of the men slept all day, and in spite of the roar of their snoring, Will and George found time to talk. At first George had avoided talk of Chartism, but one day in January he finally said, "Will, how much do you know about the Chartist movement?"

"Very little," Will said. "I know that Chartists think every man should have the right to vote."

"Aye. Every man twenty-one or older. What do you think about that?"

"It's only right, I'd say. But I'm not sure I would know who to vote for."

"Aye, but if you had the right to vote, wouldn't you find out? And what if a truly common man could run for the Parliament? Wouldn't you vote for him?"

"That's one thing I don't understand. I know there's a House of Commons, but isn't it all made up of squires and gentry?"

"Of course it is. Only landowners can vote. And there's no pay for being in Parliament, so how can a working man afford to hold office? Those are the things that have to be turned around."

Will was sitting on his cot. George's cot was so close that they couldn't sit facing one another; they had to sit at opposite ends. Will could see how much politics meant to George, and he supposed they ought to mean as much to him. But it was imaginary as far as Will was concerned. People who had power didn't give it away. He had seen only loss of rights for poor people in his own lifetime. What could change that?

"We need a secret ballot, too," George said. "As things stand, if you refuse to vote for your squire, he knows it, and no one dares to go against him."

"So how is this all to come about? The ones who run things, they won't give us any of that."

"We took a petition to the House of Commons last spring, and the members refused to consider it. They pushed us aside and wouldn't so much as hear us out. So now we have to do more. Working people have to stand together. We do the work in this country, and if we stopped, what would happen?"

"How can we stop?"

"Not easy. I understand that. But there's been some small strikes already, and the day isn't far off when we'll have enough workers joining with us that we can call a general strike across the land—and then we'll find out if we have power."

"But I've heard these navvies talk," Will whispered. "I know what they think of you and your Chartist opinions. They won't ever join a movement like that."

"These men don't have the brains to look out for themselves. It's different in Birmingham and Manchester and all the factory towns. The movement's growing, and the factory owners are worried."

"They'll clamp down, then."

"Of course they will. And that only makes the workers angrier. It's all going to turn into a war, as I see it. But when it's over, no one will have to work in conditions like this. The new labor laws say that children under nine can't work in the factories, but their fathers just lie about their age. Poor people can't get by unless everyone in the family brings in a little something. It's a crime the way the factories take advantage of women and children."

Will had seen that in Manchester. He agreed with George. Still, he doubted that anything would change. It was something for George to hope for, even believe in, and maybe it kept him going, but all Will knew was that Monday morning he would start another week, the same as the one he had just finished, and none of these navvies would ever go out on strike.

One day that week, deep in the tunnel, Will was shoveling hard and steady when he heard a voice behind him. "Say, lad, be ye here yet? Not gone home to Mum by now?"

Will didn't answer, didn't even look around. He knew it was Arnold.

"Or yo think yor a navvy now?"

"He does good work, Arnold," George said.

"Yo on'y want a lad about ye to hear yor talk. I heerd ye telling him all yor ideas when us good men was tryin' to rest up on Sunday mornin'."

George turned away. Will had stopped shoveling for a few moments, but he began again. Arnold seemed to wander about more than most of the men, and this kind of talk was the sort of thing he would start up, sooner or later, every day. Jack Kincade did nothing to stop him. The truth was, Will had come to believe, Jack was scared of Arnold, and he let him get away with more than he did anyone else.

"I don't like all that talk, George," Arnold said. "Yor makin' trouble for ever'one. Lake knows what yor sayin'. One day he's agoin' to run ye off. The lad here better take care, or he'll be gone too."

George didn't answer, and as always that meant Arnold had to push a little harder. He lived to fight, talked of it when he came back from the pub where he drank at night, bragged some days about the men he'd knocked about. "I only killt one man I know aboot," he liked to say, "but I hold myseln back. Killin's not what I like."

"George," he was saying now, "I heerd yor talk of votin' and strikin', an' I won't put up with it. So that's an end on't. Do ye un'erstan' that?"

George had warned Will not to take Arnold on, but George had some stubbornness in him, too. He might have said that he would say nothing more, and the matter might have gone away, but instead, he simply didn't answer. Will could hear Arnold behind him still, his breath coming heavier. "I axt ye a question, George. Do ye un'erstan' what I say to ye?"

Still no answer.

And then Arnold had hold of George, was spinning him about.

He grabbed George with both hands around his neck and began to choke him.

"Stop that!" Will shouted.

Arnold gave George a violent shake and then shoved him away. He turned toward Will. "You want some like 'at?" he asked.

He reached for Will. But Will, without knowing he was going to do it, drove his fist into Arnold's face. The man took the blow, but his hands dropped, and before Will thought better of it, he hit Arnold twice more—left, right. The right struck Arnold solidly in the jaw, and he fell backwards to the ground.

Will had had a few seconds to think by then, and he wondered whether Arnold would kill him. But the big man wasn't getting up. Will couldn't see his face very well in the dim light, but he thought he might have knocked him out. After a few more seconds, Arnold began to mumble, or moan, but it was at least a minute before he raised his head and tried to sit up. All the navvies had gathered close to watch, but no one spoke. Arnold finally sat up. By then Jack had showed up. "Arnold, you got what was coming to you," he said. "Now let it go."

Arnold was showing no sign of being able to get up. Will wasn't sure whether he had even heard Jack. But Will was still expecting the worst. When the man finally found his strength, he would be wild. It might even be another day before it happened, but surely his pride was destroyed, and he wouldn't let this rest.

"That's it, men. Get back to work," Jack said. "Will, are you stayin', or are you clearin' out?"

"There's no reason *he* has to clear out," George said.

One of Arnold's friends helped Arnold to his feet. The man stood still, staring, not seeming to focus on anyone, and then he turned, stumbled a few steps, caught his balance, and walked from the tunnel. Will had no idea what that would mean.

"You'll have to watch yourself every minute," George said. "He'll be waiting for you, sooner or later."

But that night Arnold was gone. He had collected his gear from the tent and walked away from the camp. The men who had been laying track outside the tunnel said that they had seen him stumbling like a drunk down the muddy road toward the nearest village. They hadn't seen him since.

Will expected him back sometime, but he never saw him again. Days passed—weeks—without his return. What had changed on the crew was that there was no bully around. The men drank at night, as always, and they argued at times, but no one bothered Will. No one seemed to be interested in finding out just how hard a punch the lad could throw. Will liked that in some ways, and he began to feel some respect. Everyone knew how hard he worked, and they knew he was quiet most of the time, not a troublemaker. Still, Will sometimes wondered what his father would think, him brawling with such a man. Will had never been in a fight in his life. He knew he was strong, but he had had no idea how hard a blow he could throw. He was sure he never wanted to do such a thing again. And yet, it was difficult not to feel a little pride in chasing Arnold off, stripping him of his arrogance.

•   •   •

In February 1840, Will felt some softening of the weather. He even heard birds sing in the morning the way he had heard them at home. In fact, some mornings when he woke and heard the sound, for a few seconds he thought that he was back at his farm, that he would arise and work in the fields. Reality was painful when he realized where he was, but at least he knew he could do the work now, and he felt some pride in himself. The men were working outside now, not in a tunnel, and that was much better. He liked to do actual road grading, not mere shoveling, and Will even used his skill with oxen some days to pull a big grader, a job that was not all that different from plowing a field. He could lose himself in grading and not feel quite so much like a stupid laborer.

Still, there was nothing to look forward to, and he knew he had to find another way to earn his living. It was clear, however, that he couldn't go back to a factory town to seek work without quitting his job, and he remembered how hopeless his search had been last time. So he told himself he would get enough money ahead to last longer this time, and listen for news that factories were hiring, and then he would search again. He had to find a job that offered some possibility of a future.

Toward the end of the month, the crew reached another hill. A short tunnel had to be blasted and cleared. That meant getting out of the weather on rainy days, but Will didn't like the dark. "It doesn't matter," George told him. "It's a change again. After a few years of this, it's the only little pleasure a man can enjoy."

George, by now, had told Will his story. He had started out on a tenant farm, the same as Will—but northward, in Cumbria, near the Lake District. His father, however, had worked more than 200 acres, and the family had been quite well off. George had gone to boarding school, and his father had hoped that he would read for the law someday, but George had loved the green hills where his family lived, and he had liked farming. He had married a young woman, another farmer's daughter, had taken over his father's tenancy, and he and his wife had had four healthy children in six years.

Life had been good, with holiday celebrations in the nearby village, good food on his table, and a substantial cottage with four rooms. But the enclosures had begun to make things difficult, and then illness had devastated his family. A fever had attacked his youngest child, a son, and then had struck the rest of his family.

George had been very sick himself, but he and his older son, Ben, had survived. The rest had died, including his wife, who had been only a little past thirty. George and Ben had managed the farm for a number of years, but George hadn't married again. He thought he wanted to, but it didn't seem to be in his heart to start all over, to feel the same about another woman. When his son was old enough and wanted to marry, George had let him have the cottage and had gone to Liverpool to seek work. He had been a dock worker and had spent a few years in a factory, but he had finally been labeled a Chartist and warned he would never again find work in the area. That was when he had signed on with a railroad crew, and that was what he had done for almost four years. He longed, now, to go back to his old farm and work with his son, but he feared, in these hard times, that unless he could bring some money with him, he would be more a burden than a help.

Will knew by then that all the Chartist talk was just that—talk. George believed what he said, but what he wanted was not to organize or strike; he wanted to go back to his land and watch grain grow and see sheep graze in the green hills he loved.

"I can hold out maybe another year, if my health stays good," he told Will. "And, thank the Lord, it's been good these many years."

But George was over forty now, and this was not work for a man that old. Will told him often that his son would welcome him. He ought to return home for the planting season. George didn't argue, but he seemed to hesitate, and Will wondered whether George and his son had parted on good terms.

In spite of what George said about liking a change, Will hated the tunnel, and as they moved deeper into the hill, he found himself thinking of his own planting time, back in Herefordshire. He wondered how all the children were doing, whether Daniel was managing all right, and how his father's knee was now. Mostly he wondered about his mother, and how much she must think about him.

Will had written to the family a few times and sent them some money, as much as anything to give them confidence that he was doing all right. He liked to imagine how blessed they would feel by a sovereign here and there to bolster their income. But he had never really admitted what kind of work he was doing. He had merely told them that he had a job and that it paid fairly well. He checked in the village sometimes, and he had picked up a number of letters from his mother at the post office. She promised him that the family was doing all right. Sarah had a serious suitor, and Daniel was working harder now that he had to. But she seemed to be holding back, as though she didn't want to tell him that it had broken her heart to lose her first son. She didn't mention Liz, either, and Will had to assume that that was because she didn't want to tell him the bad news. Will suspected that Liz was moving on with her life, no matter what he had said to her. He had written her a few letters, too, but she had never answered. It was easy enough to understand what that meant.

So Will kept doing what he had to do each day and tried to take the days as they came. He couldn't live his whole life hoping for things that were impossible. He did pray, though. He had no interest in churches, but he still believed the Lord had helped him when he had hit bottom in Manchester. Every morning, therefore, before he pulled himself out of bed, he lay in his cot and said a silent prayer. He asked for some answer, some change, some road to a happier life. What he knew now was that he would welcome a chance to be a tenant farmer, if he could manage that someday. He had thought too much about Liz and had never really understood how good it was to farm, to live with a family, to eat pretty well most of the year, to work on his own schedule, no matter how hard he worked. He believed that George was right about everything he said: England had to give the working classes some hope, or surely common people would rise up and tear down the whole system. But for now, all Will wanted was the life he had once had. Squire Riddle didn't seem so bad when compared to the men he worked with now.

One late afternoon in March, Will was shoveling in the tunnel, as he had been doing all day. His back was weary, so he straightened up and stretched for a few seconds. Just as he did, he heard a cracking sound, as though someone had stepped on a rail fence and broken it with a snap. At the same moment, someone yelled, and he felt a blow to his chest. He went down on his side and felt something strike his head. He was knocked out for a few seconds—maybe much longer, he didn't know. All was dark, and as his mind cleared a little, what he felt was pain: not only in his head but in his shoulders and arms, and especially in his right hand. He couldn't move, and he realized how much pressure was on him. A quiet realization came to him. He was buried and likely to die. Maybe the whole tunnel had collapsed, and everyone would die under the timbers and rock.

He didn't panic, didn't suck all the air out of the bit of space around his face. The thought occurred to him that at least this was the end of shoveling, of living this way. He didn't really ask himself whether he believed in another world, an afterlife, the way his parents did. He simply knew that whatever came now, he was powerless to control. And he wouldn't have to wait very long before his pain would end.

Then he heard sounds, and he knew that someone was digging for him. He could hear the scraping, the muffled voices. He felt someone take hold of his leg. The pain only got worse as they lifted the rock and timbers, and especially when they got hold of his legs and pulled him loose from the debris. When he winced and moaned, he heard someone say, "He's alive. We got him out in time."

Men were carrying him out into the sunlight. The pain was all through his body now, but he heard a man—maybe Jack—say, "Look at his hand. It's smashed." From that moment, the pain in his hand was by far the worst. He got a glance at it and saw blood and torn flesh, saw two of his fingers sticking out at wrong angles.

The men laid him on a patch of grass. Someone had hold of his arm, and he heard someone say something about his fingers and then try to pull them straight. He lost consciousness at that point.

When Will came back to himself, he was being lifted again. Men carried him toward the tent and to his cot, then laid him out again. A doctor was on his way, someone told him. Someone else had wrapped a rag around his hand, which only seemed to make the pain worse. But a new thought had struck Will. "George?" he said.

No one answered, and that told Will what he feared. George had been digging next to him, and it had been his voice Will had head heard in that last second. It was George who had knocked him down, and George must have taken the worst of the blow from the falling rocks.

Finally, Jack answered. "George is dead," he said.

• • •

Will was sitting on his cot. Two days had passed. A man who called himself a doctor had tried to set his fingers, but the bones in his hand were broken too, and there wasn't much the old fellow could do about that. "It may not heal the way you'd like," he had told Will, "but let it set for a few weeks, and then try to use it when you can. It might work fairly well for you, in time." Then he had given him brandy mixed with laudanum, and Will had slept most of the time for those next two days.

He hadn't eaten much during those forty-eight hours, and he still wasn't hungry, but he ate a little gruel left over from breakfast.

He was still sitting up, trying to get his head to clear, when Mr. Lake walked into the tent. "Well, Will," he said, "you did good work for me. I hate to lose you. But the doc said you can't go back to work for a long time—perhaps never, at this type of work."

"I trust you'll pay for my keep while I'm getting better."

"Pardon?"

"Wouldn't that be the right thing to do?"

Mr. Lake stared at Will, but he didn't answer.

"George told me what you do," Will continued. "You use people up and then you throw them aside—like an old ox that can't pull anymore."

"We gave you work, Will. And you were desperate to have it."

"That's right. And that's what you take advantage of. People can't find work, so they'll take anything. You killed George, and you ruined me, and who cares? You'll merely hire two new men and keep laying track."

"I should have known George would feed you that kind of thinking. It's always the same with these union people. They want work, but then they complain that t'isn't exactly the way they'd like to have it."

"What am I supposed to do now, Mr. Lake?" Will held up his hand, wrapped in bandages.

Mr. Lake didn't answer for a time. Finally he said, "Things happen. A man has to find his way forward when they do."

"And you don't owe me anything?"

"I'll tell you what I owe you. I owe you some good advice. Get yourself under control and stop all this labor union talk. And don't come back here looking for work. We don't want your type talking to the laborers, spreading *socialism*."

"Is that what I'm talking—or am I just hoping for a fair chance in this world?"

"That's what all you men want these days—a job you can keep whether you do the work or not, and a promise that nothing will ever go wrong. Well, son, that's not how life is. Now get on down the road. I don't want to see you around here again."

• • •

The Duncans were sitting in their parlor on a March afternoon. A pale-looking man with long side whiskers and an ill-fitting suit was sitting in a chair across from Mr. and Mrs. Duncan. Liz was thinking that the man—Wilford Woodruff was his name—must have lost weight recently. His suit of clothes looked baggy on his small frame.

Liz had protested when her father had asked her to listen to what Woodruff wanted to say. He was one of the missionaries from the Mormons—a religion from America—who were preaching in the area. They had been visiting all the members of the United Brethren, and many of those people were joining the new church. John Benbow and Thomas Kington had accepted the Mormon baptism and had allowed themselves to be immersed by this man. They were saying that this was the religion they had been waiting for. Apostles and prophets had been called again, and the ancient doctrines of Christ were being taught in their fullness. But Liz had heard that Mormons were crazy people, and she hadn't wanted to have anything to do with them.

Now, though, she was listening. Woodruff was a good man, she thought, not wild at all. He told the story of a young man with the ordinary name of Joseph Smith. "He's a prophet of God," Woodruff said, looking her parents and her sister in the eyes, one at a time, and then focusing in on Liz. "I testify that it's true. Angels have visited the earth. The Prophet Joseph has received a record—a story of ancient people who lived on the North American continent. It's another scripture, a testimony from another people of the divinity of Jesus Christ. Read the book and you shall know it's from God, not man."

Liz wasn't impressed with the words. She didn't care about a new Bible from America. But she was impressed with the man's eyes, his steady, honest expression, his confidence in what he was teaching. He may be wrong, but he certainly did believe what he said, and she found herself wondering: was it possible that the things he professed were true? If they weren't, how could he look at her and speak this way?

"Mr. Woodruff," her mother said, "how did you come to believe in this man?"

"Joseph Smith?"

"Yes."

"I didn't believe in *him* first. I read the Book of Mormon—and I knew it was from God. It was later I came to know Brother Joseph, and the Spirit told me that he was, indeed, a man of God."

"How did you hear about all this?" Brother Duncan asked.

"Well, I'll tell you. My brother and I left home to seek work, and we ended up in New York state. We met a missionary who offered us a Book of Mormon. I read it, and I knew immediately that it was genuine. No man could write that book. It is what it purports to be. Joseph received it from an angel, and he translated it with the help of God."

"But what about this Joseph Smith? What was it about him that convinced you he was more than just another preacher?"

"I walked with Brother Joseph from Ohio to the western boundaries of Missouri—that's a thousand miles. I've seen him bless people and raise them up from the doors of death. I've heard his prophecies and seen them come about, and I've heard his doctrines and know them to be inspired. The world has distorted the teachings of Christ, but the Prophet Joseph preaches the pure doctrine as he receives it from the Almighty."

The words were almost fanatical. If Liz had read them in a newspaper, she would have set the paper aside with a laugh. But this man was no liar.

Liz had changed in some ways this last year. She felt ready to believe in something—in someone. She had put in a very hard winter, resisting her father's pressure to marry men of his choice and trying to hold on to the hope that Will could somehow return to her. She had come to feel that she could live as a farmer's wife, if that was what it took, but she wanted to marry someone she loved, and she didn't feel for these other men what she felt for Will. For months now she had been praying for an answer, wondering how she could ever be happy, even if she never married, and now she had the feeling that this American might be offering her what she had been praying for.

"Will you read the Book of Mormon?" Mr. Woodruff was asking. For some reason, he kept looking at Liz.

"Yes, I would like to," she said, and her parents agreed.

Mary Ann was glancing toward Liz, seeming surprised. Finally she said, "Surely, I'll read it, if everyone else is going to." But then she laughed. "I'll let you all take your turns first."

Liz wasn't laughing. She had felt something, and she actually hoped that the book was all that Mr. Woodruff said it was.

CHAPTER 11

Abby was standing in the little living room of the house where she and Jeff were going to live in Nauvoo. She was trying hard to convince herself that the place would be all right, but it was hard to feel happy about anything in such humid heat. She actually felt as though she might pass out. "Can you turn on the air conditioning?" she asked Jeff. "And then maybe we can go somewhere until the house cools off."

Jeff had walked down the hall to check the back bedrooms. He returned now and stood across from Abby in the living room. "There's no central air, Abby. They just have window units. That's one of the things I'm supposed to do—install air conditioning."

"Did anyone ever tell me that?" She was looking around the room. The Robertsons had said the house was furnished, and it was true, there were some basic items in the living room—a couch and two chairs and a small TV in a little bookcase—but they were nothing like the furniture in the Robertsons' house in Las Vegas. This all seemed old and cheap. The carpet was a shag, faded to a gray green, with a flattened path from the kitchen past the couch and down the hallway to the bedrooms.

"I thought I told you what to expect. The Robertsons never really lived here. They told me to start looking around for some nicer furniture and just to do whatever it takes to make the place nice. They want you to start redecorating. They'll pay for it."

"How much can I spend on things?"

"I don't know. They didn't seem to worry much about the cost. If you come up with some ideas, we can call them, I guess, and find out what the limits are."

Abby sat down in a big recliner. It was worn, but not uncomfortable. Still, it felt hot and damp. Everything was damp. And there was a smell in the house like mildew. She cupped her hands over her face and tried not to take very deep breaths. She didn't want her first official act in the house to be a trip to the bathroom to vomit. "Can you turn those air conditioners on?" she asked.

"Yeah. And then, like you said, let's get out of here for a while. I didn't know air could be this *wet*. This has got to be worse than usual, don't you think?"

"Not in July. It was like this in New Jersey every summer. But we had air conditioning."

"People always talk about humidity, but I don't think I understood what it's really like." Jeff rubbed the flat of his hand across his wet forehead and hair and then wiped his hand on his jeans. He walked into the kitchen. Abby heard him fiddling with something and knew he had to be working on the window unit.

Abby had already walked through the house. There were three bedrooms, all of them small, but that meant she and Jeff could each use one as an office. The bathroom was really bad, with decaying floorboards and black mold growing on the grout between the tiles in the shower. The kitchen was tiny, with old linoleum on the floor and imitation maple cabinets, built with particleboard. She knew that the Robertsons only intended the house as a second home, and she even knew that she could do some nice things with the place if they let her use enough money. But today, with nausea coming over her in waves, she felt as though she would give anything to be back in their California apartment, as small as it had been.

For almost three months now, every day had seemed unsettled. Abby worried about money, about the baby to come, about Jeff not having a real job. She had always liked stability, even routine—knowing what her tasks for the day were and then setting out to do them. Jeff was better at handling impromptu kinds of adjustments. He thrived on change, on newness. She told herself she ought to be more like that, but even as a little girl she had liked to give her attention to one thing at a time, repeat familiar patterns, find comfort in the same activities. Part of what had attracted her to Jeff was that he seemed freer than she was, more exciting. She just hadn't realized how much his way of doing things would keep her on edge.

Abby heard the air conditioner start up with a thump and then begin to rattle unevenly, as though it were about to fail before it got started. She hoped for some movement in the air, but she felt nothing.

Jeff stepped into the living room. "Right now it's just blowing hot air. It's going to take a little while before it actually starts to cool."

"Will it always be that noisy?"

"I hope not. I'll work on it later and see what I can do. Let me get the other two units going first."

"If the one in our bedroom makes that much noise, how will we sleep?"

"You'll sleep. I'm not worried about that. I'm the one who can't handle noises."

That was true, normally, but she wondered whether she could deal with that kind of racket, not to mention a draft blowing on her. The thought struck her again: she wanted to go home, and she didn't know where home was anymore. New Jersey? Sunnyvale? Las Vegas? She didn't really have a home—but she wanted one.

It wasn't long until Jeff returned. "The one in our bedroom is fairly quiet," he said. "I'll work on the one in the kitchen when we get back. Let's go get some lunch and see if the temperature has come down by the time we get back."

"Jeff, I don't feel like eating."

Watching his face, she saw that he finally realized what was happening to her. He came to her and knelt down. "Oh, honey, you're sick, aren't you?"

That brought tears—and she didn't want him to think she was feeling sorry for herself. "I'll be okay. It's just so hot in here. And it stinks." Even the word brought the nausea back, and she swallowed hard.

"Okay. Let's get in the car and crank up the AC. We can drive down to the historic part of town and just see what it looks like. Maybe we can walk into the Visitors' Center or something. I'm sure it's cool in there."

"Okay," Abby said. She wasn't anxious to get back in the car, after spending two full days and a morning driving from Las Vegas. And she didn't really want people to see her in the Visitors' Center, as bedraggled as she felt. But she said none of that to Jeff. She wanted to prove she could handle things.

The Robertsons' house—Jeff and Abby's house for now—was on Warsaw Street, which ran along the east side of Nauvoo State Park. Historic Nauvoo was on the west side of the park. Jeff drove back through the town, which looked like most little Midwestern towns, with only about three blocks in the business district, a mix of historic buildings and rather tired-looking little businesses and shops. But at the west end, near the bluff that overlooked the Mississippi, was the gleaming temple—almost a shock to come upon, even though they had driven past it when they arrived. It was magnificent in its otherworldly design, its beautiful windows, its high spire, and its surroundings of sky and grass and gardens. They also passed the statue of Joseph and Hyrum Smith on horseback, closer to the bluffs.

Jeff was driving slowly, taking in everything. "You know what that statue is about, don't you?" he asked. "Joseph and Hyrum leaving town, heading for the Carthage Jail—on their way to die."

Tears came to Abby's eyes again, but for a new reason. She felt cooler in the car, and her insides were settling down a little. What she realized was that she really was in Nauvoo. She looked down toward the river, and then, as the car followed the curve slowly around a bend and down a hill, she could see some of the buildings the early Saints had built. She had learned this history, knew what this place had meant to the people who had had to give it up. "I've got to be stronger," she whispered.

"What?"

But she didn't repeat herself.

"It's like coming home," Jeff said. "I don't know why, but, for me, it's like returning to who I am."

"I haven't been in the Church long enough to feel that way. For me, it's more like this story I've heard is turning into something real."

Jeff pointed out the window on Abby's side of the car. "Look. That's Wilford Woodruff's house. That's one place we've got to visit right away. Wilford Woodruff was the one who taught my Lewis family and brought them into the Church."

Jeff drove a few more blocks and then turned into the historic area on Water Street. "That brick building down on the left is the

Nauvoo House," he said, "and that one on the right is the Mansion House, where Joseph and Emma lived, and the one across the street is the Homestead, where they lived when they first came here. I've been reading about all this stuff—and studying the maps." From the time Jeff had known they were moving here, he had been reading Nauvoo history.

He turned in front of the Mansion House on Main Street and headed north. "Look at the sign," Jeff said. "That's Parley Street. I can't believe this. It's like old Nauvoo never was lost." They continued down Main Street and passed through a little section of old brick buildings. On the left were a print shop, John Taylor's house, a post office, and a tin shop, and on the right was the Browning Gun Shop. Farther along, on the left, were the Scovil Bakery and the Cultural Hall.

Abby was finally taking some deep breaths. She was feeling much better.

When Jeff parked the car near the Historic Nauvoo Visitors' Center, Abby decided she looked no worse than some tourists who were walking past their car. And when they stepped inside, the temperature felt great. Abby was holding Jeff's hand, but she walked slowly and held him back a little. She liked the quiet of the place, and she especially liked the statue of Christ at the south end of the building. She saw some older missionaries in their suits and dresses, with black name tags, but it was a younger sister missionary who approached them. "Welcome to Nauvoo," she said. She was a pretty young woman with dark hair and strikingly white teeth. Abby liked her mellow voice.

"We're not just visiting," Jeff said, sounding excited, as usual. "We've moved to Nauvoo. We'll be here a few months, maybe even a year."

The missionary—"Sister Stringham," according to her name

tag—smiled even brighter. "You're going to love it," she said. And then Jeff started telling her what had brought them to Nauvoo. He was always such an open book. People liked that about him. Abby could see the delight in Sister Stringham's eyes.

But as she walked them around the Visitor's Center and explained the displays, Jeff showed another side of himself, one that worried Abby. He had questions about everything. Abby could tell that Sister Stringham was trying to stay close to a fairly scripted presentation, but Jeff wanted to know all sorts of details, many of which she didn't know. She seemed a little nervous about that. Still, when she described the martyrdom and testified that Joseph Smith had been a prophet, Jeff listened quietly. "Yes, I believe that too," he said. "We both do." He grasped Abby around the shoulders and added, as though he saw some logical connection, "We're going to have a baby. Can you tell?"

Sister Stringham blushed. "No," she said. "I hadn't noticed."

"That's because we're not too far along. This is Abby. She's actually the one who's pregnant. I'm not. At least not as much as she is. I haven't been sick at all, so far."

Abby had to laugh. She would never say such things, and Jeff embarrassed her sometimes, but still, she felt connected by his words, silly as they were, and she slipped her arm around his waist and smiled at him. When she glanced back at Sister Stringham, she thought maybe she saw a little envy in her eyes. Jeff was good-looking, and Sister Stringham must have been able to see how much he loved Abby.

The fact was, though, Abby had worried a great deal all this last month. Once the pregnancy test—and the subsequent appointment with a gynecologist—had established that she definitely was pregnant, Jeff had been nothing but happy and supportive. Still, sometimes he seemed to be trying too hard, as if to make up for his first, less-than-enthusiastic reaction. She wondered whether he wasn't feeling trapped: a family coming now, with pressure on him to provide even if he had to give up some of his personal goals.

At the end of the little tour, Sister Stringham talked about the exodus from Nauvoo—how the Saints worked on the temple almost until the day they had to leave, and how they drove their wagons down Parley Street to the landing, crossed the river, and then, at the bluffs beyond the river, looked back at their temple, knowing that they would never see it again. She had tears in her eyes as she described the suffering and death that plagued them as they crossed Iowa.

Jeff kept nodding, and he thanked her, but then he said, "You know, they didn't all cross at the Parley Street landing. A lot of people crossed at the Kimball landing, or the one up at the north end of Main Street. I was just reading that in the motel last night. I stayed up about half the night—so I'd be prepared to see everything today."

Sister Stringham nodded. She didn't say whether she already knew those things, but Abby watched her face change. She looked a little deflated, as though she had been "corrected" when she had been trying to say something that was spiritual to her.

"You know," Jeff said, "most members think all the Saints left in February and crossed on the ice. But only a few crossed after the ice formed. Some left before that, and the majority left in the spring. The last group didn't leave until September."

Sister Stringham was nodding again, but her eyes weren't engaging with Jeff's.

"What you said was all true," Jeff said. "I'm just saying, most of us have grown up hearing things that aren't *exactly* accurate."

"This is just a little introduction to Nauvoo," Abby said. "They don't have time for lots of details."

"Oh, I know," Jeff said. "You did a great job. Really. Thanks so much," and then he asked her where she was from and how long she had been a missionary. Sister Stringham seemed pleased to talk about all that, but Abby had the feeling that she was still disappointed by Jeff's reaction.

Jeff looked around at the other missionaries and apparently decided he wanted to meet them all. He took Abby's hand and led her to the senior missionaries at the desk and then to some others close by who weren't doing tours at the moment. "We've moved here," he kept telling each of them.

Abby smiled when she saw the brightness in everyone's faces. Jeff had sparked good feelings in everyone just from his enthusiastic voice and his big smile. All the way to the car he kept talking about what nice people the missionaries were, how much he would like to serve a mission in Nauvoo someday, and how he wanted to use every spare minute to get to know the place. But after he started the car and fiddled with the vents blowing the cold air, he said, "I'm not sure I liked the way that Sister what's-her-name portrayed—"

"Sister Stringham."

"Yeah. I didn't like the way she portrayed Joseph Smith. Some people make him sound like he wasn't even human. But he was a young guy, and he was impulsive at times. He had a temper, too. He was actually a lot more interesting than the way we describe him most of the time."

"More interesting to you, maybe."

"What?"

"Not everyone likes to make things complicated."

"Sure. I understand that. But to me, it's more impressive that he was a normal human being—with weaknesses to deal with—and still able to do what he was called to do. I mean, you know how I feel about him. He's my greatest hero. I'm just saying he didn't walk around with a halo over his head and sweetness in his voice every minute." Jeff started the car. "And I think it would be better to say something about plural marriage. Otherwise, people think we're ashamed of it."

Abby knew that Jeff had a point, but she also remembered, just three years earlier, trying to comprehend everything about the Church. She wasn't sure it would have worked for her to have to deal with polygamy right off the bat. Still, she let it go. Jeff could be forceful when he started arguing a point. What she did say was: "Jeff, you have to be a little careful. As we go into all these historic buildings, why don't you just let the missionaries tell the story the way they tell it? It's going to be hard if you ask them a lot of questions they can't answer."

"They need to hear hard questions. Then they can study up and do a better job next time. If I weren't a member, I would be thinking, 'These people give tours, but they don't know all that much about the place.'"

"Jeff, come on. That's not fair. How many people read the history all night while they're traveling here? A week ago you wouldn't have known some of that stuff yourself."

"I know. That's true." He was driving now, had turned the car back onto old Main Street, but partway through the area he turned left, and Liz knew he was heading back to the Wilford Woodruff house. "I'm just saying that some people who come here are going to want more detail. The missionaries shouldn't just repeat that standard stuff about all the Saints driving their wagons down Parley Street and crossing on the ice. If that girl—Sister Stringham—had just read one good history, she would have known that stuff."

"Maybe it's more important that she read the scriptures when she has time, so she has the Spirit with her and can bear strong testimony."

That stopped him for a moment. He kept driving and then parked in front of the Woodruff house. "It doesn't have to be one or the other, does it? Can't she have a good spirit and also know her history?"

Abby was looking at the red brick house, with bricks set on end in the lintels over the windows and the front door, creating a shape like a fan. It was a beautiful little house. But she wondered whether she had the strength left to climb stairs. She was feeling better now that she had cooled off, but she was exhausted. Above all, she didn't want to quarrel with Jeff. "Honey, I don't disagree with that. Just remember, you *live* for questions. Most Mormons don't know which landings the Saints used to cross the river, and they don't feel cheated if they never find out. The important thing is that the people were forced out of Nauvoo, so they went west and started over—and modern members have that to thank them for."

"Hey, I agree. Entirely. Every culture has a narrative. George Washington didn't really cut down a cherry tree, and he wasn't all-knowing or anything like that. But we tell that story, and it sort of tells us who we are. Mormons do the same thing with the Prophet Joseph. But it's okay to grow up, too, and a person can know actual history without giving up the essential narrative."

"I'm sorry, Jeff, but now you're sounding like a Stanford grad. You can get away with that with me, but if you go to Sunday School this week and start telling people who live here that they don't know their history, you're going to get off to a really bad start."

"So is that what you're worried about? That people won't like us?"

"It's not just that, Jeff." She was losing her patience. "Didn't you sense what you did to Sister Stringham? That story about the Saints finishing their temple and then being forced to leave—that was her testimony of what she feels about this place. What you told her, in effect, was, 'Of course, you're only giving me half the story. Don't you know anything?' I watched her face. She was embarrassed. You made her look bad. That's not nice, Jeff. You're a good person, but you don't realize what you do to people sometimes."

"I wasn't putting her down. I was just telling her something that struck me as really interesting when I read it myself."

"Okay. But hold back when we go in here. You probably know more about Wilford Woodruff than the missionaries do. Just hear what they have to say. Maybe you'll learn something."

Jeff stared toward the house. She knew she had hurt him, but she also knew he needed to understand how he was perceived at times. "I think what you're telling me," he finally said, "is that I'm kind of a jerk. But I never think of myself that way."

"You're not a jerk, Jeff. I love you—but that's because I know your heart. You have to let people know you before you come on too strong and scare them away."

"What does that mean? That I have to dumb down everything I say all my life so people who have no curiosity won't be offended just because I *am* curious?"

"That's arrogant, Jeff. You think about it for a while and you'll agree with me."

"Oh, I agree. I've been told that all my life, so it must be true."

"I didn't say *you* were arrogant. I said that you made an arrogant *statement*. One thing I know about you is that you have the humility to think honestly about yourself."

Jeff didn't respond, and now Abby *knew* that she had hurt him. "Jeff, don't—"

"Let's come back here some other day." He had never turned off the engine, and now he shifted the car into reverse and backed out.

• • •

Jeff didn't say anything as he drove home. He was back to a place he'd been many times in his life. As early as elementary school, he had taken a lot of teasing for being smart. He hadn't really minded that. It was the other thing that was hard for him. In his own mind, he just liked to learn things and then tell other people what he'd learned, but that wasn't what people felt from him. He knew he voiced opinions with more force than he really intended, mainly just to make the case for what he was thinking at the moment, but he loved to hear counter arguments. It was illogic that drove him crazy, or opinions based on scanty information or rumor or mere stubbornness. What Abby had said was true: he loved questions and most people preferred answers. But why was that wrong? He understood that he would never answer many of the questions he posed, but he lived according to the answers that he did have.

Still, Jeff knew Abby was right about the way people perceived him, and he was going to have to be careful when he got into discussions in elders quorum or Sunday School. But life looked long if he had to spend it trying not to say what he was thinking, not being who he was.

When they arrived back at the house, they found that the temperature had cooled considerably, though it was still muggy. At least the rattling window unit had seemed to smooth out somewhat on its own. Jeff still needed to lubricate the thing, but he could do that later. "Maybe we should give this place some more time," he said. "Should we go look for a place to eat?"

"No, that's okay. We have sandwiches left in the cooler. I think I'll lie down for a little while. You can get yourself a sandwich, and I'll probably do the same in a little while."

"Okay."

"I love you, Jeff."

He nodded, but he couldn't think what to say. Did she mean, "I love you even if you are a pain to be around sometimes"?

Jeff realized that he didn't actually feel like eating either. So he stepped outside and walked around the house. There was a big lawn that would need mowing. Brother Robertson had said that he had hired a man who would show up once a week, but Jeff felt funny about having a hired man do something like that. He thought he would probably cut it himself. He had seen a lawn mower in the garage.

He also decided he might as well start unloading the car. If he did it himself, Abby wouldn't have to be involved, and he didn't think it would be good for her to be working in the heat. They had shipped a few boxes from Las Vegas, and they had filled the car with personal items and clothing, but they didn't plan to move any of their furniture.

Jeff found the air outside oppressive all over again. He was also astounded by the sounds—some sort of bugs that seemed to scream in rhythmic unison. More than anything, he hadn't been prepared for the sweat that would pour out of him when he started hauling boxes and armloads of clothing. He was only about half finished when he came back inside and saw Abby standing in the living room. She looked scared—and pale.

"What's wrong, honey?"

"Jeff, I'm bleeding. I don't think that's supposed to happen now."

"What do you mean? Are you losing the baby?"

"I don't know. I'm so tired I can hardly stand up, and . . ." She stepped to the couch and sat down, but her head fell forward, and he thought she had fainted. Jeff dropped to the floor in front of her. She looked up at him, her eyes glazed. "I think we'd better find a doctor."

Jeff couldn't think for a moment. Was there a hospital in Nauvoo? He didn't know anyone, didn't know how to find out. He thought of calling the missionaries at the Visitors' Center, but he didn't want to take time to try to find the number. He had seen a man outside—the next-door neighbor. "I'm going to ask the neighbor where we can take you," he said, and he was already on his way.

What he learned from the neighbor was that Nauvoo had no hospital, but there was a clinic in town. Jeff ran back, swooped Abby up in his arms, and carried her out to the car even though she kept saying that she could walk, and then he drove her the few blocks to Mulholland Street and west into town. He spotted the clinic, pulled a U-turn, and parked quickly, but this time Abby was out of the car before he could come around and pick her up. So he wrapped his arm around her and walked with her into the little building.

An hour later, Abby was lying on an exam table and Jeff was sitting in a straight-backed chair, holding her hand. Dr. Birch, a tall, soft-spoken woman, opened the door, walked to the table, and said, "How are you feeling now, Abby?"

"A lot better."

"I think you pushed yourself a little too hard with that long drive, and you were probably dehydrated. The liquids we've been putting into you have obviously brought you back a long way already."

"But what about the bleeding?"

"That's not necessarily anything to worry about. It could be the beginning of a miscarriage, but in the first trimester, women often do some spotting. The best thing now is to rest up, stay as cool as you can, and keep drinking liquids. If you're losing the baby, you'll know soon. You should start seeing a gynecologist right away."

"We don't know anyone here."

"I can refer you to a very good ob-gyn in Carthage, if you'd like."

"Should we see someone today?" Jeff asked.

"No. Let's let Abby rest. Just make an appointment, but if you begin to miscarry, we'll have to get you over to the hospital in Carthage—or across the river in Iowa." She touched Abby's arm. "Do you want to rest a little longer here?"

"No, I'm fine. I feel a lot better."

Dr. Birch left, and Jeff helped Abby get dressed. He was relieved to see the color come back into her face. "Are you sure you feel okay?" he asked her.

"I'm still tired, but back at the house, I thought I was passing out."

"I know. It scared me so bad, Ab. I thought something was really wrong, like you were having a stroke or something—and all I could think was how much I love you."

"It wasn't *that* serious."

"Maybe not. But I didn't know I could be so scared. It's like you're half of me now, Ab. I didn't believe it when I used to hear people say things like that."

She laughed. "That's not what you were thinking when I was getting after you over at Wilford Woodruff's house."

"In a way it was. I don't like to think that I embarrass you."

"Oh, Jeff, don't worry about that. I saw those sister missionaries looking at you. It was like you were the grand prize in a raffle and they were holding the wrong tickets."

"Oh, come on," he said. "I didn't see that."

"I'm not kidding. Sister Stringham was—"

"Abby, I want the baby."

"I know. But if—"

"I want the baby, and I want you. The other stuff I want is not as important. I really mean that."

"If we lose the baby, I can get pregnant again. At least we know that now."

"I know. But I want this baby. It's ours. When I thought something was wrong, that was all I could think of: I want our baby, and I haven't let you know it."

"I did wonder, at first."

"Don't wonder. Don't ever wonder."

Abby put her arms around Jeff's neck and held his face to hers. "I did get the grand prize," she said.

CHAPTER 12

It was almost morning, and the cold was seeping through Will's clothes. He had no greatcoat, only the tattered suit of clothes he had worn when he left home. March was more than half gone, but rains had come almost every day lately, and nights had been cold. He had found a pile of cotton cloth—the scraps from a shirtwaist company—and had luxuriated in the softness. This was not the first time he had slept in an alley, but it was the best night's sleep he had experienced since he'd left the navvy camp. He doubted that the cotton would remain there more than a day, what with rag and bone collectors coming about so often, but at least for one night he had felt almost as though he'd had a bed. He had even pulled enough of the cloth over him to stay warm for a few hours. But now he was cold and he also needed to relieve himself. There was nowhere to do that except here in this stinking back street where many others had done the same; he had no choice about that.

In the three weeks he had been back in Manchester, he had used up much of the money he had saved while he was working. At first he had boarded in cheap flophouses—as bad as the room he'd turned down when he had first arrived—but he needed to conserve what money he had so that he could eat. He needed to hold out until his hand healed enough that he might be able to find work again.

More than almost anything, Will hated the idea of begging for his food, but he knew that he would have no choice if he couldn't work. And the truth was, his hand seemed to be getting worse, not better. It was hurting more, and stiffening. He saw no answer, no hope, even though he told himself he would have to manage somehow. More than ever, he found himself doing as his mother had advised him: he was praying often, over and over, more desperately than ever in his life.

He had seen Timothy North one day, preaching on the street in the same place where Will had seen him before. Will didn't speak to him, but North recognized him and walked over to greet him. When he saw the dirty wrapping on Will's hand, he asked about it, and Will filled him in on what had happened.

"It's not right," North said. "They use you up and throw you away."

"I had a friend named George on my work crew," Will said. "He used to say the same thing—even use the same words." Then Will told North what had happened to George. "He was a true friend," he said. "I miss him every day, and I wake up at night thinking about him."

North put a gentle hand on Will's shoulder. "You need new friends," he said. "Come to church services with me and meet some people who will be your brothers and sisters."

Will liked this man and appreciated his kindness, but he saw immediately what the missionary had in mind. This was just one more recruiting method—to find someone who was down and out and invite him to his meetings.

"We have apostles with us now—here from America. They're

like Peter and Paul of old. They preach with the same authority, and they—"

"Thank you, but, as I told you before, I have no interest." Will broke away and walked on down the street even though he had no-where to go. One thing he knew for certain was that he didn't want to hear someone preach. In spite of Will's almost constant prayers, he still wasn't convinced that God cared about him. There were lots of men like him on the streets, and women who had been pushed to even lower depths: walking the streets, offering themselves as prosti-tutes. Twice now he had slept in some corner or alley only to get up in the morning and find that another man nearby had died in his sleep. Had those men prayed?

Will had never expected to be in mortal danger himself, but a day earlier, he had stood in a queue and waited for a bowl of soup at a soup kitchen. He had realized after standing for the better part of an hour that his head was spinning, and then he had found himself coming back to consciousness on the cobblestone street. Someone had helped him sit up—a man of forty or so with a shabby beard and reddened, infected eyes. "Don't ye get up yet," the man said in a voice that sounded Irish. "You're not lookin' good. White as a ghost, ye be."

Will had sat for a time, but then he had stood, not accepting help. "I'll be fine when I get a little food in me," he had said. There were several men around him, all watching him, actually looking worse than Will. But only the Irishman seemed concerned. The oth-ers stared blankly, as though they were beyond caring.

The line finally moved and Will shuffled forward, got his soup, and ate it, and he did feel a little stronger. And that night, he had gone to a pub—one that let the likes of him come inside, dirty or not—and he had bought a full meal. It had taken more of his money than he wanted to spend, but he had known that he had to put some nourishment into his body. If his health broke, he would never find work, even if his hand healed.

Now, still lying in this pile of rags, he felt something else working on his mind. Sometime in the night, his hand had begun to throb, and he realized it was pain as much as the cold that had awakened him. He didn't dare take the bandage off, partly because he didn't want to see whether the wound had begun to mortify but also because he had nothing to cover it with once he discarded the disgusting bandage. These bits of cloth he had slept in were too small.

Will was suddenly seized with fear. He didn't want to lose his hand. And when he let that fear sink in, he realized he knew no one who could even do that for him—saw off his hand at the wrist. He couldn't so much as pay some surgeon or barber to take care of even that. He sat up, but as he did, the throbbing increased. "What can I do?" he whispered, and he knew, without exactly admitting it to himself, that he was asking God.

"Go home," he heard a voice say. He looked about, thinking someone had spoken, but he realized no one was near.

He lay there for a time, wondering about the words, trying to think what he could do. He had been telling himself for three weeks now that he could never go home again, that his family would be punished for it if he did, and he had promised his father that he would not return. But he remembered what he had felt when he was a little lad and had fallen from the old crab apple tree behind the cottage. He had broken his wrist, he thought, and he had known only one thing to do about it: run to his mum. And that was what he wanted to do now.

Will got up. He didn't know whether he had the strength to walk so far, but he heard the words again, more clearly this time and alive with truth. He had made his way from Herefordshire in the fall, and now, half a year later, he had to make that same trek back.

He knew, just as surely, that was his only hope to save his hand. Maybe his life.

Will found a dark corner in the alley to relieve himself, and then he walked to the street. He stopped at a bakery and bought a heavy quartern loaf of bread and a sizable wedge of cheese, and then he set out. The purchase took all but the last four shillings of his money, so he had to make the food last. He walked most of the day, and he told himself he would rest a little from time to time but would walk day and night. Maybe he could walk the trip in four or five days if he just kept pushing on. The pain in his hand wasn't so bad now that he was up and moving. Maybe it wasn't rotting yet. But he couldn't waste time, and the nights were cold enough that he would be better off up and going than sleeping on the ground.

That afternoon he met a farmer who was clearing a ditch alongside his field. The man greeted Will and then asked, "What's happened to ye?"

"I hurt my hand a little, that's all."

But the man wasn't looking at his hand. He was staring him in the eyes. "An' ha' ye a fever, do ye?"

"I don't know." Will touched his forehead with his left hand and he realized that he wasn't just warm from walking. His head was hot to the touch. "I'll be fine," he said.

"How far ye walking?"

"To Herefordshire."

"That's a hundred mile, I'd say."

"Aye. Most of that."

"You can na' walk so far, young man. I know that much. Stop with me a day or two. My wife can dress yor wound—get that dirty rag off your hand."

Will tried to think. Maybe that was what he should do. But he heard the words again: *Go home.* "For now, I'll keep amovin' on. I'll rest when I must."

"You'll end oop dead, I fear. An' look at them clouds. A storm's coomin'."

Will had noticed the clouds thickening, but he had assumed when he set out that he might have to walk through some rain. This old farmer, though, seemed to be seeing something more. Maybe he really should get inside for the night.

Go home.

Will nodded, as though to answer the voice, and he kept going. He did rest for a time as the sun was going down, and he ate some of the bread and cheese. By then a light rain was falling. After he walked for a time, a wind started to rise, and the rain pelted down harder and harder. Will could see no place to seek cover, so he kept trudging forward, and gradually he felt the wet seeping through his clothes. With it, the cold got through, and he began to chill. In another hour mud was forming in the road and Will was straining, shaking all over. Still, there was nothing to do but to keep going. If he was getting sick, if his hand was filling him with putrid blood, his answer was still the same. He had to make it home.

Sometime in the dark night, with rain falling hard, he came to a stone bridge that crossed a little stream. He walked under the bridge to the edge of the stream and sat down on the dry ground. He lay back and shut his eyes.

Will hadn't known that he'd fallen asleep until he awoke with a start. The cold had reached deep inside him, and he was shivering all over, his teeth actually chattering. He got up, reached out, and felt that the rain was letting up a little. He knew he had to keep moving ahead, so he climbed back to the road and crossed the bridge, but the going was worse now. His legs seemed to have lost strength, and the mud and manure in the road were getting sloppy, grabbing at his boots. After a few minutes, he wasn't shivering. He was glad to actually feel warm—until he realized that he felt hot.

Go home.

Will kept going. He reached a little village about the time the sun was coming up. He saw a lamp burning in a bakery, so he walked around to the back door. The baker opened the door and was willing to sell him another loaf of bread and even let him sit in the warm room while he ate a little. But the baker, like the old farmer, told Will that he looked sick. Will didn't argue; he let his clothes dry a little, and then set out once again.

As the sun came up the third day—or maybe it was the fourth—Will realized that he must have walked in his sleep part of the night. At least, he couldn't remember walking all night. Had he stopped somewhere to sleep in a hayrick? He thought he remembered that, but it might have been the night before. He had slept in wet hay, his nose filled with the smell, and he had thought of home, even thought for a time that he had made it there. And he had dreamed of his mother touching his forehead, telling him that he was all right now.

He had walked again after the dream, before daylight, but he didn't remember whether another night had passed since then. He knew he had passed through Birmingham, that he had gone into a pub, used a shilling of his money to eat a meal, and then had slept with his head on a table. But the proprietor had shaken him and told him to move on, and he had moved on. Had that been this night? He didn't think so. He had passed through Worcester, and that was late in a day, when the sun was just going down. A constable had stopped him. He remembered that. The man had accused him of being drunk, of staggering as he walked. Will had denied that, but then the constable, a portly man with long mustaches, had said, "You be nuffin' but a skeleton, lad. When did you eat last?"

Will didn't remember now what he had said. He only remembered that the man had called him a skeleton, and now it was another day. And rain was falling again. He thought he wasn't far from home. He had struggled uphill and made it to Great Malvern, but there were more hills to cross, and his legs were weak. He stumbled ahead for another two hours, falling down several times. Each time he was tempted to stay down, but he knew he couldn't do that. Most of the walk was downhill now; he just had to hold out a few more hours. His mother would know what to do. He had to make it to her.

But his feet went out from under him, and he fell on his face, the mud filling his eyes, his nose, his mouth. He turned on his side, fought for breath, and tried to get up—but he felt everything falling away, dark taking him.

• • •

And then he was waking up.

A man and woman were staring in his face. "He's alive," the man said.

"He won't be for long," the woman said. The man pulled at Will's shoulder, and Will tried to help, but finally it took another man—a coachman—to get him to his feet. Will was vaguely aware that the men had nice clothes that were getting soiled. He tried to walk, but mostly they dragged him past a team of big horses and lifted him into a coach. Will didn't know what happened after that, except that he was now in a warm place, and a woman—the one who had looked down at him when he was out in the muddy road—was saying, "Take a little of this soup."

Will sipped at the soup from the spoon the woman was holding. He glanced at his hand and saw that new bandages were on it.

"I cleaned your hand, but it's beginning to putrefy. You may need a surgeon to cut away some of the dead flesh."

Go home.

"How far am I from Ledbury?"

"It's only four miles. Is that where you live?"

"Near there."

"My husband can take you, when you're ready, but he's gone now for our physician. Eat all you can and the doctor will do what he can for you. Then we'll have a surgeon come too, if it's necessary."

"To cut my hand off?"

"No. I hope not."

"Excuse me, ma'am. Who are you?"

"Our name is Crawford. Our driver saw you in the road. We gathered you up and brought you home in our coach."

Will could see that he was in a fancy bedroom, in a manor house, perhaps. He needed to leave soon, but for now, he kept eating the soup, and he drank some hot tea and then ate some bread. He felt more alive as he ate, but the pain in his hand was worse. "I can walk four more miles," he told Mrs. Crawford.

"No," she said. "You can't walk another step. We'll see what the doctor can do, and then, when you're stronger, we'll take you home. She sounded almost like his mother, and he knew she was right. He couldn't walk another step.

Will spent a week with the Crawfords. Mr. Crawford—Squire Crawford—was like Squire Riddle, a wealthy landowner with tenant farmers who worked his land. His farm was near Colwall Stone, below the Malvern Hills, and it spread across a beautiful stretch of green farmland. He owned over two thousand acres and was clearly very well off. Will had never spent a night in such opulent surroundings. He slept in a bedroom by himself, in a large, soft bed. Mrs. Crawford brought meals to him herself—lamb chops, batter pudding, baked ham, and delicious sweets. Each day their physician, Doctor Wickers, called at the house, re-dressed the wound, and had Will take various herbs. He also gave Will more laudanum, which relieved his pain but kept him sleeping most of the time. A surgeon came too, and he cleaned away some of the worst of the dead flesh. Will was relieved that he didn't call for more drastic measures.

Mrs. Crawford seemed to find great pleasure in looking after Will. She was a woman of more than fifty, Will thought. She had white hair and round cheeks, and somehow she looked more like a scullery maid than a lady, but she mentioned more than once that she believed in Christian service. Maybe she considered Will one of the least of mankind, a commoner she could bless with her Christian goodness. If so, she was entirely natural about it, and she never made Will feel as though he were the wretched waif he had clearly become. She had also noticed early on that Will's speech sounded educated, and she had paid a compliment to his mother's training, observing that she had taught him well not only in his language but in his politeness.

All this was pleasant in its way, but Will still felt compelled to reach his mother. He didn't know what his father would think of that. Now that he was feeling better each day, he wondered whether he should stay away. But what would he do? He couldn't work yet, and he had no prospects. The Crawfords, from the beginning, understood that they were nursing him to keep him from dying—and then they would take him to his home. He certainly hadn't told them that Squire Riddle had run him off for poaching. They might look at him very differently were they to hear that.

More than anything, he believed that was what he had been told to do in some way that he didn't understand—*go home*—and he still had to do it. So he told the Crawfords he felt ready to travel, if it wasn't too much to ask them to help him on to his home. Mrs.

Crawford wanted him to stay a few more days, but, without explaining, he merely said that he needed to get home.

"Will your mother be worried about you? Should we send her a letter?"

Will avoided that. "I merely need to get home. She'll take good care of me."

Mrs. Crawford agreed, but when she returned to his room, she was carrying clothing. "My husband had your clothes destroyed," she said. "They were not just worn; they were infested." Finally she asked him, "William, how did this happen? Why did you leave your home?"

"I went to Manchester to look for work." He told her about working as a navvy, about the cave-in and his injury, and about his hungry walk home.

"Why did you leave your farm? Don't you like the work?"

"I didn't—not when I left. Now, I think I wouldn't mind it."

"Are you the eldest son?"

"Yes."

"Maybe you'll take over your father's tenancy, then."

"I can't do that now. I passed it along to my brother." That wasn't quite the whole truth, but it was the only thing he could think to tell Mrs. Crawford. He wondered now, would he want to take over the farm if that were ever possible again? His thoughts immediately turned to Liz and the old dilemma he had felt.

"You might think about us sometime," Mrs. Crawford said. "If you marry, and a tenancy should open, we try to be good to our tenants—more than some. Mr. Crawford likes you, and he might welcome you here. In time we'll need a new bailiff, and you just might prove yourself able to hold such a position. How long before your father might turn over his tenancy?"

"I don't know. He injured his knee and can't work the way he once did. Before I left, I had been running the farm for quite some time."

Mrs. Crawford nodded, seemed to think for a moment, then said, "Well, we'll see that you get home today. But you shouldn't work for a month or two. And Dr. Wickers wants to see you again in a week. We can send a coach for you."

"No. That's fine. I can see a doctor in Ledbury."

"But will you do it? Dr. Wickers said the surgeon might have to cut away some more of the dead flesh. I'm afraid your hand will be very scarred, and maybe not that useful to you. Some of the bones were broken, and it was too late to set them the way they should have been set."

Will had sensed that, but hearing the words was rather alarming to him. He hoped he wouldn't be crippled all his life.

"If you can return next week, we can see that the doctor cares for you."

"That's very nice of you, but—"

"We had five daughters, Will, but only one son. And he died of a fever. He was a beautiful boy, like you, and I tried to save him, but I couldn't. Your hand is far from healed, and you're not out of danger. I truly believe that you should stay another week or two and fully recover. It would be a joy to me to have you here."

"I . . . would like that. But truly, I need to go home."

"All right, then, but you must take care of yourself—for your mother's sake, if not for your own. If you can't afford a physician, come back to us. Or if you need work, we can let you do something for us until you're strong enough to do farm work." She touched his arm, tears in her eyes.

"That's kind of you, Mrs. Crawford. I'll remember that."

"My husband wanted to go with you today, but he had business to look after. We'll send you with our coachman after he finishes his morning work."

Will tried to calculate. Four miles in a coach might not take very long, and he didn't dare arrive home on a bright afternoon. He might be noticed. But Will accepted her offer, and that afternoon he asked the coachman to let him off on the Ledbury road, just north of town. He said that he would like to walk the last little way. The coachman seemed to have no preference about that, and he simply let Will off without so much as a farewell. Will walked up the valley. He longed to finish the trek by walking straight to the front door of his cottage, but he knew he had to wait for the cover of dark. What he also knew was that he was not so strong as he had thought. He was already exhausted and rather happy to step into the woods and fall asleep under a tree.

Will woke up before dark, his hand hurting again. He was also feeling apprehensive. He was excited to see his family, but he hoped his father wouldn't order him away. He knew he was breaking a promise, and he knew how much trouble he could cause for his family. He hoped he wouldn't be a hardship, eating at their table. He knew for sure that he couldn't stay with them long. But he wouldn't stray far from Ledbury. He never wanted to see a big city again.

It was another hour before he felt safe to emerge from the woods. As he began to walk, he felt his legs wobble. He walked slowly, trying to let his balance return. He was nervous, and he didn't know whether he was shaking from that or whether he was still feverish. He felt his head and knew the truth. He was still sick.

As Will approached the door, he could see a glow from the fireplace. Then he heard a voice—the deep voice of his father, he thought, probably reading the Bible out loud to the children. He felt as though he had been gone for years, not months. He wondered what had changed.

He wasn't sure how to enter. Finally he gave a little rap at the door, then opened it. "Hello," he called. He stepped inside. There were only coals left burning in the fireplace, giving off a dim light. But his father was sitting close to the fire, and a tallow candle was sitting on the hearth, casting light so that he could read. Although it was something Will had seen thousands of time in his life, he was somehow surprised to see it still happening. His father looked up at him. Will's eyes were adjusting slowly to the light.

"I'm sorry," Will said. "I know I'm not supposed to come here."

But suddenly his mother was there, having hurried to him from the corner of the room. "Oh, Will, I'm so happy to—" She stopped, took hold of his shoulders, and turned him toward the light so she could look into his face. "What's happened to you?"

"I got hurt." He held up his hand.

"But I hardly know you. Have you been sick?"

"I . . ." Will didn't know where to start. He was feeling dizzy again. And Morgan hadn't moved. He didn't know what the man was thinking. "I won't stay long, Father. I'm sorry to come here. I didn't know what to do. I thought I might die."

"It's all right," Morgan said, and he stood up. He came to Will, would probably have given him a handshake, but instead grasped his shoulder. "We've been very worried about you," he said. "Your mother has been praying every night that you would come home. I didn't think it was wise, but here you are, and I'm not going to turn you away. We'll have to keep you hidden."

"I'll go as soon as I can find . . ." But Will was finally home, and something in him was breaking down. His strength was gone. He began to sob. He took his mother under one arm and his father in the other. He was slipping down.

Someone had him from behind. He heard Daniel say, "Mum kept telling us something was wrong. She knew."

Daniel had caught him and was holding him under his arms. Everyone else was there too, and his father was saying, "Let's get him to the bedroom."

Brothers and sisters were picking him up. His head was spinning, but they got him to the bed and laid him down, and Sarah and Esther kissed him, their cheeks wet, and told him how much they'd missed him. And then his mother put her face against his and whispered, "I'm alive again, just to have you here, and you will be too. We'll take care of you."

• • •

Will slept fitfully, dreamed of strange things: of walking in mud, of rain and wind, and of his body burning. He woke once to his mother wiping a wet cloth across his forehead and neck. He had kicked all the bedding away, and he felt the cool of the cloth, but he felt the heat inside himself, as though he were full of coals. He knew the fever had come back strong.

The next day and night were much the same, but then he woke to realize he had slept well for a time. He was wet with sweat, and cool. He reached to pull a quilt back over him, and his mother moved in her chair next to his bed. "The fever has broken," she said.

His mother looked tired. It had been less than a year since he had left, but she seemed ten years older.

"You rest some more," she said.

"You need some sleep yourself."

"I know. I'll catch up. But you look much better. Seeing that will help me sleep. First, I have to get some food for you." He remembered her trying to feed him a couple of times, but he knew he hadn't eaten much. He wasn't hungry yet, but he wanted to get his strength back.

"I walked from Manchester, and I was sick. And mostly out of food."

"I know. You told me."

"I did?"

"You've talked a good deal, though I wasn't always sure you knew what you were saying."

That seemed right.

"You talked about Liz."

"Is she betrothed?"

"No."

He raised his head. "She's not?"

"She didn't want to marry the men her father brought home. She told me more than once, at church, that she missed you. She didn't say anything more than that, but I know she loves you."

"She does?"

"Of course she does. And now—I wonder—perhaps God will still find a way for the two of you."

"That can't happen, Mother. It's not good for me to think of such a thing. That's what got me into trouble before, thinking that I could do something better with my life."

"I don't know what miracles God may have in store for you, but I know I asked Him to bring you home, and He did."

"He *told* me to come home," Will said. "I heard something in my head, over and over, saying, 'Go home.'"

"When did this happen, Will—when did you hurt yourself?"

"Early in March."

"The fourth of March?"

"Maybe. I don't know."

"It was that day. I know it. A feeling came over me that day that something had happened, that you needed to come home so that I could help you. I prayed that you would come home, and the Lord put my words in your mind. You understand that now, don't you—that the Lord was in this?"

Will thought he did. And he was alive. But it also seemed a cruel turn of events. His hand was perhaps ruined, which would limit him in any work he took on. And Liz may love him, but he would never have her.

"Now, you have to pray," his mother was saying. "Pray to get better, and pray for a future. Pray for Liz, if you still love her. God can do anything."

Will truly wanted to believe that.

CHAPTER 13

A week had passed and Will was beginning to get out of bed at times. He was weak, but he had an appetite, and eating three meals a day was strengthening him. He had forgotten how much he enjoyed fresh bread, new potatoes, even oatmeal porridge and cool milk.

One morning he ate later than most of his family. When Daniel returned to the kitchen after having been out doing his chores, Nettie said to him, "You didn't eat anything, Daniel. Sit down with Will and have your breakfast now."

"I'll do that," Daniel said, smiling.

"You look like a different man," Will said. "What's happened to you?"

"I can na' say. But the work's not so bad when I take't on as me own."

Will felt some envy. He had been telling himself that once he recovered, doing farm work wouldn't be so bad—not after all those days spent with a pick and shovel, and not after his days of hunger. The work wouldn't be his own, however; he'd given that away.

But Nettie said, "Tell the *whole* truth, Daniel. There's something more adding spring to your step."

Daniel sat down at the table. He was grinning. "I'm to be married, Will. But na' just yet. Na' 'til I put some money by—and find some way to feed a family."

"You'll have this place, Daniel. What does Father say about that?"

"There's yet too many of us, Will. I could na' bring a wife home yet. An' maybe the tenancy is not mine after all, with you back home again."

"How could that be, Dan? Squire Riddle would never hear of it. I'll have to leave again, as soon as I can—before someone gets wind that I'm here."

But Daniel knew that. Will understood that this was merely his way of paying deference to his brother. He really did seem a changed man. "Well, who knows?" Daniel said. "Things can change. There was a time, I thought nothing would ever look right—but everythin' can come 'roun'."

"So, who's the lucky lass?"

"You know her. From church. Molly Drake."

Will did, of course, know her. She wasn't half so pretty as Liz Duncan, but she was a lively girl who loved to laugh, and she had a fine figure. No wonder Daniel was feeling lighter these days. "She's a good choice," Will said. "She's all ye can handle, I wager."

"And maybe a little more." Daniel laughed, as though he understood that he'd been a dour young man, hardly someone who seemed right for such a sprightly lass.

Will liked what was happening to Daniel. "Her father's a wainright," Will said. "It's possible, he'd have work for ye."

"I know. It's what Father says too. But Brother Drake hasn't spoke a word to me on that. And he has a son—his first choice, no doubt."

"Maybe there's a place for more than one. Wagons are always needed, you know."

"Some say trains will hurt the business."

"Maybe coaches won't be needed so much, but how's a farmer to do his work without a sturdy wagon?"

Daniel nodded, and there was a hint of a smile on his face, as though the mere contemplation of a life with Molly was enough to feed him with joy for now.

"And Sarah tells me that she's also found someone," Will said.

Nettie was standing at the dry sink, using a basin to wash the morning dishes. She turned around and looked at Will. Today she didn't seem quite so worn down as she had at first, but he thought he saw sorrow in her face. "Sarah has made promises herself," she said, "but it's the same problem. How are they to live? There's no work for any of the young men—no way to start life, not the way there was when your father and I married."

The front door had come open as Nettie was speaking, and Sarah stepped in. "Speak of the devil and he appears," Sarah said. She was smiling, not seeming nearly so concerned as her mother.

"Do I know this man who's turning your cheeks so rosy red? What's his name?"

"John Davidson. He lives east of Ledbury. His father is a tenant farmer, the same as us."

"He must not go to the United Brethren."

"No. He's Anglican. But he's gone to meetings with me lately. He likes the sermons he hears, and he's a born dissenter. He's ready to turn from all the nonsense he hears from his own preacher. Things are changing at church, Will, and he likes what he's been hearing."

"What changes?"

No one answered until Nettie finally said, "Will, we need to tell you about that—and we will. Soon."

Will shrugged. It was not anything he cared much about. "So what about John Davidson? Will he receive the tenancy from his father?"

"No. He must find some other way. And for now, there is none. He's twenty-three and a good farmer. He's looked all around for a vacant tenancy, but more of those close than open. You know that."

"I know more than e'er I wanted to know."

"Will . . . all of you," Nettie said. "Let's talk as we should."

Will smiled and nodded. "You can never imagine what it's like in the big cities. Men are queued up outside every factory, and no one finds work. And those who have work are angry. They're paid nine or ten shillings a week—or less. I heard plenty of talk of men going up against the factory owners, even shutting the mills down if they have to."

"What purpose will that serve?" Nettie asked.

"Things can't go on the way they are, Mum. Mill owners have every fine thing—and they keep taking more. They're starving the rest of us."

Will felt the reaction. He saw it in all the faces.

Daniel stood up. "It's time I get back to work," he said. "We're about to start planting, and we're far from ready for it." He stepped to his mother, kissed her on the cheek, and then looked back at Will. "You should get back to bed and rest yourself."

"I need to get back to the dairy," Sarah said. She followed Daniel out the door.

Will looked at his mother. "I seem to have emptied the cottage with my dangerous talk."

"You can't speak that way around your father. You know that, don't you?"

"I know what he would say. I also know more about this world than he ever will—and it didn't take me long to learn it. Sooner or later, things have to change. I have no desire to fight a revolution, but some are ready. That's all I'm saying."

Nettie turned back to her dishes. Will decided he had said enough. "Daniel's right," she said. "You need to rest now."

"I'm tired of resting. I might walk outside a little. I need to get my legs going again—even if my hand isn't ready."

But as he stood and turned toward the door, he saw that his father was standing there. "It's good to see ye up," he said. "But Will, you can na' walk outside."

"I'll only walk to the barn. No one will see me."

"We can na' take that chance. You understan', do ye not?"

"I suppose I do." But Will, for the first time, felt imprisoned. He had been so happy to be home, but home was the farm, not the cottage, and he hadn't looked out across the fields or stepped into the barn to smell the animals or touch his tools.

"Will, sit down for a little," Morgan said. "There's somethin' me and you must speak on."

Will sat back down at the table and watched his father's face. There was something coming—something that was important to his father but that he seemed nervous about.

Morgan walked to the table, his limp not much better than it had been when Will had left. He sat across from Will at the old oak table. He clasped his hands together and looked into Will's eyes, but as he began to speak, he looked down. "Will, there's been a preacher here, and he's changed the hearts of many of the United Brethren. John Benbow and Thomas Kington have accepted baptism from this man, and both ha' embraced the gospel he preaches."

"So what will happen to the United Brethren?"

"So many are acceptin' this faith, there will na' be a United

Brethren. But Will, this is the true religion we was all seeking afore. It's the same as what Jesus Christ brought to the earth. It's been restored, sent down from God to a prophet."

"So you've accepted it yourself?"

"I ha' na' been baptized yet. There's more I need to learn. But me an' your mother met with a missionary—the preacher I mentioned. He's here from America and, Will, I testify with all my heart, he's a man of God. We're holdin' another meetin' with 'im t'night, right here in this room. We wan' ye to listen to 'im. It's the gospel we seeked for, Will, the light and truth."

Will realized he had heard all this before. The man in Manchester—North—had talked of the same thing. It was the Mormons that his parents wanted to join with! Will turned in his chair. "Mum, what do you think of this American and his true religion?"

Clearly, she had heard his tone. "Don't make light of it, Will. I've never heard such sensible doctrine in my life. And he—Wilford Woodruff is his name—is blessed with the Spirit of the Holy Ghost. If you listen to him with an honest heart, I know you'll feel it."

"He's a Mormon, isn't he?"

"That's not the right name," Morgan said. "It's The Church of Jesus Christ of Latter-day Saints."

"I know about it," Will said. "I met a man in Manchester who invited me to a Mormon meeting. He said this fellow named Smith, in America, is behind the whole thing."

"Nay, Will. It's the Lord 'imself who's behind it. Joseph Smith is on'y a man—but a man o' God."

"I can't believe you would fall for a story like that, Father. These Mormons are preaching on the streets in Manchester. They claim they have all truth stopped up in a bottle, and all you have to do is buy a pint. For a pretty penny, too, is my guess. Don't let anyone sell you such rubbish."

"Will, don't start in this way. I thought you was humbled after all you been through."

"Remember what you told us," Nettie said. "You heard a voice telling you to come home."

"I heard words, Mother. I don't know that it was a voice. They were just words that came into my head."

"And where did they come from?" Morgan asked.

He was leaning forward, leering at Will, and Will didn't like that. He knew what he'd heard, but he didn't want his father telling him what to believe about it. "I don't know. I really can't say."

"That's not true," Nettie said. She walked to the table and looked down at Will until he finally looked up. "You told me that it was God who brought you home."

Will knew he had said that, but he tried to think whether he was sure it was true. "It might have been," he finally said.

"You do believe in God."

"Yes, I do. But I doubt he paid a visit to this Smith fellow."

"Would you at least listen to Brother Woodruff?" Morgan asked.

"No. I told you, I met one of them already, and he's like you. He thinks religion is the answer, but the only thing I hear from religion is sweet talk about the next life. These preachers get paid by the landowners, and that's their whole purpose—to keep poor people poor and rich people rich. I believe in God, but I don't believe in religion."

"This one is different," Nettie said. "He's not paid by anyone. And in his religion all members are equal in the eyes of God, and equal in their church."

"I'm sorry, but I don't believe that."

Morgan had already given up, and now Nettie did. A long

silence followed. Will watched his father, who was still leaning forward, looking squarely at the table, his hands clasped in front of him. "I was willin' to let you come home because Nettie prayed so hard for ye to come back to us. But it can na' be safe to stay long—never was. You knowed that when ye got here. An' yet, what worries me more is that it's not safe for the other childr'n to ha' you about. You say things that go against the beliefs of this family. I can na' let Josiah and Esther and the li'l lads hear you blaspheme so. I fear for your soul, son, but I can na' keep ye here and let ye ruin other lives."

"That's fine, Father. I'll leave tonight—after dark."

"I'm not askin' that. Stay 'til you have more strength. But talk no religion with the childr'n, or even Daniel and Sarah. An' don't be walkin' outside."

"But Morgan, what will he do?" Nettie asked.

"I do na' know, Nettie. It's the same as it were afore. I know that, but he brought it on himsel' with this talk of his. I firs' thought he were changed, but I ha' no such notions now. When he fin'ly has to eat with the hogs, like the prodigal son, then he might understan' what he's givin' up."

"I know more than you think, Father. I've been with those hogs—and I wanted to come home. But you can't welcome me. Squire Riddle wouldn't let you even if you wanted to." He sat for a time, and then he added, "When I was working with that crew of corrupt men, living in a tent, working twelve and fourteen hours a day, I wanted more than anything just to come back here and be with my family. I'm sorry I don't see eye to eye with you about religion, but I do know what I've given up." He looked at his mother. "I thought of you every day. I longed more than anything just to be here at this table to eat your meals and laugh with everyone."

"But you understan' why you can't stay," Morgan said.

"Aye. I understand. But when I'm gone again, I'll still miss this farm, and miss all of you." There was nothing more to say.

• • •

Will stayed five more days. He rested and ate, and he tried to be kind to everyone. He said nothing about religion, and even though he wouldn't come out of the bedroom to meet Wilford Woodruff, he said nothing more about the Mormons. The entire family did meet with Woodruff, along with several neighbors, not all of whom were members of the United Brethren. The talk at breakfast the next morning was all about joining the new church.

Will didn't want to ask questions, but his parents told him that Woodruff—"Apostle" Woodruff, they called him, or "Brother" Woodruff—had arrived in Herefordshire early in March. "On the fourth of March," Nettie said. "The day I had the feeling about you, that something was wrong." John Benbow and his wife had accepted baptism first, and Thomas Kington a little later, but all the preachers in the organization had accepted Woodruff's teachings, and they had already begun to teach the entire membership. The Gadfield Elm chapel, a United Brethren meetingplace across the Malvern Hills near Eldersfield, had been deeded over to the Mormons, they said, and most of the members—more than six hundred people—had either joined or were listening to the missionaries.

Morgan told Will, "I ne'er heerd a preacher who reasons so clear but who speaks wi' such faith that his words cut right to a man's heart."

Will didn't care. In time, this would all blow over like most of these "movements." Reality would set in, and disillusionment would follow.

Will didn't tell his family when he planned to leave, but he knew which day he would head out. He had thought it all through. He would leave on market day, before dawn, so he was well away from the farm when the sun came up. But he would make one attempt to see Liz, and the best hope for that was at the marketplace. He also knew where he was going. He would return to Colwall Stone and see whether the Crawfords would keep their promise and offer him work.

He decided not to say good-bye, if only because he didn't want his parents to give him money, but also because he couldn't stand to go through it all again. He had slept in the attic of the barn the last couple of nights, slipping out there after dark with his father's somewhat hesitant permission. He arose at four o'clock on Tuesday morning, wrote a note and left it at the front door with a rock to weigh it down, and then he walked away. He felt sick, worse than before, because he had some idea of what he faced, but he was more resolute this time. He couldn't come back again.

He walked toward Ledbury, staying in the woods all morning. It was almost noon when he pulled his cap down low, walked to the marketplace, and watched the people from a distance. He knew that Liz shopped most weeks, and that she and Mary Ann liked to come quite early in the afternoon. And fortunately, that was the case today. More than an hour passed before his breath caught when he finally saw her. He followed his plan. He approached a spot near the end of all the booths and waited for her to come near. When she and Mary Ann approached, he walked as though to pass her by, then stepped in front of her and said, "Hello, Liz. It's Will. May I speak to you a moment?"

Liz and Mary Ann both let out a little cry of surprise, and then Mary Ann laughed. "Are you the real Will, or his ghost? We thought Will was dead and buried."

Will looked out from under the brim of his cap, and he smiled. "I guess I'm still alive. But I might look like a ghost."

"What's wrong?" Liz asked. "Have you been sick?"

He lifted his hand, still bandaged. "I was injured. I'm doing better now."

"You look like you *were* buried," Mary Ann said. "And now you've climbed back out of the grave."

"Hush, Mary Ann," Liz said.

At the same time, Will said, "Please talk to me for a few minutes."

"What are you hiding from?" Liz asked.

"Squire Riddle. If he knows I've been back in the village, he'll assume I've visited my home. I can't have him think that. My family is scared they'll be moved off the farm."

"Then you have seen them?"

"I didn't say that, and don't either of you say that. But walk with me just a little."

"Will, that will bring more attention than anything. Just say what you have to say—and quickly. Unless you want to take that cap off and not act like some skulking criminal."

Will knew the surprise was over, and now Liz was letting him know that she resented the way he'd handled everything. "All right," he said. He took a quick glance at Mary Ann, as if to tell her that she could listen too—if she didn't speak. "There's a Squire Crawford who lives a few miles north of here, near Colwall Stone. He's mentioned that I might be able to work for him. He may not keep his promise, and if he does, I would only be a laborer. But it's better than what I suffered in Manchester, and there may be some way, still, to rise to something better. It's only a small hope, but it's something."

Liz looked confused. Finally she said, "Let's move away from this marketplace." She turned to Mary Ann and added, "Shop for us. I'll return soon."

"Liz, don't do this. You have your mind made up. Why do you want to dredge all this—"

"Just finish the shopping. I need to talk to Will." And then she said to Will, "Meet me at the church." She headed toward Church Lane. Will didn't follow her but took Back Lane, which looped wider but also ended up at the church on the hill. He knew where Liz was heading: to Dog Woods beyond the church, where they had walked before.

When Will caught up with Liz near the St. Michael and All Angels Anglican church, she walked away again into the woods, but a little way down the path, she stopped. She sounded almost angry when she asked, "Are you still hoping that we can marry?"

"I'll always hope that."

"You haven't shown it. I haven't heard from you for three months."

"For a time, I gave up. I was working long, hard days, and there seemed no way to escape doing that. And then I got hurt."

"And what's so different now? A job as a farm laborer?"

He tried to take hold of her arm, but she pulled her elbow away from his grasp. "I think the Crawfords like me," he said. "The wife suggested that I might have some opportunities with them. Maybe I could be their bailiff in time and manage their farm."

"And how long would it take to gain such a position with them?"

"I have no idea. It's only something to dream about. But I wanted you to know that there might be a reason to wait a little longer."

"My father is ready to disown me. I've turned down every suitor he's brought to our home. How long can I do that?"

"I don't know, Liz. I only know I'm still trying to find a way to rise above my station."

She stopped and turned toward him. "Will, I've thought and thought about this. I've wondered whether I could marry you if you were a laborer. My heart tells me I could, but my head tells me the truth. I would be miserable if I had to live in poverty, and I would make you miserable. I've changed since you left. I'm not so conceited as I was. I may never marry, and I've accepted that, but I still can't see myself in a farm cottage."

"But a bailiff makes a good living. If I can—"

"Can you even work? How bad is your hand?"

"It will heal. I can manage." But he didn't know that, and he saw the truth of what she was telling him. "I won't be far away this time. I'll write you, maybe pay you a visit from time to time. I'll let you know whether my hopes get any better."

Liz shook her head. "I told you a long time ago, this isn't worth it. We're only making ourselves unhappy. Let's agree to say good-bye and part."

"I won't ever give up." But even as he said it, he knew that he had given up before, and he probably would again.

"I'm sure I won't stop thinking of you, Will, though I wish I could."

"Let me hold onto a little hope. Promise me you won't put me out of your heart entirely."

"I'm not promising anything."

He nodded. He understood.

"Has your family embraced Apostle Woodruff's teachings yet?" Liz asked.

Will was taken by surprise. "Yes," he said. "They haven't been baptized, but they will any day. What about your family?"

"We've all been baptized."

"You don't believe all that about Joseph Smith, do you?"

She looked him in the eye. "I do believe it."

Will knew he had better not say anything more. This was another wedge being driven between them.

"Will, you need to read the Book of Mormon."

Will shrugged. "I could do that."

"And you need to listen to Brother Woodruff."

"Maybe I'll have a chance sometime."

"Seek the chance. The gospel he preaches is right. I feel it every time I hear him. And he is a good man. I feel that, too. What he teaches is more important than whether you and I end up together. If this life doesn't turn out so well, we have eternity to be with God and feel His happiness."

That was exactly the kind of talk Will hated. He didn't tell her so, but he knew she could feel it from him. Now he did feel his hope slipping away.

"God bless you, Will. You're such a lovely man. I wish something had been possible for us."

And then she did the last thing he expected. She slipped her hand around his neck and pulled his face to hers. She kissed him, and then held him for a long time. She had begun to cry.

"I've never been kissed," she said. "I just wanted that much to remember."

"I've never been kissed either," he said. "I'll remember this all my life." He kissed her again, but this kiss didn't last as long. She pulled away, then said good-bye and hurried away.

• • •

Will walked on to Colwall Stone and reached the Crawfords' estate early in the afternoon. The walk had taken more out of him than he had expected. When he arrived at the manor house, the Crawfords' border collie ran out and barked at him, then pranced around him. The sound brought Mr. Crawford out of the horse barn. "Will!" he said. "How good to see you. You're looking better than when I saw you last."

"I am better." He wanted Mr. Crawford to think he was much better, but he admitted some of the truth. "I'm just a little tired from the walk."

"Yes, yes. Come into the house and rest. Mrs. Crawford talks of you every day. We've prayed that you would recover."

"Thank you."

"Come inside."

"Could I ask you something first?"

"Yes, of course."

"Mrs. Crawford said that you might have work for me. I know that I can't do very much just yet, but I know farm work. It's what I've done all my life. I could be of some help to you now—if I could receive nothing more than room and board—but in time I could be a strong worker for you."

"You can do more than that, Will. Mrs. Crawford and I have talked and talked about this. Our bailiff is not a young man anymore. He could use some help. You could work as his assistant. After a time, if you prove yourself, you could possibly manage the farm for us. The truth is, I was going to let you rest a little longer, and then I was going to seek you out and make that offer to you."

"It's more than I ever hoped for, sir."

"And maybe it's more than we hoped for." Squire Crawford's eyes filled with tears. "You remind us of our son, Will. It feels a little as though he's come back to us. God works in mysterious ways, you know, but He does bless us. I hope you know that."

Will didn't answer. He didn't want to be a hypocrite after all he had been thinking and saying. But God did seem to be in this. He was not about to deny it.

CHAPTER 14

Will sat down on a bench outside the Crawfords' horse barn. He pulled his boots off and then looked off to the west where the sun was setting. It was a fine late September day, 1840, and Will had now been working on the Crawford farm for five months. The grain harvest was finished and the hay was cut and stacked for the winter.

Will was tired, but he was feeling stronger all the time. His hand was still not very useful to him, and he sometimes had to improvise as he worked, but most of his work was supervising, and that he did well. He was confident about farming, he understood what needed to be done, and he was good at coordinating all the workers' efforts. He got along well with the men he managed, too—better than he had sometimes done with his own family. He was younger than almost all the men, but they had learned that he knew what he was doing. Old Smithers, the bailiff, was a cranky man. He was always berating his workers, and he changed his mind so often that men became confused. Even Smithers had realized that Will was a better manager. He seemed ready to step back, fiddle with things in the barn, and let Will take over. The laborers liked that—even told Will that they did.

The Crawfords were happy with Will too, and they often told him so. He was the only man among all their tenant farmers and laborers who was ever invited into the manor house for meals, and he was invited often. He lived in a single room in the attic of the horse barn. It certainly wasn't fancy, but it wasn't the bunkhouse, either, where the single laborers lived. Will spent little time in that attic room, the workday being so long, but at least it was a place where he could be alone at night, and the Crawfords didn't begrudge him the beeswax candles he used. Will could write to his family, or to Liz, and he could read his Bible. He had never studied the Bible on his own, and he was questioning himself about that now. If Liz had come to feel so strongly about religion, what would she think of him if he always expressed so many doubts?

And in spite of what he had told his mother, he did wonder about the voice he had heard. Someone—or something—had told him to go home, and he had made it there. Added to that, the Crawfords had been brought into his life. When he had reached the end of his own strength, they had found him, lifted him out of the mud, and given him this work. His situation now was better than he could have imagined just a few months back.

So Will was thankful, and he felt a need to discover what he believed. As he read, what he found was that he loved the words of Jesus Christ. He read the Sermon on the Mount over and over, telling himself those were the admonitions he wanted to follow. He hadn't liked what he'd seen of religion—with all the sternness and false piety—but he did believe that following Christ was the answer to the problems he saw in the world. People should care for one another, not place themselves one above another. And religion shouldn't support divisions that claimed some people were "common" and others were their "betters."

He had written to Liz and told her that he was an assistant farm manager, that he was paid considerably better than a laborer, and that his prospects were good for managing the farm someday. He knew that would be good for her to hear, and good for her parents to know. But Liz didn't write back.

A few members of the United Brethren met in the home of a lay minister in a nearby village called Colwall. What Will was hearing now was that the whole branch had converted to Mormonism. Will knew one of the members, a man named Cornelius Williams. He was a saddler who operated his business in Colwall Stone, a larger village, also nearby. Will had taken in some harnesses for him to repair and had recognized the man from the annual "love feasts," as the United Brethren called their gatherings at John Benbow's farm in Frome's Hill. Brother Williams had encouraged Will to attend Sunday meetings. Will had avoided any promises about that, so Brother Williams had invited him to share an evening meal with his family. Will was happy to do that, but when he had arrived at the house, he discovered a motivation for Brother Williams's hospitality. He had a grown daughter of twenty or so, who seated herself next to Will at the table.

The daughter—Alice was her name—was quiet but friendly, and she wasn't bad looking. Her teeth were rather muddled, and she had a grayish complexion, but she had gentle brown eyes and a cheery manner about her. All the same, Will wasn't really interested. He compared Alice to Liz, and Liz came out far ahead. Afterward, though, as Will walked back to the farm, he told himself that he may have to start thinking differently about that. He might be bailiff of the Crawfords' farm someday, and that would raise him a little in the eyes of many, but he was not the Crawfords' son, however much they liked to have him near them. Will told himself that if he believed in the words of Jesus, he couldn't look down on Alice Williams. She was a good young woman, probably used to working hard. She would be a good mother, a good housekeeper, and she wouldn't feel compromised in marrying Will. Maybe Alice didn't excite Will, but perhaps some girl of her sort could. Maybe it was time for him to let his feelings for Liz go and to begin looking about for another nice young woman.

All of that sounded right to Will, but none of his wise thoughts reached his heart. He still thought of Liz every day.

· · ·

Will rode a horse into Colwall Stone quite often to have work done by the blacksmith, to order barrels from the cooper, or to ne-gotiate with brokers to sell his grain. When he had seen Brother Williams in the village recently, he had received another invitation for supper and almost turned it down, but, telling himself that that was the wrong attitude, he had accepted. When he returned on the following evening, he immediately realized what Brother Williams had had in mind for him this time. As he entered the Williams home—a small stone cottage, nicely furnished—he saw a stranger in the parlor seated next to the fireplace. He was a young man—in his thirties, perhaps—but sober in appearance and dressed in a dark suit of clothes. His side whiskers extended to his jaw, and a thin slice of mouth cut across almost from one set of whiskers to the other. He stood when Will entered the room.

Brother Williams said, "Brother Lewis, I want ta introduce ye to Apostle Wilford Woodruff. He's here from America."

Will extended his left hand for a handshake, avoiding the pain from a firm grip on his right hand. Woodruff was smiling, showing a row of good teeth. He didn't seem quite so serious after all. "I know your name," Will said. "You taught your religion to my parents, the Lewises, in Wellington Heath, near Ledbury."

"Yes, I know. I was in Ledbury last week and saw your family at prayer meeting. They send their greetings."

Now Will understood. Brother Williams had arranged this meeting with the encouragement of Will's parents. And the Williamses surely wanted him to accept Mormonism and then their daughter, in that order.

"Brother Lewis tells me that your family has never been so happy," Woodruff said. "Your father has been searching for the true gospel for many years, and now he's found it. Your entire family has."

Will understood what Woodruff was suggesting. He knew he was in for some strong-arm preaching.

But Brother Williams said, "Let's sit down an' eat. After supper, Apostle Woodruff can answer all your questions, Will. I 'spect you'd like to understan' what your family's taken on."

Will told himself he would not pose any questions but would excuse himself soon after the meal. Alice sat down by him again, and this time he paid her much more attention—mainly so he wouldn't have to talk to Woodruff. But Mr. Woodruff talked anyway. He told about his constant comings and goings, trekking through the Malvern Hills in three counties. He knew how many miles he had walked each day, how many people he had preached to, how many he had baptized. In less than six months, he said, "more than a thousand new Saints have entered the waters of baptism here in the Malvern Hills. We have well over three thousand members in Britain now." He seemed to like the numbers, and surely he wanted to add one more tonight.

"What about London, Brother Woodruff?" Brother Williams asked. "How did your work go there?"

Mr. Woodruff looked at Will. "I spent the better part of a

month in London," he said, "and returned here a few days ago to hold conferences in our two circuits. I'll be leaving again before long to meet with our other apostles in Manchester—but then I'll be going back to London to see whether we can further the work of the Lord in that sinful place. It's a wonderful city, with much to see, but I vow, it's the capital of Babylon." He looked back at Brother Williams. "We faced opposition at every turn in that city, but we made a few conversions. The people there need the Lord as much as in any place I've ever seen."

"The devil is at work here too," Brother Williams said. "Some of the preachers is up agin us, printing all kinds of lies."

"Yes, I've seen a good deal of that. I baptized some people one night in a pond over in Hawcross. A mob pelted me with rocks and sticks and anything else they could throw. One stone struck me on the top of my head. I almost went under, but the Lord sustained me, and I continued His work."

Apostle Woodruff took a long look at Will before he said, "But hearts can change. Brigham Young and Willard Richards, both apostles like myself, taught here for a time. One night we were in Dymock with Thomas Kington. You know him, I'm sure."

"Aye. I do."

"Well, we met Sister Mary Pitt, sister to William. Her leg had been lame for eleven years. She hadn't walked without crutches for most of that time. The three of us laid our hands on her head and rebuked the lameness. She walked from that very moment—walked all through town the next day. Some denied the truth that was right before their eyes, but many people in Dymock saw us with new eyes after that."

Will nodded, but he could only think of the similar stories told by the United Brethren. He'd heard more than enough about healings and miracles. These Mormons probably rolled on the floor, too, and danced around the room when they felt "the spirit." Will wasn't going to have anything to do with that. He turned and spoke to Alice—his way of showing, quite openly, that he wasn't impressed.

When the dishes were cleared away, all the adults, including Alice, stayed at the table. Will was about to claim he needed to leave when Brother Williams said, "Brother Lewis, all of us here ha' ta'en on the true gospel—drinked it like a cool tankard of spring water— and we're all refreshed. It's the same with your family. It's what we all been looking for all our lives. We want you to hear, from the mouth of an apostle, the words we heerd from him."

This was something new from the saddler, this poetic talk, and Will could tell that he'd prepared the little speech. It was surely something he believed, but that didn't mean Will liked the idea of being trapped this way. "And what is it that makes you an apostle, sir? I've not heard that sort of title in England. Is it common in American churches?"

"No. Certainly not," Mr. Woodruff said. "As you know, it's what Jesus Christ named those he called to witness of Him. New apostles have been called in our age, again as witnesses for the gospel. "

What surprised Will was Woodruff's matter-of-fact way of speaking. It was quite a claim to make, but he made it without sounding arrogant. The man was a true believer, however misguided he might be.

"Jesus Christ built His church upon the shoulders of those first apostles. He gave them the authority to carry on after He was gone—to preach repentance and to baptize in His name. But the apostles were murdered, the authority was lost, and with it the pure doctrines of Christ were distorted. The good news I bring is that the authority has been returned to the earth, that prophets and apostles have been called again—not by man, but by God."

Woodruff placed his hands flat on the table and looked at Will steadily. "I don't take my calling lightly, Brother Lewis. It's not a responsibility I ever would have expected in life. I'm not as good a man as I'd like to be, and I'm not a grand preacher. I'm the son of a farmer and miller, and that's the same work I've followed. But I was fortunate to hear the truth and embrace it. Why God chose me I'll never understand, but He called me through the Prophet Joseph Smith—I know you've heard of him—and I have accepted the call." He smiled rather innocently. "I was a rascal of a boy. I climbed every tree and I fell out of more than one. I almost met my death many a time when I was growing up, and yet the Lord preserved me for his purposes. I was never very religious, so you can imagine that I feel like a fish out of water now. But when God called me as a missionary and witness for Christ, I agreed to do the best I could."

He pronounced *missionary* in his American drawl, with an emphasized "airy" on the end, but something in his simple way of speaking appealed to Will. He did seem to be a farmer, not a trained minister. And something he said reminded Will of what he had been thinking lately, that the doctrines Jesus Christ had taught were not being preached in modern religions. No wonder this man was converting people. But that didn't change the fact that he was making great claims for himself. "What makes this Smith fellow think that he can speak for God?" Will asked.

"When Joseph Smith was little more than a boy, God appeared to him—stood above him in the air in broad daylight. This began the great work of restoring the true church to the earth. Later, he received authority from heavenly visitors, who laid their hands on his head and bestowed God's priesthood upon him. It is through that authority, divinely given, that he leads the Church today."

Will didn't doubt for a moment that Wilford Woodruff believed what he was saying, but Will couldn't imagine such things: God paying a visit to a young lad, "heavenly visitors" appearing.

"I know it's a lot to believe, Brother Lewis. I was skeptical when I first heard of it myself." He shook his head as though he were still a little amazed. A shock of black hair fell across his forehead. Woodruff looked like a farmer, with his pale forehead and ruddy nose and cheeks. Will could see in the man's hands, too, that he had worked hard in his life and hadn't spent all his days out preaching.

"I know the Prophet Joseph well," Woodruff said. "He's thirty-four years old—only a year older than I am—but when I look in his eyes, when I hear the words of God from his mouth, I know for certain that they couldn't come from him. He's a farmer's son like me—and you—and yet he speaks with the tongue of angels." He looked steadily into Will's eyes. "I testify to you that he *is* a prophet. I promise you that you will know it too, if you ever meet him."

"And is that likely? Is he planning to visit us here—now that you've persuaded so many in these hills to join your church?" Will had intended the words to suggest his doubt, but he found himself actually wondering whether he would have a chance to meet the man.

"I don't know where God will send him in his life. But I know this. You can know he's a man of God by reading the Book of Mormon. Would you like to do that?"

Will hesitated. He was expecting to say no, but instead he said, "I wouldn't mind reading it. I've wondered what it is." Feeling that he was sounding much too interested, he added, "But only out of curiosity. I'm not nearly so religious as my parents or the Williamses. I'm sorry to say it, but I don't think much of religion."

"Brother Lewis, you're right to doubt the versions of Christianity you've known in your life. Remember, the United Brethren are doubters about the religions of England, too, but in praying for light and truth, they prayed me here. A voice told me to come south from where I was in Staffordshire, and I followed that voice. Now

I understand why. Your people have been prepared to accept the truth."

The words struck Will, moved him more than he wanted to be moved. A voice had told Will to come home, and a voice had told this man to come here to preach—at about the same time. Will didn't say that, though. He told Brother Woodruff, "But the United Brethren are not so different from Anglicans as they think they are. They don't question the way we live here in England. Some folks sit in their manor houses and eat venison and drink fine wines while others work themselves to death in mines and factories and farms—and are looked down upon for being laborers."

"Now you've struck on a great truth."

Will couldn't have been more surprised. He had expected Woodruff to justify the ways of the world. That was what his father had always done.

Brother Woodruff seemed enlivened by the subject. He leaned forward again. He had little eyes, but they were steady as stones, and they were aimed directly at Will. "The Lord, through His prophet, and in the Book of Mormon, has taught us that when His people are righteous they will see to it that there are no poor among them."

"But I suppose the poor must wait for their reward in heaven. That's what my father always told me. I don't accept that."

"I'm not talking about heaven. I'm talking about this earth. I'm talking about *Zion*."

"What's Zion?"

"For now, it's Nauvoo, Illinois. It's the city in America where many of the Saints are gathering. It's a place where everyone can own land—and everyone does. So we all work as laborers in the field. We work to provide for our families, and when we have surplus, we help those in need."

"And what of Joseph Smith? How does he live?"

"He lives in a log house, and his wife fills the place with those who are sick and afflicted. It's the same with the apostles. My wife and children live in a humble log cabin. When I return from my mission, I will farm again, and I plan to build a good brick house—with the labor of my own hands." He smiled. "And the house will have a fireplace in every room. When I leave England, I want never to be cold again. I never do get warm here."

Everyone laughed at this. "You spend too many days walking in the rain," Sister Williams said.

"That's true. I do."

Will glanced at Alice, who seemed warmed by what she had heard, more color coming into her face. But he also saw in her what he saw in Brother and Sister Williams. They were watching him to see how he was accepting the things he'd heard. Will didn't want to deal with their expectations. He was still trying to understand. "What kind of place is this city . . . what did you say it's called?"

"Nauvoo." Apostle Woodruff spelled it out. "It comes from Hebrew. It means a beautiful, peaceful place. It's built on a big bend of the Mississippi River. It was a sickly place when we took it over, but we're draining the wet areas, and it's going to be one of the most beautiful cities in America. We have plans to build a temple of God on the bluffs above the town—and we shall all work on it together."

"And there are no rich and no poor?"

Apostle Woodruff laughed softly. "I can't claim that yet," he said. "I can promise you that no one is rich. So far, though, we're more or less equal in our poverty. Our hope is always to work together and to bring everyone to a better state. No one is placed above another, and neighbors help each other. Not everyone's as idealistic as I am, and I won't say that we don't fail in our efforts at times, but the Prophet teaches us to work for the good of the whole society."

"Is there anyone who would say to a fellow member of your

church, 'I'm sorry, but you cannot marry my daughter. My family is too far above yours'?"

"There may be some who take that attitude, but personally, I've never heard anyone speak such words. Some may come to us with more money, or with a prideful heart, but if someone tried to place himself above another, he would soon feel the shame of it. It isn't how we think."

Woodruff had a curious way of speaking—strong in his expression of belief but quiet and humble in admitting realities. Will felt his honesty. The man seemed to be describing something he had actually seen. Will liked him. He found himself wanting to reject what he was hearing and, at the same time, wishing he could believe it. He liked to think there was a place and a people that didn't divide up into social classes. "I can never own land in England," Will said.

"I know. America is different, because we're so big and new. But Nauvoo offers more than land. And more than a happy society. Our leader speaks with God. We aren't wandering about, hoping we stumble onto a truth from time to time. We are taught daily by the Lord."

That was the part Will doubted. He didn't like the idea of one man claiming to have a direct communication with God. He worried that this Smith was a charlatan, duping a whole people for his own purposes.

"I have a Book of Mormon," Brother Williams said. "You will na' find a great many in England, but—"

"We're printing more," Apostle Woodruff said. "I stood with Brigham Young and Willard Richards at the top of these hills, at Herefordshire Beacon, and we were told by God that it was time to print the Book of Mormon in this land."

"Aye," Brother Williams said. "But for now, Brother Lewis, you can borrow mine."

"Yes. That would be fine."

Apostle Woodruff explained the history of the Book of Mormon, how it had come from an angel and was translated by inspiration by Joseph Smith. Will's skepticism was only fired again by that, but Woodruff said, "Think of it this way, Brother Lewis. If this book is not true, you can forget all you've heard tonight. But if it's a genuine record, brought to earth by an angel, God will make it manifest to you."

"That's fair enough. I'll give it a read," Will said, but he tried not to seem enthusiastic.

"And will you pray about it—kneel down and ask God whether it's from Him?"

"I . . . don't mind doing that, either."

When Will got home that night he did read a little in the Book of Mormon, and then, because he had promised, he knelt by his bed—the way he had as a child—and he prayed that he could know whether it was true. Or at least he said the words. He didn't really expect an answer. He was curious about the book and about Joseph Smith, but when he got into bed, he thought mostly about owning land, about immigrating to America and, of course, taking Liz with him. It seemed to be everything he had been longing for all these years. But he couldn't run off to America chasing a lie.

After a time Will got out of bed and knelt again. "Lord, if what I heard tonight is true," he said, "show me in some way." But he sensed no answer, and he lay awake for a long time, wondering how he could ever know.

•　•　•

The following day Will was riding his horse down a lane between two fields, heading back to the barn. As he neared the manor house, he noticed a young woman approaching on foot. She had on a rose-colored dress that was like one that Liz often wore, and she was about the size of Liz.

And then he realized. It *was* Liz.

She looked up as he approached, seemed unsure for a moment, but then smiled. Will couldn't imagine what could have brought her there. He dropped down from his horse, led the animal by the bridle, and walked to her. "I can't believe my eyes," he said.

"I'm sorry. I shouldn't be here, I'm sure. But suddenly, this morning, it was what I wanted—needed, really—to do. If you can't talk to me right now, just tell me, and I'll wait until you can."

"I can talk to you, Liz. But I still can't believe I'm looking at you. Are you more beautiful than ever? Is that even possible?"

"Oh, Will, I'm not so beautiful. I'm just flushed from walking. You're the one who looks well. You've recovered your strength, haven't you? How is your hand?"

"My fingers move a little better all the time, but I can't really grab hold of anything."

She took his hand and felt the bones gently. A thrill passed through Will, his arm and chest tingling. He wanted more than anything to kiss her again. "Is your work going well?" she asked.

"Aye. I didn't think I would ever like farming so much. After my days as a navvy, though, anything seems better."

"But you're in charge here, aren't you?"

"In a manner of speaking, I am. And you know me. I like that." He was watching her all the while, wanting so badly to hold her. He was certain that he had never seen another face so beautiful, skin so rich. "But what brings you here?"

"I need to talk to you."

"All right. Let me take this horse to the barn. Walk with me, and then we can sit out here in the sun." It was a cool day, but the sun felt good. As he walked, he kept thinking to himself that something this wonderful couldn't really be happening.

He tied his horse in the barn and slipped off the saddle and bridle. Liz was taking everything in, commenting on the lovely barn, the beautiful house she had seen. But Will could hardly think what she was saying. He kept asking himself what she wanted to talk to him about.

When they sat down outside the barn, Will turned toward her on the bench. "Tell me what's on your mind."

"My father has chosen another suitor for me. He tells me he won't take no for an answer, that I'm too old to pass up this opportunity."

"Who is it?"

"He's new in our church—not the Brethren, but the Latter-day Saints. He has a trade—he's a carpenter and a joiner—and my father says he professes great love for me."

"Is a carpenter good enough for your father now?"

"I suppose so. He wants me married, and he wants me to marry someone in our church. This man—Hawkes is his name—promises that he'll build us a nice house, and he claims to be quite prosperous in his business."

"What about a farm bailiff? Would such a man be good enough?"

"Maybe, Will. I've told him what you're doing now, but he has his mind so set against you, he doesn't like to listen. He tells me you're not a bailiff yet, and it may be a long time in coming. For now, he thinks I would have to live in a farm cottage, with no servants."

"Do you expect to have servants?"

"I don't know. I haven't learned much about cooking or keeping house, but I can learn—and I wouldn't need to hire help, I don't think. But it's more than that. He's heard from others some of the things you've said about religion. He's afraid that if we married and had children, you would lead them away from God."

Will turned away a little. He shut his eyes and raised his face to the sun. He needed to think about all this. He knew what he was about to say, but he wanted to test it in his mind and heart for a moment. "Liz, I met with Wilford Woodruff last night. I liked what he said. He talked about the city in America—Nauvoo—where everyone owns land and no person is above another."

"I know. Everyone is talking about it. Many are getting ready to gather there. One group already left. But Will, you can't have faith in a city. Not if you reject the religion."

"Woodruff is a good man. I trusted him. He told me to read the Book of Mormon and pray. I read a little last night, and I don't know what to think of the book so far, but I did pray, and I asked the Lord to show me if it was right for me to believe all this." He turned to her. "And then, there you were, like an angel, appearing in my world, where I never thought to see you. When did you think to come here?"

"Last night, as I lay in bed. And then again this morning."

"It's when I prayed. I don't like to believe in such things. It seems silly to me, but lately things have been happening. God seems to be taking an interest in me. Maybe he wants us to be together in this church—and in Nauvoo."

"What are you saying? That you would leave England?"

"Gladly, if the place is what Woodruff says it is. But I need to believe. You told me that you believe in the Book of Mormon. I need to see what I think of it."

"Yes. You do. Will, I think my father might relent if he knew you had embraced the new church."

Will felt something powerful happening inside him. It was everything he had hoped for, and everything that had been impossible just a few months earlier. He wondered what the Holy Ghost felt like, whether this heat inside him had anything to do with that.

"But you can't join the Church for me, Will. If you were baptized, and then lost your faith, that would be too much for me."

"I understand that." It was all so wonderful and yet frightening. He had to keep his feet on the ground. He needed to test these new ideas. He needed to be certain before he made promises. But hadn't God already answered him? "Liz, after I broke my hand, a voice spoke to me and told me to go home—where I thought I could never go. And then the Crawfords found me and gave me a chance in life. Now it would appear that the Lord has sent you here—to me. I need to find a deeper faith, I know, but God seems to be answering my prayers. I never believed that that could happen."

Liz was nodding. "I'll hold out. I won't marry Brother Hawkes. I'll tell my father that you are studying—"

"Let me talk to him. I'll convince him."

She smiled but looked a little frightened. She was feeling what he was, Will was sure; they were about to have what they wanted, it seemed, but everything was too new to accept.

"Do you really love me, Will? I know you think I'm pretty, but I have a sharp tongue and I'm used to having far too much. Would you really be happy with me, if we were to marry?"

"Don't ask me to think of reality. I only know what you are in my mind. I've loved you since I was nineteen and you were still just a girl. It's not just that you're beautiful; it's that you fill up my head and heart. I can't think of anyone else. I've tried."

"I tried to put you out of my mind too, Will, but I couldn't. Maybe it always was what God wanted for both of us."

Will thought so. And what he felt when he kissed her this time was different from before. In his mind, she was now his betrothed. He would give the rest of his life to be certain she was always happy.

CHAPTER 15

Jeff and Abby were sitting in their bishop's office. The executive secretary had found them in their Sunday School class and asked them to walk down the hallway with him to meet with the bishop. It was only their second Sunday in the ward, but Jeff figured they were about to receive a calling.

The bishop—Wayne Harrison was his name—was rather husky. His suit was a little too tight in the shoulders, and it looked as though it had been worn every Sunday for a long time, with permanent wrinkles in the sleeves and under the arms. He had big, hard hands with some ground-in dirt in the creases. But his voice was soft, his cadence slow. "So tell me, Brother and Sister Lewis, what brings you to Nauvoo?"

"Do you know Harvey Robertson?"

"I've heard that name, but I can't say that I know him."

"He bought a house over on Warsaw Street, but he's never actually lived there."

"All right. Now I know. He came to church once. He told me

he'd bought a place in our ward. He said he'd be staying here at times, but I don't think I've seen him since then."

"He got called as a mission president," Jeff said, and then he explained the circumstances that had brought him and Abby to Nauvoo and the arrangement they had with the Robertsons.

"So you might not be around too long?"

"It's hard to say. We might be here only a month or two, but you might as well think of us as part of your ward. We could be here quite a while." Jeff wanted to have a calling. He didn't want to sit on the sidelines the whole time they were in Nauvoo.

"I wish you were staying for good."

"We do too . . . in a way. We love it here."

The bishop nodded. His sparse hair was cut very short, which made his head look the size and shape of a basketball. Jeff liked something about him. He didn't seem in a hurry. And Jeff believed him when he said that he wished they could stay.

The bishop was looking at Abby now, as though he were saying, *Does your husband answer all the questions?*

"Bishop," Abby said, "are there any opportunities for Jeff around here? Would anyone in this area be looking for a computer person?"

"Probably not in Nauvoo, but Keokuk and Fort Madison—on the Iowa side of the river—have some big companies. Or there's Quincy. But that's about an hour's drive."

"Well, I'll have to check around and see what might be available," Jeff said.

"But you're willing to serve in the ward while you're here?"

"Not only willing. We want to," Jeff said. "We keep hearing stories about all those early Saints who gathered here. We want to do our own part to build Zion."

"Well . . . I know what you mean." Bishop Harrison let his big head incline just a little to one side. He took his time before he added, "But we don't really gather here anymore. We try hard to work with the other churches—just make sure we do some good in the community."

Jeff had the feeling that some members must move there with the idea they were going to rebuild old Nauvoo. The bishop seemed a little wary of that. "I know what you mean," Jeff said. "But you have to admit, Church work these days seems rather . . . ordinary. I sort of wish we were fired up with the old zeal. The word had to be spread across the whole world, and there were only a few thousand people to do it. That was pretty intense stuff."

The bishop was smiling now, his eyes rounding and his cheeks balling up. "I guess it was. But we have enough challenges of our own. The young folks in the Church are growing up with more temptations than the pioneers ever thought of."

Jeff was nodding, but it was Abby who responded. "We have some personal challenges, Bishop," she said. "We're worried about Jeff finding a job in this economy. And we're expecting a baby."

He nodded, and Jeff heard some tenderness when he asked, "How are you feeling, Sister Lewis?"

"Well . . . I'm doing my best. But I've been sick, and the heat has been hard for me."

"I remember how hard that was for my wife when the summer heat came on. Let us know if we can help you." He looked back at Jeff. "We do try to look out for each other here. I guess that's what the gospel has always been about."

"You don't have to worry about me," Abby said. She smiled. "I'm not the first woman to have a baby."

"I know. But it probably seems like it sometimes." Bishop Harrison hesitated for a moment. "Are you all right financially for now? You have food, don't you?"

"Oh, sure," Jeff said. "Our parents would never let us starve.

Or maybe they would let *us* starve—just not the grandchild we're constructing for them. But we want to manage on our own, and I'm sure we can."

"I guess you have a college degree?"

"Yes. We both do."

"I've worked in design before," Abby said. "Interior décor and that sort of thing."

Bishop Harrison looked a little confused.

"Actually, I worked in a carpet store. I helped people figure out what couch would go with what rug."

He laughed. "Well, once again, we have a little furniture store here. But you'd probably have to look outside Nauvoo, in the larger towns. Bigger stores might hire someone like that. The truth is, though, no one's doing a lot of hiring at the moment."

"We don't want her to work right now anyway," Jeff said. "We had a little scare right after we got here. We thought she was losing the baby. The doctor told us she needs to get plenty of rest."

"But I'm fine now," Abby said, "and I might have to work, if a job doesn't come along for Jeff right away." She was looking at the bishop, not at Jeff. This had been an ongoing discussion between Jeff and Abby, and not one that had gone very well.

"So, Jeff, I guess you're sending out resumés and all that sort of thing."

"Yeah, I am. I had given some thought to going back to grad school. But this just isn't the right time for that."

"You mean, in computers or . . . what?"

"That's one option. I've also given some thought to history— you know, becoming a history professor. I think I would like that, but I need to start bringing in a decent salary, with a family on the way. So I've put that on the back burner."

The bishop nodded. "I'll tell you something I just started to realize," he said. "Life goes by fast. It seems like you're twenty and the next day you're forty-five."

"I guess that's right. I can't wait *too* long if I'm ever going to do it."

"Well . . . yes. But that wasn't what I was thinking. There comes a time, as long as you've paid your bills and raised a family, and as long as you've served in the Church and honored your commitments to the Lord, when the rest of it doesn't matter as much as you think it's going to." He leaned back in his chair. "The fact is, work is work, pretty much, and some people end up with more *stuff* than others, but when you stand before the Lord, it all won't matter. He'll want to know what kind of person you've been."

Jeff knew that. And it was good for him to be reminded. But life didn't look short to him, no matter how often he was told that by people the bishop's age—and his father's. Sometimes a week could be a long time when he was doing things he really didn't want to do.

"Well, listen," the bishop said, "let me tell you what I had in mind. I want to call the two of you to teach a Sunday School class together. It would be the older teenagers. The way we have it divided, the kids would all be fifteen to seventeen. Even if you're just here a short time, I want our young people to get to know a couple like you. You're young and smart, and you're committed to the gospel. That's what I thought about you when I met you last week, and I feel all the more that way after talking to you."

"We'd love to do it," Jeff said. "Wouldn't we, Abby?"

But Abby looked at the bishop. "I've only been in the Church about three years. I don't know whether I could answer some of the questions that kids that age have."

"Who can? But you two probably have a better chance than most of us."

"I'll let Jeff be the theologian," she said. "I'll just tell them to pray and love the Lord."

The bishop nodded. "You'll be wonderful. We'll present your names next week, but we'd like you to teach that day, too, if you could. We've been substituting that class while we look for a teacher."

"I'm excited," Jeff said. He took hold of Abby's hand and looked at her. He could see that she was pleased too, but he worried about her. She looked so pale, and she was losing weight, not gaining. Her gynecologist had told her she needed to rest and to eat small meals, more often—but that wasn't easy with so much of what she ate coming back up every day.

• • •

On Monday evening Jeff and Abby drove to the outdoor stage in the historic area, just west of the LDS church. They had been hearing about a show called "Sunset by the Mississippi," and they wanted to see it. Jeff had suggested that they wait until cooler weather, or until Abby's morning sickness was past, but Abby was feeling a little better—after being very sick earlier in the day—and she wanted to get out of the house.

They had seen the Nauvoo Pageant right after they had arrived. It had been a grand, impressive production, and they were curious now to see what the other show was all about. What surprised them was to see that most of the performers were the older couples and sisters they had been seeing in the historic sites. Many of them appeared to be in their seventies, and they were out there in the early evening heat, singing and dancing—and sweating—in their period costumes. There was also a group of younger, college-aged performers who brought some polish to the show. Abby and Jeff enjoyed the old-fashioned songs, the jigs, the silly humor. There was a kind of professional quality about the whole thing, with good lighting and sound, but the older missionaries clearly weren't experienced performers, and that was part of what made things fun. Jeff kept hooting and cheering, and Abby would say, "That's the brother we met in the blacksmith shop," or, "We met those two on Sunday. They were the guides in the Seventies Hall."

Jeff kept thinking about the things the bishop had said the day before. These people had kept their commitments, probably all their lives, and now they were serving missions when a lot of people were sitting in their rocking chairs or playing golf. They must have felt as though they were melting, with the men wearing vests and the women in their long dresses, but they gave the show their full effort. They never stopped smiling even if they had to mop their foreheads from time to time.

When the show was over, Jeff and Abby walked across the lawn to their car, which they had parked across from the church. From behind them, Jeff heard a man say, "I hope you two put on some bug spray. This lawn is a bad place for chiggers."

Jeff had already learned about chiggers the hard way. He had been scratching since the day he had walked into the state park and through the long grass. He turned around. "Don't worry, we've learned all about chiggers. We spray our shoes and socks every time we go out."

Jeff had seen the big man driving a horse-drawn wagon full of tourists, and he had watched him tonight, looking particularly self-conscious when he had to dance. His wife was a trim little woman in a fancy green calico dress. She was flushed, and her gray hair was sticking to her wet forehead. But she was smiling. "How many days have you been here?" she asked.

"Not days. Weeks," Jeff said. "We live here. We moved here two weeks ago."

"Almost three now," Abby said.

"That's wonderful," the sister said. "Don't you jist love it here? We've been here five months, and still, every time I look at the temple, I have to pinch myself to think we got sent here—of all the places in the world we could have gone." She laughed. "But it shor is hot."

"Where are you from?" Abby asked.

"Idaho. A little outside Rexburg," the man said. "I'm just an old spud farmer." He laughed. "We rented out our place and told the bishop to sign us up for a mission. We kinda hoped we'd get called to Nauvoo, but we figured it'd never happen."

"That doesn't sound much like retirement."

"You can say that again. We work all day, six days a week, and we do this show two nights a week. Then we do the other one— 'Rendezvous in Old Nauvoo'—two more nights."

"Twice a night with that one," his wife said. "We get finished, they empty out and refill up the Cultural Hall, and we go right back after it again."

"But you seem to have fun," Abby said.

"We do. But after, we jist fall into bed. I'm seventy-three, and Elder Caldwell's seventy-five." She laughed again, making a breathy sound. "We should know better, at our age, but I guess we don't."

"Do you call your husband 'Elder' all the time?"

"When we're around other people we do. President says it may be our only chance to be called 'Elder and Sister,' so we might as well enjoy it."

Jeff was amazed that people in their seventies would be so obedient to a mission president. "Well, that was a fun show," Jeff said. "We had a great time."

"We wouldn't do it, 'cept the pay is so good," Elder Caldwell said. He had a booming voice, and his laugh was twice the size of his voice.

Sister Caldwell said, "Some people ask us if we get paid. We tell 'em, shor we do, and it's good pay, too—it's outa this world."

It was an old joke to Jeff, but Abby liked it. "Well, we admire you," she said.

"Tell us your names," Sister Caldwell said. "I'm sure we'll see you again." Jeff could see how affectionately she was looking at Abby, as though she saw her as one of her own grandchildren.

"I'm Abby Lewis. This is Jeff. He's from Las Vegas, and I grew up in New Jersey. I just joined the Church a few years ago."

"Where do you live in Nauvoo?"

"On Warsaw Street."

"We live on the next street over, on Fullmer. What's your address?" When Abby told her, she said, "We're only about a block and a half away. And once the heat goes away—and this show ends for the season—we like to go out for walks. I'm sure we'll see you."

"Come and visit us," Abby said.

"We will. You're such a nice young couple—and so nice-looking."

"Hey, we were too," Elder Caldwell said. "Fifty years ago."

"No, you were a big awkward lug, and I wasn't half so pretty as Abby."

Elder Caldwell grinned. "That can't be right. 'Cause you were the prettiest girl in the world." He put his arm around her shoulders. "Still are. No offense to you, Abby."

Abby touched Sister Caldwell's forearm. "It's true," she said. "You're beautiful. Prettiest girl in the world."

"Oh, brother," Sister Caldwell said. "That's a stretch." But Jeff saw that her eyes had moistened a little.

Jeff felt Abby reach her arm around his waist, and he knew how much she was taking from this. But it was only after they had said good-bye and had gotten into their car—and gotten the air conditioner going—that she said what she was thinking. "Do you think you'll love me that much in fifty years?"

"Are you kidding me? Elder Caldwell does okay, but I'll love you *twice* that much. *Ten times.*"

"I'm serious. I think I'm driving you crazy, always getting in the way of what you want to do. I worry sometimes that you're falling out of love with me already."

"Hey, that Elder Caldwell has worked hard all his life. That's what a man is supposed to do. You have every right to expect me to do the same thing."

Jeff meant it, too. But as he drove past the temple, all lighted and glowing golden in the night, he thought again about the length of life. He wondered if Elder Caldwell had loved to farm. Maybe he had lived his dream. Maybe the guy would have fallen dead at thirty if he'd had to sit in an office all his life.

•   •   •

Later that week, on Thursday, Abby was lying down in the bedroom letting the cool air flow over her. She had not felt well all morning, but she had been trying to help Jeff in the basement. The foundation leaked when hard rain fell, and he had been reading about some material that he could use to patch the cracks. He had talked to some men in the neighborhood who said it wasn't worth doing—that the pressure from the groundwater would just break through again. But Brother Robertson was hoping to finish off the basement and had asked Jeff to look into sealing the walls. Ultimately, he would probably have to dig down outside and patch out there, too, but in the heat, he thought he would start inside.

Abby had been little help, in reality, but she had at least been cleaning up after him. Finally, though, the nausea had been too much for her. She had come upstairs and vomited, and then she had lain down—as Jeff had been telling her she ought to do. But then the doorbell rang. Wondering who could possibly be coming to see them, Abby got up, trudged to the living room, and opened the door.

"Sorry to bother you." It was the sister she and Jeff had met after "Sunset by the Mississippi." As Abby was trying to recall her name, she said, "Sister Caldwell. Remember? I wasn't sure I remembered your address, so I just thought I'd ring the doorbell and see if this was the right place."

"Come in. I'm glad to see you."

"Just for a minute. I just have an hour for lunch, and then I have to run back to the Lucy Mack Smith house. That's where I'm working today. Elder Caldwell is driving the wagon, so I won't see him all day."

That seemed to be some sort of explanation for why she had come by, but Abby wasn't sure she was making the connection. "Sit down for a minute. I was hoping you would visit us." Sister Caldwell sat in one of the recliners, near the door, and Abby took a seat on the couch across from her. She liked the woman, but she missed the cooler air in the bedroom. She hoped she wouldn't start to feel nauseated again.

"I just wanted to check on you. I kept thinking the other night, maybe you weren't doing so well."

"I have been a little sick."

"You're pregnant, aren't you?"

"Does it show?"

"Not in your tummy. Only in . . . other ways. "

Abby wasn't sure she understood that, but she was touched that Sister Caldwell was worried about her.

"I don't mean to be a busybody, but I've been a Relief Society president three different times in my life, and it's just what I do: worry about the sisters. Can I help you?"

"Not really. I just—"

"I was thinking, you may be stuck here alone when your husband is at work—and if you needed to shop, or something like that, I could maybe run you somewhere."

Abby laughed. "I don't think you have time in your schedule for that, Sister Caldwell."

"Not much. But it gets better in another month or so. Everyone says that things calm down in the middle of August when all the tourists head home."

Abby took a breath. Her head still seemed filled with fog. "Actually, Jeff is here most of the time," she said. "His job right now is to fix up this house for the people who own it. You can probably hear him down in the basement."

"I'm glad to know that. I thought I was hearing rats or something." She laughed. "I'm sorry, but I don't know whether I'd want your husband fixing up my house. He seems more like a schoolteacher than a carpenter."

Abby was actually interested that Sister Caldwell would see him that way. "Well, he's more of a technical person, but he lost his job, and he is good at building and repairing. His dad's an engineer, and Jeff has some of that in his genes, I guess."

"Is that where it comes from—from wearing jeans?"

"No. I meant—"

"I know. I'm just joking. I shouldn't say such foolish things until you get to know me. You'll think I'm some crazy old lady."

Abby smiled. "No. I'm sorry. I'm not quite all here today." What she was actually thinking was that Sister Caldwell was amazing.

She looked ten years younger than she really was, with surprisingly smooth skin.

"Usually the morning sickness isn't so bad after the first few months." Sister Caldwell's smile flashed. "Of course, that's when you get big as a barn, and you can't think of a way to arrange yourself so you can sleep at night."

"Sounds wonderful."

"I did it six times. Seven, really, but I lost one when I was a few months along." And then, without a transition, she added, "I'll bet you two are worried, with Jeff out of work."

"Sure. But he'll find something. This is a pretty nice situation for us for now—if he can get better air conditioning installed before I fall dead from heat stroke."

"It is hot in here. You can come over to my place for the afternoon if you want to. We do have central air conditioning—that's something I never did have at home."

"I'll be okay. Back in the bedroom it's cooler, and I'm going to lie down for a while."

"That's what you were doing when I got you up, isn't it? I need to get out of here."

"No, really. Stay as long as you can. It's so nice to get to know someone."

Sister Caldwell crossed the room and sat down next to Abby. She took hold of Abby's hand in both of hers. "I look at you kids and all I can think of is that time when we were first married."

"We've been married over a year now."

"Trust me. That's still 'first married.' You still have all kinds of things to figure out. It's not easy to blend two ways of thinking into one, and it takes a while to learn how to take care of each other. When we got married, the farm was so unpredictable. It was always a worry. Jack—Elder Caldwell—is a welder, too, and he used to work in town quite a few hours each week, and then he'd be working outside on the farm until after dark. Sometimes it seemed like there was nothing but work in our lives, and hardly enough money to keep us going."

"I guess everyone goes through some hard times along the way."

"Shor. But we always managed. Jack wasn't that active in the Church when he was younger, but he figured out what was really important—you know, when the boys got a little older and he knew he had to be an example. But over the years we just paid our tithing and trusted God. Everything worked out for us."

"And you have six children?"

"We *do* have six, but one is waiting for us on the other side. When our oldest son was seventeen, he rolled a tractor into a ditch. Elder Caldwell saw him go over, and he ran as hard as he could, but the tractor was on top of him and he was near dead. Jack got Larry out and got him into town, but he was all broken up, his organs and everything inside. He only lived about an hour."

"Oh, Sister Caldwell, I couldn't handle that."

"Don't say that. We do what we have to do in this life. Some of the missionaries like to say they couldn't do what the pioneers did—but what choice did those people have? When life forces us to find out what we're made of, we find out we're tougher than we think we are."

"I think I've had life too easy, Sister Caldwell. My parents gave me everything I wanted. Jeff's parents were pretty much the same way."

"It doesn't matter. Life has a way of testing everyone."

"Things are kind of frustrating right now. Everything is so up in the air. I don't know where we'll be or what we'll be doing in another year."

"Well . . . you'll work that out. God'll show you what you're supposed to do. But be good to each other. That's more important than anything else."

Abby nodded. She didn't know why she felt like crying, but she didn't speak for a time, and she held back her tears.

"You're so beautiful," Sister Caldwell was saying. "So young and so beautiful. And that boy of yours, he's got good genes—and not just for engineering. I'll bet he makes a pair of tight blue jeans look mighty nice." She laughed in a burst. "Oh, my, there I go again. I'm a missionary. I shouldn't say things like that. I'll learn that about the time I go home."

Abby was laughing.

"You go lay down now. But I'll stop by once in a while. I might do your dishes or something—or if I make up anything decent to eat, I'll bring something over. I never have learned to cook for two, and Jack hates leftovers. Not that he would ever say it." She stood up. "Give me a hug now and I'll get out of here. You need a mother. That's what you need. I'll try to be one, just a little. Or maybe a grandma."

"Thank you so much," Abby said, and she did hug Sister Caldwell. Then she went back to the bedroom. But she didn't lie down; she knelt down. "Help me to do this, Lord," she said. "Help me to take care of Jeff. I'm such a crybaby, and I'm sorry, but I didn't know everything would be quite so scary."

She stopped and thought for a time, and then she added, "I don't know what tests we'll have in life, but please help us to deal with them." She thought of Sister Caldwell, dealing with hard things but keeping her promises—and her sense of humor.

She ended her prayer, and then she lay down on her bed again. Pregnancy seemed enough of a test for now, and yet, most of the women in the history of the world had managed it. She had to stop feeling sorry for herself.

CHAPTER 16

A week had passed since Liz had come to visit Will. He was not as busy as he had been all summer, and the sun was setting earlier now. That meant that Will quit his work earlier than he had during the harvest and the hay cutting, and he spent his evenings reading the Book of Mormon. He felt the change that his reading was bringing about in him. He knew he needed to find a deeper faith, a deeper concern for his fellow man. There in his room, alone, he began to see how completely he had devoted his thoughts to his own happiness. He had come to love the Sermon on the Mount in the past few months, and now, the Book of Mormon was confirming his feelings about Christ's teachings.

What he found himself believing, without really analyzing his reaction, was that the book actually was an ancient record. It was an account no one—especially not an uneducated boy—could have faked. It was a complicated book with hundreds of names and a history of a people that covered a thousand years. And it felt real. But logic was one thing and faith was another. He still found it difficult to imagine that God would actually appear in the real world. Will had been taught all his life that God was a spirit, but this God could show up in the form of a man, could talk to a fourteen-year-old lad.

Still, there it was. He believed the words he read in the Book of Mormon—and that belief was affecting him. One evening when Will was taking supper with the Crawfords, Mrs. Crawford asked, "What's happened to you lately, Will? You seem changed."

"Changed in what way?" he asked.

"You seem quieter—as though you have something on your mind."

"During the harvest I had lots to worry about, with—"

"No. It's just the opposite of worry. You seem more peaceful."

"I've noticed that too," Mr. Crawford said. He was sitting at the head of the table, with Will around the corner on his left and Mrs. Crawford to the right. A small tablecloth had been laid out for them, but the rest of the long, mahogany table was bare. The Crawfords had a cook who had prepared a fancy meal of guinea fowl, Yorkshire pudding with gravy, roast potatoes, and claret wine. Behind Mr. Crawford, near the door, stood a footman, ready to meet the Crawfords' wishes. Will sometimes wondered that he could be invited into such a world. He had gone to his quarters with manure on his boots and the smell of his horse on his clothes, and he had had to hurry to wash and change. Mr. Crawford had been purchasing clothing for Will since the day he had arrived: a finer suit than he had ever owned, extra trousers, better boots. Will liked all of it, but it worried him a little that he did like it. He was being placed above the men he worked with, and that was something he had always opposed.

"I've had more time to read the scriptures lately," Will said. "I think that's made a difference." He didn't want to mention the Book of Mormon. He had heard the Crawfords speak skeptically of the

Mormon missionaries who were making so many converts in the area.

"What a lovely thing to hear," Mrs. Crawford said. "So many young men your age would be spending their time, now that the harvest is over, drinking at a local pub."

"I never have been much of a drinker. My father taught me that."

"He's one of these United Brethren people, I think you told me," Mr. Crawford said. "I've never quite understood what it is they believe that's different from the Church of England's teachings."

"They seek truth. That's all. They aren't happy with what they hear from the clergy—in any of the churches."

"Is that also your position?"

"I've been skeptical of religion, to tell the truth. But I certainly believe in seeking truth."

"Doctrinal disputes don't interest me," Mr. Crawford said. "I only believe in doing what's right."

"I can't disagree with that." But Will felt less than honest in saying that, so he added, "Most of the United Brethren are now joining The Church of Jesus Christ of Latter-day Saints. I've become interested in doing that myself."

"You mean the Mormons?"

"Some people call them that."

It was Mrs. Crawford who looked shocked. "Do you know about them?" she asked. "They worship some lunatic in America. He's building up his church among the poor people here—and no doubt plans to fleece them for all he can get."

"People may say that, but I don't believe it's true. The preachers in their church accept no pay for their service. No one's getting rich. If that's happening anywhere, it's in our English churches."

"I would be very careful," Mr. Crawford said, in a more

controlled voice than his wife had used. "It's one thing to make such claims, and it's another to find out what's really going on. Anyone who puts himself above others like this Smith—claiming he's a prophet—I would keep a close eye on."

"It's just the opposite, sir. He works alongside others." Will took a bite of his potatoes. He decided he had probably said enough. But he was a little disappointed in himself. He felt he had to make a better defense—if he could do so without offending. "When I said I had been reading the scriptures, I meant the Book of Mormon. Do you know about it?"

"Only what we've heard," Mrs. Crawford said. "It's a jumble of madness, from what Reverend Mason tells us."

"I don't find that true at all. You should read it, at least a little."

"No, thank you. And I think you should put it aside and return to your Bible."

Will looked back at her—looked directly into her eyes. "Mrs. Crawford, I believe it's a true record. I don't know how Joseph Smith could have translated it, except by the power of God."

She stared back at him, obviously shocked. "Will, that's utter nonsense. You must know that. Don't let these people lead you into such foolishness."

There was a hardness in her words that Will hadn't expected. To Will, the Crawfords embodied the spirit of Christ's teachings. They were the good Samaritans who had taken him in and looked after him. But now their response seemed cold and harsh. He didn't know what that was going to mean for him in the future. He did describe the Book of Mormon for them, and he told them that it taught the same gospel found in the Bible. Mrs. Crawford softened a little at those words, but the rest of the dinner felt awkward, as though everyone was straining to be polite.

But something had changed in Will. After dinner, when he

returned to his room in the barn, he couldn't stop thinking about the things he'd said. He had borne testimony of the Book of Mormon. Of Joseph Smith. And he had felt good about it.

Will continued to read the Book of Mormon. He met again with Wilford Woodruff—the fourth time in two weeks—and after that fourth meeting, he told Brother Woodruff that he was ready to be baptized. He actually wanted to meet a few more times and have more time to learn, but Woodruff said he was leaving soon, taking his mission northward, back to the potteries and then on to London again. But Will knew he wanted to be baptized, and he wanted Brother Woodruff to be the man to do it. So there was no good reason to wait.

Elder Woodruff invited Will to meet at the Severn River for the baptism on Sunday afternoon. Will thought it better that he not say anything to the Crawfords, and yet he wondered why he should concern himself about that. He didn't think they would send him away, but even if they were to do that, shouldn't he be willing to face any persecution that might come? The problem was, even though Will felt confidence in his newfound faith at times, he still caught doubts running through his mind. He had been skeptical of religion for too long not to wonder whether everything he had been told would turn out to be true. He trusted Brother Woodruff, but he still wondered what Nauvoo was really like and whether Joseph Smith was quite the man he was purported to be. Will was ready to make this commitment, based on things he had heard and the peace he felt, but in the back of his mind was a nagging feeling that he might end up disappointed—or worse, that his skeptical side would win out in the end and he wouldn't be able to cling to the faith he was now feeling.

When Will read the Book of Mormon each night, he felt reassured, but as he worked each day, his doubts and worries always came back to him. Still, when Sunday came, he walked to the Severn—a walk of a couple miles—and all along the way, he told himself that he was about to take a great step forward. He had been thinking of his sins, the things he needed to repent of, and he told himself he would put them all behind him and embark on a better life. He hadn't been one to do much evil. He didn't curse much at all, and he had never gone to prostitutes the way most of the navvies had done. But he had felt the temptation to go, and he knew his thoughts were sometimes unclean. He wanted now to live a purer life. Above all, he wanted to be more Christlike in the way he treated people. He thought of his anger in the past, his hatred of the upper classes, even Squire Riddle. He thought of his impatience with his brothers and sisters and his disobedience toward his father.

Will had had no way to get a quick message to his family, but when he reached the river, he was taken by surprise. There, waiting, were his parents and all his brothers and sisters—all dressed in their Sunday clothes. They watched him approach, all smiling and waving, and Edgar and Solomon, unable to wait, ran to him. Edgar was almost nine now, and Solomon had just turned six. Will knelt and grasped them, each with one arm, and he held them tight. "My goodness, lads, did you walk all this way?"

"Aye," Solomon said. "An' it's a long road. We walked all day."

"No, Solomon. Only part of the day," Edgar said.

"Well, it's so good to see you," Will said. "Edgar, you were baptized yourself not long ago, and now it's my turn."

"You must be good now, Will. I knocked Solomon down an' made 'im cry—not to hurt 'im but on'y runnin' through the barn too wild—an' Dad told me that was evil, doin' like that."

"I better not run through the barn, then," Will said, and the boys laughed.

They all walked on to the others, and everyone took turns

embracing Will. "I'm so pleased you made this choice, Will," Nettie said. "Now we're all together again. Or at least it feels that way to me."

"How did you know I was being baptized?"

"Brother Woodruff came through Ledbury this week. He sent word through Brother Watkins. We all cried, I think—most of us, anyway. Maybe not the little boys."

Will liked to think of that, all his family so pleased. Sarah and Daniel were grown up now, and he wanted them to think well of him. He knew he hadn't always been the brother to them that he might have been.

Morgan reached for Will's hand, but Will gave him his left hand, knowing what his dad's firm grip would do to the injured one. "'Tis what we ha' prayed for—this day. I feel angels wi' us—all the host of heaven singin' songs of gladness. Me own father and mother must be here, hoverin' about, pleased in their hearts that we've found the truth, af'er seekin' it so long."

It was the very kind of talk that made Will nervous. Will had no idea whether there were angels flying about, raising their glad voices, but he didn't like to hear his father make such claims. Wilford Woodruff had a little of that in him too, talking often of miracles and dreams and spiritual manifestations, but when he taught the principles of the gospel, he made the doctrines plain and sensible. It was the way Will liked to think of his baptism: the next sensible step, now that he had accepted the teachings he had heard.

Brother Woodruff strode across the grass, holding out his hand, and then remembering and wrapping his arm around Will's shoulders instead. "What a glorious day," he said. "Morgan, I wasn't sure that Will would come to this point. He's a questioner. But that's how he should be. I questioned mightily myself when I first heard the truth. And there's one thing I know. Truth can always hold up to any question if it's asked in sincerity and with an open heart."

He and Morgan told one another how true that was, seemed to take great joy in their own propensities to study things out, but Will wasn't sure that either of them experienced the kind of doubts he could raise. In fact, he was feeling a little out of place now, hearing them and others exult in the spirit they were feeling. Will was not sure what it meant to "feel the spirit." He felt a wonderful calm at times, and he felt satisfied with an explanation, but he didn't know that his bosom had ever burned, as Brother Woodruff liked to say.

It was Will's mother who said the right thing to him. "A voice told you to come home. And this is why. It was to meet Brother Woodruff and accept the gospel."

Will took hold of his mother's hand. "I believe that's true," he said, and then he stepped back and looked around at the valley. The sun was moving toward the western horizon, the angling light adding a sheen to the rich, green hills. He thought how much he had missed these hills, these valleys, when he had been away in Manchester, and he felt pleased that he could make his mother so happy. He looked at the sheep grazing on the hillside, the patchwork of fields divided by hedgerows, the lushness of all the growth. He had come home in every sense, and it felt right.

But he was also looking at the people who had gathered by the river. "Was Liz at services this morning?" he asked. "Did she hear that I was being baptized?"

"Yes, she did. I saw tears on her cheeks. And her father was pleased too. He told me he was. But when I asked Liz if she would come with us, she told me that she couldn't, that her father would not approve."

Will wondered what that meant. Was he still not good enough for the man?

Wilford Woodruff stood before the group and called for their attention. He gave one of his brief accounts of the progress of the Church, recounting his recent experiences in the branches of the Malvern Hills. "I have enjoyed coming back after my sojourn in London, but I must say, the opposition has become more forceful here. You may have heard, on Wednesday night at prayer meeting in Dymock, we were attacked by a mob, led by a local minister. These madmen threw rocks at the house, broke out the windows, and unleashed venomous accusations against us. But we carried on, and we won't let them stop the noble work we're doing. The elect of God are here in great numbers, and they hear the shepherd's voice when He beckons them. It's only to be expected that Satan and his minions will try every means possible to stop us. But you who have chosen to be baptized today are being gathered into the fold, and no matter the hostile forces that assail us, truth shall prevail. Some of you, I have no doubt, will gather to Zion, and there you will help to build up the kingdom of God."

Will loved more than anything to imagine himself doing that.

"I will be leaving you again before this week is over. I'm sorry to go, but there is much work to be done in various places, and I must meet in conference with my brothers, the other apostles. I promise to return before I leave England, but the day will come when you will be called on to carry the work forward yourself. There are more than four thousand members of the Church on this island now, and many more will join you. I've established more than forty branches of the Church this year, and seen more than fifty ministers enter the waters of baptism. So come to Nauvoo if you can, but if you cannot, know that the work is moving forward here, and you are part of this great outpouring of the spirit here in the latter days. I've met no better people anywhere than you good people here in the Malvern Hills."

Will saw the tears in Apostle Woodruff's eyes. The leader re-moved his frock coat and waistcoat, and then his boots, and he walked into the water. It was a cool day, and Will expected a cold walk home, wet from head to foot. But Brother Woodruff had been performing baptisms over and over for months, and he didn't seem at all concerned about getting wet himself.

He called out to the first candidate for baptism—a petite woman in a cotton dress. She took off her bonnet and shawl and handed them to her husband, and then she walked carefully into the water. Will saw her wince as her foot touched the cold. There was a shallow area, near the bank, but Brother Woodruff was standing in deeper water, almost up to his chest. The woman took his hand and stepped toward him but wobbled before she got her feet set on the muddy incline. Brother Woodruff took hold of her wrist and she grasped his, and then he raised his right hand and pronounced the baptismal prayer. He lowered her backward until her entire body was under the murky water. She came up breathless, looking star-tled, but then she pushed her dark hair back and smiled before she anxiously climbed back to the bank. One of the sisters wrapped her in a blanket, and then her husband stepped into the water.

Will was the last of five to be baptized. When Brother Woodruff called his name, Will had already taken off his outer coats and was standing in his shirtsleeves. He handed the coats to his father and stood on one foot and then the other to pull off his boots. He looked into Brother Woodruff's eyes as he took hold of the man's hand. He could see that the apostle's eyes were full of excitement, but Will also saw his love for Will—something he had noticed before.

Will slipped in the mud and had to grab Brother Woodruff's shoulder to keep from sliding much deeper into the water. "Get your feet under you," Brother Woodruff said. "This is not a baptis-mal site I plan to use again."

For a moment Will thought they both might go under, and he laughed a little, but now the cold was making its way through his clothes. He wondered how Brother Woodruff could stay in the water so long—and do this so often.

All this was not what Will had planned to be thinking about. He had promised himself that he would cast away his sins at this moment and invite a great change into his heart. What he now worried about was getting back up to the bank without falling, or without carrying the apostle with him.

But then Brother Woodruff took hold of his wrist and placed the flat of his hand on Will's back. Will felt himself calm. "When I take you into the water, bend your knees, so you go down easily."

Will nodded.

Brother Woodruff took a long breath, one that Will could hear. Will glanced to see that the apostle's eyes had gone shut, that he was summoning the spirit, taking this ordinance seriously, no matter how precariously they were perched in mud and no matter how cold the water. His hand left Will's back, and as it did, Will shut his own eyes, took his own deep breath.

"William Lewis," Brother Woodruff said, "having been commissioned of Jesus Christ, I baptize you in the name of the Father, and of the Son, and of the Holy Ghost. Amen."

Commissioned of Jesus Christ. The words seemed to work their way through Will's brain and then his body, thrilling him. He bent his knees and leaned backwards, letting Brother Woodruff take him under. The water rushed around him, the sound filling his ears and the cold striking his head and face. There was a moment of utter silence, and then he was already coming up, with the water rushing in his ears again. He felt his feet slip a little, and some panic ran through him until he caught his balance and made a quick step up, with Brother Woodruff's help. For a moment he felt only the urgency to get out of the water, to stand on firm ground again. The cold had reached him and now he wanted that blanket his father was holding.

His trousers sloshed as he stumbled to the grassy bank, and water ran down his face. He wiped his eyes, pushed his hair back, and laughed a little at the awkward procedure. But then he looked back at Brother Woodruff. He reached out a hand to him to help him out of the water. And what he saw was that his look hadn't changed. The man was still moved by the experience, after baptizing hundreds over the last few months. His eyes were still full of joy and love.

Will felt something intense—not burning, but cleansing. He felt an emotion that seemed to be in his body more than his mind. It was like the swelling of his own breath in his chest. He let the breath flow out, and then he drew in more air, and something seemed to come with it: the satisfied calm he associated with reading the Book of Mormon. He felt good. He felt clean. He felt the rightness of what he had chosen to do.

Brother Woodruff embraced him, their wet shirts pressed between them. "You've done the right thing," he said.

"I know I have, Brother Woodruff."

And now Will's family was around him again, each wanting to embrace him, congratulate him, and wish him well.

Will walked back to the Crawford farm. He was warmed by his dry coats and by the brisk walk. But he was also warmed from inside out. He thought he had never been so confident that he had chosen right—and such assurance was not something he was accustomed to.

When he reached the farm, he knew for certain what he had to do. He walked to the back door of the manor house and knocked. Mr. Simmons, the butler, opened the door. "Are the Crawfords at dinner?" Will asked.

"No. Dinner is not yet served," Mr. Simmons said.

"Would you ask them whether I could speak with them for just a minute or two? I'm a little wet. I don't know whether I should enter their parlor."

"Has it rained?"

"No. It was . . . something else."

Mr. Simmons left but came back quickly. "Mr. Crawford wants you in the parlor. I told him you were wet, and he was not concerned. My own suggestion is that you not sit down."

"I won't."

Mr. Simmons led him through the kitchen and up a set of stairs, then down a hall to the parlor. Mr. and Mrs. Crawford were sitting on opposite sides of the fireplace, Mr. Crawford reading a book and Mrs. Crawford doing needlework. They both looked up, and both appeared curious, probably because of the mention from Mr. Simmons that Will was wet.

Will's confidence was waning a little. He was more frightened than he had expected to be when he had imagined this scene during his walk home. "There was something I thought I should tell you," he said.

Mr. Crawford nodded. "Yes?"

"Are you quite all right?" Mrs. Crawford asked, and she did look concerned.

"Yes. Never better. But I wanted you to know that, after much thought and prayer, I decided to be baptized today—baptized by Mr. Woodruff, from the Mormons."

"You mean you've never been baptized?" Mr. Crawford asked.

"Yes. As a baby. But not by one having authority." There, he had said it.

The Crawfords looked disappointed more than upset. They were probably not surprised. Mr. Crawford finally said, "I thought you were going to think this over for a time."

"I've thought of little else lately, and I've asked God over and over. I know now that I've done the right thing. My heart's been changed, Mr. Crawford. I've taken on the name of Jesus Christ, and I want to be true to that all my life."

Mr. Crawford nodded. Will thought he looked impressed by Will's words. And Mrs. Crawford appeared moved by Will's profession. But no one spoke for a long time.

Finally, Mr. Crawford said, "Sit down, Will. We had something we wanted to talk to you about as well. Maybe this is a good time for it."

"I shouldn't sit down. My trousers are still damp."

"It doesn't matter," Mrs. Crawford said, and her voice sounded almost tender.

Mr. Crawford got up and picked up a fancy wooden chair, which he brought closer to the fire. He motioned for Will to sit there. "That's a chair you can't harm with a little moisture," he said.

Will did sit down.

"I have to say, I was hoping you would choose not to join with this religion. But we have known from the beginning that you've separated yourself from the Church of England, and we don't concern ourselves much about that. As I told you before, I care more about how a man behaves than about his choice of religion."

Will felt relieved. "I wish you would learn just a bit more about the Mormons—so you won't think me strange to make such a choice."

"Well, certainly. I could read something, if you have some material to give me. But Will, this is my one concern—that you not try to convince me or Mrs. Crawford of your beliefs. That would only create awkwardness between us."

"All right. I understand that." Mrs. Crawford nodded to him, as if to reassure him that she had accepted his decision.

"Mrs. Crawford and I have discussed another matter at some length."

Will waited.

"As you know, Smithers was not much help during the harvest. He's been ill off and on lately with chills and fever. I believe he has contracted an ague, and he may never have his full strength again. He's not so old as all that, but he certainly is slowing down. It might be time for him to retire, and we are ready to make certain he is comfortable in his retirement."

Will wondered what was coming next. However kindly Mr. Crawford was sounding, Will doubted that he had been on the farm long enough to take over, and he was still mulling over Mr. Crawford's dissatisfaction with his interest in Mormonism. Maybe the man was seeking a gentle way to send him away. The thought was frightening. Will didn't want all his newfound hope to be dashed on the day of his baptism.

"You've done a wonderful job for us. You have directed all the workers with skill, even though you're younger than the majority of them."

Will was sure what coming next: the word *but.*

"Normally, we wouldn't wish to hire someone so young, but your experience and skill far outweigh your lack of years. We would like you to accept our offer to serve as our bailiff. We won't offer you quite as much salary as Smithers was receiving, but we think it right to treble what you're earning now, and in another year, offer you another substantial raise."

Will couldn't speak.

"How does that sound to you?"

"It's wonderful, Mr. Crawford—more than I ever could have imagined."

"Well, then, I'll have my solicitor draw up a contract, and we can both sign it sometime this week."

Suddenly Will saw the trap. "What would be the term of the contract?"

"You mean, how many years?"

"Yes."

"I think, for now, it might be best to proceed only one year at a time."

Will nodded.

"So that's all right with you?" Mr. Crawford asked.

"Yes. But there is something else I need to tell you."

"What now? You haven't joined a circus besides, have you?"

Will laughed, and he glanced at Mrs. Crawford, who was clearly wondering what else Will might have to reveal. His fear returned. He didn't know what the Crawfords would think of him. "I'm considering, perhaps in a year or two, that I might save up my money and immigrate to America."

"To this city that your Joseph Smith is establishing?"

"Yes."

Mr. Crawford let his breath seep out. Clearly, he didn't like this. "Well, I suppose that is up to you. I would only suggest that you think, once again, very carefully before you head off to the wilds of America. Isn't this city out in the West, on the Mississippi River?"

"Yes. But I hope to marry before too many more years go by, and in America I could own land."

"You could starve on a little farm, you know. What I'm offering you is security and a good living—something to raise a family with. Let me remind you that a few months ago we picked you up out of the mud, almost dead. You didn't have work, and you didn't have prospects."

"I know. I owe everything to you. And I may change my mind

about emigrating. I would surely be happy to sign a contract for a year."

"Well, then, done and done. But I hope you'll give me a year to talk you out of this wild goose chase to America."

"And I'll try too," Mrs. Crawford said. "I want you to marry and raise your children here—where I can pretend to be their grandmother. That's half the reason I wanted Mr. Crawford to hire you."

Will loved this woman—loved both the Crawfords. He hated to think of disappointing them. But for now, what was swelling in his chest was gratitude. God was opening all the doors that had been closed to him.

CHAPTER 17

Will set his men to work on Monday, and then, early in the afternoon, he rode his horse to Ledbury. He knocked on the downstairs door, and when Sally appeared, he asked to see "Miss Elizabeth Duncan."

Sally smiled at him. "I'll ask if she can make time for a visitor," she said. "I 'spect she can."

Sally took a little longer than he expected, and when she returned, she led Will upstairs to an empty parlor. Liz soon appeared, however, looking bright but seeming a little hesitant. She stayed back, didn't approach him. She was wearing a dress he hadn't seen before, pale green like her eyes, and fitted to her slender shape. He thought that maybe she had changed her clothes quickly, that she knew how beautiful she looked. "So nice of you to call, Mr. Lewis. Were you merely in the neighborhood?"

Will smiled at her playfulness, but he made no attempt to be witty. He was too nervous for that. He had put on his better suit of clothes, not the ones he had gotten wet and muddy the day before, and his boots were shined, but he still wondered whether he smelled too much of the farm. "Liz, I was baptized yesterday. I think you heard that."

"I did," she said, and she seemed to adjust to his serious tone of voice. "I'm very happy for you, Will." They were standing apart, an expanse of carpet between them. He wasn't sure what to do about that. She motioned toward a plush chair facing the fireplace. "Sit down." She chose a chair next to his, but she had avoided the sofa, where he might have sat closer to her. Maybe she was about to disappoint him.

"I understand your father didn't want you to attend my baptism."

"That's true. He didn't. But he only said I shouldn't walk so far on such a cool day."

Will wasn't sure how to take that. Why didn't Liz just tell him what she was thinking—or what attitude her father was taking? "Something else has changed," Will said.

"What would that be?"

"Mr. Crawford has hired me to manage his farm. I'm his bailiff now, and he raised my salary threefold."

He saw her react—saw her head come up, her eyes sharpen. "Threefold?"

"Aye. Starting this week."

"That will make a big difference," she said, the words spilling like a gasp. But then she added, "To my father, I mean."

"And to you?"

"It doesn't hurt," she admitted, and she laughed at herself. Then they were left silent, both smiling, taking one another in. Will knew it was time to do something, but he didn't know how to proceed. Finally, Liz said, "Was there something you wanted to ask me?" And her eyes already said, *Yes, Will. Yes.*

"Uh . . . should I talk to your father first . . . or. . . ."

"I think you should speak with me before you worry about my father."

"All right." But still he hesitated.

"It's a simple question."

"I know. I just . . ." It occurred to him that some men knelt at such a moment, but he wasn't sure whether Liz would laugh at him. All the same, he slipped off the chair and landed on one knee. "Will you marry me, Liz?"

"Yes, I will." She was still smiling, seeming to enjoy Will's awkwardness.

"What about your father?"

"I doubt that *he* will marry you, if that's what you mean."

"No. I mean—"

"I'd suggest you come back on Sunday and talk to him. But I'll talk to him first."

"Does he still think I'm not good enough for you?"

"Probably. But it doesn't matter. We'll do as we please."

"All right . . . so I guess I'll come by on Sunday, after church."

"Yes, Will. That's what I said."

"So what do we do now?"

"We kiss, Will. Don't you know anything?"

• • •

On the following Sunday Will was standing in the Duncans' parlor again. Thomas Kington had attended church services that morning and had confirmed Will as a member of the Church. Will had received the gift of the Holy Ghost, had felt the same assurance that he had at the baptism, and he was feeling strong now. He told himself he would move forward, set his hand to the plow and not look back. The world was being opened to him, and God was in everything that was happening. Still, he had to face Brother Duncan, and the man had opposed him for years.

"Sit down," Brother Duncan said. "What was it you wanted to talk to me about?"

But of course, he knew. Will took it as a positive sign that the man was treating him with civility. "Well, sir, I think you know that I've been appointed as bailiff for Squire Crawford on his estate near Colwall Stone. I have a respectable income now, and a position of some . . . prominence."

"Yes. I've heard all this."

Brother Duncan was facing Will, sitting in an elegant red velvet chair with ornately carved armrests. He was sitting very straight and he wasn't smiling. Maybe the word *prominence* had been a bad choice. Will didn't want to sound puffed up and impressed with himself. "What matters more to me right now, however, is that I've embraced the gospel of Jesus Christ, the same as you, and the same as Elizabeth. I've told Squire Crawford that I will work for him for a year—maybe longer—but my desire is to save enough money to immigrate to Nauvoo, in America. My salary will be more than adequate, and I believe I can accumulate sufficient money to buy land when I arrive there."

"So you plan to farm again?"

"I won't be a tenant farmer. I can own my own farm. And there are other opportunities in America, where a man is not tied to a class and held down all his life."

"It seems to me you have managed to rise in station here. Perhaps emigration will only condemn you to a hard life of labor."

It was what Squire Crawford had said, and it might be right, but Will dreamed of owning land, increasing his holdings, perhaps starting a business. All that was possible in America. But he didn't want to sound naïve, so he only said, "I have risen here, but it was mostly my good fortune to meet the Crawfords. I still think I can make a better life in America—and I want to live among the Saints."

"I understand. Mrs. Duncan thinks we should do the same, and perhaps we will. But if I do, it will be more out of religious conviction than the thought that I'll be better off. For you it's another matter. You're only just starting out in life, and you must look to your security."

So that was the fear. Not Will's security, of course, but Liz's. "Sir, as I'm certain you know, I'm here to ask for Liz's hand in marriage. But we would not emigrate unless I felt confident that I could provide for her in America."

"That's easy to say, Will, but difficult to gauge. Emigrating is a gamble, especially now that you have a reasonably comfortable prospect here."

"Would you prefer that I plan to remain in England?"

Brother Duncan had been leaning forward in his chair just a little, but he settled back now. He gazed toward Will for a long time. He was a large man, not overly heavy, but tall and strong. He looked authoritative. Will could see that his fingernails were cared for, that his shirt and collar were crisp, that his hair had been cut by a skilled barber. He was everything Will was not, and surely the man could see Will's own ragged fingernails, his freshly cleaned but rugged boots, his sun-browned face. The man couldn't possibly be pleased by any of that. He was apparently asking himself how to answer, and Will felt a tightness in his chest that he had hoped he would never have to feel again. He planned to marry Liz no matter what this man said, but everything was going to be more difficult without permission.

"I can't tell you to stay here, Will," Brother Duncan finally said. "And I want you to understand that I think very well of you. You're a fine young man. What I wish is that Elizabeth would choose someone who could provide for her much better than you ever will. I have introduced her to young men of considerable means—men who would have given her the life she has become accustomed to. In the end, you are still telling me that she will be a farmer's wife— that she will have to learn household skills. What I fear is that she will gradually be worn down by long workdays, caring for children, cooking and cleaning . . . and all the rest."

"I honestly believe I can—"

"Will, she wants you and will have no one else." His eyes went shut, and he sat for a moment, as if to control his emotions. "I ought to force her to think otherwise, but it simply isn't in me to do so. I feel as though I'm condemning her by accepting your offer, but I know how stubborn she is, and I no longer plan to stand in her way."

"Brother Duncan, I promise you that I will give her a good life. I will provide for her, and—"

"Will she have a pianoforte?" He leaned forward in his chair again, stared into Will's eyes. "Will she read by the fire on a winter evening? Will she have servants? Will she have the life her mother has had?"

"She'll have a fine home in time, and I will see to it that she does not wear herself down with work."

Brother Duncan pointed his finger at Will. "Don't promise what you cannot produce. I grant you my permission, but don't expect me to be happy about it. In a few years, when she understands what her choice has meant, I only hope she never comes to hate you for what you'll be taking from her."

Will had never thought of things this way and he didn't want to now, but he did wonder how difficult life might be at first—until he could provide for Liz the way he wanted to. Maybe he was selfish to want her for himself.

"Will, I do grant you my blessing. I hope the best for you. Every father worries about his daughters when this choice comes along. I know that Elizabeth loves you. And I know that my own wife started out with far less than I was able to give her in time. I only ask you to treat her as the prize she is and to give her the best life you possibly can."

"I will, sir. I promise you that."

"All right. Talk to her, then. I shall leave and send her to you."

He stood, and Will stood with him. Will chose to offer his right hand, that seeming important at the moment, but his lack of grip seemed to symbolize the awkwardness of the moment. "Thank you," he said. There were few men who could make Will feel small, but he felt that way now. Brother Duncan walked out and shut the door quietly. Will remained standing, wondering. But when Liz entered the room, she was smiling, looking pleased—not so much excited as satisfied. "Liz," Will said, "your father gave me his blessing."

"I know."

"He's concerned that I'll make you work too hard and I won't be able to give you the kind of life you've had."

"I know. He's told me that many times." Still, the quiet smile.

"He said you might come to hate me for taking you from all you've had here."

"He told me that, too. But I want you to know that I've worried too much in the past about all the nice things I have. What I want is a man I can respect and love, and when I have him—when I have *you*—I will work as hard as I must, and I will learn the skills I need. In fact, I've already started."

"I don't want you to work hard. I want you to—"

"But work I will. And *love* I will. Now kiss me, unless that's against your will."

But Will was willing.

· · ·

When the front door closed and Will was gone, Mary Ann was suddenly there in the hallway, grabbing Liz from behind, wrapping her arms around her. "It's done. It's done," she was whispering. "Did he profess his undying love?"

"Yes, and much, much more," Liz said, but she laughed and pulled away, and she climbed the steps back to the parlor. She sat down in her favorite chair, under the light from the window. Mary Ann followed and stood hovering over her. "Actually," Liz said, "he didn't do much professing. He's worried that I may come to hate him. Father told him that might happen, once he takes me away from the things we have."

"You won't ever hate him. You love him too much."

"I won't hate him, and I will never miss this house. For the last two years, I've felt myself a prisoner here—sending away all the young swains Father brought to me. But I do wonder about America. It's what Will wants, and I suppose I do too, but the sea scares me, and I worry about getting started there, when we can take so little with us."

"Apostle Woodruff says it's a beautiful place. He says that everyone helps everyone else, and when you arrive, the people welcome you with open arms."

"I know. But will you come, too? It sounds lonely to be so far away."

"I'll come if I can find a man like Will."

"I hope you do, Mary Ann. Maybe Father will decide to come— if all the members from Herefordshire leave."

Mary Ann sat down on the sofa that faced Liz's chair. "He says that he's too old to start over. But Mother will want to go if you do. And I want to move there more than anything."

"Maybe the Prophet will send Will off on missions, like Brother Woodruff, and I'll have to raise children in a log cabin."

"Could that really happen?"

"Of course it can. Mary Ann, you think you're reading a novel. You think love will burn bright, and Will is a prince, and I'll have a castle in America. But it won't be that way. I know how hard life is going to be. I've accepted that."

Mary Ann looked concerned for a moment, but then she smiled again, and she rolled her eyes to the side. "But think of that little cabin, under a nice warm quilt—with Will."

"I do think of it, Mary Ann. All the time."

Both girls finally laughed.

• • •

Will walked back to the Crawfords' farm. Brother Duncan had given him plenty to think about, but he thought of Liz more than anything. She really did love him, and there had been a time when she was only a dream of his—one he had assumed he would have to give up. He thanked the Lord for all the things that had happened. He told himself that God had raised him this far, and God would sustain him in the future as well. Still, he knew that some marriages started out well and then turned from hardship and worry into resentment and discontent. He didn't want to think that he could carry Liz off to America only to disappoint her through his own failures.

When he got back to his room, he knelt and prayed, thanking the Lord again. He felt sure it was impossible not to be happy so long as she loved him.

But the following days and weeks were difficult. Winter was long and lonely, and now the wait seemed forever. Each month he counted his savings, and he spent almost nothing so that he could build up the money he would need. Sometimes he told himself that they should marry sooner. Mr. Crawford had offered him a cottage—nicer than the ones the tenant farmers had. He could use his savings to furnish it, and he and Liz could be together. They could worry about emigrating later, after a few more years of saving. But every time he talked to Liz, they agreed again to wait to marry until they were ready to start their new lives in a new land.

Will attended prayer meetings on Thursday evenings in Colwall, and unless the weather was terrible, he would walk the five miles to Ledbury for Sunday services. That meant he could see his family without going to their farm, and of course, it meant seeing Liz. He often had Sunday dinner with the Duncans, and he had the feeling, as winter and spring passed, that Liz's father liked him more all the time.

What worried Will sometimes was to hear the news from the branches in the villages around the Malvern Hills. Brother Duncan told him at dinner one Sunday that a brother in the Twigworth branch had announced he was a prophet, and had started teaching false doctrines. Brother Woodruff had had to see to it that he was cut off from the Church.

"What worries me," Will told the Duncans, "are the people who make no effort to follow Christ. We have members in our Colwall branch who spread rumors about each other. One sister accused a family of having the itch—and not washing as they should. That whole family has stopped coming to church meetings."

"It's always that way," Sister Duncan said. "We want perfection, but we're human beings. We have to forgive each other and do our best."

"But we had a laborer show up to church in his ragged clothes, and most of the members wanted nothing to do with him. There's no place for that in the gospel—one person thinking he's better than another."

Will hadn't been thinking of the Duncans, but the moment the words were out of his mouth, he knew they could take it that way. No one said anything. Then the moment passed, and Mary Ann said, "Brother Woodruff says that everyone is equal in Nauvoo. There's no such thing as social classes. Do you think that's true?"

It was Brother Duncan who answered. "People are people. You'll find pride everywhere, and some will always resent a person who has raised himself up a little, even if it's through his own hard work. Americans like to brag about doing away with classes, and that's all well and good, but there are always those who are more educated, more refined, more successful. And there are always some who want to pull them down."

Will decided it was a good time to eat the cut of lamb that was on his plate and not comment any further. But he still believed that Nauvoo would be different from what he had grown up with.

Will and Liz walked out together often on Sunday afternoons, but they rarely saw one another during the week. As the spring and summer of 1841 passed, their plans began to settle. Will would finish out his year's contract and then hope that Mr. Crawford would keep him on until it was time for them to emigrate—and not hold him to another full year. Will had saved enough for the crossing, and Liz would bring a little money into the marriage. He didn't want to use any of that, but Liz insisted that the money would be *theirs,* not hers. In any case, Will hoped to put together enough money himself for a small plot of land. Once departure dates for early spring 1842 were announced, they would choose a wedding date not long before setting sail. Many English Saints were departing now, and most of the rest were hoping and saving for the day they could leave.

Will worked hard through another harvest, then lived with

his loneliness for one more autumn. But he and Liz became too impatient to wait until the very end of their time in England for their wedding. They married just before Christmas, with the plan to set sail in February. The Crawfords were disappointed that Will had held to his plan to leave, but they agreed to keep him on until shortly before his voyage.

The wedding took place in a government office in Ledbury. Members of "dissenting" religions were no longer required to have banns cried for three weeks in the Anglican Church, but the marriage did have to be public, and the Saints had no church in Ledbury. Still, the Duncans invited family and Church friends to a wedding breakfast at their home, and many of the members, even from other branches, came by to wish the couple well. Then Will, with no thought of a wedding trip, took his bride back to his little flat upstairs in the Crawfords' horse barn. But they were carried there in a fine coach with a liveried coachman driving—provided, of course, by the Crawfords. Liz told Will that his humble living quarters felt like a palace to her, and the place became more than that—heaven—to Will.

• • •

It was not a busy time for farmers, and Will spent more time than usual "at home" with Liz. These were delicious times for both of them, and Liz found herself happy and hopeful about the future. When they finally took their leave of the farm, Mr. Crawford offered Will his job back if he ever wanted to return. The Crawfords also made their coach available so Will and Liz could travel to each of their homes and then back across the Malvern Hills to Worcester. From there they would take a train to Birmingham, then on to Manchester, and from Manchester west to Liverpool.

At the Duncans' house, Mary Ann was finally facing the reality of Liz's departure, which had stolen away some of her romantic en-thusiasm for the marriage. "I tell myself I can find someone like Will, but where will I find him?" she asked Liz. "I took stock of all the young men at conference last fall. There wasn't anyone like him."

It hurt Liz to see Mary Ann discouraged. She had always been so happy. They hugged one another for a long time, crying, and Liz told her, "Pray that everything will come right. It's what I did, and it happened, even when it seemed it couldn't. We'll be together again. I know we will."

"I used to think so. I'm not so sure anymore. I don't think Father will leave his work here. Or this house."

"Pray. And I'll pray too. I cannot give you up forever. I have to believe that I'll see you again." But that only set them off crying again.

• • •

Will stood off a little way. He could hear all they were saying, but he didn't comment. He felt sorry for both of them, and he felt sorry for Brother and Sister Duncan, who took their turns embrac-ing their daughter. "Please follow us to Nauvoo," Liz kept telling them, but no one promised.

Will heard poor Sister Duncan say, "Since you were born, I've never had a day without you until these last two months, and that's been hard enough. Now I keep seeing you tossed about on the ocean—and gone from my life forever—and I can hardly bear it."

Even Brother Duncan, proper as he always was, shed some tears, and Will did too, just to see the pain he was creating. But he cried even harder when he had to say good-bye to his own family. He chose to take the coach to the edge of the farm and have his family walk out to the road to see him. That was at least letter-of-the-law compliance with Squire Riddle's rule for him. He actually hoped that the squire would hear the report that Will had made one last trip to Wellington Heath and was leaving for Liverpool in a coach. The man certainly knew that Will had become a bailiff for another landowner—and Will took some satisfaction in that.

Will had once thought he would never see his family again, and he had become accustomed to that reality, but now, after being able to see everyone on Sundays, he was feeling the pain of separation all over again. His father was a hard man, and Will felt a sense of failure, as much as anything, that he had never felt close to him. But his mother he would miss the rest of his life. The family saw no way, for the present, that all of them could immigrate to Nauvoo, however much they wanted to. Will thought some of them might come, but he doubted he would ever see his parents again.

Nettie kissed Will good-bye, but she was sobbing too hard to speak. She walked inside the gate and on toward the cottage. All the children came to Will after that. Josiah clearly wanted to show he was too old to cry, but he couldn't get any words out, and he left quickly and followed his mother to the cottage. Edgar couldn't hide his tears, nor could Solomon.

Sarah and Esther were especially difficult to leave behind. They both cried hard, and Esther kept saying, "We'll ne'er see you, Will. Ne'er again."

"Maybe you will. Maybe you'll come to Zion."

"Father said we can na' pay for the passage."

"But who knows? I might get rich in America. Maybe I'll pay for all of you. Or maybe the Prophet will send me back as a missionary. Who knows what might happen?"

Morgan was standing close by. "So it is in mortal life. Families divide, if on'y when some pass over to t'other side. But we'll meet again. Ha' no doubt on that. We'll dwell with God for all eternity."

"Father, I know I was prideful," Will told him. "I did things that brought hardship on all of you. I was wrong to poach that fawn. It put a stain on our entire family."

"Aye. But you knowed it in time, and you 'umbled yoursel'. God's callin' ye ta Zion, where Saints will gather from all parts o' the worl'. Be true to the faith all your mortal days. If you do that, I can be fore'er thankful that you're my son."

"I tried to do my best for you." Will really wanted to hear that his father loved him. It was something the man had never said.

"You worked hard, son. You kept us agoin', and you learnt Daniel what to do. He's provin' himsel' now, and Josiah is comin' up, ready to follow in Daniel's footsteps. You're a noble son and I'm proud on you."

Will thanked him, and his father shook his hand. "How is that hand?" Morgan asked.

"Not so bad. I work on it all the time, and I can use it a little now."

But the truth was, the hand made everything he did just a little more difficult, and it probably had improved as much as it ever would.

There was still Daniel to talk with, and he had been staying back. So Will walked to him and took hold of his shoulders. He thought of those dark days when he and Daniel had both felt so hopeless. However sad he was today, he was happy about the choices they had both made since then. "Dan, I was too hard on you sometimes," he said.

"I had it comin'. But I do better now. I know what you'd do, an' I try to do the same."

"When are you getting married?"

"I can na' say. Not soon. How can we?"

"Will you bring Molly here to the farm?"

"Aye. It's what we talk on."

"The farm looks good. I hope you haven't had to be as hard on our little brothers as I was."

"I give 'em what for fro' time to time, but they're growin' up more like you, willin' to do what's 'spected of 'em. An' our sisters, I know of none better. We'll miss Sarah, when she marries, but her and Esther, they work from sunup 'til sundown, an' smile all the while."

Will glanced at Sarah. "Or at least most of the time."

But no one could manage to laugh at that. The time had come. Will knew that he had said everything he could say. So he looked around at everyone one last time, thanked them all with a nod of his head, then walked to the coach. Liz had said her own good-byes and was waiting there.

Then Will saw that his mother had walked back from the cottage and was standing by the gate. She hurried to him again. She wrapped her arms around Will and said, "You will always be that first baby that came to my arms. I will love you no matter where you are. Please send us letters. Tell us about Nauvoo. I always want to know what is happening to you."

"I'll try to bring you to America, Mum. I will."

"No. I don't want to cross the ocean. I don't want to change everything and start anew. I just can't do it. So tell us everything, and I'll hold you in my heart."

Will embraced her tightly, and then he helped Liz into the coach. He told the driver to head back to Ledbury and on to Worcester, and then he stepped into the coach and looked out. His whole family was waving, and once again—as he had that dark day Squire Riddle had sent him away—he felt as if the pain was more than he could accept.

CHAPTER 18

Abby was sitting in the employee lunchroom at the Walmart in Keokuk, Iowa. It had never occurred to her when she was in college that she would work at a cash register in a Walmart, but a lot of things had turned out to be different from what she had expected. She had found herself to be a kind of second wheel on a unicycle when she stayed around the house in Nauvoo, with Will busy on his repair projects or on his computer. She also wanted to start earning enough money to buy the things they would need for the baby. She was feeling much better, with the worst of her morning sickness behind her, and the weather had cooled considerably now that September had come.

Jeff had been installing central air conditioning, and he kept promising that in another day or two he would have it up and running, but Abby was starting to think that he would have it going just in time for winter to set in. Jeff always trusted that he could do anything. If he didn't know how, he would check the Internet and find the information he needed, but sometimes he got himself in over his head, and Abby wondered whether he hadn't done that with the air conditioner.

Abby was working three or four days a week, depending on the demand at the store, and after a couple of weeks of checking, and sometimes stocking shelves, she was feeling fairly confident with what she had to do. She couldn't really say she liked the work. Standing so long was hard for her, and now and again a certain fruit or package of meat would put off a smell that would bring on a wave of nausea. Only once so far had she had to call for her supervisor and then dash to the employee bathroom, where she lost her lunch. She hadn't had to say she was pregnant when she hired on, but she said it anyway, and her supervisor was a nice woman, a little hard around the edges, but actually quite understanding of Abby's condition.

In fact, Abby liked most of the people she met at the store. They were working people, the same as she was now, and she understood a little better that some people could work hard and still not have enough money to take care of their teeth or to provide new school clothes for their kids—except for the T-shirts and jeans and shoes they could get at Walmart. It had taken her only a few days to realize that in Iowa and Illinois people talked to one another. They stood in line, waiting for her, talking about the weather and high school football games as though they all knew one another. But she soon caught on that people were just friendly, liked to talk, saw no reason not to. She had lived her life on the two coasts, and she had sometimes made a comment to a stranger in certain circumstances, but it had never occurred to her to launch into a whole conversation with someone she had never seen before—just because it was pleasant to do so. But she was doing that now, and she liked it.

Most of what people said to Abby was less than fascinating. "Think it's going to rain?" Or, "The store ain't too busy today." But it didn't matter. It was a way of making a little connection, and Abby found herself talking longer with people, slowing down a little. At first, when her line built up at all, she felt compelled to scan items as fast as possible, but she soon learned that very few people were in as big a hurry as she was accustomed to. They would finish out a little conversation after she had already handed them their receipt, and she would glance back, expecting the next customer to look upset, but as often as not that next person would join in.

Now, in the break room, she was sitting at the corner of a long table when Melinda, another checker, came in and took the seat around the corner of the table from her. "Oh, brother, I need to sit down," Melinda said. "My feet feel like they're goin' to bust in half. I gotta get me some better shoes."

Melinda was a young woman, maybe three or four years older than Abby. She had a nice shape, except that her weight was a little more than ample. She had a rough voice and a way of exaggerating almost everything she said. She had been wearing the same pastel blue top every time Abby had ever seen her. Maybe Abby was especially aware of that because it had a little spot on the front. Abby felt guilty for always noticing it. The woman probably didn't have a lot of choices and couldn't afford to throw something away just because it was stained. When Abby thought of all the shirts she had brought with her into her marriage, and how many she still had in her closet, she was a little ashamed of herself.

"I know what you mean," Abby said. "My feet are bothering me today too."

"Oh, and honey, you're expecting. That makes everything hurt a little more."

"How many kids do you have, Melinda?" Abby had talked to her a couple of times before, but only with others around. She realized that she didn't know much about Melinda.

"I've got two, a boy and a girl, and somewhere in the world I've got an ex-husband. He took off about two years ago . . . and let's just say, he doesn't check in with me."

"Doesn't he pay any child support?"

"Are you kidding? He didn't do that when we were married. Why would he bother now?"

"Wow. That's gotta be hard."

"I guess. But I'm a lot better off without him. He never held a job for more than a month or two, and when he did get a check, it never made it all the way home."

Abby couldn't think what to say. She took a bite of the ham and cheese sandwich she had made that morning. She had made three and left two of them for Jeff, and had told him to remember to stop long enough to have lunch. He forgot some days.

"You don't know anything about that kind of stuff, do you?"

"You mean—"

"Has your husband ever hit you?"

"No. He would never do that."

"See, I knew that. You're educated, too, aren't you?"

Abby had never mentioned to any of the other checkers that she had gone to college. "A little, I guess," she said. "Enough to run a bar code across a scanner."

Melinda laughed. She took a big bite of her tuna fish sandwich, but when she did, she cursed and then said, "I hate this stuff. I made tuna for my kids, so I made one for myself. But I can't eat it."

Abby wondered what Melinda did eat. There was a looseness in her arms and middle that seemed to indicate that she didn't exercise at all. Abby had always liked to run, and back in California, she had had a gym membership and had worked out as often as she could. She and Melinda were from different worlds, she knew, but Abby liked her. And somehow, both doing the same work, carrying their lunches to work, and both being moms—or nearly so—Abby felt a connection to a woman she never would have known or learned to like any other way.

When Abby went back to work, she felt rather subdued as she thought about Melinda. But she was lifted when Elder and Sister Caldwell came into the store and walked over to her counter to say hello. Abby often saw the Nauvoo senior missionaries, who came in on their preparation days to shop for groceries. They came in wearing suits and dresses and name tags, not their period costumes from the sites.

"How are you feeling?" Sister Caldwell asked.

"A lot better," Abby told her, and she smiled, wanting to reassure her.

"That's good. But this is a hard job for someone in your condition." She glanced at the customer Abby was waiting on and seemed to decide not to go into all that. But she did add, "I'll drop by again one day soon. Our schedule is a lot better now." She laughed. "But I kinda miss bein' up on the stage. I got so I liked it better'n I ever thought I would. I'm kind of a ham, I guess."

"I'm kind of a rump roast, myself," Elder Caldwell said, and his laugh boomed across the whole front of the store.

"Hey, you were good," Abby said.

Elder Caldwell was still grinning. "I dance about like them big workhorses I drive around Nauvoo," he said.

"That's not true," Abby said as she turned to start checking the items that her next customer had been setting out.

"Well, he does tromp on my foot pretty hard sometimes," Sister Caldwell said, "but he does all right." She stepped away, then looked back. "Abby, you are so beautiful," she said. "I'm glad to see the color back in your face."

It was a nice thing to hear, and Sister Caldwell seemed to mean it. Abby was surprised when tears came to her eyes. Part of it was the thought that she had always longed to hear such tender things from her mother—and never had.

Later that afternoon, when Abby was well aware that she had only an hour to go and was wondering whether she could hold out that long, another woman from her ward, Kayla McCord, came in. There weren't a lot of young couples in the ward, but the McCords were close to the age of Jeff and Abby.

Kayla came to her counter when Abby didn't have a line, and Abby was glad for the chance to talk to her a little. "Only forty-eight minutes until I get off," Abby told her.

"Are you really worn out?"

"Yeah. I am."

"I don't know how you do it. When I was pregnant, all I wanted to do was sleep." She laughed. "But it gets worse. Amelia's four months now, and she's not sleeping through the night yet." She looked down at the shopping cart, where her baby was strapped into her car seat, sound asleep. "I wish she would stay awake now, and then sleep at night."

"Thanks for telling me that it's going to get worse. Just what I needed."

"Oh, it's not so terrible. At least Sophie's at a cute age, and she's been really easy so far. I have a lot of fun with her."

Sophie was sitting in the child seat in the shopping cart. She twisted to look at her mom when she heard her name. She had dark eyes, like her mom, but lighter hair, almost blonde. "You *are* a cutie, Sophie," Abby said.

Sophie turned her head away.

"She acts shy. But she knows how to get what she wants—especially from her dad." She laughed. "Look at it this way. My mom says you suffer through all this for twenty years, and then you cry your eyes out because your kids are starting to leave home."

"Not my mom. She couldn't wait for her nest to empty out."

Abby wondered immediately whether she should have said that. Mormon women usually didn't say such things, and Abby sometimes seemed to shock them. But Kayla said, "I guess whatever stage of life we're in, we wish for something other than what we have."

Kayla had a nice smile, and there was a spark to her—even if she claimed to be walking around in a haze. She was still a little plump, after the baby, but Abby was pretty sure she had been petite all her life. Abby especially liked something in her honesty. She seemed to be herself, without trying for effects.

"Jeff and I have been wanting to get to know you and Malcolm," Abby said.

"Really? That's what we've been saying too. But you two are so educated, and me and Malcolm, we're just a couple of small-town hicks. If you get to know us, you'll find out how dumb we are."

"I don't believe that for a minute," Abby said, and she felt bad that she and Jeff had given that impression. "We talked about inviting you over, but Jeff has the house so torn up that we've been putting it off."

"Hey, come to our house. I'm not much of a cook, but I have a couple of good recipes. We could just have dinner and talk for a while."

"Let's do it."

"When's good for you?"

They ended up agreeing on Friday evening, and they both admitted that they didn't really have to check with their husbands. "I'll just *tell* him," Kayla said. "He has nothing better to do."

And so it was set, and Abby was lifted. Sister Caldwell was a nice mother to have around, but maybe Kayla could be a sister. Abby needed that—especially a sister who had just had a new baby and could pass on a little advice.

• • •

Jeff had installed the air-conditioning unit above the furnace and a condenser outside the house, in back. His problem was with the wiring. He had never done much electrical work. When Abby came in, he was sitting in the living room with his laptop on his knees. "I'm trying to follow the wiring chart," he mumbled. "It just doesn't make sense to me."

Abby had come in from the garage entrance and was standing in the kitchen. "I assume what you're telling me is, we still don't have central air."

Jeff let his eyes roll, but he said, "I'm almost there. Honest."

"It'll be great for Christmas. I hate it when the house gets too hot from all that baking."

"Hush. I don't need that right now. I'm feeling pretty stupid, if you want to know the truth." But then he remembered. "Hey, do you want to run down to Land and Records with me? It closes in about twenty minutes."

One of the problems they had was that they only had one car, and on days when Abby worked, unless Jeff drove her the fifteen miles and then went back for her, he didn't have a car all day.

"What do you want from Land and Records?"

"I called Dad about this wiring problem I'm having, but we got talking about William Lewis—my ancestor who lived here in Nauvoo. I didn't realize, he was part of the United Brethren group—John Benbow and all those guys—that joined the Church pretty much en masse."

"I guess I don't know about that."

"It was in England. Anyway, he was quite the guy, from what

Dad said. A real stalwart. He was about ten times more faithful than I am." He shut his laptop and set it aside. "Come with me. I want to see what I can find out about him. I'm wondering where he lived." He walked to Abby, took her in his arms, and hugged her. "Or would you rather wait here and rest? I can run down quickly."

"No. I'll ride with you. I just don't want to stand on these two stubs. I think I wore my feet off today."

At the Land and Records Office in historic Nauvoo, visitors could submit the names of ancestors and call up information on the computer system. It had suddenly hit Jeff today that he had looked around to see where early Church leaders lived or had farms, but he'd never looked up his own grandfather—actually, his fourth great-grandfather, according to his dad.

A nice senior sister from Arizona helped Jeff find the file for William Lewis on one of their computers, and then she burned a CD for him. Since the office was about to close, he didn't really look at the information. He thanked the sister and told her he would take it home and study it.

"Where did you say you live, here in town?" the sister asked.

"Warsaw Street, east of the state park."

"That's what I thought you said. Take a look at the map on the CD. Warsaw Street was called Rich Street back when the Saints lived here. William Lewis had two properties, one in town and the other one east of the city. That was probably his farm. But I think his town lot was pretty close to where you live. Just find the red Xs on the map and you can figure it out."

Jeff was happy to hear that. When he got home and used his laptop to check out the map, it only took him a couple of minutes to realize what he was seeing. "Oh my gosh, Abby, this seems impossible."

"What?"

"His lot was right across the street from us. Right there." He pointed to the state park across the street. "Just one lot in from the street."

"That's amazing," Abby said. "It's nice to think we live in his neighborhood."

But Jeff was feeling something more than that, and he wasn't sure how to say it. The coincidence seemed too unlikely. The idea that struck him was that he had been brought to this particular place for some reason.

"Let's walk over there."

"Oh, Jeff, not now."

"Come on. It's no walk at all."

"I'll stay and get dinner started."

"No. I told you, I'm cooking tonight."

"Cooking?"

"Okay, opening up a can of soup and getting out the crackers—or whatever. You know how I *cook*."

"Hey, I'm not knocking it—as long as I don't have to do it."

"Okay. So indulge me just this much. Walk across the street with me. It's not even hot outside."

"We need to put bug spray on."

"Don't worry. We will."

He took her hand and led her out to the garage, where he sprayed her feet and legs and then sprayed his own. She added some spray to her arms and hair, and then they walked across the street. They entered the woods on a nature trail that quickly turned into a canopied passage through the tall white oaks, locusts, and hickories. Just off the trail, the underbrush was thick with ferns. Jeff let go of Abby's hand and paced ahead. When he stopped, he said, "This is about 200 feet. I don't know how wide the lots were, but they must have been something like that. So this could be pretty close to the corner of his lot—except that it's in there just a little farther." He pointed into the thick woods.

"Are you going in there?"

"Sure. Come on. You're all sprayed." He walked ahead of her, pushing aside ferns and limbs. But as they got deeper under the trees, the underbrush thinned, and it was easier to see what the land must have looked like after it had been cleared.

"I don't know what kind of house he would have had," Jeff said. "A log cabin, I would guess, and I don't know where on his lot he would have built it, but just think, he walked this land, right here. His kids must have run and played over by our house."

Jeff wasn't sure that Abby felt quite so excited as he did, but he was moved by the idea of it, that he was making this connection. He cupped his hands around his mouth and shouted, "Hey, Grandpa Lewis, we just stopped by to visit you. Are you home?" There was a wild flutter of wings, as an owl or maybe a red-tailed hawk took flight somewhere in the woods. "Hey, did you hear that, Ab? I think I heard an angel fly."

Jeff was glad to hear Abby laugh. He stepped back to her and took her hand again. Rays of sun were filtering down through the trees, and birds were setting up intense complaints, perhaps displaced momentarily by the intruding visitors. Jeff loved it, the way they had so suddenly stepped into this other world, like a sacred grove. "Just think, Abby," he said, "Grandpa Lewis might have had a chicken coop or a barn or something, right here. And Grandma Lewis—Elizabeth was her name—hung out her wash or fed chickens or hoed the garden. We might be standing right where they had a well or . . . an outhouse." He laughed.

"I wonder what they were like," Abby said quietly, as though she sensed something sacred here too.

"I don't know. There's some biographical stuff on that CD. We'll have to go back and read it."

"But I mean, what they were *really* like."

"Yeah. I don't know. Dad said Grandpa Lewis was a farmer. But I guess most people were in those days. There weren't a whole lot of computer geeks around back then."

"I wonder if he was like you."

"I doubt it. I'm not much like my dad."

"That's not true. You look quite a lot like him—especially your blue eyes."

"Well, sure, but we're different in most ways. Dad got himself a good job and stuck with it. That's probably how all the Lewis men were until the genes got down to me. It probably never would have occurred to a farmer, back in those days, that his job was boring, or that he wanted to look around for another line of work."

"I don't think they were that different from us."

"Oh, I agree. I've told you that. But those were different times. God was in His heaven and all was right with the world. Once Grandpa found the truth, it sounds like that was it; he didn't question everything and wonder what came from God and what didn't."

"What about his wife? What do you know about her?"

"I don't know anything. But she was a farmer's wife. I guess she raised a family, cooked, sewed—all the things women did in those days."

"But she was real. I'm sure that farmer's wives weren't all the same."

"That's true. Still, life was pretty much set out for them. They didn't have so many things to figure out." He thought about that and added, "Or maybe that's not true. Maybe there were always things to question."

The two stood silent for a time, and then Abby said what Jeff was thinking. "Listen to the birds."

They were chirping now, sounding less raucous. It was one of the things Jeff had learned to love in Nauvoo, the sound of birds, especially early in the morning—the songs thick in the air. He had figured out that the call he liked best was made by cardinals. He would spot them, brilliant red against the sky, sitting high in the trees. He loved to see the white-tailed deer step from the trees in the park and graze along the edge of the woods. At the river, white pelicans had shown up lately, with black-tipped wings, and coots—little black water birds—were gathering in big flocks on the water. Jeff also loved the sound of the honking Canada geese overhead, flying in Vs, landing on the big lawns in the historic district. "This must have been some place back when Grandpa was here," he said. "No wonder they hated to give it up."

He raised his voice again. "Hey, Grandpa, I don't know if you heard about it, but we've moved to Nauvoo. Quite a few Mormons live here again, and if you haven't heard already, you'll be pleased to know that the temple has been rebuilt." But Jeff's voice faded, and suddenly this wasn't funny. What would his grandfather really think—what would Brother Joseph think—to know the temple that the Saints had had to leave behind was sitting on the bluff again, looking almost exactly as it had back then? Tears filled his eyes.

Abby took his hand. "I think he already knows about the temple," she said. Jeff could hear in her voice that Abby was touched by the thought too. They stood for a couple of minutes listening to the birds. Jeff had never thought much about his ancestors, but he wanted to know more now. "We'll stop back again, Grandpa," he said out loud. "It was nice to meet you."

"And you too, Elizabeth," Abby said. She looked at Jeff. "How many babies did she have?"

"I'm not sure. Enough to fill a whole page. I didn't count exactly how many."

"I can't imagine being pregnant that many times."

Jeff looked at Abby again and saw how tired she looked. Sweat was beading up on her forehead and under her eyes. "Come on, honey," he said. "We need to go back and let you lie down for a while. I'll heat up the soup."

"I'll bet your grandma would have liked to 'heat up' some soup some days."

"Actually, that's exactly what she always wanted to do. But she didn't have a can opener. They weren't invented yet."

"Wow, you really are a historian, aren't you?"

He suddenly turned and grabbed Abby, then bent and hoisted her up in his arms. "You've walked enough today," he said, and he carried her back across the street. Along the way, he said, "You know what? It might be nice if I could find a job out here. I'd like to live in Nauvoo."

"Yeah. I know what you mean. But could you get the air conditioner going before we make a decision?"

• • •

On Friday Jeff and Abby went to Kayla and Malcolm's home on Young Street. The McCords had bought an old house and were planning to fix it up gradually, but they hadn't been able to do much yet. Malcolm put in rather long hours at his job in Fort Madison, where he managed a tire store.

The four had eaten dinner and were still sitting at a little pine-wood table. Jeff had just asked Malcolm how he had moved up into a managerial position so young. "I started out when I was just a kid with the same company up in Burlington," he answered. "That's where we both grew up."

"Don't try to impress people," Kayla said. "We've never lived in Burlington. It's way too big for us. We grew up in Augusta, a little town about ten miles from Burlington. We went all the way through school together, except Malcolm was a year older than me."

"Anyway, what I was going to say was that I worked for this company from the time I was in high school. So when they opened up in Fort Madison, they sent me down to manage the place. But it's not a big outfit. I sell the tires and all that, but I end up in the shop half the time, mounting them, too." He held up his hands. "The dirt gets in my hands so deep, it won't come out."

"That's just proof of honest labor," Jeff said.

"But we're not like you two," Malcolm said. "Every time I hear you say something in priesthood meeting, I think, 'I'm not going to open my mouth. After what he said, I'll sound too dumb.'"

"Hey, I just sit at a computer and type. It's all manual labor, however you look at it."

Kayla was holding a blanket over her front as she nursed her baby. Malcolm had slid back from the table so he could stretch his long legs out. He was tall, like Jeff, but he had a sort of throwback hair cut, short and boxed, with "white sidewalls," and he usually wore Wranglers and boots. Jeff really liked the guy, and he didn't want to give him the impression that he was some sort of know-it-all. It occurred to Jeff that he ought to tone things down in his elders quorum meeting even more. He thought he had taken Abby's advice, but maybe he was still coming on too strong.

"So did you two grow up in the Church, or join later?" Abby asked.

"I grew up a member," Kayla said. "My family joined when I was really little. But when we were in high school I started inviting Malcolm to Mutual dances and things like that. He joined before we got married."

"To tell the truth, I just sort of joined because Kayla wanted me to," Malcolm said. "It took me a while to figure things out. I didn't go on a mission or anything like that, but once we got married and I started going all the time, everything started to sink in, and I got more serious about it."

"Do you think you'll end up staying in Nauvoo?" Abby asked.

"Yeah. We think so," Kayla said. "What about you two?"

"I don't know. We weren't planning to stay long," Abby said. "But we like Nauvoo. If Jeff ever gets our air conditioning going, I might even survive here."

"You don't have air conditioning?" Malcolm asked, looking seriously concerned. He sat up straight and turned toward Jeff.

"We have window units. I'm trying to install central air, and I got it all wired this week, but the condenser doesn't kick on. I thought I hooked everything up to the thermostat right, but obviously I didn't."

"Malcolm knows everything about air conditioners," Kayla said.

"Really?" Jeff said.

"No, no. Not everything. But my dad ran a heating and air conditioning company. I grew up working for him—before I decided I'd rather work for someone else."

"But you've wired them before?"

"I've helped my dad. I know quite a bit about it."

"Malcolm, I've been praying for you to appear. And now the Lord has sent you to me."

"I don't know if I'm your type."

Everyone laughed, but Jeff was half serious. He really needed Malcolm's help.

CHAPTER 19

Will and Liz didn't talk much during the first part of their ride to Worcester. Will tried to think what would happen to his family in the coming years, whether some of them could ever immigrate to Zion. Gradually, however, his thoughts turned to the days that lay immediately ahead. He had heard frightening descriptions of ocean crossings. He hoped he and Liz wouldn't face a stormy sea. When he glanced at Liz, he could see that she was worried too. "Are you all right?" he asked. He knew how much she was missing her sister.

"Will, I'm . . . not well. We may need to stop." He watched her take a long breath and saw how pale she was. "Tell the driver to stop. *Now.*"

"Ho! Driver," Will shouted. "Pull up!" By then Liz had the door open. The instant the coach stopped, she jumped down. She hurried a few steps forward, and then, as Will was hurrying after her, she bent and vomited on the ground—once, then twice more. Will had hold of her, helping her keep her balance.

Will found a handkerchief in his pocket and gave it to her, and still he clung to her. "Was it just the bouncing of the coach, or—"

"No. I think I might . . ." She turned toward him, still holding the handkerchief over her mouth. "Are you ready to be a papa?"

Will was stunned. "Already?" he asked.

"How long do you think it takes?" She was smiling now, and some color had come back to her face.

"But the voyage. It's hard enough, without this. Maybe we shouldn't go now. We could wait until the baby comes."

"It's worse then. It's the babies that die on these voyages."

Will had thought of hardships, but not death. "Could *you* be in danger?"

"I'll just have to manage. We can't change our minds now." She turned and looked at him. "Be happy. It's a good thing."

"Of course it is. I'm happy. I just worry about you."

"Just pray for me. We'll be all right."

Will told himself she was right, and later, when they stepped onto the train in Worcester, he held Liz's arm with a firm grip to assure her that he would support her through this difficult time. He didn't want her to know that he was actually wondering whether they were making a mistake.

•　•　•

Liz seemed to be doing much better. After losing her breakfast, her stomach calmed, and she was excited about riding on a train for the first time. As it turned out, however, the third-class accommodations they had chosen were miserable. They rode in an open car where smoke, even ashes, blew in their faces, and then a drizzle of rain began to fall. They stayed overnight at an inn on the edge of Manchester, where Will didn't mind paying for decent accommodations. He remembered all too well his last days in the city when he had slept in alleys. He thought how difficult it would have been back then to imagine that he would ever return in such an improved state—and with Liz by his side.

But this trip was not easy either. Will had to hire a carter to bring his and Liz's big trunks to the inn. However clean the room might have seemed, the bed was infested with bedbugs or fleas—something that left vicious bites—and Liz was sick again in the morning. By the time they had ridden another train and paid another carter to get their trunks to the docks in Liverpool—and quarreled with the carter over the price he had offered at the train compared to the one he demanded at the port—it was all Liz could do to walk onto the ship. Will found her a barrel to sit on while he tried to find out where their sleeping berth would be.

Liz sat still, not liking the subtle movement of the ship, even when docked. She watched all the activity, the sailors and passengers and porters coming on board. All of it was exciting, but the smell was almost more than she could stand. She didn't want to vomit again, but she kept eyeing the rail and thinking that she could bend over it and not make a mess of the deck.

She had never seen a town larger than Gloucester or Worcester, and now she was looking at Liverpool, which was vast. It was a sooty, gray city, a little foggy even in the middle of the day, and the dock area was chaotic. She could see hundreds of ship masts in the quiet waters that were closed into great rectangular docking areas. There were giant, ornate buildings just beyond the docks—the customs house and the city hall, and a cathedral, farther back—and wagons, oxcarts, carriages, and omnibuses everywhere. Liz had heard pieces of conversation along the dock and knew she was hearing foreign languages. She had only seen pictures of Orientals before, but here she had seen a man who seemed to be a Chinaman or a Japanese. Now she could also see a Negro who was carrying a heavy trunk and following a white man. She wondered whether he was a slave, or whether he was merely working for the white man.

On the docks there were great piles of baled cotton and stacks of boxes and barrels. Dock workers, mostly big men wearing leather coverings over their shoulders, were carrying cargo on board. Liz thought a big ship nearby was a schooner, but she didn't know the names of the others. What surprised her most was a steam-powered boat out on the Mersey River. The engine made a racket and pumped out a steady stream of black smoke. She didn't think it would be a pleasant way to travel.

When Will returned, he said, "I met our leader. Brother Burnham is his name. We'll have a meeting on the quarterdeck before we depart. I know our berth assignment now, so I'll get some help and carry our trunks down. I think, for now, you're better off to stay out here on the main deck."

"Yes, I will. At least some air is moving. But what's that smell?"

"A man told me it's the smell of the sea."

"I've been to beaches before; they didn't smell like this."

"I'm sure you're right. Lots of things go in the water here. Dumped from the ships—and from the city." She didn't have to be told. She knew he meant every kind of waste—including human waste. The thought made her think of the rail again.

"The ship's called *Sea Bird*," Will said. "It's square-rigged, they tell me, and weighs 880 tons. I'm not exactly certain what all that means, but Brother Burnham assured me that a ship of this size can get through a severe storm much better than a small one. He also said that Captain Slater was an experienced man. He promised, too, that Apostle Young and a brother named Amos Fielding negotiated good prices. We'll have 270 of our own people on board and some others—although not too many."

Liz was glad that Will felt good about the arrangements, but she was still feeling the rise and fall of the ship—and she didn't like it. She wondered about the open sea.

"Are you all right?" Will asked.

"I will be," she said. "Nothing will bother me if I choose not to let it." She didn't want him to think she was doubting their decision—or that she was weak. "I've made up my mind, Will. We're going to America. I'm not going to whimper all the way. And when we get there, we'll have our first child in Nauvoo—and we'll be thankful for it. We should be happy to know we're expecting a baby."

"That's right. That's how we'll look at it." He smiled. She was glad for that, but his words seemed a frail attempt at confidence. She could tell that he was as worried as she was.

●   ●   ●

One of the Mormon leaders, Brother Small, helped Will carry Liz's trunk down the steep steps that the sailors called a ladder. Then he guided Will to their quarters in the middle section of the steerage deck, which was two decks down from the main deck. Couples and families bunked in the center, with single males fore and single females aft. Will and Liz would sleep in an upper berth, which seemed quite wide until Brother Small told Will that four people would share it. Two children from another family would occupy half of the bed.

Will hated the thoughts of bringing Liz down into this dark, damp, smelly hold. The lamps produced a bitter coal-oil smell, but Will could also detect the sour stink of vomit and a hint of the odor of a privy. When he saw a crewman, he asked the man why the place hadn't been scrubbed any better.

"We cleaned all day yesterday. Aye, and the day afore that besides. Too many has puked down here ever to scrub it out of every crack."

Will decided to keep Liz on deck as long as he could. But when he returned to her, she huddled against him. "The wind has turned so cold," she told him.

Will had noticed it too. He feared a storm was blowing in. Herefordshire was cold in February, but this wind off the ocean bit deeper than any cold he had felt before. He held Liz close for a time, and then she seemed to warm when her friends from the Ledbury branch, Jesse and Ellen Matthews, came on board. They were from Parkway, south of Ledbury—a good long walk—but they had rarely missed their meetings in town. They had been married a few years now. Jesse had apprenticed with a wheelwright but had struggled to find enough work once he had left his master. It was partly from talking to Will and Liz about their plans that they had decided to immigrate to Nauvoo.

Jesse shook Will's hand, gave him a slap on the shoulder, and said, "This is it, my friend. We're in for a penny, so it's time to cast in a pound." He was a firm little man who walked with his elbows out, like a strutting rooster, but there was nothing proud about him. He was a good soul, and Ellen was a happy woman, not pretty, but blessed with nice color in her cheeks and a spirited, optimistic outlook. They had three children: a little reproduction of his father, even with his father's name—Jesse, Junior—who was four; Mary, two, who also looked a little too much like her father, but with her mother's liveliness; and a baby girl, half a year old, Phoebe.

All of them were tucked together in their wool coats, the two older children pressing their faces into the folds of their mother's coat and the baby wrapped up in a blanket in Jesse's arms.

"It wasn't so cold when we first came on board," Will said. "I hope we don't sail into a storm, first day out."

"Could be excitin'!" Ellen said, and laughed.

Will knew how much it meant to Liz to have Ellen on board. There had been a time when Liz had seen herself as superior to the other young women in their branch, but during the time Liz had been engaged to Will, she and Ellen had often talked about marriage, about keeping house, and about sailing to Nauvoo. Will had known Jesse for many years, and although they had lived too far apart to be true mates, they had liked one another. Will was glad to have Jesse along—someone to spend some of the long hours at sea with.

Passengers continued to come on board all afternoon. Late in the day, Amos Fielding arrived. He moved about among the Mormon emigrants, shaking hands and greeting people. Then he asked everyone to gather on the quarterdeck, or as close to it as possible on the main deck, so he could talk to them. "The wind is brisk, but the captain says it's favorable, so he plans to set sail soon," he announced. "That's better than waiting all night. I think you know that the passage to America is much slower than the voyages coming back to England. Sailors call this passage 'uphill,' since the winds are mostly counter to the direction we are heading."

Brother Fielding was wearing a slouchy hat and had pulled his coat collar around his face. He was shouting through the opening and against the wind, his voice sounding deep and hollow. "We know that we can expect the finest behavior of our people. Please remember that you are followers of Christ, willing to greet and serve the crew and other passengers as warmly as our own. Pray daily together, follow your leaders, and hold to the rules and regulations that Brother Burnham will present to you."

He hesitated and then added, "We have young unmarried sisters aboard. Let me warn them that we have had sad experiences in the past, especially with some of the sailors. Such men are known to take shameful liberties, even with married women. Behavior of this kind should be reported to the captain, but be careful never to do anything that would encourage such men. And don't assume that young men within the fold are incapable of hatching evil designs. Unmarried men and women should never be alone together. I can warn you, once you are under sail, there will be times when some of you will feel unwell, and when that happens, parents sometimes forget what their youngsters are doing and leave them to their own devices. Let us all remember that every adult has responsibility for all our children. We can assist one another in this way."

The advice continued for a time, and then Brother Fielding introduced the six brothers who would preside over the membership of the Church on board. Brother Burnham, the presiding elder, spoke briefly, laying out some of the rules, and he introduced his five counselors. He explained that the members would be divided into six groups, each led by a member of the presidency. He then called on the members to sing a hymn together: "Now Let Us Rejoice." Almost all the expected members had arrived, so it was more than two hundred and fifty souls who raised their voices together. Coming from Saints who were packed together tight and singing with power, the hymn took on greater meaning than usual.

Will felt his spirits rise, felt strength come into him. The words "And Jesus will say to all Israel, 'Come home'" struck him with force. He told himself he wasn't leaving home; he was going home. And in the final verse, he listened to himself sing, "And Christ and his people will ever be one." He had never felt the meaning of that line as he did today. He was suddenly remembering why he had been looking forward to this day. Will held Liz, and they looked into one another's faces. He could see that she was feeling the same thing he was.

An hour later the ship was towed from the dock and down the Mersey River by a small steamboat. As the *Sea Bird* reached the open bay, the sailors, in a frenzy of activity, unfurled the sails. The ship began to move under its own power. A great cheer went up from all on deck. Will embraced Liz a little tighter. "This is it," he said. "We're under way. It's what we've dreamed of all these months."

• • •

Two hours later, out in the Irish Sea, Will wasn't cheering. No one was. The winds were favorable and the ocean wasn't terribly rough, but very few of the passengers had experienced the rocking of a ship in open water before, and Will watched people change. Many who had been laughing and talking had become quiet and pale, and eventually he saw some of them slip away—sometimes to the rail, to lean over.

Liz hadn't eaten much since she had been sick that morning, and she seemed to last longer than most of the passengers. But Will saw her begin to lose her color again. He kept her out in the cold as long as she could stand it, but after she finally vomited what was left in her, she said she needed to get to her berth and lie down. So Will took her into the hold of the ship and introduced her to steerage, which was now filled up so tightly with boxes and trunks that it was not easy to get through the rows of berths. Will let her sit in the lower berth while he pulled their bedding from one of their trunks. He laid out the feather tick the Duncans had given them and then helped Liz into the upper berth, where she lay, fully dressed. "How many days?" she asked Will.

"Brother Fielding said it could be seven or eight weeks, maybe longer. It's a long way when we sail all the way around to New Orleans."

"Will my head spin like this the whole time?"

"I don't think so. I think we'll get used to it after a time."

But he had given himself away, not only with his words but with his tone of voice. "You're getting sick too, aren't you?" Liz asked.

"Yes."

"Try not to. I'm going to need help." He heard her resolve breaking already.

"All right. I'll do my best."

"Pray for us."

"All right." He took Liz's hand and said a short prayer, asking that they could weather the illness they were feeling, that the baby would be all right, and that Liz would soon feel better. But then he had to leave. He tried to get to one of the four water closets in steerage, but others were waiting to get in, so he hurried away and climbed the ladder to the main deck. The cold air felt better, but just as he stepped on deck the ship seemed to twist as it settled, and he was thrown off balance. He felt the motion in his stomach and began to wretch. As he hurried toward the rail, he stepped in a pool of vomit and his foot slipped. He went down on his seat in the stuff, but jumped up quickly and reached the rail. Everything came up in a painful gush. He hung onto the rail then, waited, hoped for relief, but his body wrenched again, so hard that the muscles in his abdomen jabbed with pain. And still the feeling didn't end. He vomited six times before he felt the need pass. His head remained full of fog, though, and he knew the sickness hadn't entirely passed.

Will needed to get back to Liz, but he feared the hold, the nasty smell and the confined, close air. He breathed in the wind for another few minutes. All around him, people were in his same condition. There were some who were saying, "I'm all right so far. I hope I stay that way." But those were few.

A sailor came by with a mop. He was swabbing up the vomit that was running across the deck. "It happens ever' time," he told Will. "This water is a li'l rough, but we'll see worse afore we gets there."

"But we'll get used to it, won't we?"

"Some do. Some hold on sick. Ol' salts like me, we don't notice much, but then a day cooms along, in a bad storm, we can have some of it too. But think on it. You got ta keep water in ye, no matter how bad the water in the barrels is. An' you got ta eat, even if it's nothing but hardtack." Will had learned that the hard, dry "sea biscuits," as they were also called, were the staple food on board, with no fresh bread ever available.

Will made his way back to Liz, who said she needed more than a rail to lean over. She needed a water closet. So Will helped her down, and walked her to the closet, which she still had to wait for. By the time he helped her back, he was wondering whether he needed to go back on deck. But he didn't go yet. He boosted her up, and then he stayed by her, holding her hand.

By then, two children had joined them. Brother and Sister Steele were in the lower berth, with two small children beside them. Robert and Celia Steele, eleven and eight, were on the Lewises' berth, lying nearer to the wall than Liz, and both looked pale and sick. Will could see what was coming, sleeping four deep in this bed, with everyone sick, and no privacy at all. It already seemed a nightmare.

Will made sure Liz was managing, and then he went back to stay on deck as long as he could stand the cold and the wind. When he returned, he took off his trousers and climbed into the berth in his shirt. He told the Steeles, below, that all would be fine. They would make the best of things. He lay there all night like that, never sleeping, and he helped little Celia down when she became desperately afraid after a dream. She crowded into the berth with her parents, and that was a little better for Will and Liz, but poor Liz moaned all night, half asleep at times, awake at others.

At some point in the night the wind picked up suddenly, and the ship began to toss more wildly. Will could hear boxes and trunks slide across the steerage deck. Pots and pans and utensils clanked as they were tossed about. And always there was the sound of someone retching; the smell only got worse.

On the third day at sea Brother Burnham found Will on deck. It was a fair day, and the sea might have been a little calmer, but the wind was from the west and the ship was tacking back and forth to move forward against it. Will was not so sick as he had been the first night, but he didn't feel like eating. He had forced Liz to drink a little tea made from the nasty, black water from the barrels and to chew a little on some hardtack, and he had done the same himself, but in truth, he didn't think he would ever be hungry again in his life.

"Are you Brother Lewis?" Burnham asked.

"Aye."

"I need to call on you for some help."

"Whatever it is, I'm willing."

"That's good. Not everyone is feeling that way right now." Brother Burnham tried to smile, but Will could see no color in his face either. He had obviously been sick himself. "Brother Small is one of my counselors—he's over your group, as I'm sure you know—but he can't lift his head off his berth. He keeps telling me he wants to die. He might feel better after a time, but I need some help now."

"I'm feeling a little sick myself, but I can get by. My poor wife is the one who's suffering."

"I've asked around, Brother Lewis, and I keep hearing your name. Members of your group tell me, 'He's young, but he's a leader. And he's reliable.'"

"I hope that's true."

"Are you willing to serve as my counselor if I release Brother Small?"

"Aye. I'm willing."

"Are you an elder?"

"No. A priest."

"Well, I'm calling you to serve as my counselor, but I want to ordain you an elder before we set you apart. I'll get back to you about all that. For now, go ahead and get to know your people. I'll tell your group to look to you for direction. You'll lead out in morning prayers and in any meeting you decide to hold, but most of all, you'll have to solve some problems."

"What kind of problems?"

"To start with, someone has stolen some food from the Carvers, and they think it's one of our own. Talk to them and see what you can find out. If you can deal with it, do so. If you think you need to bring me into it, I'll try to help, but I have a few matters to deal with myself."

"All right. I know who the Carvers are. I'll look into it."

Will liked to think that some of the Saints thought he was a leader, and he was flattered that he would be called upon. He went down to the hold and checked on Liz first, telling her what Brother Burnham had called on him to do.

"I'm proud of you," Liz told him. "You'll do fine."

But Will thought he heard something in Liz's voice. "You sound like you're not so sure."

"No. I am sure. But don't overstep. You know what I mean?"

Will smiled. She had been with him on the farm for the last two months, and she knew how he dealt with slackers among his farm laborers. He sent them down the road. But there was no road off this ship, and dealing with people in the Church was surely different from farm work. "I'll be careful," he said. "I know I need to be more patient with people."

It wasn't long before he had to work to remember those words. He found the Carvers on deck, both of them standing by the rail, looking off at the horizon. Will had heard passengers say that that was the best way to keep from seasickness: to stand in the cool air, watch the horizon, and not concentrate on the rise and fall of the ship.

Brother Carver was from Preston, where many of the people in Will's group were from. He was a bold, outspoken man who liked to profess what he believed. Will had heard him talking to a crewman before the ship had set sail, already trying to convert the man by testifying of Joseph Smith and the Book of Mormon. Will knew that was probably something to admire in Brother Carver, but he had sounded so zealous, he had run the sailor off.

Since the ship had been under way, Brother Carver had not spoken out so much; the motion of the sea had taken some of the zeal out of him. When Will approached him, he didn't want to look around. "I'm watchin' the sky," he said. "It helps a li'l."

Sister Carver said, quietly, "*Very* little." But at least she looked back and smiled.

Will stepped to the rail, next to Brother Carver. "I've been asked to take over for Brother Small, who isn't doing well."

"An' why could they na' find a grown man for the job?" Carver asked.

That stopped Will for a moment. But he only said, "I don't know why he chose me. I just answered the call."

"Maybe you're the on'y one who's not pukin' aw day."

"Maybe." He didn't tell the man that he was fighting the same affliction everyone else was. "Brother Burnham tells me that someone stole some food from you."

"Not *som'un*. It was James Bedford. He's from our very own branch in Preston."

"How do you know? Did you see him?"

"No. But he asked us for food, and when I could na' share the little we had, he gone ahead and took it aw the same."

"How do you know that?"

"He's the on'y one wiffout food. Somethin' happened to his boxes. They ne'er made it on board."

"We'll have to help him, then."

"Fine. You help him. But I'm just hopin' I ha' anough for my family. I can't part with nuffin'."

Will watched the horizon for a time himself, partly because he was still fighting to keep down the little he had eaten that morning, and partly to control himself. "How much have you eaten so far, Brother Carver?"

"Very li'l."

"And I think that's true for all of us. We probably brought more food than we really need. If we all share, we can help the Bedfords get by."

"An' if'n we get blowed off course, then what? These voyages can take longer than we 'spect."

"So you plan to eat whether someone else starves or not?"

"I'm lookin' out for my family. If you want to give Bedford your food, go ahead an' do't."

"Henry," Sister Carver said. "Don't be like that. We could all spare a little, and—"

"Hold your tongue, Sarah Ann. This is my decision to make, not yours."

Will grasped the rail and told himself not to lose his temper, not to say something he would be sorry for. "I *will* give him some of my food," he finally said. He turned to walk away, but then stopped. "Did you bring a Book of Mormon with you?" he asked.

"Aye. I did."

"And have you heard of King Benjamin?"

"Yo know I have."

"Read his sermon, Brother Carver. And then repent. Or if you don't, I hope you choke on your own food. We can hold a burial at sea for you."

Will hadn't meant to go quite that far. Those last words had popped out of him before he could get them stopped. Still, he couldn't resist a little pleasure at having said them. What he soon learned, however, was that he wasn't any better satisfied with Brother Bedford. "Aye, I took some food," he said. "I asked for help, but he wouldn't spare so much as a biscuit for my li'l childer. So I helped myseln. He had it cooming."

"But we need to plan for you. Brother Carver tells me your food didn't make it on board."

"Aye. Some of it didn't."

"Only *some* of it?"

Brother Bedford looked at the deck. He didn't seem to be sick at all. He was a stout man, dressed in a great coat that was buttoned tight around his expansive middle. Will thought he hadn't missed a lot of meals in his life.

"I had nuffin' my childer could eat an' hold down."

"But you told Carver you had nothing at all?"

"Aye. I zed so. But I know Carver. He's self-righteous—thinks his soul is made o' gold. I guessed before I asked he'd say no."

"Well, then . . ." But Will was getting ready to start casting insults again. So he stopped himself and only said, "Do as well as you can with what you have, but don't steal again. Come to me. We'll make sure you have enough."

Will left and sought out Brother Burnham on the main deck. When he reported what he'd learned, Brother Burnham shook his head in disgust. "I thought it would be something like that," he said. "Those two are always butting up against each other like old rutting goats."

"Why did they join the Church, Brother Burnham? Don't they believe in the gospel?"

"Sure they do, Will. But we are who we are, and when we find the truth, we don't always change so easily as we should."

"I don't think they understand the doctrines they say they believe."

"Do any of us?"

Will didn't know how to answer that.

"Missionaries throw out the net, Will, and they gather in the catch. But it's one thing for those we teach to join the kingdom, and it's another thing for them to break from their old ways and take on the ways of God. We all fall far short."

Will nodded. He knew that about himself, had even seen it in the last hour. But he still found himself hoping that Carver and Bedford would choke just enough on their biscuits to ask themselves whether they understood whose biscuits they really were.

• • •

Later that day, Liz, with Will's encouragement, made her way to the main deck. Will kept telling her that she needed to move about, get used to the motion of the ship, and eat and drink enough to sustain her—and the baby. So Liz climbed the ladder and stood at the rail on the main deck. Will stayed with Liz for a time, but then he said he had some other matters he needed to take care of. He would be back in a few minutes. Liz rather liked being cold, but she hoped that he wouldn't be long. She felt too weak to stand for very long.

Ellen Matthews appeared at Liz's side after a time. "Will asked me to look out for you," she said. "Are you ready to go back to your berth?"

"I am," Liz said, "but I was just thinking what a long night it would be again. Ellen, how are we going to do this?"

"I'm feeling much better," Ellen said. She laughed. "Or at least I keep telling myself that. I think we'll feel better as we go along."

Liz hoped so. She tried to think of two months of feeling like this, and it was more than she could stand to imagine. Twice now, Will had found her sobbing in their berth. But she hadn't told him how homesick she was already, besides seasick.

"Will told me your secret."

"He shouldn't be talking out of turn. We don't even know for certain."

"A woman knows."

"Yes. I suppose I do know." She fought back the urge to cry. "Ellen, it's not just that. I tell myself not to look back, but when I try to look ahead, I don't know what to expect. I wish I knew where I was going to live—and *how* we're going to live."

"God's called us to Zion, Liz. He'll know how to use us."

"I know. That's what I tell myself. But it's hard to think right when I feel so sick. I keep thinking, Will had such a good position on the Crawfords' farm. Maybe we should have stayed there."

"I know. During the night, I think all those things. But last night I kept praying, and God calmed me. We just have to trust that we're doing what God wants, and He'll watch over us."

Liz believed that. She remembered the promises she had made to herself—and to Will. She had vowed to be strong. She just hadn't known how very weak she would soon feel.

CHAPTER 20

The weather turned much better for most of the next two weeks. Liz was able to keep a little more food down, but just when she was starting to feel that she was gaining strength and becoming able to stay away from her berth more hours each day, everything changed again. Winds from the northwest began to pick up; for three days, they kept getting worse. The ship was tossed about ever more wildly, night and day.

Will kept trying to get food into Liz, but she resisted, knowing full well that anything she ate would only make her sick again. He tried to reason with her, but she was getting so weak that she wasn't thinking well. On the fourth night of the storm, Will could see that she was failing. He frantically worked with her, forcing her to sip some tea and nibble a bit of hardtack, but she hardly seemed to know what was happening.

Will could see what was coming, and he was terrified. Everything he had dreamed of and prayed for was slipping away from him. He *had* to make her eat. He let her sleep for an hour, and then he tried to get a little more food into her—with hardly any success. "Don't,

Will," she kept saying as he tried to dribble water into her mouth and place bits of biscuit on her tongue. "Don't do that."

"Sleep a little more. And then we'll try again," he told her, and he held her against him. But Will was exhausted. He had slept very little during the storm. He was losing touch with reality himself. He didn't know he was slipping into sleep until he awoke with a start. He had suddenly sensed that something was wrong. Liz's muscles seemed to collapse, and she clearly wasn't breathing.

Will shook her hard. "Wake up, Liz! Wake up!" he shouted into her ear. "Liz! Open your eyes." He heard her gasp and knew she was alive, but she didn't respond, didn't open her eyes. "Liz! Don't do this. Don't give up."

He let go of her, struggled to straddle her, and then he slapped her face, once, twice, and shouted at her again. "Open your eyes, Liz."

He heard someone say, "Give her a blessing, Brother Lewis. Command her to arise."

Will had never administered to anyone, hadn't had the authority until recently, but he knew immediately it was what he needed to do. He placed his hands on Liz's head, the way he had seen the brethren do. "Elizabeth Lewis," he shouted into her ear, "I command you, in the name of Jesus Christ, to come back to me."

He felt a little jerk of response, and then he heard another breath, long and rough, maybe a death rattle.

"I command you to stay with me," he said, as firmly as he could. But his voice had begun to break. "Oh, please, Liz. Please. Don't leave me."

He could only see the shadow of her face in the dim lamplight. But he saw her eyelashes move, and he heard her moan. "Don't, Will," she said. "Don't."

"I won't let you go!" he shouted. "I can't lose you."

"I can't. I can't."

"Yes, you can. I command you to stay with me." He watched her eyes go shut again. He wasn't doing this right. "In the name of Jesus Christ," he said again, "I command you to live!"

Her eyes opened again, and she said, in a sigh, "I'll try."

"Get me some water," Will shouted to anyone who would listen. "And a biscuit."

But someone in the dark had already known. "Here." It was Ellen Matthews. Will took a tin cup from her and held Liz's head in the crook of his arm. Her mouth was open, and he dribbled in a few drops of the brackish water. Liz choked a little, but then she swallowed, and he gave her some more. Ellen had broken off a bit of the hardtack. "Give her some of this," she said.

Will took the piece and set it on her tongue, then added a little more water. And he kept at it, like feeding a baby bird, for at least an hour. After a while, he felt the difference. She was trying now. He gradually felt her breath against him coming in a more regular, longer cadence. So he let her sleep.

It was then that he heard a little voice. "Is she better?" It was Celia Steele. Will had forgotten she was there, next to them all this time.

"She is," he said. "She needs to sleep a little more."

"Might you bless me, too?"

"Are you sick?"

"Aye."

"And scared?"

"Aye."

"Let's let my wife rest a little while, and then your father and I, we'll give you a blessing. But the wind has settled a little. Things should be better now."

"Might you bless Robert, too?"

"Yes. Certainly. Robert, how are you doing?"

"Not very good."

"I know. We all feel that way. But don't worry. We'll get through this."

From the lower berth Will heard Brother Steele say, "It's not so bad now, children. The sea is calming. We've passed through the worst."

"Where's Mum?" Celia asked.

"I'm here. Come doon to us now."

So Will got the Steele children down from their berth, and then he and Brother Steele placed their hands on their heads and blessed them. They did the same for Sister Steele and their other two children. And then Will made his way through the nearby berths, where the people in his group were, for the most part, still in bed. He asked all of them how they were faring, and he administered six more blessings before he was finished. He knew that this was something he had laughed at before—Brother Watson trying to heal his father's knee and getting no results. But all these people seemed to be comforted, and some said they felt new strength.

The day passed, and Liz stayed in her berth most of the time, but she didn't vomit, and by evening she was speaking to Will in little sentences. "I wanted to go," she told him. "You wouldn't let me."

"I know," he told her. "I couldn't face life without you. I just couldn't."

"I must remember the baby," she said.

"Yes. So do your best to eat all you can."

"I will."

Will held both her hands and whispered a prayer of thanks.

When he ended the prayer, Liz said, "Thank you, Will. I'm glad you're an elder now. You had the power to call me back."

"But I did it for myself. It was selfishness more than faith."

"It's all right. I'm glad you love me so much. And I felt the power, Will. It came from God."

Will thought that was true. It was desperation more than faith that had prompted him; still, Liz had felt God's power, and she was alive. The Lord had used his hands, his voice. Will felt changed, knowing that could happen.

• • •

Eleven days passed, the weather holding fair. Liz was feeling much better, and she was keeping her food down, at least most of the time. But the crossing would take another three or four weeks or longer, and surely there would be other storms. She prayed a dozen times a day—more—that her baby was still healthy inside her, and that she would be up to the next storm.

And then one afternoon, when she was taking some air on the main deck and actually feeling almost normal, Captain Slater, from the quarterdeck, used a voice horn to announce to all those on deck, "There are dark clouds off to the west. We're in for another bad blow. Make your way to your quarters and tie everythin' down secure. If we have to, we'll batten the hatches to keep water from filling the lower decks." He looked toward the Mormon passengers, who often gathered in a group. "Those good at prayin', pray for us now."

Will met quickly with Brother Burnham and then talked to some of the families. Liz heard him tell one man, "If things get bad, strap your children down. In that last storm, some of the little ones got thrown off their berths."

Liz was frightened, but she was also proud of Will. He was working hard to make certain everyone was cared for. He had always been reliable, but lately she had noticed more kindness, more concern for those in his charge.

He came to Liz after he had looked after the others, and they took one last look to the west where the clouds were boiling up, green and evil. The wind was rising already, the waves beginning to bulge. "Let's go below," Will said, and he helped Liz down the ladder. Once in steerage, Will worked his way through the families assigned to him, made sure boxes and barrels were secured, and told people to eat and drink a little now, before it would be hard to get to the food. And then, as the waves began to toss the boat more violently, he called on Brother Carver, of all people, to say a prayer.

Liz understood. Will was treating Brother Carver with respect, trying to bring the best out of him. The man had continued to complain about almost everything, and Will had had to reprimand him for his harshness with some of the other Church members. Still, asking him to pray was an invitation to think of the entire group, not just his own family, and that showed some wisdom on Will's part.

Brother Carver offered a mighty prayer—but just the kind, Liz knew, that Will didn't like. Will didn't think of prayer as an opportunity to use fancy words. It was a time to humble oneself before God. She had heard him say that, even specifically about Brother Carver's prayers. Still, the man did plead with the Lord to stay the elements and to protect His followers who were making their way to Zion.

And, as it turned out, Liz felt the prayer was answered. The ship tossed all that evening and all night, but not as badly as it had in the last storm. The Saints were not as seasick as they had been in the last storm, and the night was not full of cries of fear. Liz realized how weak and tired she still was when she drifted into sleep in spite of the storm.

By morning the weather had calmed a good deal. Liz awoke to

the slapping of the waves against the hull, but she didn't hear the creaking sound in the wooden beams that they had heard before. She heard muffled voices on the deck above her, showing that sailors were obviously moving about, unfurling sails that had been tied down the night before. It would be a good day, Liz told herself. She felt blessed and told the Lord so in a silent prayer.

And then someone screamed.

It was a long shriek—a woman's voice—and then Liz heard the sister plead, "No. No, Lord. Please, no."

Will jumped down from the top berth. He had never taken his trousers off the night before, having thought that he might be needed in the night. "What is it?" Liz heard him call, and she rolled onto her side to see that he was working his way to the next set of berths, aft in the steerage. He called again, "What's happened?"

"She's cold!" a sister was screaming. "I only slept a little, and she's already cold."

Liz knew the voice. It was Ellen Matthews.

"Sister Matthews," Will was saying, "what do you mean—just that she's gotten cold, or—"

"My baby's dead," Ellen wailed. "Little Phoebe, she's died, layin' right here next ta me." Liz heard her cries turn into sobs. "I never should ha' gone ta sleep."

Her husband told her, in a gentle voice, "It's not your fault, Ellen. She was pukin' up everythin' you fed 'er. She were just too weak."

Liz thought of dressing, but she didn't take the time. She climbed down in her underclothing and made her way to Ellen. There was silence in the beds, but Liz knew everyone was awake. More often than not, she knew, there were deaths on these ships, babies dying more than others. This was the first on this voyage, but many of the people had children. She knew what they were thinking: *What about my child? How many more will die?*

Liz found Jesse and Will next to each other, and Ellen still in her berth. Liz couldn't see much in the dim light, but she made out the shape of Ellen. She was turned on her side, clinging to Phoebe, who was still wrapped in a blanket.

And then Liz heard Jesse, Junior, in the bunk below. He had begun to cry. "Phoebe's dead," he said, probably speaking to his sister Mary. "Just like ol' Brownie, she's gone and died."

Liz dropped to her knees and found little Jesse. She pulled him to her, held him tight. "It'll be all right," she told him. "Phoebe's gone to heaven to be with God."

But Ellen cried out, "Why? We prayed and prayed, and God told us to go to America. Why would he take Phoebe? 'Tisn't right."

"It's the way of life," Will said. "We don't know why. But it does no good to question, either."

"'Tisn't right, Will. And do na' tell me 'tis. We gave up everythin' for Zion. An' look what God done to us?"

Little Jesse was still sobbing in bursts, but trying to get control. Liz continued to hold him.

"Don't ask those things right now, Ellen," Jesse said. "We can't break down. Think of Junior, and Mary. We have to carry on."

"I don't *want* ta carry on. I *can na'*. I prayed and prayed, an' God closed His ears. I want ta go 'ome."

"That's anough now, Ellen," Jesse said, rather firmly. "Don't talk right now. Cry aw ye need to. It's aw right to hurt. But do na' blame God."

Ellen sobbed for a time, but then she whispered, "I know. I know, Jesse. But she were so li'l. Why did I fall asleep?"

"You could na' ha' done anythin', Ellen. Once they lose so much water, they just can na' live."

Liz reached across young Jesse and touched Mary's face. The poor little girl hadn't made a sound, but she grasped Liz's hand and clutched it as though she were deathly frightened. Liz pulled her from the berth and held her close. Then she stood, still holding Mary, and she rubbed her hand over Ellen's hair, patted her face. "I'm so sorry," she said.

"Brownie died an' we digged a hole an' put him in the groun'," little Jesse was saying.

But that brought on another little screech. "I will na' let 'em put her in the sea," Ellen said. Her voice was less strident now, but hard.

Will didn't say anything. No one did. It was time for Ellen to cry some more. Liz carried little Mary with her and set her on her berth while she slipped a dress over her head.

She sat down and tied her shoes, but by then Mary had begun to cry. Liz held her close again, told her that everything was all right and that she would take her back to her mother. She made her way to Ellen. The ship was still rolling more than it sometimes did, and it was always a trick to walk in the dark. She grabbed the berths with her left hand and held Mary in her right arm as she was tossed off balance time and again.

"What can we do for Ellen?" a sister in one of the berths asked.

"I don't know," Liz whispered. Liz had been asking herself the same thing. She didn't know what anyone could do, but she knew that every woman in the hold was feeling Ellen's pain, and they all wanted to help.

When Liz reached the Matthewses, Jesse had taken little Phoebe from Ellen's arms. He was holding the tiny bundle to his chest. "This is hard," he told Liz. "We worried on this, but we had our answer. God wanted us to go."

"He did," Liz said. "Don't doubt that."

Will whispered to Liz, "I need to make a few arrangements. Stay with them for now." He made his way forward and climbed the ladder to the main deck.

There was not much that Liz could do. Jesse was taking over. He laid Phoebe next to her mother again, and he took Mary, who was still crying, from Liz. He talked to Jesse, Junior, and to little Mary, and he held them both in his arms. Liz stroked Ellen's hair again, but Ellen wasn't even crying any longer. She was lying on her side, staring past Liz. Liz had the feeling that she was talking to herself, calling up her will to do what she must do.

Will came back after what seemed a rather long time. By then many of the Saints had risen from their beds, dressed, and come to Ellen. They had told her how sorry they were, and she had thanked them in a quiet whisper.

"Could I ask everyone to go out on deck?" Will said. "See about some breakfast, and give us just a little time here."

Not all were ready to make their way up to the main deck. Some of the children were still asleep, and some of those still seasick were not able to pull themselves up. But Will had brought a lamp, and the light created a little circle. That was as close to a private place as one could find on the ship. Will told Ellen, "Sister Matthews, take as much time as you need. We'll look after your children today."

"An' what will ye do with Phoebe?"

"Ellen, we can't keep a body on the ship. It's not healthy. I'm sure you understand—"

"I will na' give her to the ocean. You can na' make me do it."

"But if you were on dry land, you would give her to the earth. It's the same thing."

"No, 'tisn't. A grave is spot o' land—some'ere I can come to and some'ere I can sit and talk to her. I will na' let her drift with the waves."

"She won't drift. They sew her up in something like a shroud, and they put weight in the bottom. Little Phoebe will sink down to the earth beneath the sea."

"Nay! I will na' let 'em do it."

"Ellen," Liz said. "I understand. I really do. I've thought what I would want, and I know I wouldn't want to put my baby in the sea. But I wouldn't want to put a child in the ground, either. The only way I could do it is to know that it's only flesh in the sea or in the ground. Her spirit is already with God. And that's a glorious thing to contemplate. She's blessed to be where she is."

"But I miss her. I'll allus miss her." Ellen broke down again, sobbing.

No one spoke for a long time, but eventually Will knelt down next to Ellen and, in a quiet voice, said, "My mother lost some of her babies. When I was thirteen, my little sister Christina died. She was two. And a few years later my mum had a baby boy, Thomas. He only lived a month or so."

"I know it happens," Ellen said. "But did your mum toss any of 'em in the sea?"

"No. She didn't. What I'm telling you is that my mother will miss those babies all her life. She's told me that many times. But sometimes we just have to do what's necessary. We go on—for the sake of our other children. And we trust the Lord."

"I did trust—an' look what's happened. What next? Will more of us die?"

"Ellen, you can't do this," Jesse said.

"She can do it for a day," Liz said. "Let her be angry today. She knows what she has to do, and she'll do it."

"That's fine," Will said, "but it's important, Ellen, that you not build this up in your mind the wrong way. You decided to emigrate, and you believed it was the right thing to do. Losing Phoebe doesn't change anything. Most families lose a child before they're all grown. There's just no point in asking why. We live on earth, where there's illness and pain. There's also death, and some die before others. That's just the way things are."

Will's voice was tender, but to Liz, his words seemed harsh. She didn't know what good it did to tell Ellen such things—at least right now. "There's a reason for everything," she told Ellen. "We just don't know what it is sometimes. Maybe someday you'll know. Maybe Phoebe is the blessed one. She can go home to God without facing some of the hardships the rest of us will live through."

"We're talking about things we don't understand," Will said. "I don't think God makes everything happen. I don't like to think of the world that way. I'd rather believe that death comes when it comes, and the blessing from Jesus Christ is that we'll rise from the grave—or from the sea—and live again."

"We'll be aw right," Jesse said. "Ellen's strong, an' she has great faith. She cares about her children more than anythin', so she'll move ahead."

Ellen was staring again, and Liz had the feeling that she had heard enough of these men offering their philosophies. Their words didn't change anything. Ellen wasn't ready yet to give up what she was feeling. She needed some time to come to that place.

"Could we give you a blessing?" Will asked.

Ellen looked back at Will for a long time, as though she weren't sure, but Liz saw the look in her eyes gradually soften. "Yes," she finally whispered.

Liz had noticed that Will had come down from the main deck with a little vessel of oil. "I would be happy to anoint you with this consecrated oil," he said. "Your husband can—"

"I'm not an elder, Will," Jesse said.

So Will stepped out. He returned with Brother Burnham, who rubbed a drop of oil onto Ellen's skin near her hairline and said a prayer of anointment. Then he and Will placed their hands on her head, reaching rather awkwardly into the upper berth. Will spoke quietly but with strength. He proclaimed Ellen whole and asked the Lord to deliver her from the anguish she was feeling. He blessed her with strength to carry on, and he commended little Phoebe to the Lord.

Afterwards, Ellen only said, "Thank you, Will," but Liz heard in her voice that she was starting the long process of accepting her new reality.

· · ·

Later that day, when Liz and Will were alone, she asked him, "Do you really think things just happen willy-nilly, and the Lord doesn't care?"

"I didn't say that."

"You said that things just happen."

"That's because I don't want to think that the Lord sits in His heaven and makes everything happen. I don't want Him to be the one who chooses to take Phoebe and leave another child with its parents, and I don't like to think that I have no control over my own actions. I want to make my own mistakes, not blame everything on God."

"But isn't there a reason for everything?"

"I don't know. Is there? Every year, on the farm, we would pray for good crops, and some years we got them, and some years we didn't. Was it God or the weather that made the difference?"

"Doesn't God send the weather?"

"I hope not. I'd rather think the wind sends the weather, and God doesn't bless one farmer and curse another."

"If I had died, would you have listened to someone who told you, 'Things just happen. Make the best of it'?"

"Is that what I said?"

"More or less."

Liz watched Will for a long time, until his eyes filled with tears. "There's a lot I don't understand," he finally said. "But I don't know what I would have done if I had lost you."

"Would you have turned against God?"

"I don't know. It's too terrible to think about." He rested his hand on her shoulder. She knew this was his way of caressing her without drawing the attention of everyone on deck.

"I just trust in God," Liz said. "That's all I know to do."

Will nodded.

"But you know what you told me. When you were hurt—and could have died—God told you to go home. You listened to His voice, and God blessed you. That means God cares about you, that He wanted you to live—and wanted us to be together."

"I do believe that. But I also know that terrible things happen in this world, and I don't want to blame them all on God."

"Do we have to understand everything? Isn't it good enough to know God loves us and that He cares what happens to us?"

"I suppose," Will said. "But I'd like to understand."

She could see the confusion in his eyes. She wondered whether the two of them would ever really understand one another, let alone understand the world they lived in. "I'm just so happy that your faith is growing," she said.

"But it's never steady. I feel it—and then it leaves me again."

"That's all right, isn't it—to believe and to have questions, too?"

"It would be easier not to fight with myself the way I do. Life is supposed to be hard, I think. But I wish it weren't quite such a struggle."

"I know. That's what I was thinking all the while the wind was blowing."

• • •

Will didn't press the issue about the burial the rest of that day, but the body couldn't be kept on board any longer. So after breakfast the next morning Will called the people from his group together on deck. Most of the Saints on board joined them. Parents and children stood together, all in the same clothes they always wore, but brushed a little better, and hats in hands. Brother Burnham presided, but he let Will conduct the meeting. "Brothers and sisters," Will said, trying to lift his voice above the rush of wind in the sails and the slapping of the water on the hull of the ship, "we're gathered together this morning to wish farewell to one of our little ones. We've clung to her body for a day, but we know her spirit actually departed yesterday. It has returned to its heavenly home. When Mary Magdalene arrived at Christ's tomb, she was told by an angel, 'He is not here; he is risen.' So is it with Phoebe. Her spirit is not here, and her body will rise from the sea and join her spirit in the resurrection."

Will had thought about the words all night, and now he watched Ellen and hoped that she might be consoled. He could see in her eyes that she had softened overnight, had accepted things, but he could also see her terrible sadness, and he thought again of Liz and how unprepared he would be to let her go. "I tried, yesterday, to explain to Sister Matthews that death has no sting when we believe in the Lord and His resurrection. But I know she is still feeling the sting of separation—and so are Jesse and Jesse, Junior, and little Mary. That's a sting we can't take away from them, but we can all bless this family with our kindness, and we can all pray for them."

Will thought he was only saying what people always said. He wasn't sure any of it mattered—or helped. But he added something he hadn't thought through very well, hadn't prepared. "We all talk as though we know the mind of God. But I'm not sure any of us do. My Liz told me yesterday that her answer is merely to trust the Lord. I'm not very good at doing that, but I guess it's what I have to do. I think that's also what Ellen and Jesse have to do now—trust, and move forward. They must go on to Nauvoo and continue the great work they've begun. And all of us must continue to call on God—for them, and for all of us."

Will then asked the members to sing "Prayer Is the Soul's Sincere Desire," a hymn that the United Brethren had often sung, and that was now in the new hymn book. The Saints sang softly, but the combined voices created a quiet power.

Will loved the words: "Prayer is the burden of a sigh, / The falling of a tear, / The upward glancing of an eye / When none but God is near." No matter how many questions he raised, he did believe in prayer. It had kept him going when he had had nothing else to rely on.

After the hymn, Brother Burnham came forward and said a prayer over the restless "resting place" for Phoebe, and then two brothers carried a tiny canvas bag to the rail of the ship. They placed the shrouded baby on a plank, stepped back, and then lifted the other end. The little bag slid down the board and dropped. The sea was noisy enough to mask the sound of little Phoebe splashing into the water, and from where Will stood, he couldn't see the bag sink into the darkness. But he was watching Ellen. She was crying, not wailing, not blaming, not challenging God. Clearly, she had made up her mind to carry on.

The wind was blowing across the deck, spraying the people with a cold mist. But no one walked away. The Saints stood together without speaking. Will thought they seemed more unified than they had been before.

CHAPTER 21

Another week passed with the weather holding clear. Early in the voyage, the wind off the sea had been cold, and no one had stayed out on deck very long. That meant far too much time in the dark steerage cabin. But spring was coming on, and the farther south the ship sailed, the warmer the weather. Will stayed on deck much of the time, just sitting on a box or on a pile of extra spars and watching the sea or talking with the other men. Most people had overcome the worst of their seasickness, but Will noticed a languor in their eyes—a deep tiredness. Liz came out on the main deck at times too, but she never felt entirely well, and she still spent many hours lying in her berth. She was able to eat a little more now, and she looked much better, but Will knew how weak she still was, and he never stopped worrying about her.

The most common discussion among the passengers was speculation about how much longer the passage would take. Captain Slater seemed to know better than to make his own estimate, so all the talk was based on shared ignorance and wishes.

The children had become livelier than at first, and they found games to play, but they were too confined in steerage and were sometimes rather foolhardy on deck. The younger girls and boys liked to run about or climb the masts. This frightened Will, who feared one of them would fall and get hurt or end up in the sea. Some of the sailors were friendly and liked to joke with the children, even feed them tall tales about great monsters at sea or mermaids combing their hair in the moonlight, but others were harsh, shouting at the children or cuffing them. Will told the crew to report to him when the children got out of hand but not to knock them about. One of the sailors stepped closer to Will and shouted in his face, "I'll not put up with these rascals foulin' my lines and spillin' our scrub buckets. You tell 'em to mind what they do or I'll throw the lot of 'em overboard."

Will thought of answers—even threats—but he didn't voice them. He promised he would talk to the ones who were getting too wild.

Food had now become much more of an issue than at first, back when no one felt like eating. Steerage passengers were expected to cook their own food in a shed on the main deck. The stove was a large plate of iron, big as a table, with a coal fire started under it each morning with flint and steel and tinder. A big kettle was used for boiling, and passengers could use a net to hang their meat, beans, or split peas into the water, each item marked with the owner's name. But with so many trying to cook at the same time, there were sometimes disputes about how much time a cook had taken, what food belonged to whom, or whether some were eating well while others suffered. And then, when the sea would become more restless, cooks would be jostled and sparks would fly—both the sparks of the fire and sparks of temper.

Worst of all was looking into the dining room where the cabin passengers ate. They had paid much more for their passage, and they sat at great feasts every day. When the "lower class of people" looked in at them, the waiters would tell them to move on, not to gawk.

What Will could see was that the passengers—Saints and others alike—were weary, restless, and still not feeling entirely well. He thought they were quicker to be harsh with one another than they might have been in other circumstances. But he knew what they felt; it was what he was feeling. Steerage was crowded beyond belief, with nowhere to escape to oneself. They would lie in berths that weren't high enough for sitting or sit on boxes and barrels and trunks, or even stand up, for want of room. Children grew cranky, babies cried, and the rumble of voices, with the crashing of the sea and moaning of the beams, all left a person bedraggled and short-tempered. There was no chance for a family to gather together quietly, no moments of privacy, little chance for couples to share intimacies.

When the sea calmed and the weather was nice, the deck became almost as crowded as steerage was in bad weather. There were coils of rope or spare spars, but little else, so most people, when the deck was crowded, had to stand, and the steady swinging of the ship, with sudden bumps and twists, made standing tiring.

Will watched his people grow increasingly irritable. They had shared much, been lifted at times, unified in many ways, but their patience was being tested. Some men became harsh with their wives and children. Some good brothers became hostile toward the sailors or the gentile passengers, denouncing them for sins and insults that seemed at least half imagined. The captain was a competent man, but taciturn. Passengers pumped him for information he simply wasn't going to give, and that became frustrating to some. And no one was worse than Brother Carver. Will worked to please the man, to praise him, to bring the best out of him, but finally, sometimes, there was nothing left but to reprimand him. And Brother Carver was too proud to accept any kind of correction.

Will also worried about some of the single members of the Church on board. A few romances were blossoming, and that was all right, but two of the young women in his group were known to flirt with the gentile passengers or even the sailors. Will hated to think of the dangers for these girls. He finally talked to them but received some rather haughty retorts. One father even told Will that his daughter had done nothing wrong and he had no right to accuse her. Will apologized to the young woman and to her father, but it took all his self-control to do it.

One Sabbath morning Will asked his group to gather on the quarterdeck. It was a fine morning, and Will thought he saw the Saints being lifted as once again they sang "Now Let Us Rejoice." They were crowded tight, as usual, but the music seemed to remind them of their common purpose. After an opening prayer, they sang "Jesus, and Shall It Ever Be," and then Aaronic Priesthood holders broke sea biscuits into small morsels and passed tin plates among the Saints. They blessed water, too, in tin cups, and passed the cups. The water was from the same barrels as usual, but maybe it had aired a little longer, or maybe the little sip wasn't enough to taste foul. In any case, Will didn't notice the burnt-wood taste that usually bothered him.

After the sacrament, Will gave a brief sermon. It was something he had been thinking about, and something, he thought, the members needed to hear. "In the Sermon on the Mount," he said, "Jesus taught His disciples in the following words: 'Ye have heard that it was said by them of old time, Thou shalt not kill; and whosoever shall kill shall be in danger of the judgment: But I say to you, that whosoever is angry with his brother without a cause shall be in danger of the judgment.'

"Brothers and sisters, I hope we remember how important these words are. We are gathering to Nauvoo—the city we consider Zion, at least for now. But Zion is more than a place. It dwells in our hearts. I know we are tired, and I know many of us still do not feel well. Some have suffered terribly. But we must find the will to control our voices, soften our words, and deal with one another with patience and understanding."

Will looked at Liz, saw her nod to him.

"I confess to you that I have sometimes been quick to judge my brothers. Sometimes I may have used harsher words than I needed to, even harsher than I intended. When we're sick, or just very tired, we sometimes say things we later regret. I fear that I have insulted some of you. I mean to do better. Let's all ask ourselves to do the same. Let's be patient with the children, kind in sharing what we have, and ready to raise up the arms that hang down."

He talked more specifically about arguments in the cooking shed, suggested that a schedule be worked out so that everyone wasn't crowding in the little enclosure at the same time. He pointed out that Christ taught that His followers should agree with their adversaries quickly. He knew that wasn't easy, and it wasn't easy for him, but it was important that they be more careful.

Before he closed, he said, "Brothers and sisters, we are being watched by other passengers and by the sailors on board. If we are to bring the gospel to the world, people must be able to observe the fruits of discipleship. If we cannot treat one another as Christ taught us to do, how can we expect others to see us as the Lord's people?"

Will saw people nodding, agreeing, and he thought he saw some of them resolve to do better. For a closing hymn, he asked that the congregation sing "How Firm a Foundation," one of the Saints' favorite hymns.

Will called on Jesse Matthews to say the closing prayer. He knew that the man had been purified by his grief and strengthened by his struggle to cling to his faith. He gave a gentle prayer, exactly what the members needed, and as they filed from the quarterdeck, many of them thanked Jesse for his prayer, Will for his fine sermon. Will felt that they had turned a corner and things would be better now.

Brother Carver grabbed Will's hand and shook it heartily. "Thanks so much, Brother Lewis," he said. "I accept your apology for the things you've said to me. I've been offended on this voyage, time and again, but I've bit my tongue, knowing that not a single one of us is perfect. You are very young, Brother Lewis, but I see some growth in you."

"Thank you, Brother Carver," Will said. He shook hands with Sister Carver, too, who was holding onto her husband's arm, looking pleased about his generosity. Will was holding on too, knowing that he couldn't say any of the things he was thinking.

"One thing, though," Brother Carver said. "We can agree with our adversaries, but only up to a point. That first mate hates us. He told me that we were nothing but madmen on a fool's errand. I told him that God would curse him through all eternity for speaking of God's ordained in that way. I felt justified. The man's a devil."

Will knew there was another side to this story. Brother Carver spent most of his time telling the gentiles on board that they needed to humble themselves and accept the restored gospel or they would be damned. The first mate seemed a fair man to Will, but he was probably out of patience with Brother Carver. Still, Will only said, "Let's be patient with unbelievers. We've only come to this belief recently ourselves."

"I'll be as patient as Jesus Christ when he threw the money-changers out of the temple. I won't be accused of madness just for following a prophet of God."

Will nodded and let it go, but he wondered what he would have thought about the Church if Carver had been the first Mormon he had met.

Will let everyone file out, thanking them all, and then he noticed that Liz had waited for him there on the rising plain of the quarter-deck. He went to her, watched her swaying before him, smiling. "That was wonderful, Will," she said. "Just what all of us needed."

"Just what I needed. I've been short with you sometimes."

She was clinging to the rail with one hand, but she touched the other to his face. "I'm glad we had some time together before we set sail. I know how kind you are. We're all worn out now. I've been no joy to be around myself."

Will thought how much he would like to have her alone for a night, together in a bed that wasn't tossing and rolling, and where there was no smell of sickness and unwashed bodies—and no children from another family. "Are you all right, Liz? Your eyes have looked so tired lately."

"I am tired. I've never been so tired in my life. How much longer will it be until we reach New Orleans?"

"Another week or two, I think. But it could be longer. Captain Slater admitted to me that the winds have held us up. It could be an eight-week passage. That would mean three weeks still to go."

He saw what the words did to Liz. "I was hoping it wouldn't be so long. I don't know whether it's the sea or the baby, but I never really feel well."

Will took her in his arms, something he wouldn't normally do out here where so many could see them. But he didn't care. He still wondered whether he had been wise to bring Liz onto the ship in her condition. He wondered about the cost of the voyage not only to her but to all their people. There were other babies who were looking very weak. And there had been a new illness, not from the sea: a fever and cough that was racking some of the people.

"I can make it," Liz said. "I've never done anything really hard before. It's good to learn that I can come up to the mark when it's asked of me. The Lord brought you back to me in Ledbury, and when I was on the brink of death here on the ship, you called me back. Now it's my turn to show the Lord I can be strong." She laughed. "And your turn to be gentle. You're learning it, aren't you?"

Will wasn't sure, but he was happy she thought so.

"I'm going to have to go back to our cabin," Liz said. "It's too hard for me to be tossed this way—and to cling so hard to the rail. I'll rest a little on the Sabbath." She smiled. "That's all I seem to do every day."

Will helped her down off the quarterdeck to the main deck and then down to steerage. He helped her all the way to their berth and lifted her up to it. But he didn't stay in the dark. He went back outside, taking his Book of Mormon with him. He sat on a barrel and read for a time, but that soon brought on some queasiness in his stomach, so he watched some flying fish along the starboard side of the ship. He let the wind whip through his hair, and he watched his shadow lengthen as the day passed slowly away.

Will did spend some time talking to Brother Burnham, comparing the sermons they had given, which turned out to have been almost the same. When Will told Brother Burnham what Brother Carver had said, Brother Burnham laughed. "I doubt the man will be satisfied with the celestial kingdom—if he manages to get there," he said. "He'll hand over a list of improvements the Lord should make in order to meet his needs."

The sun was beginning to set, much later than when the voyage had begun. Will was thankful for the additional light. He felt a glow within himself when he could watch the orange ball of the sun sink into the sea. He had always loved the beauties of the world, but he had often been too sick to take much pleasure in them on the ship. Still, he had enjoyed watching porpoises play alongside the ship, and he had seen a whale one day, diving and emerging, making a great spout each time it broke the surface. The ocean was beautiful in its way, too, the never-ending tossing and rolling, the whitecaps glistening in the sun. It would only be better if his stomach would settle completely, and it never did that.

One more week passed, and then one afternoon Will saw a line of fat black clouds in the west. Will wondered what was coming, but he understood when he heard the captain command his crew to furl the canvas on the main masts. It was late that night, after Will was asleep, when he first felt the rocking increase. He could hear the rush of the wind across the hatches, and he could feel the boat rise and then crash back into the waves. It was a good blow, but not as bad as the ones that had struck early in their voyage. Will hoped this one would pass away quickly.

But it didn't pass. It became worse all night. By morning the ship was tossing enough to keep most of the passengers out of the cooking shed. They huddled below and ate a little hardtack and drank a little tea. Will saw a few people heading for the water closets, looking pale, but it wasn't as bad as he had feared, not yet, and he continued to hope that the storm would soon pass.

By midday, however, the wind was howling louder than he had ever heard it. Will climbed the ladder to have a look. The wind caught him as he emerged and almost knocked him down. He grasped a rigging line and clung to it, but a sailor shouted for him to let go. The sailors were even pulling in the jibs and staysails.

The sky to the east was black, and the ship was being pushed hard to the lee side. The first mate was shouting to Will, but Will couldn't hear him. He cupped his hand around his ear, and the man worked his way closer. "Get below," he shouted. "Tie everythin' tight. We'll cover the hatches afore much longer."

Will climbed back down the ladder and spread the word. But things were tossing about enough already that it wasn't easy to secure them, and in the next hour the crashing sounds, the wild rocking, only got worse.

Will began to see brilliant flashes of lightning, and then he heard the sound of violent rainfall. A wave rolled over the deck and sent a gush of water down the hatches through the latticed covering. Shortly after, the sailors covered the openings with tarpaulins and tightened them down with strips of wood called battens. Children were crying by then, and now and then someone would scream as the ship lurched especially hard. Will wished he could do something, but he could only cling to the berth and to Liz. "Can we do this again?" she asked.

"Yes, we can. This will pass, and we'll make it again, same as last time."

But hours passed and the storm only became more furious. The boat seemed to jump and fall, even spin at times. It was hard to tell what was happening in the dark, with only a distant lamp swinging about, sending wild shadows through the cabin. From time to time, the ship would roll so far onto its side and hold there so long that it seemed it would never right itself. Several times Will thought it had gone under, but then it would bounce back and almost throw him off his berth.

Boxes and chests and barrels had broken loose and were sliding, crashing against the berths. At one point something metallic struck Will hard in the side of the head—a ladle, he thought. It bounced off the post of the berth and then struck the deck and tumbled away. Will held his head, wondering whether he was cut and whether he should chase the thing down, but he knew he could never manage it.

Now and then, the wind would quiet a little and the rolling would slow. Each time, Will hoped that the worst was over. But it was then that people, no longer clenching so tight, couldn't hold back their sickness, and splashes would hit the deck. The smell was overwhelming when Will had time to notice it, but then the tossing would increase again, and nothing mattered except that the ship stay afloat.

Celia and Robert Steele had been terrified of riding out another storm, so Brother Steele had let them into the bottom berth with him and his wife and other two children. The six of them were spooned together, holding tight. That gave Will and Liz more room, but they were gripped to each other tightly too. Will had wrapped his arm around Liz so he was holding her from behind. He didn't know what else to do for her. "We'll be all right," he would tell her. And a couple of times he shouted to anyone who could hear, "Keep praying. We'll make it through this." But he had been praying since he first saw the black clouds, had prayed for hours, and nothing had changed. The thought came to him again that the Lord didn't intervene, that He would let the wind blow until it was finished. He wanted to trust, but he knew very well that the ship could founder in such a sea. Every year ships went down in this ocean; the captain had admitted that himself.

Gradually, however, Will did feel that the storm was letting up. He thought they had made it through, and he told Liz it was almost over. "Oh, Will, thank the Lord for us. I thought I wasn't going to make it. I'm so sick. So sick."

But Will had only begun to pray when a blast struck the ship and tossed it on its side. The ship stayed there as boxes and baggage fell more than slid, then it finally flipped upright, but the fury of the wind seemed to multiply. And the ship went over again.

"We're sinking," Liz screeched.

There was a long pause, and Will was sure the ship was swamped, but it bounded upward one more time.

"Help us, Lord," Liz begged.

Will repeated her words. He knew the ship couldn't take much more. The roar of the wind and the ocean was all around him, filling his ears, but at times the vessel would lift high and seem to hold for a moment. It was then that Will could hear the wailing—children in hysterics, babies screaming in fear.

Above it all, Will heard Liz scream at him, "You've got to stop it, Will. We're going to die if you don't stop it."

He couldn't think what she meant. Stop what? The storm? How could he do that?

"Use your priesthood," she shouted. "Now. You have to do it now."

Will had never imagined himself having power over the elements. What did Liz expect of him?

"Do it! Do it now! Command the winds to stop."

"Liz, it will pass. We'll be all right." But he doubted she had heard him. He didn't want to yell such weakness at her.

"Will, now! I'm going to die if this doesn't stop."

Will swung his feet over the side of the berth and dropped to the deck. At that moment the ship swung on its side and Will was thrown down. He tried to get up, only to be tossed against the bottom berth. But he grabbed the side board and hoisted himself up, then clung to the post at the corner of the berth. He wanted to be standing. He didn't feel he could do this groveling on the floor.

Will lifted his right hand in the air, and, with his other arm wrapped around the post, he bellowed as loudly as he could, "In the name of Jesus Christ, I command the winds to cease. I command the storm to abate. Now!"

The ship rolled again, and Will found himself back on the deck. He had his answer. He clambered to his feet again, but he was humiliated. All the doubts he had been harboring rushed in upon him, and he realized that he didn't believe there was any such power in him. He was a sham, and now Liz would know. Everyone would know.

He clung to the berth and tried to think what he should do. Should he try again? Should he climb back into the berth and tell Liz he was sorry? It even struck him that it might be better, now, if he climbed the ladder and flung himself into the sea.

But something was changing. He wasn't being thrown about so violently. The sound of the wind had quieted a little. He thought for a moment that it was only another lull and the fury would be back. But it didn't happen. The rocking and tossing continued to calm. A few minutes passed, with Will just standing in the dark but now able to keep his balance. The sound of the wind was falling off. Even the people had fallen silent. It was really happening. The storm was ending.

And then someone in the dark said, "Thank you, Brother Lewis. You saved us."

But Liz said, maybe only loudly enough for Will to hear, "Will didn't do it. The Lord did."

Will let that sink in. The Lord *had* done it. It was true. He reached for Liz, and she grabbed his hand, pulled it to her lips, and kissed it. "Thank you," she said. "Thank you, Will. I love you."

She was crying. Will had begun to sob too. He had been trying to believe for such a long time. Now something stronger was coursing through him, seeming to fill up his body. God had been there all along, and He had known about the ship, about His people, about Liz and the baby. He had listened when Will had called. Will knew that now, would always know it, and that changed everything.

•   •   •

Two hours later the sun was shining in the sky. Liz climbed the ladder with Will just to see it. She wasn't hungry, but Will made her eat a little breakfast. Then they both climbed back down to steerage to pick things up, to swab the deck, to talk to the people and make sure they were all right. Not everyone had heard Will, the storm having been so loud. But everyone knew what had happened by now, and all of them thanked him. Liz could see that he was embarrassed by the praise.

Will made his way through steerage to make sure everyone was all right. Liz wanted to stay with him, but now that the quiet had come, weariness had struck her. She was walking past a lower berth back to her own spot when she heard a woman crying softly. "What is it, Sister Walker?" Liz asked. She knelt down next to her.

"It's Andrew. He's dying," she said. "He's hardly breathing now, and there's nothing I can do."

"The brethren can bless him," Liz said. "They can bring him back."

"He's had four blessings. But he only gets worse."

Liz looked at the baby in Sister Walker's arms. She couldn't see him very well in the dim light, but she knew he was only a few months old. He had been a happy baby when the Walkers had brought him on board. Brother Walker had bounced him on his knee in the beginning, and little Andrew had always laughed. But he had begun to spit everything up after the first big storm, and he had never improved much. Will had told Liz a week before that Andrew was in grave condition.

"Why not bless him again?" Liz asked.

"Last time, my husband said, 'Thy will be done.' I told the Lord I wanted my baby, but I would accept His will."

Liz realized that it wasn't in her own nature to accept. She had commanded Will to command the Lord, and that had seemed right. But what if she had to pass through some dark time and not get what she wanted? She had the faith to believe in the Lord's power to change things. She wasn't sure, however, that she could accept the will of the Lord when it went against her own.

• • •

Will worked hard to help the members of his group get their part of steerage cleaned and hunt down items that had been thrown about the deck. But he wanted to be alone. He needed some time to think. So he climbed the ladder again and found a place by the rail where he could stand by himself. He prayed out loud, thanking the Lord that he and Liz and the baby were all still alive, that the ship had been spared. He knew that troubles were not over for this group, but knowing that the Lord was with them, come what may, made all the difference.

After a time, he felt a touch on his arm and knew that Liz had come to share this moment with him. "Are you all right?" she asked.

"I'm fine. I'm thankful."

"There's some dried blood in your hair."

He touched the side of his head and remembered the ladle, or whatever it had been. But it was not important. "We saw a miracle today," he said. "It's not something I've believed in much before."

"There's something else you know now, Will. You're a man of God."

"It was God, not me. You said that yourself."

"But God worked through you. And now you know He can."

That was what Will had been thinking.

"Will, you need to come back to steerage now. The Walkers' baby just passed away. They need you."

Will had known that was coming, but it struck him hard. Still, he chose not to set one experience off against the other. God knew little Andrew, too, and knew the Walkers. That was the trust Will had never found it easy to accept, but he felt sure he could do it now.

CHAPTER 22

Autumn was beautiful in Nauvoo. The town was full of fall colors, and the historic area, with all the varied trees, was so breathtaking that Abby and Jeff drove down almost every day to have another look. Near the LDS Visitors' Center, several sugar maples were brilliant, almost neon red, and seeing them took Abby back to her days on the East Coast. She had missed those colors in California. She felt at home here with the angle of the sun, the clarity of the air, and the cooler temperatures, especially in the mornings. The trees along River Road, south of town, were subtler, mostly yellow, but the vistas out across the Mississippi made driving, for Abby, almost dangerous, as she gawked at all the beauty.

She made that drive many times a week on her way to Keokuk, and also when she drove to Carthage to see her gynecologist. Her baby was due in February, and in the last couple of months she had gone from "showing" just a little to being rather "great with child." She was not very big herself, and the baby had nowhere to hide. At first she was self-conscious about showing up at work in one of only two maternity outfits she had, so Jeff talked her into buying a couple more. Still, she didn't want to spend a lot on clothes she would only need such a short time. She spent most of the money she made on baby things, and she was surprised at how much everything cost.

Abby was becoming eager to see her baby. She had learned that it was a boy, but she hadn't really cared what sex it was, and Jeff had actually wanted a girl. "There's just something about a daddy and his little girl," he had told her. "But we can make more—the same way. I don't mind trying until we get us a little girl."

Abby was not so sure she wanted a lot of kids. She knew that some Mormons had huge families, but she had a hard time picturing herself with a houseful of little ones. It seemed impossible to her to love so many and give all of them the attention they deserved.

Abby had heard mothers speak before of loving the baby they were carrying, and that had been hard for her to imagine. But she understood now. When she had looked at the sonogram, had seen that little shape with arms and legs and a beating heart, she had understood "flesh of my flesh," and loved the little fellow instantly. She felt him now, squirming and thrusting his feet as though to seek his freedom, and she knew that a long adventure was ahead. She sometimes worried about the things that could happen, the choices a son might make someday, but her instinct was that she wouldn't let bad things happen. She would love him too much, teach him, and he would be like Jeff—tender and good and smart besides.

• • •

Halloween in Nauvoo was something of an extravaganza, with jack-o'-lanterns lining Mulholland Street. It was a yearly city project, she had learned, and lots of townspeople, along with some of the LDS missionaries, worked for two full days to carve all the pumpkins. These weren't the homemade type, cut with triangle eyes and noses. They were works of art. The event brought lots of people to town, and there was a charm in it for Abby and Jeff. Jeff helped with the carving and, in his usual enthusiastic way, came home talking about all the great people he had met and how much he liked living in a little town.

Thanksgiving turned out all right too. Abby and Jeff spent the day with Malcolm and Kayla and their little girls. Abby went over early and helped Kayla with the turkey and all the other preparations. She enjoyed that. But as Christmas decorations started going up in town, Abby longed to be with family. She and Jeff had had long talks about that. Jeff was all for driving to Las Vegas or New Jersey, since the cost of a flight was out of reach. Abby had hinted what her mother had suggested: that her parents would fly them home. But she was wary of doing that; she knew Jeff was against it. He didn't like the feel of turning to parents for money now. Abby's reasons were more complex. She wasn't sure she wanted time with her mother right then. She knew her mom had been against their having a baby so soon, and she didn't want to hear her say things that would make her feel bad about this baby that she was now so excited about. Abby also didn't like the idea of driving that time of year, almost eight months pregnant, with the weather so unpredictable.

Once Abby and Jeff agreed they would stay in Nauvoo for Christmas, Abby accepted the idea, and gradually she came to like it. It would be a quiet time, just her and Jeff for the last time in their lives, and Nauvoo was turning out to be charming. The little downtown area was decorated with Christmas trees in front of the businesses and with a larger tree by the Hotel Nauvoo. The temple fence was decorated with pine boughs and red ribbons, and there was a nativity scene on the lawn, all in lights. Abby also loved to drive through Historic Nauvoo and see all the quaint old houses with their fences and doors decorated in green bows and ribbons and with electric candles in all the windows.

Kayla and Malcolm held a little party in their home a couple of weeks before Christmas. They invited the younger couples in the ward with all their kids. Jeff had great fun with the kids, and, after rolling on the floor with some of them, he told Abby, "Hey, I'm thinking I'm glad the baby's a boy. I understand boys. For guys, life is all about wrestling and slugging and twisting arms. Girls never seem to get that."

"You won't bend my little baby's arms."

"Well . . . not at first. I'll play basketball with Malcolm until my son's big enough to beat up. You have to understand, pickup basketball is just an excuse to hammer each other."

This was said loudly enough for Malcolm to hear, and he turned around. "Yeah, but it's not much fun when I have to play with a sissy like you."

Jeff pretended to throw an elbow at Malcolm. "That's Malc—the elbow swinger. He brings down a rebound and then he clears the gym with his elbows."

And on it went. But Abby was glad Jeff had found a good friend. The two had worked out the problems with the wiring on the air conditioner only in time to be of help for a week or two before the weather cooled, but Malcolm had kept coming over. He liked to putter in the house with Jeff, to figure out a way to string a new wire or, especially, to tear out a wall. The two of them never stopped talking about the possibilities with the house. They were supposed to listen to Abby, who was the official decorator, but she hardly got a word in as they planned a new kitchen design or talked about the basement. They had enough rooms thought up to fill two homes that size: a big entertainment room with a projector and surround sound, an exercise room, storage, more bedrooms, and their favorite, a "man cave" filled with power tools.

What Abby didn't like so much, and Jeff hated, was the bitter cold that had struck Nauvoo in mid December. Jeff had done some skiing as a boy, traveling to Utah or Colorado to ski resorts. He said he had thought he knew about cold, but he had never felt the moist air blowing off the river. Abby worried that they didn't really have adequate coats: she felt penetrated with cold even just walking into church from the parking lot. Jeff and Abby had walked a lot that fall, but he gave up the idea entirely in December.

One cold night, Abby and Jeff drove to the Catholic church near the temple. A choral group from Quincy University was performing, and Abby had read in the *Journal-Pilot*, a county newspaper in Carthage, that the choir was very good. She and Jeff still missed the performances and lectures and film festivals they had been able to attend at Stanford, so they watched for anything that would bring back some of those opportunities.

Abby and Jeff had stepped into the Catholic church one day when they had been out walking. It was a beautiful old structure with vaulted ceilings. What had taken them by surprise was that someone was rehearsing on a magnificent pipe organ. It was the organ, as much as the singers, that attracted them to the concert, and the performance was everything they had hoped for. The precision of the voices and the power of the organ were exactly what Abby needed to feel that Christmas was coming.

As they were leaving, a young priest—a tall, athletic-looking man, and very good-looking, Abby thought—shook hands with them and thanked them for coming. "I haven't met you before, have I?" he asked.

"No. I don't think so," Jeff said. "We moved here last summer. A man hired me to fix up his house."

"Where are you from?"

"California. Las Vegas. New Jersey. Here and there."

"You're LDS, aren't you?"

"Yes." Abby wasn't sure why he had seen that in them—especially in her.

"I was out in Utah a couple of years ago. I went skiing and saw a lot of my friends. I've gotten to know the cast members from the pageant your church puts on here. They showed me all around."

"That's great. Did you like it?"

"I really did. I'm friends with a lot of the LDS people in town, and we have a good interfaith partnership. You've probably seen some of the things we do together—like the service we hold on the night before Thanksgiving."

"We read about that," Abby said. "But we didn't get there."

"Come next year. You'll enjoy it."

"I'm not sure we'll be here that long, but if we are, I'm sure we'll do that."

They thanked the priest, and then they walked back out into the cold. From the front of the church, Abby could see down into the river valley clear over to the lights of Montrose across the way, and then, as they walked up the street, she looked up at the temple with all the floodlights on it. The thought struck her again: she felt at home here. She felt welcomed. She liked a place where a Catholic priest was a friend to local Mormons, and she liked the feel of this town, even in the bitter cold.

"I kind of hope we are here again next year," she told Jeff when they reached the car.

He started the engine and fiddled with the knobs on the heater control, but then he turned and looked at her. "It's funny you say that. I was thinking the same thing."

"Isn't there *some* way you could find a job around here?"

"I could find something, maybe. I might have to drive a few miles, but I wouldn't mind that. It's just that it would probably be a dead-end job, and I doubt I'd make very much."

"Maybe we wouldn't need so much if we stayed here." It was a strange new way of thinking for Abby. She had always had nice things growing up—nice clothes, a beautifully decorated house, piano lessons. Could she raise a family and not give them such things? She wondered how much they mattered.

"I don't think I've ever chatted with a priest before," Jeff said. "It felt right to me. Kayla and Malcolm went to a Catholic fund-raiser on conference weekend—a taco dinner or something. They said a lot of the Mormons go to that. Half the missionaries were there."

"I can't picture that in most places," Abby said, then added, "You like Malcolm, don't you?"

"Sure."

"But he's not your kind of guy. He doesn't know much about history, or good books, or politics—any of the stuff you like to talk about."

"I know. But talk is one thing, and . . . I don't know . . . Malc is just a good guy. And he's really smart. He knows about things I know nothing about. The guy can fix anything."

"Kayla's background is completely different from mine. I noticed it all the time, at first. But now—I don't know—it doesn't matter."

"I know. That's what I'm saying." Jeff drove the car past the temple, but he didn't turn toward their home. He turned on Mulholland to the west, and drove down the hill to Historic Nauvoo. Abby knew why. He liked to see the decorated houses as much as she did—especially when they were lighted at night. "When is the heater going to kick in?" he wondered out loud.

"So maybe you should look for a job around here, and not send your *vitae* to all those big cities you've been trying."

Jeff didn't respond for a time. She knew this wasn't easy for him. Finally, as they reached historic Main Street and turned south by the Cultural Hall, he said, "I got a call this week from Jerry Phelps, my friend from Stanford. I guess I should tell you what he and I got talking about."

"Yes. I would think so." It really did bother her when he worked on their future without sharing the possibilities with her.

"Well, it's just this vague possibility, not any kind of offer. So nothing is likely to come of it."

"What are you talking about?"

"Jerry's in grad school at Princeton now. He knows a history professor there who's applied for a big grant. I don't know what's involved exactly, but Jerry says the guy is looking for someone with a background in history but also in computers. I guess the study he's doing is going to require some pretty sophisticated programming, and the professor has no computer background at all."

"Wouldn't you have to be in the history program yourself?"

"Well, yeah. That's the whole idea. Jerry told him about me, and how I've thought about going on in history—and that my education is in computers. The professor told him he thought I would be a good fit. They could maybe work out a fellowship for me, and the grant would pay for me to go to school."

"So you're still thinking about going back for your PhD in history?"

"I wasn't—not until Jerry called. But if I could get paid to go to school, that might be too good to pass up. I would have to apply to Princeton for grad school next fall—and do that right away—but I would probably have the inside track on the appointment."

"But you don't have a degree in history."

"I know. And that might knock me out. But Jerry said that the professor thought we could work around that. I guess Jerry made him think I was some sort of genius."

Abby tried to let all this sink in. She wasn't sure how she felt about it. "I like Princeton—I mean the town, not just the university—but it's nothing at all like Nauvoo."

"It's pretty small, and—"

"It's Stanford all over again. It's a way of thinking as much as it is a town and a university."

"Sure. I know. But no matter how much we like it here, Princeton is more who we are than Nauvoo is."

"I thought we were just saying the opposite."

"Not necessarily. I'm glad I like it here so much—and who knows, maybe after grad school, I could find a teaching job at a small college in a little place like this. We've found out we don't have to be in Chicago or LA."

Abby wasn't sure what was making her so uncomfortable, but part of it was that she had begun to feel she had found a home, and now they were already talking about giving it up.

"You'd be close to your family," Jeff said.

"I think that's maybe what I don't want."

"Really?"

"Jeff, you've only been around them for a few days at a time. They've learned to tolerate you, so they seem all right, but I don't think you understand how much I disappointed them by joining the Church. Every decision I make is foreign to them now. They questioned our having a baby, and they'll question every one we add to it. If we have more than two, my mother will want to have me declared legally insane."

She saw Jeff nod. He supposed he did understand. But she was surprised at how upset she was feeling. Jeff turned left on Parley

Street and started back toward their house before Abby realized she hadn't really looked at the decorations.

"The thing is," Jeff said, "the way grant money is drying up, chances are, nothing will come of this. But don't you think it would be the right answer for us if it did come through?"

"How many years would it take you to get your PhD?"

"Maybe five. Maybe more, if I have to get more undergraduate credit."

"Would the grant last that long?"

"I don't know. I keep asking that, and Jerry doesn't know. But he says I could get a teaching assistantship at some point."

"Could we go on with our family, or would we have to put that off?"

"We just wouldn't put it off, but things might be tighter for us than it is for most students."

"I just want to put first things first, Jeff."

"I know." But he stopped talking.

Abby knew what she had done to him. "I'm not against it, Jeff. I'm really not. But when you find out things, tell me. Let's talk about all of it."

"Okay."

"Jeff, have you really been looking for a job? I mean, seriously?"

"I've sent out applications all over the place."

Abby knew that was true, but she also wondered how much effort he was putting into those applications. It was hard to believe there weren't *any* jobs for someone with his training. She wondered if he had only tried for positions that were actually outside his range right now.

"Look, Ab, I understand the situation. I've got to start making more money. The contract work just isn't coming in the way I thought it would, and you need to stop working at Walmart right away."

"I'm feeling a lot better than I was at first. I've gotten used to being on my feet."

"Yeah, but you can't be standing at that scanner when your water breaks. You need to get out of there in a couple more weeks."

It was Abby who had suggested that timing long ago, but she was scared of stopping now. Life was going to be more expensive with a baby, and Jeff was right: he hadn't been bringing in much income. "Let's just see how I feel next month."

"Here's what I'm going to do, honey. No one is hiring right now, but as soon as Christmas is over, I'm going to start hitting the pavement in the towns around here. If I could get a forty-hour-a-week job, with benefits, then I could do the work on the house at night and on Saturdays. I've got to start making a decent salary."

"But you'll hear any day about Princeton?"

"Yes. But it doesn't matter. I won't start until fall, if that comes through, and between now and then I've got to act like a daddy and provide for my son."

Abby always felt guilty when the conversation came to this, but she also felt relieved. She did hope he could find something.

• • •

On the following Wednesday, Abby had her appointment with her ob-gyn. She had talked Jeff into driving with her to Carthage, as he sometimes did. He actually had been working very hard on the house, and she knew he didn't like to stop when he was busy, but a little snow was falling, and she felt better with him driving on the winding road along the river.

Along the way they didn't talk about work or grants or graduate school, but it bothered her a little that she had heard him talking to his friend Jerry twice since the weekend, and she could feel how excited Jeff was about the possibility. She told herself she really wasn't opposed, but she did see a lot of years ahead that would remain unsettled, and then another move after that. Her instinctive feeling was that her only real job now was to make sure her son had a good start in life. Five more years of survival wages and uncertainty just didn't sound like the life she wanted her baby to have. But she didn't say any of that. She knew she had to let Jeff explore all his possibilities.

At the doctor's office, Jeff, as always, got very interested and asked more questions than Abby ever could have thought of. Dr. Deerfield had clearly liked Jeff from the beginning, and once again they talked too long, with Jeff asking about placentas and the biology of gestation. But Dr. Deerfield gradually lost interest in the conversation as he began his exam. "Tell me something," he asked Abby, "do you feel as though you're getting bigger lately?"

"I don't know. I'm *huge*. But I've been that way for a while."

"When I look at these measurements, I don't see an indication that the baby has grown much this last month. Just to be careful, I'm going to have the nurse give you an ultrasound."

"Do you think there's a problem?"

"Not likely. But let's be sure. Let me look at the pictures and we'll know a lot more."

He left, and Abby looked over at Jeff. "I don't know if you've gotten bigger," he said, "but I wouldn't worry about it. You said yourself, the baby's really active."

But Abby didn't like this. She was nervous as the nurse performed the ultrasound, and she felt worse after she dressed and sat down next to Jeff. He kept trying to say the right thing, to calm her down, but the doctor was taking a long time, and that worried her more. She didn't want to talk; she just wanted to hear that everything was all right.

Dr. Deerfield looked much too serious when he returned. "Do you have time to run down to Quincy today?" he asked.

Abby didn't like the tone of his voice. He was a balding man with a long, narrow face. When he smiled, the corners of his lips would rise up almost vertically—and he was almost always smiling. But not now. Something in his voice seemed to say, "Don't scare these kids. Sound relaxed."

"What's wrong?" Abby asked.

"I'm not sure. I'm seeing something that doesn't look quite right. It's probably not a big problem, but I just think it would be better to check it out."

"*What* doesn't look right?" Jeff asked.

"It has to do with the baby's heart on one side. The right chambers seem larger than the left ones. But an echocardiogram can provide a better picture, and you need to see a specialist for that."

"Are you talking about a heart defect?" Jeff asked. But Abby was too startled, too panicked to say anything. She was not sure she wanted to hear the answer.

"It's possible. About eight babies in a thousand are born with some sort of heart abnormality. Most defects are minor and can be corrected easily. But I think you'll be better off to find out today if something really is wrong—and not have to wait and wonder. I called Dr. Hunt down at the Heart and Vascular Center, at Blessing Hospital. He's a pediatric cardiologist, and he's very, very good. He said you could come down right now."

"But if one side of his heart is bigger than the other, could that be a *major* problem?" Jeff asked.

"Well, yes. Of course. But the baby has been developing normally, so I doubt it's anything you need to worry too much about. I just want you to see a specialist who can take a better look at what's going on."

"What if—"

"Let's just see what we're dealing with and then we can talk again. Or it might be that Dr. Hunt will be the one you would end up with. He'll be able to explain all the options. My hope is, he'll tell you that I'm just imagining things and send you back to me."

Abby didn't want to talk. She just wanted to get to Quincy as fast as possible and find out what was wrong with her little son. It was a half-hour drive, and all along the way, Jeff kept trying to say things to console her, but Abby didn't want to hear any of it. She felt as though she had come home to find her house invaded, or as though someone had beaten up on her baby. She didn't know how bad this was, but she couldn't relax, and above all, she didn't want to speculate. She just wanted to be told that nothing was wrong after all. And so she prayed, over and over, and asked the Lord to make everything all right.

She was equally silent in Quincy, and she continued to pray during the test. Then she sat in the office and finally told Jeff, "Let's not talk about it yet. Let's just see what he says."

Dr. Hunt seemed a confident man when he walked in—with a crisp blue shirt and bright yellow tie—and he didn't seem worried. He smiled and shook hands, and then he said, "You should be glad that Dr. Deerfield picked up on this. Most gynecologists wouldn't have bothered to give you a second ultrasound."

"Picked up on what?" Jeff asked.

Abby offered one last, quick prayer: *Please don't let it be serious.*

"Your baby definitely has a heart defect. At this point, though, it's a little hard to say exactly what's going on. His left ventricle looks undersized, which could indicate hypoplastic left heart syndrome. But it could also merely indicate an aortic coarctation, which means that the aorta is pinched or underdeveloped. It's something we can correct with surgery."

"Do you mean open-heart surgery?" Jeff asked.

But Dr. Hunt was looking at Abby, not at Jeff. She had clapped her hands to her face and was trying hard not to cry.

"Possibly. It depends on—"

Abby couldn't hold back a little sob. "Cut his little chest open?"

"That's right. But I'm thinking we won't have to do that. If it's the aorta we need to correct, we'll make a little incision in his back. We won't have to open up his chest."

"But what if it's the other thing—the hypoplastic thing?"

"That's more difficult." The doctor pulled a chair over to Abby and sat down in front of her. His voice had become softer. "Hypoplastic left heart syndrome is a serious defect. It's usually dealt with in a series of three surgeries. And yes, we would have to go through his chest. But infants recover from that kind of surgery much faster than adult patients do."

"But *three* times?"

"Yes, but remember what I said. I think we're dealing with aortic coarctation, and that's a fairly simple matter. We may only need to make that correction, and he'll grow up strong and healthy—and just have a tiny scar on his back."

It was Jeff who asked the question that was in Abby's mind. "If it is the other thing—the left heart thing—will he still develop normally?"

"Possibly. If everything goes well, the child can do fine. But it's much more involved, and early development is certainly slowed."

"What if things don't go so well?"

"Some hearts are simply beyond repair. It's important you know that. In those cases, the babies simply don't survive. But it's a big mistake at this point to speculate about all that. Right after the baby is born we'll take him out and do another echocardiogram. We get a clearer picture once he's no longer *in utero*. It's conceivable that we'll conclude he doesn't need surgery, that the aorta will correct itself, but chances are, a few days after his birth, we'll correct whatever problems we find."

"Will I have to have a C-section?" Abby asked.

"No. Just a normal birth. A fetus's heart doesn't start functioning the way yours does until a day or two after the birth—and we can stretch that time with medication. But there won't be any strain on his heart during the birthing."

"So what do we do now?" Jeff asked.

"I want to see you every week, and we'll keep watching this. If you notice anything changing, any sign that the baby is moving less, I want you to come here directly. Just call ahead and we'll take you in immediately. But I have no reason to think anything like that will happen."

Nothing about this sounded good to Abby, not slicing her baby open, not facing the worst possible outcomes, not even facing the best. She had four weeks to worry, and she had never been good about dealing with uncertainty.

Jeff kept asking questions, and Abby wanted to shout at him to shut up, to think about her baby—not some theoretic "fetus" he and the doctor had begun to talk about. She stood up. "Thank you, Doctor," she said, in the middle of one of Jeff's sentences.

"Listen, Mrs. Lewis—is it Abigail?"

"Abby."

"Abby, things like this happen much more often than you can imagine. I know it's a shock when you find out, but assume the best, not the worst."

But Abby knew what the "worst" was. Her baby could die. She couldn't just skip out to the car and tell herself that the glass was half full.

Jeff was talking again—all the way to the car—telling her how much confidence he had in Dr. Hunt, telling her that she needn't worry too much.

"Aren't you worried?" she finally asked him with heat in her voice. And then she began to cry.

Jeff reached for her, stretched across the front seats and held her in his arms. "Yes, I am. Of course I am." She heard the strain in his voice and knew he was close to tears himself.

"They'll cut him open, Jeff. He'll hardly arrive in this world, and the first thing they'll do is cut him open."

"Maybe not. Maybe they won't have to."

"Give me a blessing and make him all right. God can fix something like that."

"I will give you a blessing."

Abby sat back. If she had as much faith as those Nauvoo pioneers, her baby could be healed. She drew in some air and made up her mind that she would put this on the Lord—let Him take care of her baby. But the thought of the early Saints had brought another image into her head: all those babies who had died of fevers and ague. All those women of faith praying for their babies, and hundreds of their little ones dying. The only thing she was sure of was that she wasn't as strong as they were. She couldn't let go of her little son and then just go her way. Those early sisters were made of different stuff.

• • •

Jeff *was* scared—much more frightened than he wanted Abby to know. He thought things would probably be okay, but he was frightened at the idea of blessing Abby. She wanted a miracle, and he didn't want to disappoint her. If he administered to her and then things went badly, what would that do to her?

Back in Las Vegas, when he had been a teenager, a boy in his ward, Chad Walters, had been hit by a car on his bicycle. Jeff's father had been the bishop then, and he had hurried to the hospital and given Chad a blessing. Dad came home and said he felt sure the Lord would bless the boy, that he would be all right. But that night Chad had died without ever regaining consciousness. At the funeral, the family had said it was all right, that God had taken him home. But Jeff had wondered ever since that day: why hadn't his father's blessing worked? Somehow it was easier to think that the doctor knew his stuff, could make a correction and make everything all right. It seemed easier to pray for the doctor to do his job right than it was to pray for the heart to correct itself.

But he couldn't let Abby down. He had to have more faith.

CHAPTER 23

Will spent some time with the Walkers, but he decided this time not to say too much, since they were handling their loss quite well on their own. But he needed to make arrangements for another burial at sea. He climbed to the main deck, where the crew was almost finished replacing a broken spar of the foremast. To Will's surprise, the other masts were still standing. Will walked to the quarterdeck, where Captain Slater was conferring with his first mate. Both turned as Will approached. "Well, Lewis," the captain said, "your people are telling quite a story. They say you commanded the winds to stop—and the winds obeyed."

Will decided not to respond to that. He suspected that Captain Slater was skeptical of such things. "Is the ship all right?" Will asked.

"Thanks to you. What did you do down there?"

"When things got really bad I asked the Lord to stay the storm."

"And the storm let up?"

"Soon after. Yes."

Captain Slater smiled. "It's good to know we have a man on board who can quell the seas and command the winds. I should take you along all the time. Next time, work your magic just a little sooner."

Will didn't need this kind of sarcasm. "I'm glad we made it through," he said. "You were right to furl the sails when you did." He turned to walk away.

"Lewis."

Will turned back.

"I don't know whether you people have the power you claim to have. I suspect the storm merely blew itself out and you picked the right time to say your prayer. I'll say this, though. We should have gone down. I've never passed through a storm quite like that one. And yet we only lost the one mast. We rolled so far over three or four times, I thought the end had come for all of us."

"Well . . . I'm glad we made it through."

"I've heard captains say, back in Liverpool, 'It's good to have Mormons aboard. Their ships never sink.'"

Will stepped back to the captain and spoke quietly. "I don't know about that, sir. We've just lost another baby this morning. So I know that we aren't spared some of the grief this world offers. But I do believe that God directs our work. I have no power as a man to quell a storm, but the priesthood I hold can call down the powers of heaven. I've doubted that myself at times, but I saw it happen this morning."

The captain wasn't smiling now. "Well, thank you," he said, and he shook Will's hand. The first mate did the same. They both gripped so hard that they hurt his painful hand, but he didn't blanch. He appreciated their gratefulness—and he felt good about proclaiming his belief.

What Will learned in the coming days was that the ship had been blown farther off course. The arrival in New Orleans was set back again, and supplies were dwindling. It meant that everyone would have to cooperate and share, and some had to be taught to do that, but even Carver had been softened by all the days at sea and the shared difficulties. It took a request from Brother Burnham, but Carver acceded to it and gave food to some who were especially short on supplies.

As the ship sailed past Cuba, dark-skinned people from the island approached the ship in small boats and offered fruits and vegetables for sale. The Saints didn't have much ready cash, but they bartered some of the household goods they had brought—plates and silverware—that now didn't seem so important. In this warm, clement weather no one was suffering any longer with seasickness. Quiet April winds delayed the arrival a little more, but everyone knew that the voyage would end before long, and that brought on lots of longing, lots of watching, but also hope for better days ahead.

Will knew something had changed when the blue-green waters of the Caribbean began to change to yellow-brown. This was the muddy Mississippi water, and a clear sign that the end of the voyage was near. A steamboat met the ship and attached ropes, then towed the ship, with furled sails, up the river to New Orleans. But it was slow going against the current, and another day passed with everyone anxious for the landing.

When New Orleans was finally spotted, it appeared to be nothing but masts of docked sailing ships and smokestacks of steamships. The crowd of passengers soon grew thick on the main deck. The captain had to shout, over and over, for people not to collect on the port side of the ship, but for some to stay starboard. Will stayed back, but he understood the desire of the others. As the ship was towed past the many docks, he could see all sorts of people and things he'd never seen before. Half the people here had black skin. They were slaves, Will assumed, and they were toiling with the cargo, loading or unloading ships, or carrying luggage, following well-dressed white families—men in top hats and frock coats, women in colorful dresses.

There were elegant homes not far from the wharves, two-story structures with wrought-iron balconies. But Will had also seen shacks along the river that seemed too flimsy for a family to live in. And he had seen children dressed in little more than rags playing or feeding animals outside those shacks. Similar children, along with destitute-looking adults, were begging on the streets by the docks. He also saw women who were clearly streetwalkers, and sailors staggering about, drunk in the middle of the day.

Brother Burnham called a little meeting of his leaders, and then he assembled all the Mormons on deck. He announced that no one should leave the ship until arrangements were made for their transfer to a riverboat. "When you do get off the ship," he said, "you must be very careful. There are pickpockets hereabouts, and people who would knock you over the head and cast you in the river, all for a decent pair of boots or a gold watch. Stay together, and we'll carry our trunks to the riverboat only after we have struck a good bargain with acceptable fares. Those who don't have the strength to move your own trunks, stay on the ship, and men will return to help you after they have moved their own luggage. Get your things on the boat, and then we can bargain for food for the river trip. Let us help you with that, too; we can get the best prices."

Will stayed on board and made certain none of the Mormons left the ship. When Burnham returned, he told Will, "We have to hire two riverboats. We can get a hundred and fifty of our people on one boat—the *Eloise*—at four dollars a passage to Nauvoo. It's a good price, but there wasn't room for all of us. The others will have to take the *St. Louis*. It's a larger boat, but it was more fully booked. I convinced the captain to let us fill it up for the same price."

"Is that the price for steerage class?"

"No. It's worse. There's no steerage space on these shallow boats. We're all going to be deck passengers. We sleep out in the open. It's a hardship, but usually the trip to St. Louis only takes about a week, with another day or two on to Nauvoo. The river isn't running high so far, so the boats make pretty good progress upriver—six miles an hour or so."

Will knew the members would be relieved to learn that the passage was cheap. There were some who had little money for groceries. But he also wondered how they would manage on the deck. He hoped the weather stayed warm—and dry—as the boat progressed to the north.

The transfer went smoothly. Brother Morris, one of the counselors, was asked to lead the smaller group, and Brother Burnham took the larger one. The larger group was divided into four districts, and Will, under Brother Burnham's direction, continued to lead the same people he had directed on the ship. Will soon heard the engine of the *St. Louis* being stoked up, and then the boat departed in a great roar of smoke and pounding pistons. But Captain Rupp of the *Eloise*, the boat Will and Liz were taking, stayed at the dock all day, the captain promising every hour or so that he would soon get started. As it turned out, he didn't leave that day at all, and the next morning he began to promise again. What Will realized was that even though he had claimed to be booked, he was still trying to stack as many passengers as possible onto his boat. He had wanted the Mormon business, at a cut rate, but he had saved room to stuff more people on at higher prices. Brother Burnham talked to him, extracting a promise to leave soon, but it was late in the afternoon when Captain Rupp finally ordered his firemen to stoke up the boiler fires, and it was getting dark when the boat finally pushed off.

Will watched his people give way to frustration during all the waiting. It had seemed as though the agony was over when the Saints had stepped off the *Sea Bird*. But this wait in the humid warmth, with no berth, only a deck to sit on, was a test of whatever patience the people had left. Children were tired and grouchy, and the ship was much too crowded. Worse, the food purchases had been calculated for eight days of travel, but now another two days had been added. Will had had to go about telling his people to be careful to make their food last. It was mostly dried beef and pork, and rice, which Will could see already would be difficult to boil with so many people competing for the galley.

Will had never encountered such a mix of people. He saw men in buckskin clothing who talked in growling voices and bragged to each other about heading up the Missouri and on "out west." Or at least he thought that was what they were saying. He only picked up about half of the talk in their strange dialect. Most of them chewed tobacco and spat on the deck, where people had to walk in their black spittle. That was disgusting enough, when there were spittoons everywhere and a railing to spit over, but what shocked all the English members was the tendency for well-dressed men in silver cravats and fancy, striped waistcoats to do the same thing. Splotches of tobacco spit were everywhere already, and this was the deck where most of the passengers would sleep.

There were, however, cabins for the better-off travelers, and a sizable salon, where these same passengers would take their meals. While deck passengers were making do, eating their dried meat, Will watched the cabin passengers assemble for a repast that was like a Chrismas feast: meats of every kind, potatoes, rice, vegetables—a large red ball of a fruit called a "tomato," which Will had never seen before—cold milk, wine, beer. Will watched through an open window and saw the passengers attack the food like birds of prey, reaching and grabbing, gulping. They had made short work of all the food in ten minutes, and then the men settled back to smoke cigars.

Simply finding a place to sleep and dealing with the air that never really cooled at night was disheartening. Poor Liz was suffering. Will hoped he could make things better for her soon. She didn't complain—not about the hard deck itself—but he saw in her eyes that she was wondering what kind of world she had entered.

Everything seemed a little more hopeful once the boat was under way. The pounding sound of the steam engine was bothersome, and the stories passengers told of boiler explosions—and the rush they made to avoid proximity to the boilers—did make the trip frightening. But at least the riverbanks gave people something to look at, and there were no waves to make a passenger sick. Most important, this time the trip was only a week, not sixty-six days—the time it had taken to cross the ocean.

On the second day out of New Orleans, Will climbed to the promenade deck—the first deck above the main deck—to have a little better vantage point to see the countryside. The promenade deck provided a walkway around the entire boat, so while Liz was resting on the main deck, he could move about a little and relieve some of his restlessness. He looked out across the swampy areas near the banks to the thick forests beyond. It was an unimaginable country, such vast areas open to settlement, but it was so overgrown with foliage that he wondered how anyone could clear the land. He did see pockets of cultivated, dark soil, but in those cleared areas were shanties hardly fit for humans. He knew this was the West, not Boston or New York, but he somehow hadn't expected the United States to appear quite so primitive.

Will had seen Indians on board, not dressed in the regalia that he had seen in pictures, but sometimes dressed in suits of clothes, like other Americans, and sometimes in buckskins. He had also heard at least half a dozen languages spoken on board—Swedish, he thought, Italian, French, and others. People were apparently immigrating to this area from all parts of the world. Many of them were like his English friends, looking less than prosperous but neat. The ones who had been in the country longer—the ones who seemed most "American"—were often dirty and smelly. Will had discovered that outside the water closet was a hairbrush hanging on a little rope. It was there for all to use, he assumed, but Will couldn't imagine sharing such a thing with a whole boatload of people. Worse was a community toothbrush, but Will had the feeling no one used it. He had never smelled such powerful, stinking breaths or seen such stained and decayed teeth.

Will was wondering about all that—whether this wild land made people less refined, turned them into ruffians—when a man spoke to him. "Good day," he said, in a style and accent that seemed almost British. "Are you English?" the man asked.

"Yes, I am," Will said. "Are you?"

"No. I cannot make such a claim. My heritage goes back to the south of England—Cornwall—but I have never crossed the ocean to visit my family there."

Will could hear now that his speech, though a little more careful than some he had heard, was clearly American. It was broader, seemed to come from a rounded, hollow mouth, and emphasized the letter *r* much more than he was accustomed to. "Do you live in this part of the country?" Will asked.

"No. I haven't done, not until now. But I'm moving west from Delaware, where I was raised. I plan to locate in St. Louis and be part of the great growth of these western regions. And may I ask, sir, what brings you here?"

"I plan to locate, with my wife, in Illinois."

"Ah. I understand now. You're one of the Mormons on board."

"Yes, sir, I am."

The man seemed prosperous. He had the mannerisms of an

English gentleman, and he wore the clothing of a well-off American: a dark frock coat, a stovepipe hat made of beaver skin, and a gray waistcoat. His clothes were clean, too—or at least better than most. Clearly, he had brushed his coat, even if it was wrinkled from much wear.

"Would you mind taking a moment to tell me the essentials of your beliefs?" the man asked.

"Not at all."

"But tell me first, how should I address you?"

"Will Lewis is my name."

"Mr. Lewis, I'm most happy to make your acquaintance. My name is Major Preston Harcourt."

"Are you a military man, Major Harcourt?"

"I have been. I served in the Light Infantry Brigade of Dover, Delaware. I have left that post, in my move west, but no doubt will serve in some such capacity again."

Will was not quite sure how the military operated in America. He had heard a number of the better classes of Americans introduce themselves, and they all seemed to be colonels or majors or captains. He wondered whether they were all using titles that were only associated with local militias, like Harcourt. "I suppose, Major Harcourt, I should say first that members of our faith are often *called* 'Mormons,' but that is not the true name of our church."

And with that start, Will described the Book of Mormon and explained that the church of Christ had been restored to the earth through a prophet of God. Major Harcourt listened for quite some time before he said, "Tell me more about this Smith who is your leader. I've heard of him before. Some style him as nothing more than an imposter intent on building his own kingdom on the Mississippi. Those who hold this opinion claim that men like you are nothing more than dupes, and Smith is emptying your pockets to fill his own."

"If that were so, sir, he would live in a palace and he would lord himself over his followers. But in fact—and I know this without having met the man, but by all reports from those who have—he lives in a humble log homestead. His wife takes in the sick and indigent and nurses them, and he takes off his frock coat and chops wood as well as any man in his society."

"Is that so? That's good to know. And I stand corrected." Major Harcourt had been looking out toward the east, gazing at the rich green countryside. But now he looked in Will's eyes. He was a fleshy man with a heavy nose and eyes almost hidden by a constant squint. "Tell me, if you don't mind," he said, "how was it that you, living so far away in England, came to believe in this man?"

Will answered with his eyes as much as his voice, looking directly into Harcourt's gaze. "It's not a man I believe in," he said. "I believe in Jesus Christ. What Joseph Smith has brought to us is a pure doctrine that had been lost from the earth."

"But how do you know? What makes you so certain that this doctrine is any better than what others believe?"

Will had to think about that. He wished he knew how to speak with the power that he had experienced when he had met Wilford Woodruff. He had never tried to be a missionary, but Major Harcourt seemed sincere, and Will wanted to bring some authority to what he said. "I met a missionary in my village in Herefordshire. What he taught made sense to me. I had long doubted some of the standard teachings of Christian churches. But I needed to know that Joseph Smith really had talked with God, as this missionary claimed."

"Talked with God?"

"Yes, sir." Will told the story of Joseph's search for truth and the vision he had experienced, and then he told how the Prophet Joseph had received the Book of Mormon. "When I read that book, I was certain that no man, and especially no farm boy like myself, could have written it. It was scripture, as important as the Bible."

"Is there a way I can obtain this book and read it?"

"Of course." But Will immediately asked himself where he could find a copy. "I could lend you my copy for a day or two, if you would like to read it."

"Certainly. I have some time for the next few days. I would love to read this book and see whether I'm as convinced as you are that it truly is the word of God."

Will felt a surge of excitement. "Wait here, sir," he said. "I'll bring my copy to you in two minutes, not more."

Will hurried down the steps and found Liz sitting on the deck, leaning against one of the poles that held up the promenade deck. She seemed to be dozing. Will didn't want to disturb her, but as he began to rummage through the leather valise he used to carry his personal items, she opened her eyes. "Liz," Will said, "I've proclaimed the gospel to a man I met. He wants to read the Book of Mormon, so I'm taking mine to him."

"That's good, Will. It's your first missionary work."

"Yes, it is. And this man—Major Harcourt is his name—seemed not only interested but quite taken with the testimony I bore to him."

She nodded again, but she didn't seem quite as excited as he was. In fact, she added, "Make sure you arrange to get your Book of Mormon back."

"Of course," Will said, and then he hurried back to Harcourt, delivered the book, and made arrangements to meet him the next day.

All that evening and even late at night, when Will was trying unsuccessfully to sleep, he thought of things he should have said to Major Harcourt, and things that he would say next time. Late in the night, he realized that he had come a long way. The experience on board, leading and helping others, and commanding the winds to stop—all this really had changed him. He hadn't wavered in the testimony he had borne.

He had arranged to meet Harcourt at the same spot on the promenade deck right after dinner the following day. Will got there a little early, he realized, since the cabin passengers were still eating, but he waited, and in time he saw Harcourt making his way through the crowd on the main deck. He looked up to the promenade deck and gestured for Will to come down. Will hurried down and met Harcourt at the rail, where he had taken up a place. "We can talk better here," he said. "The promenade deck becomes very crowded after the noon meal."

Will couldn't imagine that it was more crowded than the main deck, but he didn't mind being among the deck passengers. He had only assumed that Harcourt liked the higher deck better. "Did you have time for some reading, sir?" Will asked.

"Yes, indeed I did. As you say, this hardly seems a book that a young farm boy could write. It reminds me very much of the Bible, and I like its teachings."

"What impressed you, sir?"

"Well . . . everything. This young man who praised his parents. I liked that for instance."

"Nephi?"

"Yes. That's the one."

"Did you read very far into the book?"

"Not as much as I had hoped. I made some other acquaintances at supper last night, and I ended up sharing a bottle of port with some gentlemen, which led to another and another. You know how that happens, I'm sure. By the time I got back to my cabin, I was a little too foggy to read long. Still, I want to hang on to the book a little longer, if I may." He held it up to show that it had been tucked under his arm, protectively.

"Of course. Keep it another day or two."

"Tell me about this city," Harcourt said. "The place where you plan to live in Illinois. What is it called?"

"Nauvoo. It's a Hebrew word. It means a beautiful and peaceful place."

"And how much is it built up so far?"

Will liked that Harcourt was taking an interest in Nauvoo. That had aroused Will's first interest in Woodruff's teachings. "It's a place where everyone is equal," Will said. "People support one another. It's a gathering place. We're building a society based on love and harmony."

"That's remarkable. I must visit this place as soon as I get settled in St. Louis. Tell me this. Do you know what land will cost there?"

"I don't. But I'm told that it's being made available at a fair price."

"I see." Will saw something he didn't know how to read. Harcourt glanced away, nodded to a man across the deck, and then placed a hand on Will's shoulder. "It sounds as though you have a nice opportunity there, but you also strike me as a young man with great ability and a desire to make the best of things for your young wife."

"Yes. That's true."

Harcourt lowered his voice. "I've learned about an opportunity. It's what brought me to the West. But it's not been announced officially just yet."

"What kind of opportunity?"

"Land is opening up. Free land. It won't cost you—or any of

your fellow travelers—a single penny. I know you like the idea of settling in this town you're traveling to, but if Smith is asking a 'fair' price, that may not be the best way to make an advantageous start. Supposing a plot of land could be had for nothing, and your people could move onto it and set up a society of your own?"

"But that's not what we came here for."

"I understand that. But this is rich land, prime for farming, and not far from St. Louis, where the two great rivers, the Missouri and the Mississippi, join. This is the most vital spot in the West, the area most likely to grow. Land there will take on value immediately and then multiply many times in a few years. In England you may have farmed on another man's land, but as landowners here in this country, you could end up becoming gentlemen in no time—rich as those squires you pay so much honor to over there."

"We came here for religious reasons, Major Harcourt—not merely for land."

"I understand all that. In fact, if I continue to be as impressed with the Book of Mormon as I have been so far, I might want to join with your people. What we could do, then, is spread the word back in England, and in a few years we could establish a place twice as desirable as Smith has built up. There's money to be made, Mr. Lewis—money you could use to further spread the very doctrines you believe in."

Will felt his muscles losing strength, the air draining out of him. "Let me ask you this," he said. "How much would it cost us to obtain this *free* land?"

"I told you. It's all free." But those squinty eyes of his remained averted, not quite ready to take on Will's skeptical stare.

"So you will let me know how to have this land—merely as a kindly gesture—or would I have to cross your palm with a little something?"

"Please, sir, don't think I'm in this for the money. But I could certainly serve as your agent. I'm trained as a lawyer, and I could file all the papers for you."

"Yes. And that would cost me nothing. Is that what you're saying?"

"Of course not. There would be legal fees, payment for my work, but all of you could pool your money, and—"

"How much money?"

"That could all be negotiated, Mr. Lewis. I would certainly treat you well. You are new citizens of our great land, and I want nothing more than to make you welcome."

"You're unwilling to look me in the eye, Mr. Harcourt. I don't trust you, and I don't trust your motives. Could I please have my Book of Mormon now?"

"You have misjudged me, sir. I wish to read the book. You may well have found a convert to your beliefs. I want to hear everything you have to preach. Were we to join purposes, as I have suggested, we could both benefit. Surely, you hoped to prosper in our land, and—"

"May I please have my book? I don't like a man who pretends to religious belief only as a way of picking my pocket. I was warned about sharp men in this country waiting to take advantage of new-comers. I didn't know that I would meet one quite so quickly."

"Wait just a minute, young man. Speak to me with more re-spect. I have friends on board this boat. They don't appreciate that kind of talk."

Will was suddenly heated. "Give me my Book of Mormon, thief," he demanded.

"Here's your book," Harcourt said. "Keep it and be damned. But don't ever speak to me with disrespect again." He handed Will the book, but he turned his head and nodded, and in a moment a rough-looking character in tattered shirtsleeves and coarse woolen trousers came pushing his way through the crowd. He was no taller than Will, but his shoulders and chest were enormous, and beneath his slouched cap and bushy eyebrows was a pair of dark, angry eyes.

"I'll give you the respect you deserve," Will told Harcourt. "The same I would give a highwayman or a train robber. There are many kinds of thieves, but at least some of them are not liars besides."

Will realized his voice had risen and the crowd around him had turned, even pushed back a little to make half a circle. They were clearly expecting a fight to break out. Will glanced around, saw some of his own friends, and wondered whether they would help him if these two tried anything. But then Will noticed, rather deep in the crowd, Liz's face, looking frightened. He didn't want her to see him at his worst.

Will took the book and tried to leave, but Harcourt grabbed his arm. "You best watch yourself every moment from now on," he said in a harsh whisper. "You could find yourself floating facedown on the river with a knife between your ribs. In this country we teach people like you to respect their betters."

Will still had it in mind to walk away, but he couldn't resist saying, "You're no better than anyone. You're as low as the mud at the bottom of this river."

Harcourt grabbed Will's lapel. "You're going in the river, boy—food for catfish." He tried to push Will toward the rail. But Will braced himself, then knocked Harcourt's hand away and grabbed the man's coat. With a sudden jerk and twist, he flung Harcourt against the rail, and then he drove forward and bent him backwards. Just as quickly, he turned back to the man behind him. "Don't make a move," he said, "or your partner goes into the river."

"Back off, Tony," Harcourt gasped.

Will saw that the big man had his hand on a knife that was

stuck into his belt. Will gave Harcourt another shove, so that he was bent back farther over the rail.

"I tell you, back off. He'll throw me in the river."

Tony moved back a step, and as he did, Will jerked Harcourt upright, but he still held his lapel with his left hand. He spun him around and shoved him at Tony. "Now leave me alone," he said. "And don't threaten me again. You may have a knife, but I have God on my side. And the two of us can throw both of you in the water."

This brought a laugh from the crowd. Harcourt only mumbled as he walked away, pushing Tony ahead of him. By then Will was thinking he had done the wrong thing, and when he found his wife's eyes again, he could see how frightened she was.

• • •

Liz was scared. But she was proud, too. Will was not a ruffian, but neither was he a man who would ever let himself—or her—be taken advantage of. She didn't know exactly what had started all this trouble, but she knew, in the end, that he had stood up for what was right.

Still, she wondered what would happen next. The man named Tony was frightening, and he carried a knife big enough to kill a bear.

She made her way to Will, and he took her in his arms. "I'm sorry," he said. "The man is a thief, and he travels with his own set of thugs."

"How can we protect ourselves?" Liz asked.

"We'll stay with the Saints. We'll stay where his men can't get to us. They aren't the type to do their deeds in the open."

"I'm afraid they'll come for you at night."

"Not where we sleep, surrounded by so many people."

But Liz wasn't sure.

"I'm sorry, Liz. I should have turned the other cheek."

"No, don't say that. You stood up against evil men, just as you ought to do."

But still, she worried all night, hearing every sound and never really sleeping. And the next morning, when she visited the water closet, she saw Tony, along with two other men, not as big but just as coarse and dirty. She didn't know that they knew who she was, but Tony growled, "Food for catfish, little lady. We'll keep our promise."

Liz had never experienced such a thing in her life. She wondered what kind of country she had come to.

CHAPTER 24

Will kept his eye out for Harcourt and his men, but two days passed and none of them made a move toward him, although he saw them watching him at times.

The trip up the river was tedious. The English Saints had longed so much to reach America that they hadn't quite prepared themselves for the slow progress up the Mississippi. But all in all, Will enjoyed seeing this vast land, and he liked the great river, nearly a mile wide in some places. One morning he climbed to the pilot's cabin to ask about the progress of the boat and when it might arrive in Nauvoo. "There's not a good answer about them things," the pilot said, a statement Will wasn't quite sure he understood.

"I was only asking how far we've come and what day you think we might arrive in St. Louis."

"I know what yor a-askin', and I know what I'm a-sayin'. Things change fast on the river." He stared ahead for a time, and Will thought maybe he had said all he was going to say, but then he pointed off to the left, upriver. "See that little break in the water right thar. Ain't much, is it?"

Will wasn't sure what "break" he meant, but he said, "No, it isn't."

"And yet, it can put a boat like this'n on the bottom—if we was to run on it, full speed."

"That ripple of water?"

"Not the ripple. What's makin' it look like 'at."

"Which is . . . ?"

"We call 'em snags. It's a tree what's washed downriver, and it's got itself stuck in the mud. If it pokes up so a pilot can see it clear, it ain't no problem. But when it stays low, hides out under the skin of the water jist a little, it's only them ripples what tells about it. If I have me a smoke, or jist don't watch real good, we could end up wrecked on that snag, and it don't matter how far it is to anywhar. But then, ain't no man knows where he's truly goin' or when he'll get there. There's snags in every river, them with water and them without."

Will couldn't help but laugh. He liked this man. He seemed something of a philosopher. But he was a hard-looking one. He was a little man, between shaves, with oily hair and bloodshot eyes. He wore no coat, only a linen shirt that had been stained with sweat many times. It had big circles of yellow under each arm and halfway to his waist. He put off a smell of tobacco and bacon and, underneath that, the insistent odor of an unwashed body.

"I suppose an experienced pilot learns to spot snags like that," Will said.

"He reads the river like some men reads a book. And it's not just snags. It's sandbars what move from one trip to the next, changin' where the deep channel is. And it's clouds what bring a change in the weather, maybe one that turns into a cyclone. And it's knowin' what another boat will do afore it know its own self."

"I've heard that the boilers on these steamboats will blow up sometimes."

"You heerd right, too. But that's somethin' a good pilot can protec' against. Too many tells the fireman to pour coal to the fire an' stoke it good, jist to get somewhar ahead of some other boat, never thinkin' what kind of pressure they's puttin' on them tired ol' boiler walls. A good pilot hears what's happenin' in his boat an' knows when he's askin' too much of it. Young fellers think everythin's a race, and they kill a bunch of people jist to say they had a faster boat. Me, I like to read the river, love it like she's my new-married bride, an' hear that ol' engine's heart beat, like a good doctor do."

Will didn't want to laugh, but he couldn't resist, and he caught an impatient glance from the pilot.

"You be one of the Mormons from England, ain't you?"

"Yes, sir."

"I wouldn't worry so much about *when* you land som'eres. I'd worry about where it is you think you're a-goin'."

"We're going to a town called Nauvoo."

"I know all about that. You ain't the first Mormons to board this ol' boat—not by a long shot. An' I've stopped in at Nauvoo half a dozen times, at least. I hear people talkin' like it's that parcel of land—that bend in the river—that's going to give them peace an' glory. But it's just land, not heaven, and wet land at that. It's a sickly place, if you want the whole truth."

"Our people are draining off the wet areas."

"That's all well and good, but I still say, peace don't come from land, an' happiness don't neither. Them things comes from what's inside the people, an' as far as I can tell, folks is mostly pretty much the same, no matter what land they choose to settle."

"I think we understand that."

The pilot continued to stare ahead. His eyes were scanning the river. A wooded island lay ahead, and already the pilot was turning the wheel, slowly, angling the boat into the curving channel. "But here's what I'm a-sayin'. Mormons like to climb up the ladder to my cabin and tell me what ladder I gotta climb to get to heaven. An' I 'preciate that they wanna look out for me. But if you ask me, the ladder don't matter nearly so much as the climber. It's hard to get to the top if yer allus lookin' down, sayin', 'Look at them poor souls down thar. They ain't half so high as me.'"

"I think you have the wrong idea about us," Will said. "We like to preach the gospel, and we mean well in doing it. But we certainly don't mean to say that we're better than other people."

"Here's what I think. People is people. Some is jis awful bad, an' some, like my ol' mother, considerable better, but we all got feet stuck in some of this ol' Mississippi mud when it comes to runnin' fast up the ladder."

Will agreed, and then he climbed down to the hurricane deck and on down to the promenade deck, and from there down another ladder to find his way back to Liz. But he thought for the rest of the morning about the things the pilot had said. It was the people, not the place. He had always understood that, but he had learned on the voyage that people always struggled to be what they wanted to be. He vowed to finish off this final leg of the trip with the right attitude—to be the leader he had been called to be.

• • •

In the afternoon the boat stopped, as it did twice a day, to take on wood. Will had watched this operation a number of times. Men—sometimes families—lived on the banks of the river in shacks surrounded by great piles of cut logs. When a riverboat pulled up at the teetering docks by these shacks, a storm of activity always began. A dozen or so men, mostly Negroes, carried the firewood on board and stacked it on the main deck just outside the boiler. Will didn't know whether these men were slaves, but he assumed they were, and he was disgusted by the sight of them laboring so hard while their white bosses sat at their shacks and didn't lift a hand. He didn't know how men could think that they "owned" other human beings. England had been involved in the slave trade itself not so long ago, but its leaders had recognized the practice as wrong and had made it illegal.

Will was thinking about that while the deckhands tied off the boat against the dock. He decided to hurry down to the gangplank that was now being set on the dock. He walked off the boat, glad to use his muscles for a short time but, even more, to show that he was willing to help the Negroes with their work.

He walked to the pile of wood, filled his arms with the short logs, and then joined the line of workers. He made several trips that way, noticing that people on the boat were watching him, clearly curious about what he was up to. He kept at it until the boat was loaded. The day was not particularly warm, but he felt the moisture in the air, and he found himself sweating hard. Still, he liked that, too. He had worked all his life, and he needed to be active again. As he stood at the woodpile on the deck and put down his last load, he turned to one of the Negroes. "Thanks for bringing the wood on," he said. He reached his hand out.

The black man seemed unsure what was happening. He didn't raise his eyes to look Will straight on. He mumbled, "Yes, suh," and turned away. Will didn't understand. He must be a slave, but couldn't a slave even shake hands with a white man? Will turned to another of the men. "Thanks for your work," he said. But the man only nodded, then also turned away, leaving Will's hand hanging in the air again.

Will looked around to see that a number of passengers were still watching him. "I just needed to feel useful," Will said. "We spend too much time sitting around on this old boat." He laughed.

A couple of the men nodded, as if to say, "To each his own." But then Will heard a voice behind him. "I'm glad to know you've found your place in this country."

Will knew the voice. He turned around to see Major Harcourt standing with his thumbs tucked into his waistcoat, looking very sure of himself. Tony was by his side.

"I'm a working man," Will said. "I was in England and I will be here."

"Yes. I see that. You work well with niggers. You fit right in with them."

"God loves all his children, sir. I'm not ashamed to work with any man."

"That's generous of you, Lewis. But the niggers seemed just a little ashamed to work with you." He turned and looked at Tony. "I always thought niggers were the lowest form of life I'd come acrost. But these Mormons might be one step lower."

"They both 'bout as low as hogs, wallowin' in filth," Tony said.

"Let's move on before we get some of his smell on us," Harcourt said, and then he stepped forward, purposely banging into Will's shoulder as he passed him by. Will acted before he could think. He kicked a foot out in front of Harcourt and nudged the man with his elbow. Harcourt tripped and went sprawling face-first onto the deck, down among the tobacco spittle and splotches of mud. He rolled over and jumped up with more sprightliness than Will had seen from him before. But Will, just as quickly, stepped up close to him. "God does love all his children," he said. "But unless I miss my guess, he *likes* some much better than others."

Will turned toward Tony, almost dared him to make a move, but Harcourt held up his hand. "This is not the time or place, Tony," he said. "But I'm not finished with you, Lewis." He reached in his trousers pocket and pulled out a white handkerchief, which he used to dab at the spots on his waistcoat. "Mark my word. You won't get away with this." He turned and walked away as regally as he could. But some of the passengers were laughing, and Will knew he had struck deep at the man's pride.

Will knew already that he had let his lesser self come out again, just when he had wanted to show that he was willing to love all of mankind. He wondered whether he ever would become the man he needed to be.

A young man nearby said, "It's what he had coming. He lords it over everyone on this boat."

Will turned to the man, who was standing with his wife. They were clean young people, but they were deck passengers, like the Mormons. Will had seen them before. He had found that most of the deck passengers who were not immigrants were heading to Missouri or Illinois—or farther north—and had either purchased land or were seeking a place to settle and farm. But this man wasn't muscled like a laborer, and his speech sounded more refined. He was a fine-featured man, clean shaven, but with little beard to worry about, and he was wearing a better tailored suit of clothes than anyone on the boat—except perhaps, Major Harcourt.

"He's a thief," Will said. "Don't trust him if he tries to sell you land."

"He already tried," the young man said. "But we saw right through him. I'm afraid our country has far too many of his kind—especially here in the West."

"Will Lewis is my name," Will said. He held out his hand and the man shook it. But as Will dropped his hand, the man glanced down to look at it, apparently curious about its stiffness.

"My name is Andrew Cook. This is my wife, Sally. We're from

Pennsylvania, near Philadelphia, but we're heading to St. Louis. I've taken a position with a shipping company. I'll be keeping their books for them."

"I won't be so far away."

"Yes, we know. We've talked to many of your people. And we've heard about the large chapel that's planned for this city of yours."

"It's a temple. But it's only just begun. That's one of the things I hope to help with when we arrive."

Just then Will saw Liz coming out of the crowd. She looked tired, and her dress was anything but neat and clean after four nights of sleeping on the deck. "Will," she said, "I hear you've been making a spectacle of yourself." But she was smiling.

"He may have bumped a man accidentally," Cook said. "A man who had an accidental bump coming to him—and maybe a good knock over the head. Most all of us were only too happy to see him flattened on the deck."

"I shouldn't have done it," Will told Liz, but he knew he felt more satisfaction than he should. He introduced Sally and Andrew to Liz, and then he said, "I was just telling them about the temple we're building." There was a stack of cotton bales under the promenade deck. Will motioned to them and said, "Let's sit down for a few minutes, and I'll explain a little what we're trying to do in Nauvoo."

So each couple picked a bale and slid it out a little so they could face one another, and they sat down. Will liked Andrew already, and he thought Liz would like Sally. He wished the Cooks were on their way to Nauvoo. "We have no chapels for church meetings in Nauvoo so far, or so we're told," Will said. "But we're working hard to build a magnificent temple. It's a holy place, like Solomon's temple in the Old Testament."

Andrew nodded, and was about to say something, when Sally

spoke first. "What draws you all the way from England to this place?"

"We want to live together in harmony," Will said. "We believe our church is the restored Church of Jesus Christ, and we want to live according to Christ's teachings."

"But is that possible?" she asked. "We went to a church in Pennsylvania—and listened to fine sermons. But those who acted the most pious in church were usually the worst rascals. Or they were like this Harcourt, a so-called man of business, but not someone you could trust."

"I know what you mean," Will said. "But most people mean well. They're just not as righteous as they want to be."

Liz said, "But in a place where everyone is trying hard to do what's right, we can help each other."

"It sounds like a noble idea," Andrew said. "Once we get settled in St. Louis, we'll pay your city a visit. I want to see whether you still feel the same when you try to carry out the dream—not just imagine it."

"I hope you come," Will said. "But you have to understand, we didn't just think this all up. A prophet has been called by God, and he receives revelations. He gives us the true word of God. We can fail, as people, but the gospel never can."

As soon as he spoke the words, however, he thought of what the pilot had told him: "It's not so much the ladder as it is the climber." He wished he could present himself as a better example of what he believed. It was fine to say that the truth was in the Church, and a prophet was guided by the Lord, but the fruits also had to be obvious to anyone who looked upon the members. And sometimes, at sea, he had seen too much bickering, too many jealousies, too much harshness in the judgments members made.

Andrew wanted to know more about Joseph Smith and the

doctrines of the Church, so Will answered as best he could, with Liz's help. And Andrew and Sally seemed impressed with the things they heard. Will had tried to bear testimony before, but this time he felt a sincere interest from the Cooks. He was feeling this joy when he looked up to see Harcourt, with Tony, standing over him. "Mr. Lewis, you made a mistake in attacking me. I don't exchange blows with people of your class. I don't have to. I have men who look out for me."

Will saw Harcourt's other two men standing just a few feet behind. Apparently, he wanted all his men by his side, not just Tony, when he finally faced off with Will.

Will stood up. He wasn't sure what was about to happen.

"You're much younger than I, Mr. Lewis. You took advantage of that and used me badly. But let's see how you handle yourself with someone closer to your own age."

Will wondered what would happen if he did have to defend himself against Tony. Would the other two step in as well? "You insulted me, Major Harcourt. You compared me to a swine. I'm afraid that I was unforgiving. As a follower of Christ, I should have let you pass me by. I apologize for what I did."

"I'm sure you do feel regret—with Tony standing here. It turns out, you're nothing but a coward."

"I'm certain that it appears that way—and I admit, I don't want to fight a man who's carrying a knife—but I'm speaking honestly when I say that I regret having tripped you."

"Give me the knife, Tony," Harcourt said. Tony handed it over. Harcourt looked back at Will. "That puts you on an even plane. Now let's see who can throw the other into the river. I'll put my wager on Tony."

Deck passengers had seen and heard what was happening, and they began to gather around. Will saw some of his Mormon brothers, and he hoped he was not entirely on his own against all of Harcourt's men. But Will was still thinking he could talk his way out of this one. "Major Harcourt, we've had our disagreements, but surely we can respect one another enough—"

Tony suddenly bulled ahead and grabbed at Will. Will jumped back, and his left fist, as though by its own volition, struck Tony a quick, sharp blow on his right cheek. Will had never fought a boxing match in his life—not for real—but he and Daniel had watched pugilists at the Ledbury fair, and they had sparred at times, not hitting hard, just trying their skills. Will knew that boxers used one hand to keep a man off balance and then followed with a crushing blow with the other hand. But Will had only one good hand. He wasn't sure he could even use his right.

Tony took the blow without much reaction, except to stop his charge for a moment. Around them, the crowd formed itself into something like a boxing ring. Will hoped that one of the deckhands would step in and stop the fight, but he saw a couple of them turning to watch, their eyes bright with excitement. He heard Liz behind him pleading, "No, Will. He's too big for you. Don't do this." But he wasn't aware that he had a choice.

Tony was coming again, reaching. Will shot out his left hand again—once, twice—as he retreated. But the cotton bales were behind him, and he ran out of space. Out of instinct, he threw the right and caught Tony hard on the mouth, but Will felt pain shoot through his wrist and up his arm. He still couldn't make a tight fist with his right hand. It would be a mistake to use that hand again.

Tony kept coming. He grabbed Will and wrapped his arms around his body. Will tried to twist loose, but Tony managed to get his hands together behind him, and then he jerked hard, lifting Will and squeezing the air out of him. He spun around and headed for the rail, stumbling, but moving fast.

Will kicked and struggled, throwing Tony off balance enough that the two tumbled to the deck. In the fall, Tony's grip came loose and Will worked an arm free. He drove his elbow into Tony's face. He saw blood splatter and he heard the bone in the man's nose snap. Will rolled away and jumped to his feet. The crowd cheered for his little triumph, but no one tried to stop the fight—which was what Will still hoped for.

Tony came up in a wild scramble, blood covering his whiskers and his shirtfront. He charged again, but this time Will had room. He jumped aside and then slammed the man in the back of the head with a downward chop with the side of his hand. Tony landed on his chest and skidded on the deck. But he didn't seem fazed. He was up again quickly. And now, instead of charging, he came forward slowly, ready for Will, who realized he had to get away from the rail. He tried to work his way around to the left.

Tony was sucking for air, his breath raspy. Twice he spat blood. But he had his arms wide, and the crowd wasn't backing away enough to give Will room for escape. As Tony reached for him this time, Will threw his left hand, but Tony blocked the blow with his forearm and grabbed hold of Will's sleeve. Suddenly he was whipping Will around like a toy. When he let go, Will careened across the deck and felt his back slam into the rail. Tony was bearing down on him.

Will kicked out and caught the big man in the shin, hard. Tony's leg went out from under him and he fell next to Will. Will clambered onto his knees quickly and sent a crushing left-hand blow into the side of Tony's head. Then he drove his right forearm into the man's face. He saw the light go out of Tony's eyes. He jumped to his feet and waited. But Tony was still on the deck, his eyes closed.

"Get up," Harcourt was shouting. "Get up right now."

Others were cheering for Will.

Tony opened his eyes and shook his head. Then he worked his way slowly to his feet. Will knew he should attack quickly, try to finish him off, but he didn't like any of this. He still wondered why no one stopped what was happening.

"Use the knife," Harcourt said in a quiet, cynical voice. He stepped to Tony and handed him the long dagger.

Tony took the knife, moved it to his right hand, looked at Will. Will had no idea what to do now.

But Tony looked back at Harcourt and said, "No. I won't kill this man. He's beat me, fair and square."

"You'll take him now, Tony. Either that or lose your place with me."

"I don' care. I quit. I'll fight a man, but I won't use a knife on 'im when he has no weapon."

Harcourt was looking to the other two men. "Take the knife," he said. "One of you, take the knife, and finish what Tony wouldn't do."

Will saw the two wavering. But Tony said, "I'll not give it to 'em. I'd jist as leave cut your throat instead. The world would be better fer it, too. No doubt."

This brought an enthusiastic response from the onlookers and a retreat by Harcourt, off in the direction of his cabin.

Will walked over and sat down on a bale of cotton. He was breathing hard, still frightened by the thought of that knife, and feeling now the pain in his right hand. He wondered whether he had broken it again. Liz was there immediately. "Oh, Will, I was so afraid," she said. She caressed his head with her hands.

"I was too," he said, not loudly enough for her or anyone else to hear.

But Andrew was saying, "Well done, Will."

Others were slapping him on the shoulder, telling him what a man he was. But Will was thinking that he had brought this all on himself with his impulsiveness. He never should have tripped Harcourt. There was still something in him that he hadn't conquered. How could he show up in Zion with blood on his hands?

· · ·

Liz understood why Will was disappointed with himself, but she felt almost as much pride in him as when he had rebuked the storm. He hadn't chosen to fight, but when he had had to do it, he had fought like a lion. She had the feeling that life was full of fights, and Will was a man who could protect her and her children. He would never back down from the evil in the world, whatever form it took.

As the sun was going down that evening, she was sitting by herself on the deck while Will was checking on all his group members. This was hard for him, she knew, because he didn't want to be praised as a fighter. But she still had to smile when she thought of how athletic he had been, how able to take on the big man. When Sally came to her and sat by her side, she said, "Are you still a little shaken by all that happened today?"

"I am," Liz said. "When I saw that knife, I told myself I would have to help Will somehow. I was looking around for something to use to knock that man over the head."

Sally laughed. "You seem too much of a lady for that. I would never think of trying such a thing."

Liz wondered about herself. She certainly had never hit anyone over the head in her life, and she could hardly imagine that such a thought had come to her. But she rather liked to think that she could fight if she had to. "I suppose we learn about ourselves when someone tries to hurt the ones we love."

"I guess we do. But you should know, Andrew told me the same thing. He was not going to allow that man to kill your husband.

He was preparing to step in and help him. Maybe there's a little friendship there, already, but mostly, my husband believes that some things are right and some are wrong. He told me he wouldn't want to see Will stabbed and know that he stood by and let it happen."

Liz finally let the tears come. She was only just realizing how upsetting the day had been. "I was thinking that America is a very frightening place. But you and Andrew make me feel better about it."

"America is everything, Liz. It is frightening, and it can be cruel, especially here in the West. But people also believe in honor, and they stand up for it. Most of them do."

"I'm not sure I belong here. I didn't understand what it would be like."

"You have to trust in your city. I'm sure it won't be like the America you see in New Orleans or on a riverboat."

Liz had no idea what to expect now. She needed to feel safe, and she hadn't felt that since she had left her home.

That night, as Liz lay on the deck on her side, she felt her middle with her hand, and she thought of her baby. She was so glad it was Will's baby, this man she loved more than ever, but she was uneasy when she thought of the different life her child would have from the one she had grown up with herself. She had to trust her own city, Sally had said. Liz hoped she could do that.

CHAPTER 25

During the night, deck passengers on the riverboat began to get sick. Will awoke to the retching sound that had become so familiar during the ocean crossing. He got up and moved toward the sound. A man—Brother Chitester from Preston, he realized—was leaning against the rail on the main deck. Just as Will approached, he began to slump, still clinging to the rail. Will tried to catch him but was too late. He knelt down and touched Brother Chitester's shoulder. "What is it, Brother? How long have you been sick?"

"Mostly it's weakness I feel." He took a breath, as though the words had cost him too much effort. "I've been to the water closet over and over in the night. And now this."

Others were soon there, kneeling next to Brother Chitester. And then Will heard Brother Burnham, who was in the midst of the Saints. "He's not the only one," he said. "Two of the Tubbs children are sick, and so is Sister Hamilton."

Will had heard that diseases could spread quickly on these boats. He hoped this wasn't the beginning of something terrible.

"There's been cholera along the river already this year," one of the brothers said.

Brother Burnham didn't respond to that, but he made his way over to Will. "He's right. This could be cholera," he said. "It hits suddenly and hard like this, and it sometimes kills quickly. One of our emigration groups was struck down with it last year, here on the river. They lost a good many."

In the next few hours the contagion was clearly upon the deck passengers. More and more were falling ill. The rush to the water closets was too great, and that placed people in the humiliating circumstance of family and friends holding blankets around the afflicted, without so much as chamber pots. No one seemed to be in much pain, but some began to speak incoherently or to drift into unconsciousness. Their bodies were losing water fast, and Will could see that some of them were failing quickly. Those who were still feeling all right tried to help the sick drink as much water as they could, but Will wondered whether it wasn't the water itself that was contaminated.

The first death came early the next morning. Louisa Evans, just three years old, faded away quickly, and her parents could do nothing for her. She had been a lovely child, with big eyes and deep dimples. Will had marveled at her good nature on board the ship, even when she had been seasick at times. He wondered how much the voyage had weakened her. "We'll take her with us to Nauvoo," her mother told Will. "We won't cast her into this filthy water. We'll bury her where we can go visit her."

Will wasn't sure that was a good idea. But he didn't tell Sister Evans. He climbed the ladder to the captain's cabin and told Captain Rupp that he hoped the Evanses would be able to take the body on to Nauvoo.

"We can't have that," the captain said. He looked more refined than the pilot, his clothes cleaner, his face shaved more recently, but he was no philosopher. Will had heard him curse his crew in a voice like the noise of rolling rocks. "If it was only a few hours, maybe we could allow it. But we have more'n two days, at the rate we're steamin' up this river. It ain't healthy to keep the dead on board."

"What can they do, then?"

"Most people don't like to dump their kin in the river, and I don't blame 'em for that. They can git off and dig a grave, or do whatever they want once they're off the boat, but they cain't just pack the little girl along."

"What did she die of, sir? Is it cholera?"

"Don't start spreading that idea around. There's no proof that's what it whar. You jist tell the family—when we stop for wood next time—they can git off an' bury her there. That's a hour or two upriver."

"But it must be cholera. I talked to a man today who has seen it before. It has all the signs: diarrhea and vomiting, death coming before anyone can do anything."

"There's other things that come on thataway. It can't be helped. And don't start blaming the water we got on board. It's good spring water."

"Spring water in New Orleans?"

"You don't know where we git our water. It's sweet water, pure as a rollin' stream. That's all there is to say about it. Sickness hits us on the river sometimes—but I didn't talk you into sailin' here from England. That was yor idea."

Will said nothing more. He climbed down the ladder. Back on the main deck, he learned that Brother Chitester was dead. Will spoke with Brother Burnham, and then they visited with the Evans family and with Sister Chitester. They would have to get off at the next stop, bury the bodies, and then catch on with another boat.

Someone would be assigned to stay with Sister Chitester, help her with the grave, and assist with her three small children.

Will had thought he understood the dangers of traveling to Nauvoo, but he hadn't imagined anything quite so terrible as this. Sister Evans and Sister Chitester were stoic, their eyes disconsolate at first, but he watched them accept that they had no choice in the matter. What he didn't see, however, was any strength left in them. They were devastated, hardly able to stand, and Sister Chitester's seven-year-old son had begun to pass the same kind of watery stools. There was a distance in her eyes, as though she were frantically searching for some explanation, some justification, some way to tell herself that God had not abandoned her. But she said nothing. She just listened to Brother Burnham and nodded.

So the Evans family and the Chitesters made arrangements to get off at the next firewood station. By the time the boat reached that stop, three more were dead—two babies and another little girl. So three more families got off the boat, but Will didn't see that. By then, he had felt his stomach cramp, suddenly, violently. He had tried to get to the water closet, only to realize he was too late—which was humiliating.

Liz helped him back to their little spot on the deck. She asked others to protect his privacy with blankets, and she helped him take off his trousers. She told Will she would wash them out if she could get some water. "I'll be all right," he told her. "I don't feel very sick. Brother Brown vomited twice and then started feeling better."

"I know. You'll be fine," Liz said. He saw no resignation in her eyes, felt none in her voice. She was ready for a fight. "You have to drink water," she said. "You won't keep much of it in you, but you have to keep drinking."

"It might be the water that's making us sick."

"I know. But I talked to a physician—or at least a man who

treated soldiers when he was in the army. He said that it's cholera, for sure, but many who get it survive. The water can't hurt you any further, even if that's what made you sick. The danger is, if you lose too much water from your body and don't replace it, you die from that."

Will nodded and then raised his head as she held a cup to his lips. She stayed beside him, urging water on him as much as possible, for hours. He didn't try to make it to the water closet again. But he was sickened by his own stench and by what Liz was willing to do to keep the mess around him cleaned up. She kept giving him more water even when he became so weak he couldn't raise his own head.

It was a long night, and there came a time when Will became confused and frightened. Strange dreams, like visions, spun through his mind. He saw storms again, the wild ocean, and yet the ocean was brown as the Mississippi, and when he felt someone pushing at his lips, he fought back, only to come clear again and know that Liz was still there. He would gulp at the water and gag, and sometimes the water made him vomit, but Liz would not quit.

And then, when light had come again, he heard a voice speaking into his ear. "Wake up, Will. Wake up!"

He tried, but his eyes wouldn't come open. Then something warm was on his head, like a cap.

Hands.

And someone, a man, was speaking in a loud voice. "Will Lewis, I command you, in the name of the Lord, to arise and walk."

Arise and walk. He tried to think what he was supposed to do.

"Wake up, Will. Get up," Liz was saying. She was crying.

Arise and walk.

He couldn't get up. He knew he couldn't. But he knew, more than that, that he couldn't die. He couldn't leave Liz now.

He tried to turn, to roll onto his side, but all the turning was in his mind, and he realized that he hadn't really moved.

Arise and walk.

Zion.

They were almost there.

He made it to his side, tried to find some way to use his hands or legs, something to get him up.

"That's it, Will. Don't leave me. Think of the baby. Think of Nauvoo." She was pulling at his shoulder, trying to lift him.

Will rolled onto his chest, his hands under him, and he pushed up. But he couldn't do it, couldn't raise himself.

He felt the spin again, saw the wild images. Waves. Wind.

"Will, you told the wind to stop, and it stopped. You can do this. You can get up."

Arise and walk.

And now it was happening, as though she suddenly found the strength to lift him. He made it to his knees and then to his feet. Liz grabbed hold of him, pressed herself against his chest, slipped her arms around his back. "Stay up," she said. "You can rest in a minute, but stand up long enough to let us know you're back with us."

"Walk," he said. He pulled back from her. He took a step—two, three, four. Then he stopped and caught his balance.

"You'll be all right," Liz said.

Will was dizzy, and he was very weak. But he knew where he was. And he hadn't known that for a long time—a day and a night.

• • •

It was early May, 1842, when the riverboat *Elouise* finally put in at the lower Nauvoo dock. Liz could see a crowd of people gathered by the river. A brass band was playing. Someone said that the large log cabin was Joseph and Emma Smith's house. It was simple, but

Liz thought she could live in a house of that kind. And from the river, Nauvoo looked as beautiful as everyone had told her it would be. Everything seemed as green as England, with thick woods on the rising bluff, away from the water. She knew the temple would be built on that higher land, but she couldn't see it yet. "That pole sticking up, that's a crane," someone said. "That's where the temple is being built." But Liz could see no walls, not from the river.

"What a perfect place for it," Will said, "sitting above the city." Liz thought so too, and imagined it, white and gleaming, the way Wilford Woodruff had said it would someday be.

But as the boat drifted in closer, she saw that the street that led down to the dock was full of mud and standing water. She knew it had rained the night before, but she hadn't expected anything quite so primitive. In the distance she could see scattered houses, almost all of them log cabins, many of them painted white, but very small. This was hardly a "city." It was better than the shanty towns they had seen along the river, and the setting was lovely, but compared to the villages around Ledbury, this seemed a squalid little settlement.

"They let their hogs run wild," Will said, and Liz heard the disdain in his voice. But she had also noticed an old sow, with some pigs, rooting in the mud not far from river, and more of them were wallowing on what seemed to be the main street of town. Only the poorest of farmers in England would have let hogs wander into the streets.

Liz was holding Will around the waist, helping him stay on his feet. He was still weak, but he had promised her a dozen times that he would not give up. He would live. Six more had died on the boat, and some were still sick, but the company had finally arrived. Liz sensed that all the members were trying their best to find joy in the arrival, but surely, they were seeing what she was. She heard someone say, "The mud will be over our shoes." It was what Liz had been thinking.

The gangplank was soon set, and the party began its little procession into the city of God. Liz waited with Will, so he wouldn't be jostled. She found, though, that many others were doing the same. Some were carrying sick children, and some were helping friends. Little groups moved forward, huddled together, like soldiers teetering home from battle.

Liz did see something that lifted her heart. As families made their way to the riverbank, they were greeted by the brothers and sisters from the city. Strong men were coming forward to carry the trunks and luggage. Other people were leading the arriving families around the deepest mud, and then guiding them somewhere—she thought it must be to places where they could stay for now. She hoped there was a place for her and Will. She wondered how they would survive until Will was strong enough to work and to build them a house.

"That's the Prophet. That's Joseph Smith," Will said. Liz saw where Will was pointing, off toward Joseph and Emma's log house. She saw a tall man with big shoulders, dressed in a frock coat but wearing no hat. He was walking toward the dock, not minding the mud, greeting people, smiling, even laughing. She could see his light hair blowing about in the breeze, and there was something in his way of walking, his bold way of waving and calling out, that made him seem less refined than she had assumed he would be. Still, there was something remarkable about him, too. Maybe it was only that everyone crowded around him as he reached the dock, but Liz thought he would draw attention anywhere simply for his smile, his confidence, the power his mannerisms communicated. She supposed she had expected someone a little more clerical, like an English rector, someone not quite so youthful looking, not so gregarious and outgoing. Not quite so handsome.

Will and Liz finally made their way to the gangplank. The pilot was standing close by, but he didn't shake Will's hand. "Good to see you back on yor feet," he said.

"Thank you," Will told him.

"So what are you thinkin' of it? Is it what you 'spected?"

"It's not in the ladder; it's in the climber," Will said.

The pilot laughed. "Yes, a wise man once said so. But some of the rungs 'round here look busted to me. I hope you kin shinny up aroun' any footholds that's missin'."

Liz didn't know what any of this meant, but she didn't like the pilot with his disgustingly dirty clothes and his stinking breath. She certainly sensed that he was making fun of Nauvoo, and she told herself she wouldn't be disappointed. It was a new place, just building up, and it would be much better in time. What she had noticed by then was the sound of a hammer, more than one of them, and the steady pull of a saw blade. Many had come to greet the new arrivals, but others were still working—building houses, turning this place into the Zion that they all believed in. It would be a good place, Liz told herself; she had to think about it right.

At the bottom of the gangplank a man and woman stepped forward. "I know ye," the man said. "You're Brother Lewis, if I remember right."

"What's left of me."

"Aye. I see that you've suffered. I was not much better mysel' las' year, though I was only done in, not ill."

"I've seen you," Liz said, "but I don't remember your names."

"We're the Bakers, from Dymock. We saw you both at Frome's Hill conferences. You were only newly betrothed when we set off for Nauvoo."

Liz did remember, but they seemed remarkably older than she remembered them. They had always been a nice couple, neat and orderly and a little prim. But their clothes had aged even more than they had, and both of them appeared weathered and brown.

"How is it, living here?" Will asked.

Brother Baker laughed. "It's a growin' town," he said. "E'en Zion needs time to establish itself."

"But it don't do nothin' *itself*," his wife said, and she laughed too. "It's all hard work what makes it."

Liz glanced up the street at the mud. She saw cabins and sheds and privies, all built with rough lumber, and she saw fences built with split logs. What she didn't see was anything that looked at all like an English village. She had imagined stone cottages, picket fences, flower gardens. But none of that mattered. They had arrived, and Will had survived. She had prayed her husband back to this earth, just as he had done for her on the ship. Now she had nothing to complain of. She would make the best of things with what she had. She told Sister Baker, "I'm ready to work. And Will can work before long." She tried to smile, to appear as strong as possible, but she heard the confidence go out of her voice as she asked, "Is there someplace for us to stay for now?"

"You can stay a night with us, if you like," Brother Baker said, "but we have six more at home, and we're stacked in mighty high. We heerd yesterday that the Hartleys finished a new house. They moved out and left an ol' cabin open. It's a poor li'l place, but it would keep a roof over your heads 'til you can get somethin' built for yorsel'."

Sister Baker laughed again. "Yes, a roof over your heads, but one that leaks every time it rains."

"We can manage with that," Will said. "I'll be able to start building in a few days."

"We'll see about that," Liz said, "but for now, we need to get him to a bed. He can't stand up much longer. How far is it to the cabin?"

"Right up this way. I'll carry your trunk and then come back for the other things."

"But I want to shake hands with the Prophet," Will said.

Liz looked to see that Joseph was still in the middle of a crowd, still talking and laughing. "We'll have to meet him later," she said. "You don't have the strength to wait right now."

And so the Lewises followed Brother Baker, who knew where the mud was not so deep, but the soil was like nothing Liz had experienced before. It was mostly clay, and it clung to her shoes until she thought she would lose them. She and Will followed Brother Baker up Water Street to Partridge, and then three streets north to Kimball. It was not far, but it was twice the walk that Will was ready for. Liz had to help him all the way.

Brother Baker finally stopped in front of a drooping cabin with decayed chinking. The roof was shingled but appeared ready to collapse. Liz's first thought was that no one but hogs or chickens could live inside. "I'm sorry for this," Brother Baker said, "but the Hartleys made do with it for a whole winter and it held together."

"We can manage for a time too," Liz said. She waited until she was inside and the Bakers had left; she waited until Will was lying on a sagging old rope bed with a tattered straw mattress; she even waited until she heard him breathing steadily, exhausted and asleep—before she finally let herself cry. She told herself not to think of home, not to think of her sister and mother, her parlor, of High Street in Ledbury. But she had nothing to look at but windows covered with oilcloth, no glass, and a dirt floor. She placed the palms of her hands against her middle, as she had done so many times before. "I'm sorry," she told her baby.

• • •

The next two weeks were difficult. After another full day in bed, Will tried to get up each day and work a little on the cabin—tried to repair the door and fill in the missing chinking. But an hour or two of work would put him down again. He had lost a lot of weight, and he felt as though he'd lost all his strength. But he knew he would get all that back in time. He was much more worried about Liz than he was about himself. He watched her every day, trying to sound happy, trying to convince herself that everything would be all right, but she was living in a so-called house that was little better than a cow shed. She needed to see him up and doing, getting started on a better cabin. More than that, she needed to see more reason to hope. He had promised her a nice home someday, and he was certain that somehow he would keep that promise, but at the moment he couldn't see the plan that would make it possible.

As the weather warmed a little, nights in the cabin weren't quite so bad as they had been the first few nights. The fireplace didn't draw well, and it left the cabin smoky, but it helped when the fire wasn't needed quite so long each day. Liz talked to neighbors and learned what she could cook in a kettle hanging over a fire, and she was starting to do all right with that. What she hadn't mastered was making bread in the ashes of the fire. Will, not wanting to admit to Liz how bad the bread was, did his best to eat it. But it was part of the reason he wasn't eating enough, and part of the reason he wasn't gaining weight. Liz certainly knew that. He had seen tears run down her face when she had sometimes sliced her bread and found it doughy in the middle, burnt on the outside. He had eaten some of it anyway, but mostly to show her his love.

Will was also worried about money. It had cost more than he had expected for Liz to start housekeeping in the little cabin. She had brought a few of her favorite china plates from England, but she feared using them, and had had to buy tin plates and cups and earthenware crockery. The fireplace hadn't been equipped either, so Liz had purchased what she had been told was the minimum number of kettles and andirons, with a crane to hang the kettles on. They had brought bedding for themselves, but Liz was already worrying about a crib for the baby, along with nappies and blankets and clothing.

Will held her off on all that for now, but the baby would be coming in the fall—October, Liz thought—and naturally, she wanted to be ready. Will wanted to buy a building lot, and that would give them enough land to grow a garden and maybe keep a cow and a few pigs. That would help them survive, but he needed to earn money to buy a farm, and he needed to build a house. He worried that he would have to ask Liz to spend a winter in this broken-down cabin. When he watched her at night, sitting by the fire without any books to read or pianoforte to play, he wondered what she was thinking. Maybe, already, she was beginning to resent him for what he had asked of her. He wondered whether she would ever hate him for it, as her father had predicted.

Neighbors knew of the Lewises' plight, and many of them stopped by to help. Brother Hanson, a Swede with a strong accent, helped Will finish the chinking, which stopped most of the draft. He told Will that once he had a lot, men would help him cut logs and raise a better home quickly. Will's friend Jesse also helped him till the garden and plant some potatoes and peas. Will kept at it after that and got some other vegetables planted, and there was an apple tree near the house. Will knew he had to get some animals, but again, he was worried about having enough money to buy land, and he wasn't sure what a lot would cost.

Wilford Woodruff lived close by, Will and Liz soon learned, and one evening he brought Phebe over to meet them. He was more of a farmer than Will had realized, and he talked of crops that Will might want to try and fruit trees that prospered in the area. He also spoke of Joseph's recent sermons, which he had recorded. "We've lost far too many children to fevers in this place," Brother Wilford said. "Phebe and I lost a little one of our own. But Joseph says we shouldn't mourn. Children are taken straight to the Lord, and the only difference in our death and theirs is that they spend a longer time in heaven."

Will appreciated seeing his old friend, but he wondered why Brother Woodruff had chosen that doctrine to relate. It was almost as though he were warning of things that could come to pass for Liz and Will, with a baby coming that fall. Still, Brother Woodruff offered to help him get started, promised to work alongside him to build a house, and Will was reassured to know that the man's promises, back in England, were not mere words.

Will finally mustered the strength to walk to Joseph Smith's office in his store. He found William Clayton, from England, there. Brother Clayton assisted Willard Richards, an apostle Will had once met in Herefordshire. Brother Richards was serving as secretary to Joseph Smith, but he and Joseph were both away for a meeting of the First Presidency and the Twelve. Brother Clayton got out the city plat and advised Will about choosing a good lot, but he told Will, "You might want to talk to Brother Joseph about this. Brother Richards can sell you a building lot—or there are other agents who can do it—but Brother Joseph takes *everything* into consideration, and he adjusts the prices sometimes."

"When could I find Brother Joseph here?" Will asked.

"That's difficult right now," Brother Clayton said. "Have you heard about John Bennett?"

"Isn't he the mayor?"

"He was." Brother Clayton hesitated. "Brother Lewis, there's a good deal going on right now. The prophet was elected as mayor this week, so he's busier than ever. But I'll tell him that you want to see him. Perhaps I can send someone to let you know when he's available—so you won't walk all the way here and miss him again."

"But if he's mayor now, in addition to everything else, maybe I shouldn't bother him."

"No. It's all right. He'll want to meet you. It's just that he has a great deal on his mind right at the present. It's not something I have permission to talk about."

Will thanked Brother Clayton, but he left with an uneasy feeling. He wondered why Brother Clayton didn't feel at liberty to say what had gone wrong. Will walked home, and he waited each day to be summoned, but he didn't hear from anyone.

One afternoon Brother Benbow stopped by. Liz opened the door and thanked him for visiting. She invited him to come in and sit down on one of the two teetering chairs that had been left in the house. Will had been resting, but he got up and shook Brother Benbow's hand. "I heard you're living east of town somewhere," Will said.

"Aye, that's so. Many of the English Saints live out that way, about six miles east. You should think about it yourself. Some of us have ditched the area and planted hedges. I've put up a little barn and a shed and planted a garden and an orchard. It's starting to look a little like our farms in Herefordshire."

Will was wondering how some of the poorer English Saints were managing. Brother Benbow had been well-off at one time, but he had given much of his fortune to help others come to Nauvoo. Will didn't know how people with lesser means could get off to any sort of start. Will sat on the bed and left the other wooden chair for Liz. "I'm trying to get back on my feet as quickly as I can," he told Brother Benbow. "We'll soon have to decide where to locate."

"I'm sorry you have to be here in this little shack. If you would like, you could come and live with Jane and me, just until you get your strength back." He looked at Liz. "That might be better for you, too, Elizabeth."

"That's a nice offer, Brother Benbow," Will said, "but we have our garden in, and we've outfitted the place a little. We'll get by until I can build something better."

"I hope you're not disappointed with Nauvoo. It's especially muddy this time of year, and . . . well . . . I suppose, back in England, we all imagined something a little more built up."

"We're not used to log cabins, of course," Will said. "And I suppose everything does seem a little different here in this country."

Brother Benbow laughed. "Yes, I would say so. But you have to look at the city that will stand here someday, not at the one we see now."

Will knew he had to think that way. He watched Brother Benbow, who was a simple man in his way. His hair and beard were a little whiter than Will remembered, and he seemed more rumpled. His eyes had appeared tired when he had arrived, but now, as he thought of the Nauvoo to come, Will saw him brighten.

"I've noticed that a few people are building brick homes," Liz said. "Those could be very nice, I would think."

"That's exactly right. This won't be a log cabin town forever."

Will liked to think of that. Once he had a lot, maybe he could get a log home built, and then, in a year or two, put up a much nicer home. He could lay the brick himself. "It's the people that matter," Will said. "If good people work together, we'll not only build better homes, we'll build a society like none other."

"That's right," Brother Benbow said. But he didn't sound as confident as Will would have expected. "Of course, there's work to do in that regard, too."

Will waited. He wasn't sure what that meant.

"Some who join the Church bring their old ways with them. We see selfishness at times, and you know how people can be. They spread rumors, criticize, argue over doctrine—all the things we've seen in the past. Some have even turned against Brother Joseph."

"But why?" Liz asked.

"They arrive here expecting Joseph to be a god, not a man. One family left Nauvoo because they said Joseph lost his temper with them—and I'll admit, I've seen him do that a time or two. But he's been pushed to the limit by all the worry about everything—paying the bills he's incurred for the Church, for one thing. And then . . . there are other things. Some people believe every rumor about him, no matter how far-fetched."

Will heard something in Brother Benbow's tone of voice that reminded him of Brother Clayton's hesitancy to describe all that was going on. "What's happened with the mayor?" he asked.

Brother Benbow shook his head sadly. "Bennett's a rascal if there ever was one. He worked his way into Joseph's trust, and then he proved himself to be conniving and immoral. He's tried to take advantage of young women in the Church, telling lies to gain their trust."

"Has he been cut off from the Church?"

"Aye. But the man is dangerous. He's out for revenge, and it's no telling what lies he'll spread now."

"So that's the way of it," Will said, but he still wondered why William Clayton had seemed to unwilling to say more.

"Well, Zion has to be built," Brother Benbow said. "And God only has mortals to work with. We're a sorry lot, we are, but we cannot ever let go of the ideal we strive for."

Will nodded, but it was difficult to accept the reality of what lay ahead. When Brother Benbow left, Will lay back to rest, but he couldn't sleep. He thought of the good position he had held with the Crawfords and the future he might have had with them. He didn't want to admit the idea to himself, but it was hard not to think that maybe he and Liz should have stayed in England.

•   •   •

After Brother Benbow left and Will drifted off to sleep, Liz sat and wondered about the things she had heard. She had been fighting against her homesickness, but now she gave way to it a little. She had always known that things would not be perfect here, but she didn't like to think that a man like Bennett could work his way into the highest levels of the Church and turn out to be so evil. She wondered why Joseph, as a prophet, hadn't discerned what the man was capable of doing.

What she told herself, though, was that she had to grow up. There were always things wrong in this world, and she couldn't expect perfection here any more than anywhere else. And most important, she couldn't give way to self-pity. She had promised Will that she would be strong. She knew she had been a pampered young woman, but this was a new world and a new time. She had to make the best of things. So she got up and worked on a meal for dinner.

On the following morning, Liz was hanging out wash when Sister Coombs, a neighbor, walked by. She and Liz struck up a conversation. "Sister Coombs," Liz said, "let me ask you something." She set her basket of wet linen down.

"Shor. Ask all you want. I jist don't know much, so don't set yor heart on getting any answers." Sister Coombs laughed. She was a big, red-faced woman who stretched all her vowels out long and growled all her "r's."

"I've washed clothes this morning—boiled and scrubbed them—and it's not something I like to do very much," Liz said.

"But I was wondering, if other women don't like it either, maybe some of them would pay me to do it for them. My husband and I are spending money but not earning any—and that can't go on forever." She tried to smile.

Sister Coombs laughed, nodding all the while. "Here's the trouble with that," she said. "It's about the first thing that comes to mind when folks step off the boat in this town. We already got us too many sister warsherwomen, and not enough women who have two bits to pay someone for warshing."

Liz had not wanted to wash for others, but it had been the only idea she had come up with. She was actually relieved to think it wasn't worth pursuing. "Is there something that I *could* do? My husband is still sick, and we have costs coming up."

"Some sisters sew. Others make little things they can sell. But there's never much money around here, and one thing gets worse as the summer comes on. More and more people get sick, and more of 'em get despert to find somethin' they can do."

Liz nodded. The little hope she had started to work up, thinking about the laundry, was gone now. She felt her worry returning.

"What about teaching school?" Sister Coombs asked.

"Me?"

"Shor. You talk like a fine lady. You musta been edicated back in England. There's schools in town already, but with more children comin' all the time, people look for someone to larn their young folks. No one can pay much, but if you take on a few pupils, there's a few dollars in it. Or if they can't pay ready money, they'll pay you in corn or chickens or candles or some sich thing. That's mostly how business is done around here."

"Where would I teach?"

"Some jist have their schools in their houses, but you don't have no extra rooms in yor little place. I guess that's something you'd have to figger out."

"But it's an idea," Liz said.

"An' let me tell yuh something else. No one will ever go hongry around here. We're all poor, but we do look out for them that needs a little extra help. Someone's always got a little flour they can spare, or they'll slaughter a hog and hand over a ham to yuh. We'll all do jist fine in the end, but for now, we have ta share everythin' around. And we do."

Liz didn't want to accept help, but she liked the idea of people looking out for one another. And she felt lifted by Sister Coombs's attitude. She had never thought of herself as a schoolteacher, but she had been a good student. Anything was better than spending her days in this little hovel, worrying about what was coming next. She would advertise herself as a teacher, and she would find a place for her school. She wouldn't tell Will just yet. He thought he had to provide for her in every way. But she was going to take a step forward, even if it was a small step, and the more she thought about it, the more she liked the idea. It made her feel good about herself. It made her feel strong already.

CHAPTER 26

Christmas didn't feel quite right to Jeff. Over the years, except during his mission, he had always been able to go home for the holidays. A return to Vegas had always offered time to take life easy, to not worry about school, and to bask in the warm weather. But it was not the cold that bothered him this year; it was the worry, which wasn't going to go away for a while. Abby was constantly telling him how sure she felt that the baby was all right—that he probably wouldn't need surgery. Jeff wasn't nearly so sure. He had blessed Abby—and the baby—with Malcolm's help, and he had said the words he wanted to say, but before he had closed the prayer, he had also said, "May the Lord's will be done." He had felt the need to say that for some reason, and afterward, it had troubled him. Why hadn't he commanded the baby to be healed and left it at that? Why had he hedged?

His bishop at Stanford had told Jeff once that the art of prayer was to ask for the things the Lord already had in mind for us. The logic had seemed strange to Jeff, but the idea was that God's will had to be done, and that meant that those who pray—or give blessings—should seek the Spirit, recognize the will of God, and then ask for that. Prayer wasn't a good-luck charm, he had said. It was a means of discovering God's will.

Jeff hadn't been entirely happy with the idea then, and he was rather frightened by it now. What he wanted was for the defect in his son's heart to heal, and he wanted Abby to be comforted—and rewarded for her faith. He didn't know what he would say to her if things didn't work out the way she wanted.

Malcolm and Kayla had gone home to Iowa for Christmas, so there wasn't really anyone to spend the day with. Elder and Sister Caldwell had stopped by with a poinsettia, and that had really pleased Abby, but the Caldwells were actually working that day, since the historic sites were open for a few hours. Jeff wished they could stay around longer; Sister Caldwell always made Abby laugh—and provided a little mothering when she needed it.

Abby had called her mother that morning but had not looked happy when she set her phone down. Jeff had been able to tell, from hearing one end of the conversation, that Olivia was disgusted that Abby was working at Walmart this close to her due date. She had been pressuring Abby to quit for at least a month now. Abby had told her parents about the heart defect right after they had heard about it. Since then, both of them had tried everything to talk Abby into coming home. They didn't like the idea of some small-town doctor handling such a delicate operation. Abby had told them over and over that she was seeing an experienced pediatric cardiologist at a very good hospital. She had finally been forced to tell her mother that the discussion was over. The subject had slipped back in a few times all the same, and Jeff was sure it was Olivia's disagreement with everything Abby and Jeff were doing that lay behind the force-ful advice about getting out of Walmart.

So it was a hard day. Abby cooked her first turkey, and it was okay—just a little dry. But she was disappointed with it, and when she disappeared into their bedroom, Jeff went to check on her and found her crying. "It's not the turkey," she told him. "It's just that . . . I don't know . . . it's just everything."

"Are you worried about the baby?"

"No, Jeff. You healed the baby. You said that."

Jeff's breath caught in his chest and seemed to stay there the rest of the day. But the next day he felt he had to do something to lift Abby's feelings. Before Christmas he had been searching online and noticed a job announcement that he decided he should follow up on. He drove to Fort Madison, Iowa, and talked to the personnel director at a manufacturing company that was a branch of the Siemens Corporation. The company built blades for wind turbines and was apparently doing well. Jeff caught the personnel director, a man named Darrell Schoenfeld, on a good day, when things didn't seem very busy. After the two talked for a time, he told Jeff, "If you'd sent in your resumé, I probably wouldn't have paid any attention. I always think a guy from a place like Stanford is going to think too highly of himself—and not be satisfied with support work."

"That's actually what I did in my first job," Jeff told him. The work really was similar to what he had been doing in California, and the truth was, he wished it weren't, but he didn't say that.

"Some of what you would do here would really just be IT work—troubleshooting for managers and office people when they have software problems."

"Yeah, that's a lot of what I did in California. But what are the possibilities down the line? I'm actually trained in program development, and I would especially enjoy that kind of work."

Mr. Schoenfeld lifted his coffee cup and took a tentative sip. "Here at this plant, I'll admit that it's mostly grunt work—but

Siemens is a huge international company. So there's room to move up in the corporation."

"That makes the job all the more interesting," Jeff said.

"But what if it doesn't go that way? Are you planning to put down some roots here and stick around?"

"We like Nauvoo," Jeff said. "We've been talking a lot about staying here. And it only takes about twenty minutes to drive over. So yes, we might settle here and buy a home."

Jeff ended up with an invitation to return for a second interview, and three days later he had a job. He liked what that did for Abby, who said she would give her notice at Walmart and quit right away. "Things are finally working out," she told Jeff, and he told her it was true. He did think it was a blessing that he had shown up at the right time to get the job. It just felt as though he were forcing his own will a little to comply with God's will—and his wife's. He told himself that it was all right, that he was doing the right thing, but he still felt a little disappointed.

All the same, he was relieved, and he really was convinced that God had had something to do with the whole thing. He felt even more that way when he got a call from his friend Jerry Phelps. "Hey, Jeff," Jerry told him, "sorry to give you bad news, but that grant at Princeton didn't come through. No one is funding much of anything right now. It might develop into something next year, but it's dead in the water for now."

"It always did sound a little too good to be true."

"Not really. I still think you ought to apply to grad school out here. If you get in, they would work with you on your finances."

"Well . . . I know. But I found a job across the river in Iowa. It's not a lot of money, but for this area, it isn't bad."

"You don't want to stay out there, do you?"

"Actually, it wouldn't be that bad. It's a way to support my family, and that's what I need to do right now. Besides, it's a company that makes blades for wind turbines, which is something I believe in."

"Sure. I know what you mean. But you love ideas. I know you'd love to teach. It's hard to imagine you doing anything else."

"Sometimes, though, you start to wonder whether all the academic discussions really matter. Right now, the main thing I want to do is make Abby happy." He hesitated, and then he added, "Jerry, we found out our baby has a heart defect. He might need surgery just as soon as he's born. I have interim insurance that I can convert over now, and be covered straight through. I don't know how that would work if I were back in school. Besides, I don't want her working at Walmart. I really want her to know that I'm willing to take care of her and the baby."

"Sure. But with more education—"

"I know all the arguments, Jerry. But this is safer. And maybe it's more important to produce clean energy than to question someone's theory about the significance of the Napoleonic Wars. You know what I mean?"

"Sure. I've heard that there's a real world. I just don't like to have too much to do with it."

The problem was, Jeff knew exactly what Jerry meant. He knew he would miss the academic world forever. But after he clicked his phone off, he felt confident he had made the right choice. Things really were working out.

• • •

On New Year's Eve, Malcolm and Kayla spent the evening with Jeff and Liz. Liz was happy to have them, and she was feeling much better. She was relieved that Jeff had found work. She felt sure that he had been prompted to visit the company in Fort Madison and not just send in an application. That had made all the difference. Now she was sure that God would look after their baby, too. Everything was going to be all right.

Kayla and Malcolm had brought Sophie and Amelia with them. Little Amelia went to sleep after Kayla nursed her, and Abby and Kayla put her down between two pillows on Abby and Jeff's bed. Abby still hadn't bought a crib she could let Kayla use, but she had picked one out, and she had been getting the extra bedroom—the one they had used mostly for storage so far—ready for her son. As she watched Kayla with her little girls, she imagined herself trying to be a good mom. She wanted to be as attentive and patient as Kayla always seemed to be.

Sophie was three, and rather a quiet little girl. She lay on the floor and colored—or sort of scribbled—in a coloring book that Kayla had brought, and then, as the evening wore on, she climbed onto her daddy's lap and fell asleep. Abby watched Sophie, with her sweet face against Malcolm's chest, and she pictured what life would be like next Christmas with a little guy around, maybe even walking by then. She was sure he would love Jeff the way Sophie loved her daddy. She couldn't wait to see what he looked like. More than anything, she wanted to hold him. She wanted to tell him that he was loved and that he would be just fine.

"Have you decided about the baby's name yet?" Kayla asked.

"Yes," Jeff said. "His name is Mahonri Moriancumr. But we plan to call him 'the brother of Jared,' for short."

"I guess your next son will have to be Jared," Malcolm said. He allowed himself a sly grin.

"Not really," Jeff said. "I mean, who *is* Jared? The brother of Jared plays second fiddle to the guy all his life, and yet, for all we know, Jared could have been a horse thief."

"Camel thief, from what I've heard," Malcolm said.

"You guys are reaching a little too hard now," Kayla said. "I think it's time we get these girls home to bed."

"Aren't you going to stay until midnight?" Abby asked.

"We haven't made it to midnight on New Year's Eve since Sophie was born. We're just so glad to get some sleep, any night, we get it when we can."

"I guess that's how we'll be next year," Abby said.

"Do you really think you'll still be here in a year?"

Abby had stretched out in her recliner, trying to give her baby some room, but no position felt good for very long. She pulled herself up a little straighter. She could hardly believe how huge she was, or how awkward she felt all the time. "Who knows?" she said. "We've talked a lot more lately about how much we like it here, and with Jeff's new job, we might be here quite a while."

Sophie squirmed, and Malcolm moved her so she was lying across his legs with her head on Kayla's lap. Malcolm said, "Jeff tells me, though, if he wants to move up with the company, he might have to transfer somewhere else."

"I know. But that might be way down the line. By then, we could maybe buy a house, and we might decide we'd rather stay."

"I'll tell you what I've been thinking lately," Jeff said, but he didn't continue immediately. He seemed to be considering what he wanted to say.

Abby was watching Kayla and Malcolm on the couch, with little Sophie lying across both of them. She felt a goodness, a rightness, that she hoped Jeff was feeling too.

"I've been thinking," Jeff continued, "that my family came here once, and they got forced out. It's just kind of cool that we would end up coming back. I keep thinking that old Grandpa Lewis is excited about it. I'll bet Joseph Smith likes the idea of some of us coming back here too—you know, having wards here and everything."

"I hope so," Kayla said. Sophie had taken her shoes off earlier in the evening, and Malcolm was holding one of her little bare feet as though to keep it warm. Abby was touched by that.

"So what are you saying?" Abby asked. "That we ought to stay here?"

"Maybe." Jeff leaned back in his chair, rested his head on its back, and talked more to the ceiling than to anyone in the room. "I'm starting to feel *connected* to Nauvoo. It's partly because of the people we've met—especially you two." He waved his open hand toward Kayla and Malcolm. "But also, I keep thinking, there's no spot on earth that has more significance for us—or at least for me. It's not only the city that the Saints considered Zion at one time; it's the place my family came to when they immigrated to this country. Do you get what I'm saying?"

"Sure," Malcolm said. "We don't have family history here, but when I got the job in Fort Madison, we decided we wanted to live over here. There were more members on this side of the river, but there's also the temple and the pageant and everything."

"Yeah, I get all that," Jeff said. "But I'm also talking about walking the streets where prophets walked—and where my Grandpa walked—and trying to find out what I can learn from that. Does that make any sense?"

Malcolm finally laughed. "Not really. Not to me. But I don't understand a lot of things. My biggest mental challenge is rotating tires and remembering which one goes where."

Jeff laughed too, but then he said, quite seriously, "Sure. We all have to take care of the tasks before us. I'm just wondering if there's some reason Abby and I are supposed to be here. We've been feeling that way lately, but we're not really sure why. Maybe we can learn something here that we can't learn anywhere else."

"When I get feelings like that," Kayla said, "I just follow them. I don't try to figure them out."

Abby liked that. "That's how I think too," she said.

"I know. I think too much," Jeff said. "But here's where my mind's been going lately. I want to know what Zion is. Joseph Smith called Nauvoo the 'cornerstone of Zion' after we had to give up Zion in Missouri and come here. So Zion was here for a time, and then we called Utah Zion. So we talk about it like it's a place. But what is it, really? What's the point of it?"

"Wasn't it a place to gather and build up the Church?" Abby asked. "You know, create some strength and then build up the worldwide Church from there?"

"Sure. But that's kind of explaining the function of Zion. It doesn't say what it is—or what it's supposed to be."

"I've thought about that too," Malcolm said. "It seems like it was God's way of teaching people how to bring the gospel into the real world—you know, make it more than just an idea."

Jeff sat up straight. "For a guy who says he can't remember which way to rotate tires, that's pretty good stuff."

"I actually can rotate tires. I was lying about that."

But Jeff was obviously not going to be sidetracked. Abby knew how much he loved to pursue these trains of thought once he started. "So there's no such thing as goodness alone. You have to be good *to* someone. You have to turn spirituality into a practical reality."

"So what does *that* have to do with us staying here?" Abby asked. "Nauvoo isn't Zion now. Our old bishop used to say that we're supposed to create a Zion society wherever we live." In a way, she didn't want to talk Jeff out of his idea, since she wanted to stay in Nauvoo, but she really didn't understand what he was saying.

"I'm sure that's right," Jeff said. He was staring past Abby, obviously still thinking. "But my grandma and grandpa lived right across the street, and it feels to me like God sent us here to meet them and find out who they were. And every time I take a walk down on the flats, I feel like I've come home. I just think we need to explore that for a while."

"Explore it? How do we do that?" Abby asked.

Jeff looked down, resting his elbows on his knees. "I don't even know, Abby. I should take Kayla's advice and go with the feeling—not try to analyze it so much. I just keep thinking that I need to understand what Zion is. Grandpa Lewis gave up everything to come here—to gather with the Saints in Zion—and most modern members don't even give the idea much thought. I never had until we moved here."

"Maybe most of us just don't think as deep as you do," Kayla said.

"But that's the thing. It's really not very deep at all. Last year at this time we didn't even know that you two or your little daughters existed. And now, you matter to us. That's probably Zion, step one. Malcolm helps me on this house, and now I plan to help Malcolm on yours. That's Zion, step 2. It's pretty simple. For all I know, that might be the whole thing. I just keep feeling like Grandpa Lewis must have seen a lot more in it than I do."

"I'll bet he really just followed *his* feelings," Abby said.

"I know. That's probably right. And as usual, I talk too much."

That seemed the end of the conversation. Malcolm took Sophie in his arms and stood up. But after he did, he said, "I was reading in Fourth Nephi the other night. It tells how after Christ came to the Nephites, the people lived in harmony for two hundred years. They all looked after each other, and no one put himself above anyone else. It even says that there were no poor people. I guess Zion must be like that, but I don't know how we ever get to that point."

"I don't either," Jeff said. "That's exactly the kind of stuff I've been thinking about."

"So help me fix up my house. That's where you can start." Malcolm smiled.

"That is where I want to start," Jeff said, and he sounded serious.

Malcolm carried Sophie to the car, and Jeff walked to the bedroom and got Amelia and walked outside with Kayla. When he came back to the house, he asked Abby, "Did I get too carried away?"

"Of course. It's what you do. But I liked thinking about all those things." She pushed back against the backrest and made the recliner into something of a bed. "For me, though, it's not that complicated. In a year, little Mahonri, or whatever we decide to call him, will—"

"Hey, let's go with that name. I like it."

"Okay. You be the one to tell my mom."

Jeff laughed. "Scary thought," he said.

"Anyway, a year from now he'll be running around the house. But we'll sit here with Kayla and Malcolm, and we'll love them even more than we do now. To me that's just friendship, and it's the best thing in life. I don't think it matters whether you call it Zion or not."

"When Joseph Smith wrote to Emma, he would call her his 'dear, dear friend.' We've kind of lost the meaning of that word— what it meant to people in the nineteenth century."

"Oh, Jeff. We do have different ways of thinking."

"I know. I'm sorry. I shouldn't turn everything into some big deal."

"No, no. That's you. I love the things you talk about, and I love how carried away you get . . . and I love *you*."

"And I love the way you say 'talk'—towak—like you grew up in Joisey."

"I do not."

"A little, you do."

He was smiling, but he leaned back and shut his eyes, and Abby watched him, wondering still whether he weren't just trying to make things okay for her. "Are we all right, Jeff?" she finally asked him.

"We love each other. We're friends. And we're in Zion, trying to figure out how to be Zion people."

"But are you trying to convince yourself? After all you said tonight, wouldn't you still rather be a professor than a computer programmer?"

"I don't know. I just know that I don't want to leave Nauvoo *yet*. And I want to do what's best for you."

"Then let's think about our lives here. Do we want to buy a house? Do we want to think that we're permanent—until later notice?"

"Yeah. I think we do."

"Okay. Let's start thinking that way and talking that way. Let's not always be saying 'if' about everything."

"Okay."

"Jeff, tell me something else. And I want you to be honest."

"Okay."

"Do you feel like our baby is going to be all right?"

But Jeff didn't answer for a long time, and that made Abby uncomfortable. She pushed in with her heels and made the recliner come back up a little. Finally, he said, "I trust your faith more than my own, Abby. And you feel good about it."

"Jeff, that's not what I need from you."

"I know. But bad things happen in life, and I think some of those things will happen to us. I just don't know that we can pray away everything we'd rather not have to deal with."

"So you're not sure?"

"I know what I told you in the blessing. But I also said that the

Lord's will should be done. We have to accept that it might not be what we want."

"Why would He want to take away our baby, Jeff?" She brought the recliner all the way up.

"I'm not saying that He would. But so many babies died in this city, Abby. Hundreds of them. What makes us different?"

"What's different is that those mothers were strong and I'm not. I couldn't give up my little son now. I just couldn't."

She watched Jeff. He came to her and put his arms around her, but he couldn't bring himself to tell her that everything was going to be all right.

• • •

Jeff and Abby tried to stay awake until midnight, but Abby didn't make it. So Jeff put her to bed, and he told her he was going to read a little and wait up "for all the excitement." After giving her a few minutes to fall asleep again, he put on the new winter coat that he had bought with the money his parents had sent him for Christmas, and he stepped outside. He almost gave up the idea when he felt the wind, but he pulled his chin into his collar and walked across the street. There was a little snow in the woods, under the trees, but not much. The bigger problem was the dark, along with the tangle of vines and ferns. But he made his way into the little open spot he had chosen to imagine as the heart of Grandfather Lewis's building lot. He stood in the center of it and looked up at the sky. A bit of moonlight was making silhouettes of the black branches and casting a silver light across the thin clouds.

"Grandpa, I came to say hello again," he said, but not loudly this time. He was feeling disgusted with himself. He had babbled on and on, as usual, making lots of noise and saying very little, but when Abby had really needed him, he hadn't been able to assure her.

"I'll bet you were the strong, silent type," he told his grandfather. "I'm probably a huge embarrassment to you."

The wind came up a little, and he turned his back into it. He could hear the click and rustle of bare tree limbs, and he felt the cold air seep into him, but he wanted to be here on his grandparents' land for a few minutes tonight. He wished he could actually talk with them.

"Grandpa Lewis," he said, "if I'm supposed to stay here, I want to do it, and not wander off. But maybe I'm just making all this stuff up about being gathered here to your old neighborhood. You may not even know that I'm here. You people probably have better things to do than try to track all your grandkids all the time."

He stood in the quiet and tried to think what his grandfather might be like, what sort of man he had been when he had lived here. These winter nights in a drafty little log cabin must have been hard for Grandma and Grandpa and their kids.

"I do have the feeling we're supposed to stay here, but I pray about it every day and change my mind just about as often." He stopped and listened, wished that a voice would sound in his ears. But he heard only the gentle winter noises.

"I feel like our baby will probably be all right, but I couldn't get myself to say that, and now Abby's going to be worried again. People always say they feel 'prompted' to do this or 'inspired' to say that. All I do is toss things back and forth. I really need to get to the point where I know the Spirit better than I do right now. What did you do about that? Did you figure all that out?"

Jeff wished he knew more about the old man. His dad had an old photograph of him, made when he was seventy or so. He'd had a white beard and a solemn look in his eyes. He probably didn't have much patience for Jeff's hand wringing. If he could hear all this right now, he was probably wishing he could give Jeff a good swift kick in the rear. Strong men didn't mumble and plead and feel sorry for themselves.

The wind picked up stronger again, and from somewhere in town Jeff heard firecrackers, or maybe someone shooting off a gun—something to celebrate, even though midnight was at least an hour away.

"Anyway," Jeff finally said, "if there's some way for me to know that this is where I'm supposed to be right now, that would help a lot. I don't expect you to figure out everything for me, but I'd just like to feel like I'm not entirely on my own."

And then, in the dark, he heard a flutter of wings. It must have been that bird—that owl or hawk—he and Abby had heard the first time they had come here. He looked up at the sky, the silver layer of clouds, and then he saw a great bird, dark against the clouds, its wide wings barely moving. It drifted across the opening above, slowly turning. Jeff lost his breath. He stood watching, in awe, as it made another circle before it lifted upward and out of sight—as though it were an angel carrying his words to heaven.

Jeff chose not to doubt. He knew what he felt.

He made his way out of the woods and back across the street. What he believed was that he and Abby were exactly where they were supposed to be.

CHAPTER 27

Will ate his breakfast, and, even if it was only cornmeal johnnycake and coffee, as it had been every day lately, he was feeling stronger. He had been in Nauvoo over three weeks now, and he was feeling a little better each day. Today he was going to work in his garden, and then he wanted to seek out Joseph Smith even though William Clayton had never sent the messenger he had promised. Will simply had to acquire a building lot so he could start to clear land and get a house built—and get Liz away from this leaky, smoky cabin.

He was eating with a plate on his lap, since he and Liz still didn't have a table, when a loud knock came on the door. Liz got to the door first. When she opened it, Will saw that Joseph Smith himself was outside, standing head and shoulders taller than Liz. "I understand you want to see me," Joseph said. He was smiling as though he were enjoying some joke that Will didn't really understand.

Will got up and hurried to the door. "Yes, yes," Will said, "please come in." Liz was speaking at the same time, saying the same thing.

Brother Joseph stepped into the room and looked around. The

only light was from the windows and the open door. He was wearing a frock coat and holding a tall hat in his hand, but his clothes were well worn, his boots muddy. His skin looked youthful, but he hadn't shaved for a few days, and the stubble gave him the look of a working man. But none of that mattered. The Lord's Prophet was standing in Will and Liz's humble little cabin; Will could hardly believe it.

"I'm glad you found this fine palace," Joseph said. He laughed. "Just the thing for a lord and his lady."

"Let's say that the rent reflects the value of the property," Will said, grinning. "But thank you. Thank you for coming to see us here."

Joseph's voice softened. "I'm sorry that we couldn't fix you up better than this for a start," he said. "There are so many coming and there's so much work to do. We all have to manage as best we can for now." He took a closer look at Will. "I understand you've not been well, Brother Lewis."

"I was struck down on the boat, Brother . . . or President Smith. I—"

"Go ahead and call me Brother Joseph. It's what everyone calls me, and it's what I like."

"I will, then. And call me Will."

"Was it cholera, do you think?"

"Yes, I do. But I'm getting my strength back. I called on you because I'm ready to purchase a building lot—if I can afford it."

By then, Liz was saying, "Please, sit down, President Smith." She moved one of their chairs, set it closer to him.

He laughed again. Will thought it was because she hadn't called him "Brother Joseph." "And where will you sit, Sister Lewis?" Joseph asked. But she was closer to the door now, and he seemed to see her more clearly in the light from outside. "My goodness, Sister Lewis, you're reputed to be a beautiful woman—Emma told me so—but that was faint praise indeed."

Will put his arm around Liz's shoulders. He knew that she didn't feel pretty these days, with only one dress that would fit her now, and living in this squalid place. She had bought a tin tub, and she bathed and cared for herself as best she could, but nothing was easy with a dirt floor and only a small hand mirror to look at. "I took her away from a better life, Brother Joseph," Will said. "I need to make things right for her again."

"I'll sit over here," Liz said, clearly hoping the conversation would turn away from her. She sat by the fireplace on a little bench—a rustic piece of furniture, but one that had been offered with love by a neighbor.

Joseph sat in the chair Liz had offered and Will sat in the other, in front of him. Joseph seemed to be studying Will, as though to take the measure of him. Will was surprised by the intensity in those eyes, how open and direct the man seemed. "What are your plans, Brother Will? Have you a trade?"

"I'm just a farmer."

"He's too modest, President Smith," Liz said. "He managed a large farm for a wealthy squire. He's a leader, and once he gets his legs back under him, he can work as hard as any man you'll ever meet."

Joseph nodded to Liz and then looked back at Will. "Yes. I see all that," he said, and Will wondered what he meant exactly. "You're right to want a building lot here in Nauvoo. That's easy enough. Come to my office today and choose a lot on the city plat. But you'll need a farm, too. You can keep some animals here in town, and you can grow a fine garden, but you'll need more acreage than that for a good farm."

"But how much does farmland cost?"

"For the present, here's what I would suggest. We have a large plot about six miles out on the prairie—on the road to Carthage. We consider it common ground. Any of our brothers can claim a parcel there. If you can get the prairie grass plowed as soon as possible, there's still time to plant this year."

Will had heard something about this, but he saw no way to make it happen. "But how could I plow it? I have no horses or oxen and probably not enough money to buy any."

"That's why we all have to work together. As you get your health back, you can offer what you have—your youth and strength—to plow that deep prairie grass for men who need the help. Then they can make a trade by offering you their animals to plow your own ground."

"Yes, I could do that. I'm not quite ready to work from sunup until sundown, but I can put in a few hours each day."

"But it's six miles," Liz said. "How could you walk that far twice each day—and plow fields besides?"

Will grasped his knees and leaned forward. "I'll just do what I have to do. I'm improving fast now."

"But you'll be down again if you try to do something like that."

"She's right," Joseph said. "We've seen it plenty here. We've had more sickness than I've ever seen before, and it comes back on people. I've seen men try to get going too fast and put themselves in early graves."

"Why are so many sick?" Liz asked.

Joseph got up and walked to her. "Come, sit on the chair. I'll move this bench over and sit on that." What surprised Will a little was that she complied, but there had been something more than politeness in his voice—a kind of authority. Joseph pulled the bench over, sat down near Will and Liz, then said, "It's mostly the ague that people suffer with here. They tell me it's bad air that does it—miasma. It's caused by all the standing water hereabouts. But we drained off a great deal last year, and we're working at it again now. It won't always be like that."

"Brother Joseph," Will said, "tell me the names of some men I could talk to—men who have work animals and who might need my help. God helped me get this far. He'll help me move forward. I need some way to provide for Liz—and for the child we'll soon have."

But Joseph didn't answer for a time. He sat straight on the little bench and folded his arms over his big chest. "I'm thinking about this just a little differently now," he said. "Did you bring some money—enough to buy a building lot?"

"I think so. I don't know what the lots cost."

"Supposing you made a small down payment on your lot and agreed to pay the balance off, a little each year? It's something we allow when it seems the right thing to do. And remember, it's a full acre, which you may not want here in town. You could sell off part of it, and that helps to get it paid for."

"Would I have interest to pay on the debt I would owe?"

"No. We don't charge interest. But I would have to have something from you each year. I need money to pay off the loan I took to buy all this land. But supposing you took the balance of that money, and you bought three or four teams of oxen. The land out there on the prairie can't be broken by a single team. It takes at least three teams, pulling together, to get under that deep-rooted grass. The problem is, there's no one man who owns that many oxen."

"But would I want that many once I'd opened my land the first time?"

"Not for yourself, you wouldn't, but here's what I'm thinking. Every man who starts a farm on the prairie faces the same problem. If you had three or four teams, you could hire out to plow ground for newcomers. You could set yourself up in a good business. Most people couldn't pay you in cash. Around here, we pay off our bills in corn, produce, eggs, bacon—whatever we have. Or a shoemaker makes you a pair of boots or repairs your harnesses—all that sort of thing. If you had those oxen, you would have valuable trading power. At the same time, you could plow your own field and harvest some grain this fall. If you raise some produce in town, and fatten some animals, you would eat all right and still make the payment on your land. In time, you could buy your own farm, not just use the common ground. "

"How much would all this cost? What's the price of an ox in this country?"

"I'd say fifty dollars would buy you an excellent team. If you bought three or four teams, you might get yourself a better price than that."

But it was more than Will had expected. "That would take everything we have, just for three teams. And then we'd have nothing to live on. I also need some of my money to buy hogs and chickens."

"It's what everyone is up against, I'm afraid. I'm sure it's the reason no one else has started a business of that kind."

Will tried to think what he could do. He glanced at Liz and tried to sound confident, so he wouldn't worry her. "I worked a little as a stonemason in my home country. I'm not very skilled, but I can build a wall or a shed. Is there any work of that kind here?"

Joseph laughed softly. "You shouldn't tell me that, Will. I'm likely to put you to work on the temple every day."

"I want to work on the temple."

"I'm glad to hear it, and we ask that you work one day in ten. We even pay people who know the trade, but we can't pay much, and it wouldn't be much to support a family. Still, there are times when someone needs rock work here—and especially bricklaying.

It's something else you can trade on. That's how people live here, at least for now. They do some farming and they add a little to that by plying whatever skill they have."

"I'm thinking—could I lay brick and earn enough to buy those oxen?"

"Maybe. In time. But that won't help you much for this season."

"I understand that. I'm just trying to look ahead, think what I can do."

"And what about your hand?" Liz asked. "Can you grip well enough to lay brick?"

"I think so. I could . . . well, maybe not yet. I'm not sure."

· · ·

Liz was immediately sorry she had asked. She saw how discouraged Will looked. She had been listening to all this talk, hoping to hear an answer that would satisfy Will and maybe even inspire him with more hope than he had had lately. But as she watched him now, she saw the worry in his face. She couldn't let him sink any further. "I have some money," she said. Joseph looked at her. "My father gave me a little money before we left England."

"So you came with a dowry, did you?" Joseph laughed.

"Actually, yes. Though a small one. But I could buy those oxen."

"We aren't going to do that, Liz," Will said. "He gave you that money for a house. And I promised him that you wouldn't have to live in a log cabin very long. If he saw this place you're living in now, he would grab you up and carry you home."

"But Will," Liz said, "if you start a business, you can multiply the money. What I have now is not nearly enough for a nice home."

"But it's a start. I won't touch that money."

Liz had known exactly how Will would react. But her mind had already moved quickly ahead. "President Smith," she said, "now that

I'm in America, I'm thinking of becoming a woman of business. What I want to do is buy some teams of oxen and start plowing for farmers in the area. Can you put me in touch with someone who has oxen for sale?"

Joseph smiled. "I could give you a name or two. Yes." He turned a little more toward her, and his smile became more pronounced. "But how do you hope to handle all those oxen? Have you had much experience with plowing, Sister Lewis?"

"Not any at all, sir. But I know a fine young man—strong and experienced—and I think I could hire him to do my work."

"Liz, no," Will said. "We can't spend your money that way."

"This is of no concern to you, Mr. Lewis. I'm doing business with Mr. Smith here—*Mayor* Smith. I want to buy myself some nice-looking oxen, and I don't see that you have anything to say about it."

Joseph was still laughing, but he said, "It's something you two do need to talk over, but Will, I don't think I would cross this little lady. She seems to know what she wants. I'm married to such a woman myself, and I've learned that being mayor—or even Lieutenant General of the Nauvoo Legion—doesn't impress her much. When she sounds the bugle and makes a charge, I go into quick retreat."

"I'm learning that too," Will said. "But I made promises to her father."

Joseph nodded. He got up from the bench. "Those are things you two will have to decide," he said. "But I hope you don't look straight down at the ground as you walk ahead. You need to see a little farther up the path."

"The path does look a little muddy at present," Will said.

"I know. But all your decisions should take into account what this city will be like in ten or twenty years. Try to see this place the way I do. I picture Nauvoo when the temple is finished, the streets are paved, businesses have built up, and we've all built ourselves better homes. You have to remember what Zion is all about: we're going to raise each other up by working together—not by climbing over one another, the way it's done most of the time in this world."

"That's what Apostle Woodruff taught us, back in England," Will said. "It's what brought us here."

"Brother Wilford has the vision," Joseph said. "Those who have means must concern themselves for those who don't. We must support one another, offer our talents to the Lord and to each other, and live together in harmony." He looked at Liz. "Have the members offered help to you while Will's been sick?"

"They have. Everyone stops by to make sure we're getting by. Two sisters came this week from a relief organization. They brought us some bedding and promised quilts for the winter."

"Yes, that's the Female Relief Society. It was just formed this spring—while you two were crossing the ocean. It's not just a ladies' society like you run across in most towns. It's built after the manner of the priesthood, and it will change all our lives in time. My wife Emma is the president."

"Yes, they told me that. They also suggested that I plan to join them when I can."

"Now, that's a compliment, Sister Lewis. They see something in you, that's for certain." He smiled and looked at Will. "We men never quite grab hold of anything the way the sisters do. They'll have us living right if they have to pull us along by our lapels."

"That's the way of it," Will said, "but, Brother Joseph, I've been hearing that everything's not as harmonious as it should be. I hear about people criticizing, complaining, even giving up and leaving."

"I know." Joseph suddenly looked solemn. "The net we throw out is always going to bring in a few stinking fish. We try to change them, get them to see what we're doing here, but some never quite grasp it. And there's something I need to warn you about." He looked down at the dirt floor for a time and seemed to think, as though he needed to choose just the right words. "In the next few weeks, you're going to hear things about me that will test your faith in everything you've been taught. I simply ask you not to believe what you'll hear."

"We won't pay attention to lies," Will said. "We've heard some of that before."

Joseph nodded, then stepped to the door. But he turned back and said, "Do you know about John Bennett and the things he has been saying?"

"We know he was cut off from the Church," Will said. "And we know you replaced him as mayor."

"Yes . . . well . . . he's begun to spread lies. I hate to think of all the trouble he's going to cause us."

"The Saints know the truth. They won't believe his lies."

He looked down again. "But distortions are even more dangerous than outright lies. He's crafty at making things that are right and true sound evil. There are those, already, who believe him, and they are publishing his distortions all across our land. The worst is, some of our own people have been misled by what he's saying."

"Don't worry about us. We'll stand by you no matter what lies he tells."

Liz stepped up next to Will and said, "That's right. We shall."

Brother Joseph smiled a little, but his demeanor had changed since Will had posed his question. Will thought he looked sad, even tired. "I'm glad that young people like you keep coming here," Joseph said. "You're willing to work, willing to be equal with your neighbors, willing to lift up the hands that hang down. We're going to build something extraordinary, something the world has never seen. And we won't be stopped by men like Bennett. The Lord will see to that."

Liz felt a surge of confidence—and love—for this man. He seemed a little rougher than she had expected, but he was good. She felt that. And she also had a glimpse, now, of the burden he was carrying, leading the Church as such a young man.

"Some come here," Joseph said, "and they see the body of this place, but they need to see the soul. Find a way to do that, Brother and Sister Lewis. God brought you here for a reason. For now, you need a little help to get started, but the day will come when you'll bless the lives of those who come after you."

Liz liked to think that she would be able to do that. She had spent her life living too much for herself, thinking too much of her own comfort. She didn't want to live in a broken-down cabin very long, but she did want to see the soul of this place, as Joseph said. She wanted to serve, and she wanted to do her part to take a little of the burden off Will.

• • •

Will stepped closer to the Prophet. "Thank you so much for coming by to see us," he said. He felt stronger already just to have spent some time with the man, and he had some ideas now about how he might be able to manage. He didn't really like the idea of using Liz's money, but he knew she would buy those oxen, whether he wanted her to or not, and he was also thinking she was right. He could multiply her money by adding his hard work, and maybe build her a house all the sooner. Her father might think he was taking away what was hers, but he promised himself he wouldn't do that.

"I hear you're a powerful young man, Will," the Prophet said.

"I look like a skeleton now, but there was a day, I could heft about as much as any man." He grinned.

Joseph grabbed him by the arm, as if to feel his muscle, but then he nudged him just enough to make Will take a step to catch his balance. "Well, build yourself up, Brother, and then we'll wrestle a round or two. But I must say, I believe I can throw you."

"I keep hearing that you've never been thrown." Will pretended to size him up, looking him up and down. "So far."

Joseph laughed in a great burst. "The real truth is, I must admit, I've met my match a time or two." He took hold of both of Will's shoulders. "Well, yes, you've got some muscles in those shoulders. You might make me work just a little—before I throw you."

Will liked this man. There was nothing pious or stuffy about him. And Will had the feeling that if he ever did throw him, Joseph would be the first to slap him on the back and congratulate him. Will had heard the spirit and power in Joseph's voice when he had talked about Zion, but now he seemed the kind of fellow Will might have chosen for a friend when both of them were lads.

"Give me a month or two of wrestling with those oxen, and then I'll be ready to see what I can do."

"I'll plan on it," Joseph said. "And I won't underestimate you." He looked at Liz. "I heard how he took on that scoundrel on the riverboat and gave him his due."

Will was shocked to know that Joseph had heard about that. "I shouldn't have fought the man. I—"

"You're right. You shouldn't have. No question about it. But then . . . I shouldn't have enjoyed the story so much. I heard what he did and said, and I heard how you set him right. I know it's better to turn the other cheek, but now and again, maybe a man like that deserves what he gets."

Will knew he had taken too much joy in his triumph, and he

knew the Prophet was mostly just joking, but it was hard not to feel a little pride in Joseph knowing about it.

"There's a better story going around about you," Joseph said.

"About me?"

"Yes, sir. I talked to a man who sailed with you. He told me that you stood forth in the steerage of that ship, raised your arm to the square, and commanded the winds to cease. And the winds obeyed."

"It was my arm and my words," Will said, "but it was Liz's faith."

Joseph looked over at Liz. "That's how it is with most of us," he said. "But I'm very much pleased with both of you. You're going to do mighty things in your lives. I feel it in everything you do and say."

Will was too moved to say anything. He put his arm around Liz. He had the feeling they were going to be all right.

"Things might get worse before they get better, but I've seen some of the future, and I know we'll become a great force for good in this world. The gospel will go forth to every tongue and people. I promise you that." He nodded firmly, and then he added, "This morning I had something else to do, and I was heading out to do it. But a thought came to me that I needed to stop here—and I've learned to obey those kinds of promptings. They come from God."

"It was good that you came," Will said. "We needed some hope, and you've given us that."

Joseph shook hands with Will, and then he touched Liz's arm. "Bless you and your baby." He smiled. "And bless your plowing business."

He left.

Will and Liz walked to the door and watched Joseph mount his big black horse and ride away. He waved, and they waved back to him, and then they continued to stand in the open doorway.

"He *is* a prophet," Will said. "We did the right thing in coming here."

Liz turned and wrapped her arms around Will, pressed her face to his chest.

• • •

Later that day Will and Liz chose a building lot. It was on the bluffs, away from the river. They thought it might be a healthier place to live—where the soil wasn't so boggy and the air didn't smell of decay. The plat map they looked at placed the land just off Rich Street, but so far, not many had moved to this upper area of Nauvoo, and Rich Street was more a line on a map than it was a street. Still, Will and Liz had hiked up Parley Street and then worked their way north through the thick woods until they found the lot, marked with stakes, that seemed the highest point of land in the area. Will kicked away grass and dead leaves on the ground and found dark, rich soil that he knew would produce a fine garden, and he judged that there were enough white oaks on the lot to use for building logs. So he and Liz had returned to the red brick store and signed the deed for the property.

Early the next morning, Will said to Liz, "Let's go back and look at our lot."

"You'll wear yourself out, walking up there again."

"No. We can walk straight up this time—not go clear around to Parley Street. I just want to stand on the land again and look it over a little more."

So after breakfast, they hiked up the hill and walked all over their land. Finally Will pointed to an open space in the trees and said, "I think this will be the best place to build a good home. But we can build a log cabin right next to it, and then till up a garden where it will be close to the cabin but also close to the brick house, when I get it built."

"Oh, Will," Liz said, "it's so much work. Can you clear all this growth this year and build a cabin, too?"

"There's more than that to do—if you buy those oxen and then hire me to be your plowboy."

"Maybe we should plan to stay one winter where we are. We could manage. I don't want you to work so hard that you ruin your health."

"I'll be all right. And I've had at least a dozen men promise to help me cut the timber and raise a log house. But I want to use hewn logs and plaster the walls—so it won't be too bad of a place, even if it's just for the first year or two." Will liked the idea of working from sunrise to sunset again, the way he had always done, and he felt sure he could soon do it.

He stood among the oaks and hickories and pictured himself felling those trees, opening up a bigger clearing in these woods. He pictured pens and coops for his animals, tried to think where he might place them. He finally said what he had been thinking—and feeling—since he had signed the deed. "We own land, Liz. It's our own land."

"It's what you've always dreamed of, isn't it?"

"Aye. All those years I farmed for other men I wondered what it would be like to have land of my own. And it feels good. It truly does." He turned to look at Liz. "But I will say this. It's not the land that matters to me so much as I thought it would. It's being here in Zion. I keep thinking about the things Brother Joseph said yesterday—about seeing the soul of Nauvoo, not the body."

"What has stayed in my mind is the way he looked right into us and told us we were some of those who would make Zion what it's supposed to be."

Will took hold of Liz's hand and they stood close. He hoped Liz was seeing the same things he was envisioning. Not just the farm, but the family they would have. He had thought at one time that none of this could ever happen, and now he had everything—even if most of what he was seeing resided only in his mind. Above all, he had Liz. It was still a wonder to him that she loved him, that she had stuck with him through everything.

"Will, I've been feeling something new for a day or two." She placed her hand on her middle. "I think our baby has started to move."

"Is that so?"

"It's just a little flutter I keep feeling, but I'm almost sure it's the baby. I felt it again just a moment ago."

"Have you been worried about the baby?"

"I have. It seemed that I should have felt it by now, so I've been waiting. On the ship, I wondered whether the poor little thing could stay alive."

"I know. I—"

"Oh! There it is again." Liz took Will's hand and placed it flat against her. They stood like that for a time, waiting.

And then Will felt it—one little bump.

"That was it," Liz said. "The strongest yet."

"I know. I felt it."

They looked at each other, and Will saw Liz's eyes fill with tears. "We're all right," she said. "All of us. We made it here together."

Will took her in his arms and held her. Tears were on his cheeks too, but he hardly knew how to tell Liz what he was feeling. This child was the beginning of their posterity, and they were standing in this holy place—their own little portion of Zion.

"I hope our children will understand what this place means," Liz finally said. "I want them to see the soul of it too."

"Aye. And their children. I keep seeing the generations marching out from here. I hope they always know what they're part of."

Will finally stepped back from Liz, and the two looked across the land again. Just then a huge bird with wide wings—an eagle, Will realized—swooped down through the trees and landed in a tree not far from them. It stood on a limb majestically, its white head bright in the sun.

"It's so beautiful," Liz whispered. "It descended like an angel."

Will had thought the same thing.

They stood looking at the bird for some time, but then, with a little leap and the powerful lift of its wings, it flew up and away from the clearing and into the sky. They kept watching until it was out of sight, and then they looked out across their land again.

"Let's have a prayer," Will said.

So they knelt in the woods among the ferns and bracken, and Will thanked the Lord for their arrival, for their baby, for each other. And then he dedicated their little plot in Zion as an everlasting home to their family.

AUTHOR'S NOTE

The Winds and the Waves is the first book in a series. The double story of Liz and Will, Abby and Jeff, will continue through two more volumes. Or at least that's my plan for now.

I have long been interested in Nauvoo, Illinois, but that interest expanded when my wife, Kathy, and I were called by The Church of Jesus Christ of Latter-day Saints to serve for two years as the public affairs representatives for Nauvoo (from the fall of 2008 to the fall of 2010). While there, we did research on our ancestors who lived in Nauvoo in the 1840s. What we knew—but learned much more about—was that our Nauvoo relatives were part of the United Brethren organization that was converted, almost *en masse,* by Wilford Woodruff and other apostles during the second apostolic mission to Great Britain. My third-great-grandparents, Robert Harris, Jr., and his wife, Hannah, surely knew Kathy's third-great-grandparents, Thomas Henry Clark and his wife, Charlotte. They lived on opposite sides of the Malvern Hills, in Herefordshire and Gloucestershire, but Thomas Clark was one of the leaders of the United Brethren and a lay minister who traveled throughout the preaching circuits. He certainly admonished my ancestors to righteousness (just as Kathy continues to "encourage" me).

We became interested not only in the lives of the Clarks and Harrises in Nauvoo but in their home setting in England. We've traveled to the beautiful Malvern Hills, which lie west of the Cotswalds near the Welsh border, and I've spent a couple of years researching not only the United Brethren but the midlands of England in that era. I decided not to follow the life stories of either the Harrises or Clarks, but to draw upon the many experiences recorded in journals and life histories of the Saints who emigrated from England to Nauvoo. My distant cousin Darryl Harris has followed the life of Robert Harris, Jr., in his *Light and Truth* series (Harris Publishing, Inc.), which he began publishing in 2003. I saw no reason to cover the same ground.

This book is a historical novel. Some authors tell history in a "fictionalized" style and narrate the way a movie camera might, shifting from place to place and including events that no character in the book observes. I have chosen, however, in any given scene, to write from the point of view of one of my four main characters. I believe this creates a sense of reality and offers an insight into the way people of the time might have felt and thought. A history book offers a broader, more general picture of a time; I hope this novel looks underneath the facts and figures and renders the fears, aspirations, and motivations of some representative people (even if they are people of my own making).

When I portray historic figures, such as Wilford Woodruff or Joseph Smith, I try not to put words into their mouths that they wouldn't have said. When these characters are merely making conversation, I stay true to their personalities, based on what I've learned about them, but when they express opinions and attitudes—especially theological ones—I base those on actual statements I have read in their journals or sermons.

For the last few years, in an attempt to portray these times and places accurately, I've steeped myself in English and Mormon history. If you would like to do some "steeping" of your own, let me recommend some of the books and sources I've used. A good starting place is: *Truth Will Prevail: The Rise of The Church of Jesus Christ of Latter-day Saints in the British Isles, 1837–1987,* ed. V. Ben Bloxham, James R. Moss, Larry C. Porter (University Press, Cambridge and Deseret Book, 1987). An additional help is *A Century of "Mormonism" in Great Britain* by Richard L. Evans (Deseret Book, 1937; reprinted by Kessinger Publishing, 2007). More specifically focused on the two apostolic missions to England is *Men with a Mission, 1837–1841: The Quorum of the Twelve Apostles in the British Isles,* by James B. Allen, Ronald K. Esplin, and David J. Whittaker (Deseret Book, 1992). A provocative work that adds insight to these times is *Audacious Women: Early British Mormon Immigrants* by Rebecca Bartholomew (Signature Books, 1995).

Wilford Woodruff's detailed journal is the source of much of what is known about British missionary work, especially in the Malvern Hills. The entire journal is not readily available, but *Waiting for World's End: The Diaries of Wilford Woodruff,* edited by Susan Staker (Signature Books, 1993), provides a rich selection of his personal record. Also, a biographical work that uses his journal and quotes from it extensively is: *Wilford Woodruff: History of his Life and Labors,* by Matthias F. Cowley (Bookcraft, 1964). A collection of essays, edited by Alexander L. Baugh and Susan Easton Black, *Banner of the Gospel* (Deseret Book, 2010), also draws on his journal and provides biographical insights. One essay in that book, "Wilford Woodruff: Missionary in Herefordshire," by Cynthia Doxey Green, was especially helpful in my research.

William Clayton's journals are crucial for details about the British missions, but also for Nauvoo history. George D. Smith has published the journals with extensive explanatory notes under the title: *An Intimate Chronicle: The Journals of William Clayton* (Signature Books, 1995).

While individual journals provided me with specific details that were helpful, collections that draw upon journals and family histories are the most easily accessed. In studying Mormon ocean crossings, an essential resource is *Saints on the Seas: A Maritime History of Mormon Migration, 1830–1890,* by Conway B. Sonne (University of Utah Press, 1983). A book written for children, but useful to anyone interested in this aspect of Mormon history, is *I Sailed to Zion: True Stories of Young Pioneers Who Crossed the Ocean,* by Susan Arrington Madsen and Fred E. Woods (Deseret Book, 2000).

My specialty during my years of teaching literature was the Victorian novel. Years of reading and teaching Dickens, Eliot, Thackeray, Hardy, and others taught me a good deal about the British caste system, their money, their food, and so on, but I learned that when I wanted to be specific I had to search out details I hadn't known. There are dozens of books written on life in Victorian England. I focused on the midlands as much as I could, and on the 1830s and '40s. Books that helped me most were: *Daily Life in Victorian England,* second edition, by Sally Mitchell (Greenwood Press, 2009); *The English Countryman: His life and work from Tudor times to the Victorian Age,* by G. E. and K. R. Fussell (Orbis Publishing, 1981); *The Rural Life of England (1840)* by William Howitt, a reprint of a work published in 1840 (Kessinger Publishing reprint); *What Jane Austen Ate and Charles Dickens Knew: From Fox Hunting to Whist—the Facts of Daily Life in 19th-Century England,* by Daniel Pool (Simon and Schuster, 1993); *Inside the Victorian Home: A Portrait of Domestic Life in Victorian England,* by Judith Flanders (Norton, 2003); *A Writer's Guide to Everyday Life in Regency and Victorian England, from 1811–1901,* by Kristine Hughes (Writer's Digest, 1998).

I'll talk about the best resources on Nauvoo history in my next volume, but certainly the starting place is Glen M. Leonard's definitive work, *Nauvoo: A Place of Peace, A People of Promise* (Deseret Book, 2002).

Dialect is tricky—especially dialect from a distant era. I knew that the dialect in Manchester differed from that in Herefordshire, but the distinctions are not easy for someone who speaks "A-*mare-uh-kun*" English. I was fortunate that Dickens, along with Elizabeth Gaskell, wrote novels set in Manchester in an era very close to the time I was writing about. I tried to follow their rendering of the Manchester dialect, but I softened everything a little since dialect can be tiresome to read. I learned in my research that dialect in southwest England might not have been too different from that in Herefordshire, so I took my chances with the Hardy novels, set in Devon. I will probably hear from Anglophiles who will tell me I got something wrong, and I'm sure I did, but I was trying to suggest a voice rather than render the speech exactly.

My wife and I had a great adventure in the Malvern Hills. I drove on the left side of the narrow roads while she programmed the GPS, and we tried to visit all the towns where Wilford Woodruff preached. That was much harder than we had assumed, with names changing, towns disappearing, and some villages having been engulfed by larger cities. Still, Ledbury and Wellington Heath, where I set the novel, must look much the way they did 170 years ago, and Herefordshire Beacon, where Wilford Woodruff, Willard Richards, and Brigham Young stood as they conferred on the decision to publish a British edition of the Book of Mormon, has not changed. Truly, there cannot be many views in the world more verdant, bucolic, and timeless than that one. Those who love Mormon history should make the trip, see the Benbow farm and the Gadfield Elm church, and drink in the feel of the region. We picked up local history books, walked the streets, and met the wonderful people. We also drove north to Birmingham, Liverpool, Manchester, and Preston, and we used the museums, local maps and books, and local experts to learn more about all those places in the nineteenth century.

People sometimes compliment me for working hard to get history right in my historical novels. I like that image of myself: the hardworking, blue-collar drudge. But here's the real truth: The research is great fun, the travel to the sites is even better, and it's only the blasted process of trying to get the story written that is making an old man of me. I hope I make it through three volumes!

I wish to thank Emily Utt of the LDS Church Historic Sites Division in the Church History Library and Archives. She offered her own expertise and provided me with research notes and documents that proved invaluable. David J. Whittaker of the L. Tom Perry Special Collections in the Harold B. Lee Library at Brigham Young University allowed me use of his personal notes from his extensive research on the United Brethren and the apostolic missions. Emily Watts and Cory Maxwell, at Deseret Book, read my outlines and helped me develop the form and concept for the series, and Emily has served once again as my editor, as she has done many times before. I've now been publishing with Deseret Book for thirty-three years, so I feel a great kinship with the entire staff.

Kathy has always helped me on my books, but she worked overtime on this one, and I'm indebted to her for all she did. Not only did she join me in our adventure to England, but she read the entire manuscript three times, at various stages. Frankly, she is a *tough* reader, and therefore, a big help. More and more, as I develop plots, I turn to her and we brainstorm my outlines together. If I get stuck, I go to her for consultation, and she's often the one who comes up with the right answer. But still, some of the ideas in the book are mine. Honest.